VIGILANTE

BY THE AUTHOR

THE COUNTDOWN CHRONICLES
Kiss of the Mandarins
The Warehouse
Never Go Back
The Deception Covenant
Endgame

THE ORGANISATION

ORIGIN TALES
The Brotherhood
Rise of the ACF

VLADIMIR SERIES
Vladimir's Diary
Red Empire
Fifty Years to Paradise

THE VAV CHRONICLES
Vampires And Victims

OTHER WORKS
The Prophecy Illusion
Trinity

VIGILANTE

MARTIN M.
McSHANE

The Book Guild Ltd

First published in Great Britain in 2024 by
The Book Guild Ltd
Unit E2 Airfielod Business Park
Harrison Road, Market Harborough
Leicestershire, LE16 7UL
Freephone: 0800 999 2982
www.bookguild.co.uk
Email: info@bookguild.co.uk
Twitter: @bookguild

Typeset in 11pt Adobe Garamond Pro

Printed and bound in Great Britain by
CPI Group (UK) Ltd, Croydon, CR0 4YY

ISBN 978 1835740 583

British Library Cataloguing in Publication Data.
A catalogue record for this book is available from the British Library.

Vigilante:

Somebody Who Takes The Law Into Their
Own Hands To Punish Criminals For
Their Crimes.

CHAPTER ONE

It's half one on a Sunday morning and Danny Deacon is lying fast asleep, fully clothed, along the edge of his bed looking like he's about to fall onto the floor at any moment. He's been lying like this since arriving home eleven hours ago, drunk as a skunk, from a four-day birthday Beano with his drinking buddies, Gaz and Jacko. He'd only come home to replenish funds, intending to return to The Manor, their local pub, and continue the birthday celebrations. After loading his pockets with the last dregs of loose change from the bottom of his savings jar, Danny laid down to "rest his eyes for a few minutes" but at his age the Beano has proven too much for him and within seconds he's dead to the world, snoring like a train. However, had he made it back to The Manor he'd've found neither Gaz nor Jacko there because they too, just as he himself had, succumbed to exhaustion as at their ages a four-day Beano is just too much for them.

For the past nine years, Danny has occupied the ground-floor flat of a converted house in the unfashionable eastern end of Camden Town in North London. There are eight "abodes" in the building but Danny's is the only one with a bedroom; the others being bedsits where single men live out grim bachelor existences. Danny's existence is just about the same as theirs but he, at least, has a bedroom. Not that that's saying much because, to him, it's just another room to heat and clean, not that he does much cleaning as

1

evidenced by the state of the flat. Danny's children, three boys and two girls, keep telling him he drinks too much and that he should look after himself better. Danny's inner voice tells him *you drink too much*; to be truthful, even he thinks he drinks too much and if his flat could speak, it too would tell him he drinks too much because he drinks too much. In defence of his anti-abstinence stance, Danny tells everyone that drinking in The Manor with his mates is the only comfort he has left in life but it's far, far, far more complicated than that.

*

When Danny was in the army, he could never have imagined things working out the way they have; twice divorced, scraping by to make ends meet, living in a butthole of a flat in the rear end of Camden with no hope of ever escaping. The entire building reeks. Of what, no one is certain. Most residents think it's blocked drains causing the smell but none of them, including Danny, is sure what it is or do anything about it; neither does their landlord. Danny's children, apart from Brad, his youngest son who he'd named after a buddy of his that died in Vietnam, hate visiting the flat and whenever they come to London they stay with friends or pay to stay in a hotel rather than stay with their father.

On leaving the army, on wife number two's advice, or rather demand, Danny's expertise in conducting interrogations along with his considerable resourcefulness and demonstrable self-reliance should've made him the ideal candidate for a variety of well-paid careers on Civvy Street but at the back of Danny's mind were his old Sergeant's words of warning for him to keep a low profile. And so, in order to keep his family safe, Danny took on a series of low-paid jobs but, following his second divorce, Danny did what a great many former soldiers do, he became a postman. Danny loved everything about being a postie; the hours, the outdoor nature of the work, the lack of supervision, absolutely everything, especially talking with other ex-soldiers. Despite keeping most of what he did while serving to himself, Danny was always happy to hear what Gary "Gaz" Croaker and Peter "Jacko" Jackson had gotten up to in the army; though compared with Danny there wasn't very much to brag about. Over the years, the three posties became drinking buddies and continued drinking together after they retired, meeting regularly in their local, The Manor in East Camden. Sometimes, when out delivering the post, Danny pondered on what the people he was posting bills and cards and letters to would think if they knew what he had done in the military, particularly while serving in Vietnam as a "voluntary" member of IPEF. He hardly believed it himself now but, nevertheless, it was true, it happened, all of it, every last bit of it! More recently, he's been pondering on what his old IPEF buddies are doing and whether any of them have sunk as low as he himself has. Danny's existence since leaving the army has been thoroughly miserable. He'd been happy in the army, he was someone when he was in the army.

*

It's now a quarter to two and Danny's mobile phone ringing wakes him. His ringtone, being exactly the same as his alarm, makes him think he needs to get up for some reason. What, he doesn't know, but when he looks at the screen it's an incoming call and not an alarm at all. He's angry with himself that he hadn't, as he normally does, put his phone on silent because, being such a light sleeper, thanks to his time in the army, he wakes at the slightest sound, even after going to bed blind drunk. The screen says: "Unknown Caller". *Who the hell's calling me at this hour! It'd better not be one of those people trying to scam me! If it is I've got bad news for them, I've got nothing worth stealing and I'm flat broke!* But then he thinks, *I bet it's Gaz and Jacko pissed up and messing around!* He's convinced it's them.

"Thanks for waking me up you pair of idiots! It'll take me ages to get back to sleep!"

"Am I speaking with Mr Deacon?" asks a man on the other end of the call.

"You'd better not be one of those scam-callers I see on the telly!" warns Danny.

"Good morning Mr Deacon, my name's Tony Wilson and I'm calling from St Thomas' Hospital." At those words, Danny goes cold believing this is the type of call no parent ever wants to get.

"Yes, I'm Mr Deacon, what's this about?" mumbles Danny, fearful of what the caller might say next.

"We found your number among your daughter Lucy's belongings," says Mr Wilson. On hearing those words Danny's world implodes. "Do you live in London Mr Deacon?"

"Yes, why?" he whimpers in dread of what Mr Wilson will say next.

"In that case, can you make your way to St Thomas' Hospital? I'd come straightaway if I were you," says Mr Wilson, giving the urgency of the situation but not the reason.

"Yes… okay… I'll get a taxi. No, I'll… I… is there parking there at St Thomas'? Anyway, what's happened to my Luce? What's wrong with her? Has she…" Danny stammers breathlessly.

"Please, Mr Deacon, whatever you do, don't panic, just make sure you get here in one…"

"Don't panic! Don't panic! You call me at stupid o'clock in the morning and tell me not to panic! I need you to tell me right now what's happened to my daughter because I'm not leaving here until you do!" yells Danny, his anger rising because he hates not being in control of situations and it's causing him to panic.

"I can't give you many details, Mr Deacon, because I don't have them. All I can see on the computer screen is your daughter was admitted a couple of hours ago following an incident and she's currently being treated in the ICU… the Intensive Care Unit. When you arrive at reception a member of staff will be able to give you more details. Are you okay Mr Deacon? I realise this…"

Danny ends the call because he needs to get to St Thomas' Hospital straightaway. While searching for his wallet, which he's left in The Manor, Danny recalls when the children were little and a teacher or parent or a friend or whoever would call to say that one or other of them had cut or grazed this or that and been taken to hospital, "as a precaution". *Bloody kids!* yells Danny's inner voice. Danny's angry that Lucy hadn't told him she was in London, but, then again, he knows she and the others come to London all the time without letting him know in case he asks them to stay or spend time with him. Danny's youngest son, Brad, however, always tells him when he's coming to town and whenever he does he always stays at his flat, despite the smell, and always takes his old dad out for a pint. Unlike the others, Brad loves his dad's company and always has.

*

It's barely three miles to St Thomas' from Danny's flat. He calculates he could walk it in about an hour or, at that time on a Sunday morning, drive it in about ten minutes. A taxi is out of the question as "those legalised thieves", as Danny refers to taxi drivers, will charge him an arm and a leg at that time of a morning. He can't afford taxis anyway. Getting the tube is out the question as they won't start running again for three hours yet and he'd stopped using night buses a while back after an argument with a drunk and, being drunk himself, both were removed from the bus by the police and served with a ban. "No, decision made! I'll drive to St Thomas' and think about where to park after I get there." The worrying thing for Danny is St Thomas' is inside London's Congestion Charge Zone but as it won't begin operating again until seven in the morning, he's hopeful he'll be back outside it by then.

Arriving at the hospital's car park, Danny drives up to the barrier and peruses the parking charges but, being unable to afford them, he reverses back onto the road and drives to a nearby side street he knows. He's parked there before, not that it's actually a parking space; it's the pavement but people park there anyway. He has his fingers crossed that nobody's there. The space is empty but newly installed concrete bollards make parking a tight squeeze. Manoeuvring between the bollards and the wall, Danny scrapes all down the sides of his van. After parking up, he writes a note for parking wardens explaining that he's visiting his daughter in the ICU at St Thomas' Hospital and left his wallet at home in the rush, and sticks the note on the dashboard facing the windscreen. Opening the driver's side door, Danny finds he can't get out of the van because it's parked too close to the wall. Climbing into the passenger seat he tries that door with the same result, so he climbs over the seats into the back of the van and exits via its rear doors. Inspecting the latest damage to his vehicle, despite it already being covered in scrapes and scratches and dents, Danny's angry because the latest damage is very noticeable and it will take weeks to blend in. *What will people think of my driving? Who cares what they think!*

After arriving at reception, a security guard signs Danny in and hands him a floor plan of the hospital, drawing a circle around the ICU with a ball-point pen. He points Danny towards the lift concourse and tells him to check in at the nurses' station before entering the ICU to make sure it's okay for him to go in. At the lift concourse, Danny presses the up-arrow call-button on the control panel mounted on the wall. As it illuminates, he looks to check to see which floors the lifts are on. They're all between the eighth and tenth floors, according to the indicators above each individual lift. After thirty seconds none of them has moved; *C'mon. c'mon, c'mon, c'mon!* After waiting a further minute, still none of the lifts are heading to the ground floor, so Danny presses the call-button again, harder this time. One of the lifts starts making its way down but stops at the seventh floor. *Bugger!* Danny's internal voice wanted to say "*fuck*" but it, like Danny, doesn't use bad language. Another lift begins making its descent but stops at the fifth floor. *Bugger! Bugger! Bugger!* Danny presses the call-button again in case "the computer" has forgotten he's there. A third lift starts its downward journey; seventh floor, sixth, fifth, fourth, third, second and stops on the first floor. Danny considers running up the emergency stairs next to the lift concourse to the first floor to catch the lift. He's about to do just that when two lifts commence downward journeys. They both stop on the third floor. The lift on the first floor starts going up. Danny curses himself for not running upstairs to catch it. The lifts on the third floor start moving; one up, one down. At last, a lift arrives on the ground floor. The doors open and one person gets out. A man enquires, "Going down?" Danny says he's going up. The doors close and the lift continues down to "Basement level -1". Danny's anger and frustration is at 10. He's about to kick the hell out of the beautifully polished stainless-steel lift doors when the "ding" of a lift arriving on the ground floor echoes throughout the concourse. He turns around to find two sets of lift doors opening simultaneously behind him. Miracle of miracles, one of them is going up. Danny runs across the concourse, enters the lift and presses the button for the fifth floor. The doors take an age to close and when they do, the lift rises so slowly that Danny wants to smash it to pieces with his bare hands. The speed of ascent, however, gives him time to check the map. It's then he realises that he's misread the floor plan and the ICU is situated on the first floor of the East Wing and he's in a lift going to the fifth floor of the West Wing. Danny punches the lift's internal stainless-steel panels to vent his anger. It's then that he notices the CCTV camera; he smiles at it to show whoever's watching that he's not a nutter and doesn't need removing from the building. *If anything else goes wrong my brain's going to explode!* screams his brain. Then he gets a break. His lift stops at the first floor to let someone in so he leaps out of the lift and there, straight ahead of him, is a sign saying "East Wing". He asks a passing nurse for directions to the ICU. She looks at him with the look of someone who's rushed off their feet and doesn't have time for idiots asking stupid questions; "It's there... right in front of you... where it says ICU," she replies wearing a fake smile and continues walking without breaking her stride. Danny shouts, "Thank you", at the nurse's back but she's gone already.

Nearing the doors to the ICU, doctors and nurses, dressed in what Danny likens to military grade bio-hazard suits, are rushing in and out. They pay him no attention. Now he's there, Danny doesn't know if he can go through the doors because he's scared of what he'll find on the other side. *But if she's in the ICU then she must be alive at least,* he reasons. Danny's just about to go into the ICU when there's a tap on his shoulder. He turns to find a man standing there.

"Danny Deacon?" the man asks.

"Yes. I got a call…"

"I'm Detective Sergeant Paul Dean of the Metropolitan Police. I've been waiting for you to turn up. Before you go in to see your daughter, can I have a word in private first?" asks DS Dean, directing Danny to the "family room". Being an avid viewer of reality TV programmes, particularly those about the Emergency Services, Danny knows this is where people are taken to be given bad news about their loved ones. "What have you been told so far?" the detective asks mechanically.

"Not much. Nothing really. I…"

"Your daughter… Lucy?" says the detective. Danny nods. "Well, around midnight, she got mugged for her mobile phone by a couple of youths on a motor scooter; Scooter Muggers we call them." *That doesn't sound too bad, maybe Luce is okay and they've put her in the ICU as a precaution.* "We get about ten scooter muggings a night around where your daughter was attacked, it's an epidemic. She was standing at a bus stop making a call when two youths rode up on a scooter, she wouldn't've heard them coming because they coast in close to their victims without revving the engine or making any noise, grabbed her phone off her and in doing so knocked her to the ground. There were a couple of people who witnessed what happened and called for an ambulance. She was treated at the scene by paramedics and then brought here to St Thomas'. The witnesses couldn't give much of a description of the muggers because it was all over in the blink of an eye. Ah, here's the doctor. I'll leave you with him but here's my card. I'll be in touch but call anytime."

The doctor tells Danny that Lucy received a serious blow to her head resulting in fractured skull and at least two bleeds on her brain. Danny wants to see her but the doctor hasn't finished. He tells Danny that Lucy has been put into a medically induced coma to stop her fitting and to regulate her breathing. Danny asks about brain damage. The doctor says it's too early to make a diagnosis as they're waiting for the drugs to stabilise Lucy before carrying out tests on her. Danny asks again to see his daughter. The doctor nods and calls for an ICU nurse to take him in. "Prepare yourself," she whispers, taking Danny by the arm.

CHAPTER TWO

This is the first time Danny's been inside an ICU. He's seen battlefield versions of them before but they're nothing like this. The incessant beeping of monitors and the rhythmic pneumatic hiss of ventilators freaks him out. To his right is a row of eight beds. The patients occupying them are connected up to more tubes and wires and surrounded by more machines than he could've imagined possible and somewhere beneath it all were people unconscious of receiving life-saving treatments. "Your daughter's in the last bed on the left," whispers the nurse and parts the curtain surrounding Lucy's bed. He doesn't want to look but he knows he has to. When Danny sees his daughter lying there with all sorts of wires and tubes sticking in and out of her, his knees give way and he collapses onto the floor. The nurse helps Danny to a seat. He leans his elbows on Lucy's bed, rests his head between his hands and weeps uncontrollably. The nurse puts an arm around Danny's heaving shoulders to comfort him. It's then he realises he hasn't called anybody to tell them about Lucy. He tells the nurse this and asks if it's okay for him to make a call. "Okay," she says, "but keep your voice down," she whispers with a caring smile.

"Hello son, sorry if I woke you," croaks Danny, his hand covering his mouth.

"Shit dad, it's three in the morning! You sound terrible! What's wrong?" Brad croaks in return.

"Sorry son, but it's Luce, she's been hurt. I'm with her at St Thomas' Hospital."

"Is she okay?" Brad asks, now wide awake and terrified that his sister is in hospital and his dad is calling him at three in the morning.

"No, son, she's not okay. She's in the Intensive What's-a-name Unit; you know, the one where they put people when they're very poorly." Poorly's not a word Danny normally uses and this further alarms Brad.

"Shit Dad, that sounds serious. What happened to her? Was she in a car accident or something?" Brad asks. Danny pauses before answering.

"No, son, she wasn't in a car accident... she's been mugged. Now I know you'll want all the details but I can't talk right now because I'm at her bedside in the Intensive Care Unit. I'm not supposed to be making phone calls, so what I want you to do is call your brothers and sister and tell them that Lucy's in the ICU at St Thomas' Hospital and they should come straightaway."

"Straightaway? Shit! Is she going to die, Dad? Is she?"

"I don't know son but she's in a bad way. I can't talk anymore. Love you boy," sobs Danny, overcome with grief.

It's only after talking with Brad that Danny takes his first look at Lucy's face. It's completely unmarked. She looks beautiful lying there like she's asleep. Asleep with her eyes taped to keep them closed. Seeing his daughter's eyes taped shut brings more tears to Danny's eyes. He recalls the day she was born and in his mind begins plotting revenge on the bastards who did this to his daughter. *You're old, so what can you do? What can I do? What can I do?* This thought percolates around and around inside Danny's head until it turns into loathing for the man that is and longing to be the man he once was. *If this had happened forty... twenty... years ago I'd've... I'd've known what to do... yeah, I'd've definitely known what to do!*

A consultant neurologist doing the ICU rounds enters through the slit in the curtain surrounding Lucy's bed and introduces herself. Danny introduces himself and asks if it's okay for him to stay. The CN smiles and pats him on the shoulder as a way of giving him permission to stay and then grabs Lucy's charts from the foot of the bed, examines them briefly and, after checking the patient's vital signs, updates the chart. "We'll be taking your daughter down to theatre in about half an hour," the CN whispers and goes to leave. Danny asks, "Is she going to be okay? I mean, is she going to live?" The CN repeats to Danny what he already knows; that Lucy has a fractured skull and at least two bleeds on her brain and at the moment she's in a medically induced coma to stop her fitting and to regulate her breathing. The CN holds Danny's hands in hers, looks him in the eye and tells him straight that Lucy may never regain consciousness and if she does there's likely to be brain damage but it's too early to tell. Hearing this makes the blood drain from Danny's face. He feels as if he's going to faint but regains his composure and thanks the CN for being honest with him. She says they have to hope and pray for the best and leaves.

The moment the CN departs, Danny's ex, Joyce, appears through the slit in the curtain. Despite their mutual detestation, Danny and Joyce hug one another. Joyce's latest husband, Jeff, appears, followed closely by a nurse who tells them there's a maximum of two visitors allowed at a time. Danny looks at Jeff, he thinks that's his name, and nods at him to scarper. Jeff looks at Joyce. She knows how unpredictable Danny can be and, not wanting a scene, tells Jeff to leave. After Jeff departs, Danny whispers, telling Joyce about what happened to Lucy.

"I know you Daniel Deacon and I remember the promises you made when the children were little and I know the types of things you got up to in the army!" Joyce hiss-whispers. *Oh no you don't!* thinks Danny. "Look, Danny, please don't you go doing anything stupid because at your age all's that'll happen is you'll end up getting yourself hurt or killed or…"

"What do you care if I get hurt or killed?"

"I don't but in case you've forgotten, you've got five children and eight grandchildren who need you!"

"Need me? Need me! You're joking aren't you? Lucy was in town without telling me. They're all the same! Apart from Brad. None of them bother letting me know when they're here. I only get to know about it afterwards when they mention something! Anyway, how did you find out? Did Brad call you?"

"No, Steph did. She and Lucy were supposed to meet up with the boys and when she didn't show she got worried and called the police who told her…"

"Oh, so the boys are in town too are they? Well, that's just great! They all did a great job of looking after their sister!" Danny hisses contemptuously.

"Don't you dare go blaming Steph or the boys for what happened to Lucy!"

"Sorry," says Danny, calming down.

"Wow, 'sorry'! That's a word that doesn't pass your lips very often, Daniel Deacon. Sorry, Danny, that was mean of me," Joyce adds sarcastically.

"Look, I'm going, so your bloke Harry can come in," says Danny with a sly grin. Joyce laughs.

"You're a bugger you are, Danny, a right bugger. You know very well his name is Jeff," says Joyce, kissing Danny goodbye on his unshaven cheeks. She rubs a finger on his bristles as if to tell him he needs to shave more often. He likewise rubs the bristles on his chin, then smiles and leaves.

As Danny passes through the ICU's outer doors he shoulder barges Jeff who's on his way in, "Sorry mate, didn't see you there!" Danny says with a grin. A nurse calls to him saying, "We'll let you know if there's any change in your daughter's condition." Danny pauses and replies, "Like if she's dead or something?" which he immediately regrets saying. "Sorry, nurse, it's been a rough… I'm feeling a bit… you know… sorry." The nurse says she understands and goes about her duties.

Outside the ICU, DS Dean is sat dozing half-awake on a metal-framed chair with a padded seat which has had most of the sponge picked out of it by tiny fingers. He's been waiting to speak with Danny and jumps up when he sees him. Danny asks if he hasn't a home to go to. He says not since his divorce and asks Danny if he wants to go for a beer. It's nearly four in the morning but the DS says he knows a twenty-four-hour drinking club nearby. Danny says okay and the pair head off together.

The drinking club DS Dean takes Danny to is one of the roughest places he's been in for a while. It's not spit and sawdust but not far from it. The twenty or so people in the bar, including two bleary-eyed bartenders, acknowledge DS Dean as he and Danny walk in. Looking around, Danny wonders what the punters do for a living if they're out drinking at four in the morning. As most of the clientele are much younger than him, he doubts that any of them are retired or even anywhere near retirement. Dean introduces Danny to everyone, adding that he isn't a grass and nobody is to go thinking or saying he is or he'll sort them out. The bar staff and the clientele all laugh and chant manically in unison, "Danny isn't a grass and if anyone says he is Deany will sort them out!" and then continue drinking, smoking and talking about whatever it is they're talking about. There are no females in the club. Danny isn't at all surprised by this, considering the state of the place. He gets a whiff of something familiar.

"Yep, that's ganja you can smell," says DS Dean as casually as if he's talking about garden mint. "If you ever need to score, the stuff they sell here is premium gear." The DS orders two pints of London Pride, and he and Danny go and sit at a table furthest away from everyone. "Cheers," says DS Dean, clinking Danny's glass with his own.

"Cheers," Danny replies mechanically. "Listen, Sergeant Dean, what can you tell me about the scumbags who mugged my Luce?

How old are they, what do they look like, what colour were they?" DS Dean's intrigued by Danny's intensity when asking questions and thinks he could prove useful to him.

"Now, Danny, I can't comment on what colour they are because that's considered 'racial profiling' and I'd be had up. You never know who's listening... even in here!" says the DS, sounding "official". "We've got lots of words and phrases these days that we have to be careful about using or the Word Police will hang us out to dry. And, by the way, call me Paul or Deany whenever we're... y'know... socialising."

"Tell me about it! My kids are in the Word Police. I think they're Generals in it!" laughs Danny. "If I say something that I think is okay, and they don't, they correct me or say I'm a casual this or a casual that. They drive me crazy. By the way, just so you know, I'm not a racist and don't know why I asked about what colour the scumbags were who attacked my Luce," says Danny to clear up any misunderstandings. DS Dean just shrugs his shoulders and laughs.

"Yeah, my kids are the same as yours I think. And because I'm in the police they're a bit ashamed of me. It's all, 'the police are this' and 'the police are that'. Everyone's the same. Nobody stops to think about what it'd be like if there weren't any police! I say to them, 'come out on patrol with me and show me how to do my job,' that usually shuts them up. But when one of them gets burgled or one of them's been attacked or one of them's had their motor stolen... who do they call? Not fucking Ghost Busters that's for fucking sure, it's the fucking police they call and then they're all sad and crying and asking for help and then the next thing is they ignore you when they see you on the street. I shouldn't tell you this, but, if certain people report a crime, we put it to the bottom of the pile," laughs the DS.

"Don't blame you!" Danny replies, lying to win DS Dean's trust.

"What do you do for a job?" asks Deany.

"I'm retired... a pensioner... but I do a bit of painting and decorating on the side. Don't tell nobody though," jokes Danny who then realises he's just told a cop he does a bit of hooky work on the side and doesn't pay tax on it.

"Don't worry," Deany laughs, "your secret's safe with me. What did you do before you retired?"

"I used to be a postie!" says Danny proudly but as he doesn't want to talk about his background, he changes the subject. "So, Deany, do you know who mugged my daughter?"

"I do. Know all of them very well in fact… all of them!" repeats DS Dean with emphasis. "Right nasty bastards they are! I shouldn't go telling you this but they're a bunch of wannabe gangsters from the local council estate. Going back to their ethnicity for a minute, I'd describe them as being like a box of liquorice allsorts… mix of black, white and a few brown shades in between. Just so you know, last night, in the same area where your daughter got mugged, they did about a dozen other muggings."

"So, if you know who did it, why don't you arrest them?" asks Danny.

"Listen, Danny, the amount of evidence that's needed nowadays to get the CPS to raise a charge is un-be-fucking-lieveable! Criminals like this gang are forensically aware and no one will make a statement against them so the CPS can't raise charges. People'll tell you who it is but they won't put anything down in writing or go to court and testify… too dangerous. Mind you, they're fucking idiots! Who do they think's burgling their houses or stealing their cars to break up and sell to buy gear off the same people who do the scooter muggings? Estate rats, I call them and they're worse than any vermin you can imagine!" Danny sees DS Dean is getting worked up. "Anyway, it won't be my problem for much longer, I retire in a couple of years and I can't wait!"

"What about the people who were at the bus stop, didn't they make a statement?"

"I've told you before, they said it happened so fast they didn't see anything. And, before you ask, CCTV has been checked and came up with a big fat zero!" Just then, DS Dean's phone rings. He leaves the table to answer it.

When the detective returns to the table, he tells Danny it was one of his informers on the phone and has told him which gang members it was that mugged his daughter and that the ones who did it are both white. Danny says he really doesn't care what colour they are, he just wants them arrested. DS Dean repeats what he told him previously about the CPS not being able to raise charges because there's no evidence and no one on the estate is prepared to go to court or make a statement. "It's like being in an arse-kicking competition with your legs tied together. Sometimes I wish we could go back to doing things the old way," he adds, looking into Danny's eyes. "We got things done and the streets were safe." DS Dean and Danny descend into a deep conversation about how things used to be and how things are different these days and how people don't have any respect for the police or the law or anything.

"When we were kids, you had to earn respect. It was something people had for you because of the kinds of things you did and the way you acted, you never asked for it or demanded it, it wasn't like that then," says Danny.

"Yeah, but, in those days, people treated one another with respect, not like nowadays. These days everyone thinks they have a right to respect but it's a different kind of respect they're talking about," explains DS Dean morosely.

"You're pissed," says Danny, who, glancing at his watch, adds, "I've got to go otherwise I'll get a parking ticket or get caught by the Congestion Charge if I don't get a move on." As Danny stands to leave, he offers his hand to DS Dean and as he takes hold of it Danny pulls him in close, "Listen, before I go, tell me the names of who it was your informer said mugged my daughter. If you don't it'll play on my mind! It'll drive me mad!"

"You know I can't tell you that."

"Then at least tell me where she was mugged."

"If I tell you, promise me you'll stay away. It's a dangerous place and if you go snooping around asking questions it won't end well for you," says DS Dean hoping Danny will do exactly the opposite.

"I promise I won't go doing anything stupid," Danny answers cryptically.

Clamping Danny's hand tighter, DS Dean pulls him closer and whispers to him which bus stop Lucy was at when she was mugged. Danny grips Dean's hand even tighter and insists, for his peace of mind, that he gives him the names of the muggers and will keep hold of his hand until he tells him. DS Dean makes no attempt to break the handshake, instead he gives Danny the names of the gang leaders; "Tomic and Pitbull are the street names they go by. Tomic's the main one. They're vicious thugs, suspected of at least two murders, so keep your word and don't go doing anything stupid! I don't want you going all gangster on me!" says DS Dean with a laugh, hoping Danny will immediately go looking for Tomic and Pitbull. *Then I'll get them after they get him!* thinks the detective.

*

All too often, DS Dean has seen parents in Danny's situation and he intends "helping" him bring Tomic to justice, something he himself has failed to do for well over eight years. He badly wants Tomic off the streets before he retires and time is running out. DS Dean's used people as bait before, with mixed results, but believes this time he's chosen well with Danny Deacon. He'll keep watch over him, as much as he can, but, unbeknown to DS Dean, this time he's chosen a stooge with a military mind perfectly formed for all types of warfare.

*

Once outside the drinking club, Danny thinks he might have time to pay Lucy a visit before the Congestion Charge kicks in, plus, St

Thomas' Hospital is on his way to the van. Arriving at the ICU, a nurse tells Danny that Lucy already has two visitors with her, "and that's the maximum," she says, leaving no room for discussion. Danny tells her that he's on the clock with the Congestion Charge and if she wouldn't mind telling that to whoever it is with Lucy, he suspects Joyce and Jeff, he'd appreciate it. Just then, Danny hears his sons' voices calling from behind. They tell him they've been trying to call him for ages. He tells them he had his phone on silent because he was being interviewed by the detective assigned to Lucy's case. They ask him, then, why he smells of beer? He says he needed a drink afterwards to calm his nerves. Danny's sons want to know all the details about what he spoke to the detective about what happened with Lucy.

"You can tell us outside," says Kelvin, "I need a cigarette! There's a smoking shelter near the hospital's entrance," he adds, leading the way to the lift concourse.

"You need to give them up," says Danny.

"You say that every time you see me smoking," replies Kelvin but, unusually, Joey, Danny's second eldest son, agrees with his dad that Kelvin should pack in smoking.

"How did you hear about Luce being here?" Danny asks.

"Brad called me and I called the others," Kelvin says matter-of-factly. "He said he'll get here as soon as he can but with that piece of crap he drives who knows when he'll show," he adds sarcastically. "Anyway, what's the story, Dad?"

"There's not much to tell to be honest. Luce was just standing at a bus stop making a phone call when a couple of scumbags riding a scooter coasted up behind her, grabbed her phone and knocked her to the floor. She banged her head on the pavement or the kerb or something and has fractured her skull. That's it!"

"That's it? Didn't this detective tell you anything else?" Kelvin asks.

"He said there were a couple of people at the bus stop but it all happened so fast they didn't see anything... anything useful anyway."

"That's all?" Joey asks in disbelief.

"Weeeeeeeell… he did kind of tell me where it all happened… you know… the bus stop where they mugged Luce," says Danny nonchalantly. This news concerns Joey.

"Listen, Dad, you're not in the army anymore… and you're getting on a bit… so don't you go doing anything stupid! Okay?"

"You sound like that bloody detective," says Danny laughing.

"Look, Dad, leave everything to the police. Don't get involved!"

"Leave it to the police? Leave it to the bloody police! Are you having a laugh? They've been after these scumbags for years but they can't do anything about them because nobody will testify against them or give a statement or anything!"

"Doesn't that tell you something about them? They're not the type to go messing with. Just leave it to the police!"

"Anyway, I'm off home before the bloody Congestion Charge kicks in," Danny says, looking at his watch.

"Don't know why you're looking at that thing, it hasn't been right since the day you got it," says Kelvin snootily.

"Don't worry about the Congestion Charge, Dad, I'll pay," says Joey.

"You're a good lad, Joebyjoe, but the van's parked somewhere it shouldn't be and I don't want it getting towed away," says Danny, giving him a fatherly hug of farewell.

Before Danny leaves for home, he, Kelvin and Joey agree to meet back at his flat after they've visited Lucy. He knows they don't like visiting him, and they refuse point blank to stay with him whenever they're in London, so Danny's surprised when they agree.

"I'm worried that Dad'll do something stupid, Kel," says Joey as soon as Danny is out of earshot.

"It wouldn't be the first time," says Kelvin. "But you know what he's like, he'll do whatever he's going to do. He loves a crusade!"

"Yeah, but this isn't like fighting a council, Kel, or complaining to a company about something that didn't work properly, this is serious. If he goes snooping around where Luce got attacked he could end up getting hurt."

"He can take care of himself," says Kelvin, flicking his cigarette butt to the ground and squishing it flat beneath his shoe.

"Kel, Dad's a pensioner! He won't stand a chance against a street gang!"

"Who said he's going up against a street gang? He probably just wants to have a look around to satisfy his curiosity... you know what he's like."

"Kel, he thinks he's still in the army for crying out loud! He even buys his clothes from the army Surplus Store!"

"Only as cheap work clothes!" says Kelvin. "C'mon, let's go and see Luce. If Mum and Jeff are still with her I'll tell the nurse to kick them out!"

*

As Danny opens the front door of the building, a familiar stench assaults his nostrils. He's almost gotten used to the smell after all these years but still wonders what it can be. He knows it's not the smell of death because he's smelt that smell many times but can't imagine for the life of him what can possibly create such a powerful odour over so long a period of time. It's not damp, it's not any chemicals he knows of, it's not drains, the landlord's had them flushed several times over the years, it's not anything that anybody in the building recognises or is prepared to own up to. Tenants have come and tenants have gone but the smell has remained throughout all the time Danny has been living there, and for years prior to him coming to live there, apparently, according to the house's longest-standing resident; who, rightly, is everyone's prime suspect.

Knowing Kelvin and Joey are coming round to see him, Danny sets about tidying his flat. Despite his meagre income, Danny enjoys the "occasional" takeaway; his flat is littered with the evidence, which he adds up the cost of while stuffing cartons into a black bin bag. "Wow! I need to cut down on the old takeaways," Danny mutters under his breath when he reaches four hundred pounds. *But think of all the money I save on gas and electric by not cooking and all the things I don't have to buy like hoisin sauce and mango chutney!* "Maybe I'll cut down to having just one or two a week," he says but he knows that as soon as he leaves The Manor after a night on the booze with Gaz and Jacko, he won't be able to stop himself getting a Chinese or Indian takeaway on the way home.

After a bit of tidying up, Danny sets about doing a bit of cleaning, starting with the lounge, but gives up less than halfway through, *I'll get a cleaner to come in once a week... or... once a month and I can have one or two extra takeaways a week with the money I save! Yes, once a month'll be fine.* Danny knows neither scenario will ever happen as he won't be able to afford the £30 an hour it costs for an agency cleaner. The last thing he does while waiting for Kelvin and Joey to arrive is turn the cushions over on the settee. One of them is so badly stained with curry sauce he flips it back over again. Just as he's dropping off to sleep, the buzzer sounds at the front door of the building. Danny peers through the spyhole and, seeing Kelvin and Joey standing outside, he shouts, "Not today thankyou," and laughs. Kelvin rolls his eyes at Danny's old joke and says, "Good one Dad, haven't heard that one before!" but Joey likes to play along; "Are you sure, Madame, it's three for fifty pence this week," he says in a comic voice. Danny laughs and opens the front door to let his sons in.

"Shit Dad, that smell's still here!" says Kelvin, pinching his nose.

"Don't know what you mean, son, what smell? Fresh as a daisy here," insists Danny.

"Bloody hell, Dad, it's getting worse!" says Joey gagging. "You probably don't notice it because you live here but it's definitely getting worse!"

"I've tried everything, the landlord's tried everything, everyone's tried everything, but no good, no one can find where the smell's coming from."

"Have you had the council out? What did they say?" asks Kelvin.

"Said it's nothing to do with them that's what they said; useless they are, useless. Anyway, come on in, I've been tidying up."

When Kelvin and Joey enter Danny's flat, they look around in disbelief of their dad's claim that he's been tidying up, as everywhere looks greasy and grimy. Instead of sitting down, they perch on the edges of the arms of the settee, despite them not looking much cleaner than anywhere else in the flat.

"Dad, you need to look after yourself better," says Joey concernedly.

"Don't worry about me, son, I'm alright. Tea? Coffee? Whiskey?"

"So," says Kelvin, "you have enough money to spend on whiskey but not enough to spend on furniture or keeping this place clean?"

"Sorry, son, I lied about the whiskey," Danny lies, "it's just tea or coffee."

"None for me thanks Dad, I've done nothing but drink tea and coffee for the past four hours," says Joey.

"Not for me either thanks Dad," says Kelvin, knowing his dad's coffee will be the cheapest instant variety and the cleanliness of the crockery and cutlery questionable.

"So, how come you're down?" asks Danny.

"We're here for a christening… Pete and Melinda's latest. I'm staying with them and Joey's staying with Malcolm and Hilary… you know, from uni?"

"Can't say I know any of them but it sounds like you're all sorted so no need for me to sleep on the couch so you two can have my bed," says Danny with a sly grin. Kelvin shudders at the thought of sleeping on what he presumes will be grimy sheets. "Anyway, that explains how you got to the hospital so fast from Bristol," Danny adds bitterly. "Were you planning on dropping in and seeing me or what?"

"Look, Dad, it's just a flying visit. We were supposed to be going to go back to Bristol today but with what's happened to Luce we'll be staying in London for a while."

"I suppose Luce was… you know… invited to this christening too?" asks Danny.

"She was. Look, Dad, you know very well we usually stay with friends whenever we come to London. This place is just too small to accommodate…"

"But that shouldn't stop you from letting me know you're here or taking me for a pint or dropping in to see me!" There were various things implied in what Danny said, including if they'd told him they were in London things might've turned out differently for Lucy.

"It was a flying visit for Christ's sake! Luce and Steph's businesses take up all their time and Joey and I have very demanding jobs! But you wouldn't understand that because you don't know what it's like to have responsibility! We don't get much free time and when we do we have to make the most of it. Sorry," says Kelvin bitterly.

"So, where's Steph?" Danny asks.

"She's on her way back to Scotland, you know what she's like."

"Yeah, I know what she's like… self, self, self, first, second, third for always and forever!"

"That's not fair, Dad, she's got a lot on since the breakup of her marriage!"

"What! She's got so much on she can't hang around to visit her comatose sister in hospital? And by the way, I know what it's like when marriages break up so don't pull that one!"

"She said she wants us to… you know… keep her informed, as they say."

"Well, if you two don't want any coffee, I do!" yells Danny, leaving the room so he doesn't have to bear the sight of his sons for a few minutes.

Returning more calm after making coffee, Danny reminisces with his sons about what Luce was like as a child; always bright and bubbly and bouncy, always "doing stuff". They call to mind family camping holidays and how miserable they made them, all of them, including Danny, who'd enjoyed "tenting it" when he was in the army. It's not long before the conversation turns to the attack on Lucy. Joey can tell by his dad's tone of voice, the things he's said in the past and the things he's saying about whoever attacked Lucy that they will probably get off with a slap on the wrist, "if they get caught at all," he says growing angry and getting angrier by the minute. Joey attempts to change the subject but Danny wants to talk about how society cares more about criminals than victims. Kelvin disagrees with his dad and trots out a stream of facts and figures and statistics about crime, punishment, justice, redemption and rehabilitation which Danny labels WAGNERs; "Wild Assed Guesses Not Easily Refuted," he adds by way of expansion of meaning. Joey laughs at this, saying he remembers him saying exactly that when they were kids. Kelvin isn't in the mood for laughing, nor is he prepared to back down, and continues to make his point. "Listen, Professor Plum," says Danny insultingly, "you just wait until you've got someone like them doing to you what they did to Luce and see what you think then! You'll soon change your tune then!" yells Danny into Kelvin's face. Joey steps in to avert a full-blown argument and after a moment says, "Dad, the way you're talking it sounds as if you know who Luce's attackers are!" Danny shrugs his shoulders. "Dunno, how would I know who attacked Luce?" he answers defensively. "I bet that detective told you more than you said he did, didn't he? What else did he tell you, Dad?" Danny denies DS Dean told him anything more than where the attack took place. "So... going by what you just said, there was more than one of them!" says Joey accusingly but Danny denies this.

The rising sun gleaming on dewy rooftops and shining through the windows of Danny's flat makes them all feel tired so Kelvin and Joey take their leave of their dad but not before Joey warns him, once more, not to get involved and to leave everything to the police. And, just as he'd said to DS Dean, Danny promises he won't do anything stupid. *Depends on what you mean by stupid!* Danny thinks as he shuts the door behind his sons.

Alone in his flat, Danny contemplates going to bed but he's far too wired to sleep and so watches TV instead. The television is still blaring away when he wakes up. His poor old neck is stiff from falling asleep on the settee. He looks at the clock; it's half past nine. *Too early!* Tired out, and feeling like he's been hit by a train, Danny crawls into his bed. After ten hours' fitful sleep Danny wakes with a start. All that has happened since the two o'clock phone call floods into his consciousness. *I need to see where it happened!*

*

Alighting from the bus, Danny glances across the road to the spot where Lucy was mugged. Standing statue-like on the pavement, he notices a dark stain on the kerbstone. It looks like dried blood and he should know, he's seen enough of the stuff in his lifetime. Walking trancelike towards the stain, Danny steps out in front of a delivery lorry which only just stops in time before hitting him. The driver blasts his horn at Danny who takes no notice, so the driver leaps out of his lorry to confront him and sees from the look in Danny's eyes that something's not right.

"Are you okay mate?" the lorry driver asks, concerned for Danny's welfare.

"What? Yeah, mate. No. I'm fine," Danny answers, his voice weak and trembling.

"You don't look fine to me. Do you want me to call an ambulance for you?"

"My daughter was attacked last night... over there," Danny says, pointing. "They knocked her over and she hit her head. She's in St Thomas' in a coma... all for a mobile phone..." By now a crowd has gathered.

"C'mon, mate," says the lorry driver, "let's you and me go and sit in my lorry."

"I should've been there to protect her. If I was there it wouldn't've happened."

"Do the police know?"

"Oh yeah, the police know alright. They even know who did it but they can't do anything."

"I know what you mean. Look, mate, there's a caf I go to just around the corner, why don't you and me go there for a cup of tea and a talk?"

"No thanks, I'll be okay. It was just the shock of seeing where it happened. That stain over there," says Danny, pointing again, "that's my daughter's blood that is. She shouldn't've been here! She was supposed to be… Whenever she comes to London she never tells me but if she did and I know she's here I can tell her where's safe and not safe to go. I'd've told her about what it's like around here then s-she wouldn't've been here!" The lorry driver thinks Danny needs looking after.

"C'mon mate, I know you're upset and you've got every right to be. Look, why don't you go home… I'll even drive you."

"Thanks, but I don't want to go home. I came to see where it happened and I want to stay for a while but thanks, I'll be alright. Don't worry, I'll be alright."

Danny leaves the lorry driver and crosses the road to where Lucy was mugged. Arriving at the scene of the attack, he looks up and down the road to see who's around but refuses to look down at the bloodstain. He takes his mobile phone out of his pocket and starts using it to try and attract the attention of Scooter Muggers. Typical of a soldier like Danny, he's thought it through and positions himself in such a way that the muggers will have to pass between himself and the road to snatch the phone. Having excellent peripheral vision, he's confident that he'll see them coming, no matter which direction they come from. He has it planned that when they make a grab for his phone, he'll shove them into the road, *hopefully right in front of a bus! Yeah, hopefully flatten the lives out of them!* If the Scooter Muggers don't get hit by anything, he knows they're likely to come for him but he's thought this through too. If they're wearing crash helmets, he'll knee stamp them, but if not, he'll deploy whichever of his "moves" seems best depending on whether it's both together or one at a time. If there are more than two, he plans to take the first two down hard, knowing any others will likely run away. He has no plans to run away or run after anyone.

After thirty minutes waiting for the Scooter Muggers to show up, Danny's phone is almost out of battery. *I need to get it charged up. You should've charged it up before you left the flat!* Just then, Danny notices a youngster of ten or eleven cruising up and down the pavement on a bicycle on the opposite side of the road. He's on his phone and all the while looking directly at Danny. *He's a spotter!* The cyclist tries to appear nonchalant but it's obvious from his body language he's no such thing. Five minutes later, Danny's phone battery dies and with no light showing to attract Scooter Muggers, he puts it away and then crosses the road to confront the spotter. As soon as Danny gets close, the spotter ends his call, puts his phone in his hoodie pocket and cycles away at speed. Despite Danny heard some of what the spotter was jabbering, he has no idea what it was he said but assumes it must've been street slang which, he supposes, means he's in a street gang. *I should've run after him!* Believing the evening is a bust, Danny looks around for a pub because he's gasping for a drink. He doesn't accept he's an alcoholic but he can't go more than a day without at least having a couple of pints of beer inside him.

Just on the corner is a pub called The Oak. Danny thinks it looks okay and goes inside where he finds he's one of only three white faces. The bar is packed with locals and, going by the banter flying between them, the atmos is friendly, so Danny orders a pint of beer and takes a seat at the only empty table in the whole place. As he sits, he wonders why the table is empty.

"You don't want to sit there man," advises a massive black guy.

"Oh, why's that?" Danny enquires of the absolute unit standing in front of him. *Reminds me a bit of Taylor.*

"Because, my friend, it's next to the dartboard and they're all terrible shots in here," the man says, laughing.

"I've had worse things than a few darts fired at me," responds Danny casually.

"Oh really? What you had fired at you then?"

"You name it: RPGs, every type of round from two two to a forty-five, shells, mortar rounds and the odd crossbow bolt!"

"Who'd you upset to get that lot sent your way?" jokes the man.

"Hi, I'm Danny," he says, holding out his hand.

"I'm Albert, Alby to my friends," says the man-mountain. They shake hands. "So, you were in the army?"

"Yeah, over twenty years until the missus made me pull the plug. Divorced me a year later."

"Who were you with?"

"Tank Regiment... mostly," Danny lies.

"Royal Anglian!" says Alby, saluting and he and Danny shake hands again. "My missus divorced me too. She said she hated the army but as soon as I left she decided it wasn't too bad after all. Kids?"

"Five!"

"Four!"

Danny and Alby reminisce about their time in the military, though Danny's careful not to give too much away. It wouldn't do for him to share his secrets, as it could prove to be dangerous to those he shared them with.

"Haven't seen you in here before," says Alby, suspicious that Danny could be undercover police. "Not many people jus' drop in here for a beer. Have you just moved into a house or somethin'?" Danny realises Alby's sussing him out.

"Nah, I live in Camden. I... I... I came to see where my daughter got mugged. It happened just around the corner from here. They were after her mobile phone and now she's lying in a coma in St Thomas' Hospital. The doctors say she might never come out of it."

"Shit man, that's rough! But why you here though?"

"To be honest, I was using my mobile to try and bait the scumbags who attacked her so I could dish out some justice on them," says Danny, hoping to convince Alby he's no narc. "They were on scooters... Scooter Muggers the cops call them."

"Yeah, you see them ridin' around here all the time but baitin' them is stupid. My advice is don't do it, they'll probably stab you or somethin'. Stay away!"

"The detective I spoke to said the police know who it was that did it but they can't arrest them because they don't have any proof and nobody'll give a statement about them."

"You can't blame people for that. Anyone talk to the police around here gets branded a grass and bein' a grass on a housing estate, especially like this one, is a dangerous thing! Snitches get stitches, as they say!"

"Same around our way."

"Then you understand! Even though they're only kids, everyone's scared of them. They all carry knives… some of them carry guns and they're not scared of usin' them! An' they're not jus' into muggins, they're into everythin'… burglary, protection, nickin' cars and breakin' them up… drugs… especially drugs… everythin'!"

"Same in Camden… minus the scooter muggings… though I dare say some of that probably goes on too."

"It definitely does! My advice is to leave it to the police otherwise you'll end up lyin' next to your daughter in St Thomas' Hospital in a coma or dead!"

Danny and Alby spend a couple of hours drinking and putting the world to rights, talking about how drugs have ruined society and what can be done about street gangs. They conclude that until the police and local communities learn to trust one another and work together, ordinary people will continue to suffer and things won't improve until they stand up to criminals despite that it's dangerous to do so. As Danny and Alby share the same values, a kindred spiritship sparks between them and they swap mobile phone numbers. Before Danny leaves The Oak to wander home, he tells Alby that if he's ever in Camden he's to drop in and have a pint with him at his local, "The Manor it's called. Do you know it?" Alby says he does and promises he'll see Danny there one day.

CHAPTER THREE

The morning after his night drinking in The Oak with Alby, Danny wakes with a hangover and feeling out of sorts; his tolerance to alcohol is not what it used to be and all it seems to take these days is a couple of beers to fill his head with cotton wool the following day; *pathetic*, is the word that springs into his mind whenever he's like this. Having not eaten for almost forty-eight hours, the smell of frying bacon for his breakfast makes Danny retch; *I'll try a piece of dry toast instead and see how that goes.* After nibbling at half a slice of burnt, dry toast, Danny plugs in the electric kettle and places an "own-brand" teabag into his favourite mug which Brad had bought for him many years ago. It has the words "World's Best Dad" printed on it. Despite the mug being chipped and cracked, Danny wouldn't part with it for the world. He loves the things his kids have bought for him over the years and keeps them in a box inside the chest of drawers in his bedroom with the word "Treasures" written on a label stuck on it. Inside the box are gifts and knick-knacks and mementos given to him by his children when they were young. He's often thought that if he should ever get burgled, and the treasures box gets stolen, he'd track down the scumbags who stole it and dish out some righteous justice on them old-school style.

Feeling fragile, Danny settles down on the settee to watch whatever is on TV, nibble his dry toast and drink his mug of tea without sugar; *bloody sugar! I knew there was something I forgot* to get while I was out shopping. *I should've written a list! I knew I should've written a list! Something else to forget!* The midday news has just begun. "He's not worth the licence fee… none of them are!" Danny shouts at the TV and points at the newscaster. It's just the usual items today; the government are saying they're doing things about this and that and the opposition parties spouting platitudes about it being "too little too late" and the like. *As if that lot've got any idea! They're useless, every one of them!* After several international news items about oil, famine and disease, followed by sport, there's the weather before the regional news programmes take over. As the London news comes on, Danny goes into shock seeing Lucy's face filling the screen and the newsreader saying how she's the latest victim in the growing number of people being robbed for their mobile phones by Scooter Muggers and now she's lying in a coma in the ICU of St Thomas' Hospital. The screen switches to a reporter standing outside St Thomas'. She's interviewing Detective Sergeant Dean; the caption at the bottom of the screen names him. He's saying how attacks like the one on Lucy are all too prevalent on the streets of London and he urges people to be careful when using their mobile phones in public. Danny's furious and wants to know why he wasn't told that the attack on his daughter was going to be on the news. Within minutes, an angry Danny Deacon is washed, dressed, out the door and on the tube to St Thomas' Hospital where he's hoping he'll bump into DS Dean. When Danny arrives at St Thomas' there's no sign of DS Dean but there's a "DI Christine Haynes", according to her visitor badge; *she'll do! Yeah, she'll do!*

"Excuse me, I was just watching the BBC news," says Danny, without introducing himself. DI Haynes recognises him from the photographs in Lucy's case file.

"Ah, Mr Deacon, at last! We've been trying to get hold of you," says DI Haynes, rubbing Danny's coat sleeve sympathetically.

"Well, you couldn't've been trying very hard!" Danny snaps back.

"We kept calling but your phone kept going to voicemail. Did you play the messages? I left several myself. I'm so sorry about…" Danny realises what the problem is. His battery had died the previous night while he was out trying to bait the Scooter Muggers and he hasn't charged it back up.

"I've been having a bit of trouble with my phone lately and my voicemail is… anyway, I saw my daughter's face on the news and came as quickly as I could in case there's been a change in her condition," says Danny, thinking on his feet and not wanting to answer any questions about his phone.

"As far as I know, there has been no change but you'll need to speak with the doctors. I was about to go up to the ICU ward. Shall we go together?"

"Do you know a Detective Sergeant Dean?" asks Danny, gritting his teeth.

"I do… I'm his boss. He's waiting outside the ICU for me."

"I see," says Danny, taken aback. "So is it you or him that's in charge of the case?"

"Detective Sergeant Dean is the lead IO, Investigating Officer, for the case but he reports everything directly to me as the SIO, Senior Investigating Officer, so I can focus resources, and so forth, to best effect. Working in this way ensures we achieve maximum results through solving crimes in the most expeditious manner," says DI Haynes, speaking in a serious voice and wearing a serious face. Danny's heard this type of "duck-speak" many times before, and in his mind, labels DI Haynes a greasy-pole climber.

"That's erm… very reassuring," says Danny, smiling as he used to to officers when really he thought they were idiots, and lots of people, usually civilians, were going to die.

*

As Danny and DI Haynes exit the lift, they come face to face with DS Dean. Danny tells the DS he saw him on the BBC lunchtime news and he's angry at not being told about Lucy's case being broadcast. DS Dean repeats what DI Haynes had said, insisting he tried to contact Danny about the interview in order to prepare him, but couldn't get hold of him. Danny asks, in which case, as he wasn't contacted, why the interview went ahead. Dean says he cleared everything through Lucy's mother. Seeing the expression on Danny's face, DS Dean surmises this isn't something he wanted to hear. DI Haynes, however, is angry with her DS for different reasons. As his boss, she thought it should've been her who'd given the interview as a way of boosting her profile within the Met and to advance her career at the same time. She'd come to St Thomas' specifically to reprimand DS Dean.

Before either DS Dean, DI Haynes or Danny can say another word, the consultant neurologist who Danny had met on his first visit emerges from the ICU flanked by interns. Recognising Danny, she beckons him to join her in the family room. This is the second time he's been invited in there and wonders if this time it'll be better news. While the CN brings Danny up to date with his daughter's condition and treatment, DI Haynes orders DS Dean to join her in a walk along the corridor, during which she informs him that, in future, should it be deemed necessary and appropriate, it will be she who will give TV interviews concerning the Lucy Davies case and he's to clear all requests, whether for TV, press or anything else concerning the case, through her, in writing, beforehand. "Do you understand?" asks DI Haynes sternly. DS Dean says he understands perfectly, then adds that this wasn't a request from the media, the interview was his idea as a way of highlighting the growing problem of scooter muggings and he'd arranged it through an old contact of his at the BBC. This revelation makes DI Haynes even more angry. She's sick and tired of old fart lags like Dean doing things their way, the way they'd done things for years, and resolves to speak to the Chief Superintendent, a personal friend of her father, about bringing his retirement forward by two years, and get rid of him straightaway. As the DI storms off, DS Dean chuckles quietly to himself. *Idiot. She'll have to get up pretty early in the morning to get one over on old Deany!*

*

Following his talk with the CN, Danny goes to enter the ICU but he's prevented by a nurse from doing so, "There are already two visitors with your daughter, Mr Deacon, so you'll have to wait until at least one of them leaves," she says. Danny asks who the visitors are. She says Mr and Mrs Baxter are with Lucy. Danny asks her if she'd be so kind as to tell Mrs Baxter that he's here and would she mind telling her husband to get lost so he can visit his daughter. The nurse smiles and says, "You're just like my old dad you are. Hang on a minute and I'll go and tell them they've had their turn and other family members are waiting." Danny thanks the nurse and tells her that she's just like his daughter which makes them both smile. "Couldn't charge my phone, could I?" Danny asks, waving his mobile in the air. The nurse takes Danny's phone and plugs it into a charger. The minute Joyce and Jeff depart the ICU, Danny hotfoots to Lucy's bedside. He sits down, without looking at Lucy's taped eyes, and takes hold of her hand. It's warmer than he expected. He notices a deep rumble he hadn't noticed during his first visit. He listens carefully for a minute before deducing it's the collective drone of hushed tones of visitors talking with their loved ones. Drawing the curtains around Lucy's bed, Danny hopes he can talk to her in private without being overheard by anyone.

"Hello Luce love, it's Dad here. I just wanted to…" Danny pauses for a moment, choked with emotion. "I just wanted to let you know what's going on and what I've been up to. I spoke to the doctor just now and she says there's no change for the moment but I know you, you'll pull through. Everyone's here, you know, the boys, well Kel and Joebyjoe, I think Brad's on his way but, according to Professor Plum, Brad's car's a load of old rubbish so he might not make it… sorry, this is boring… for you I mean, not for me!

"Kel said Steph's gone back home to Edinburgh but he's 'keeping her informed', as they say. Your mum's here with number four. I reckon the reason she's been married so many times is because she loves wedding cake so much," Danny jokes, gives a little chuckle and then continues. "Remember when you were a little girl? You used to come to me for everything. I remember one Sunday morning when you were about four you asked me to teach you to ride your bike without stabilisers. We went to the little cul-de-sac just around the corner from the house. It was always empty but that morning it was full of cars parked all down one side. I looked along the line of cars and said, 'There's plenty of room,' you looked doubtful but you had that determined look on your face and set off pedalling with me holding the seat. After a couple of goes you were ready to try it on your own. I kept hold of the seat for a few yards but then let go. Do you remember what happened next?" Danny asks and looks at Lucy's face for the first time. She looks so peaceful lying there. Beautiful. He wants to remove the tape holding her eyelids closed but stops himself from doing so. Instead he squeezes her hand and tells her that he loves her. He's sure he feels her squeeze his hand back, so he squeezes her hand again. Nothing. Again. Nothing. Again. Nothing. Again. Nothing for the fourth time, so he continues his story about teaching her to ride her bike without stabilisers. "You went wobbling off down the road and ended up scraping your pedal all down the side of a shiny, new silver Mercedes. Do you remember what I said? I said, 'Well, if you go leaving your shiny, new silver Mercedes where kids learn to ride their bikes then you've only yourself to blame.' When I looked round you were halfway home. We never told Mum that one.

"Remember when I taught you to dive at the local swimming pool during the school holidays? You did some big belly flops at first but you never gave up. In and out, in and out the pool you were. Once you got the hang of it, though, you were perfect. Perfect. You dived into the water without making so much as a splash... like a little water nymph you were. All your friends were jealous you were so good so you taught them how to dive. You were always good like that. Remember when…

"Listen, Luce, I found out from the detective investigating your case, Detective Sergeant Dean's his name, where you were… you know… attacked, so I went to see for myself. Joebyjoe knew that's what I'd do and he warned me not to do it but I did it anyway. He told me not to get involved but I had to. You understand, I know you understand because I made you all that promise when you were kids. So… I went and stood where you stood and took out my phone to attract the Scooter Muggers but nobody showed up. There was a kid on the opposite pavement who I reckoned was a spotter so I went to speak with him but he cycled away. My battery died so I went for a pint in a local pub and met a big black geezer called Alby. Anyway, we had a chat and it turns out he used to be in the army too and his missus made him leave and then divorced him just like someone else we know!" Danny attempts a laugh to lighten the mood but can't. "Anyway, me and Alby, we have the same sort of values… same sort of attitudes… same sort of standards type of thing. Before I left, we swapped phone numbers and I told him that if he's ever around Camden to drop into The Manor for a pint." Out of fear for where his daughter is and what might become of her, Danny's emotions get the better of him and cause him to cry out in pain and anguish, "Wake up Luce! Please wake up my little darling! I wish you'd wake up Luce. I wish you'd wake up! Wake up girl! C'mon girl, wake up!"

A nurse comes to investigate what all the commotion is and finds Danny kneeling at the side of his daughter's bed. He looks as if he's praying. *I'll get them, Luce, I'll get them, don't you worry girl, I'll get them!* This is Danny's silent prayer and pledge to his daughter. Taking in the scene, the nurse disappears and returns with a cup of tea. "Don't suppose you've got a couple of sugars to go with it have you?" Danny asks after taking a sip. The nurse returns with a bowl of sugar while swivelling Danny's phone in front of her like she's winding a clock.

"There's a Detective Sergeant Dean on the phone for you," says the nurse. "You'll have to take the call outside I'm afraid."

"Hello," says Danny, speaking quietly into his phone from the lift concourse.

"I heard you went snooping around where your daughter got mugged," says DS Dean, sounding none too pleased but not angry.

"So what! I wanted to see where it happened so I could get things right in my head," replies Danny unapologetically.

"I don't like being taken for a mug, Deacon! You promised me if I told you where your daughter was mugged you wouldn't go snooping around."

"No, Sherlock, I said I wouldn't do anything stupid. That's a completely different thing and, as it happens, I didn't do anything stupid!"

"Oh really? Then what do you call standing in the exact same spot where Lucy was mugged with your phone lit up like Harrods at Christmas? What were you doing? Baiting the muggers?"

"So what if I was? It's a free country. In any case, I can look after myself!"

"Listen, Danny, I know what you're going through, I see it all the time, but these street gangs are ruthless. They carry knives, axes, machetes, acid, all sorts of things… some even carry guns! Don't get involved, I don't want to see you getting hurt or killed," the detective lies because he doesn't give a toss whether Danny gets hurt or not, he just wants Tomic behind bars and is prepared to do anything to put him there before he retires.

"Anyway, who was it grassed me up?"

"It don't matter. What matters is, you staying away from where you shouldn't be! Understand? If you do anything like that again I'll arrest you for obstructing a police officer in the course of his duty."

"You don't frighten me Dean. You told me these gangs do what they want and they get away with it because the police can't get any evidence against them. Well, when I get my hands on them, I'll get your evidence for you! I'll get your statements for you!" Danny screams down the phone.

"I'm warning you Danny, don't go sticking your nose where it'll get bitten off!" says DS Dean, pleased he's got himself a hot-head who'll go and do something stupid and, if he gets injured, be a witness to lock up Tomic or, if he gets killed, be a source of DNA evidence to send him away for life: *winner, winner, chicken dinner!*

*

After his phone conversation with DS Dean, Danny is absolutely fuming. He races round to The Oak to confront Alby, convinced he must've grassed him up to Dean. Entering the bar, he spots Alby and gives him a nod to join him over by the pool table. Alby tells Danny he's a pretty good pool player but if he fancies his chances he'll play him for £1 a frame. Picking up a pool cue, Danny tells Alby that someone grassed him up to DS Dean about him visiting the spot where his daughter was attacked. Alby gets the gist straightaway and warns Danny not to accuse him of being a grass as, while it's not true, and he insists that it's not, just being labelled a grass on a housing estate like his is dangerous. "There are always people lookin' for any excuse to do you in," Alby whispers. Danny whispers back asking how a guy as big as him is afraid of anyone! Alby lifts his T-shirt and shows Danny his stomach. It's been sliced and stitched to hell and looks like a bad road map. "Eleven times I got stabbed. I only just survived. No matter how big or how tough or how strong you are you can still get stabbed or shot or axed or anythin'. The ones who did it were around fifteen! Fifteen! I revenged on their older brothers. Afterwards everyone agreed that justice had been done and there'd be no more revengin'... all quits. That's what we said, that's what everyone thinks, but they'll come for me on any excuse... but I'm ready for them," Alby says with iron resolve.

Danny wants to believe that Alby isn't a grass and so takes him into his confidence as a way of testing him. He tells Alby that he wants to do more than just bait the Scooter Muggers, "I want to disappear them," he says matter-of-factly. Alby scoffs at the idea and repeats what he said to Danny before about leaving it to the police. "Don't mess with these people man, I'm tellin' you! Look what happened to me!" Alby says forcefully. Danny asks if any of the ones who stabbed him are still around. "Yeah… one or two. One goes by the street name Tomic. He's the latest wannabe Mr Big! He's got a sidekick, an idiot that goes by the name of Pitbull. Pitbull, I ask you? What an idiot!" Hearing Tomic's and Pitbull's names again so soon after hearing them for the first time shocks and astonishes Danny. He says he thinks he's heard their names before. Alby says he's not surprised. Danny tells Alby about DS Dean telling him that the Scooter Muggers that attacked his daughter are both white and asks Alby if he knows who they are. Alby says quite a few of them are white. "Yeah, but, would you know who might be the ones who attacked my daughter?" Danny asks. Alby tells him, for the third time, to leave it to the police. "Listen, Danny, if you go all gangster, you'll end up getting killed. I mean it man!" warns Alby. Danny says he reckons himself more of a vigilante than a gangster. Alby reckons he likes the sound of being a vigilante and says he fancies himself for the job.

"You know Alby, you're built like a brick outhouse yet you stand by while a bunch of skinny kids terrorise your streets and don't do anything about it, none of you do!" Danny says, looking around the pub. "As a former soldier, you shouldn't be scared of anything, I'm not!"

"Who says we don't do nothing? We're just careful what we do, that's all. It's the difference between stayin' alive and not."

"So, tell me then, what you do?"

"Better not, it might give you ideas. Now, shut up talkin' and let's have a beer and shoot some pool. Okay?"

"Okay, but tell me about Tomic and his gang while we play," Danny insists.

"They're the worst of the worst of the street gangs. It's like they're tryin' to outdo the others to keep them in fear. On the surface there's only about ten of them but behind them are about a hundred wannabes who'll do anything to get noticed by Tomic so they can join the 'Numbers', as they call themselves. Listen man, these kids don't have any boundaries. They think nothin' of shootin' someone or throwin' acid in the face of someone who's 'disrespected' them!" says Alby, making air-quotes around the word 'disrespected'. "They don't know nothin' about respect!" hisses Alby. Danny nods in agreement. "In fact, I'll tell you somethin', most people around here who go missin' hasn't run away or nothin', they been took by these wannabees doin' Tomic's dirty work!"

"Listen Alby, tell me, man to man, where can I find this Tomic or his mate Pitbull? What do they look like?"

"Take a look out the window," says Alby, nodding towards the road. "See those two at the traffic lights ridin' on a scooter? That's Tomic and Pitbull. Tomic's the one in front."

Danny trots over to the pub window and outside, not twenty feet from him, two scrawny-looking youths are sat smoking weed on a scooter waiting for the traffic lights to change. They're laughing and joking and yelling at passers-by as they rev the hell out of the scooter, making it spew a stream of choking blue smoke. Danny assumes, going by the state of the scooter, it's stolen. He's not wrong. This is just one of over forty scooters Tomic and his gang have stashed in and around the estate. Many of them are kept out of sight inside people's houses. They don't necessarily have anything to do with Tomic or his gang but they're too afraid to refuse when asked to do things like stash scooters or drugs or guns. Danny asks Alby if he's sure it's them. He says he is. Danny asks how he knows. Alby says he knows it's Tomic and Pitbull because he's known them since they were kids, "Which isn't so long ago," he adds with a rueful smile.

Taking out his mobile phone, Danny snaps a quick pic of Tomic and Pitbull at the precise moment they turn to face him. Realising his photo is being taken, Tomic throws the scooter to the ground and he and Pitbull make for The Oak, scattering pedestrians everywhere. Booting the pub's door open T&P march in like they own the place. Terrified locals at the bar turn their heads away; they know what's about to happen and don't want to get involved. Tomic orders the bar manager to turn the CCTV off and wipe the recording and then orders everyone in the bar to switch their phones off. Danny's moderately impressed with the way these two little gangsters took charge and asserted themselves; *reminds me of me when I was running ops in 'Nam.*

"What the fuck do you think you're fuckin' doin' takin' a pic of me and my bro you fuckin' wanker?" yells Tomic, trying to make his voice sound tough but failing miserably to do so.

"I wasn't taking a photo of you, I was taking a photo of your scooter, actually," says Danny mildly. "I love scooters I do. Love everything about them. Love taking photographs of them. Always have. I couldn't tell what type yours is though. It's a bit rough. Have you given it the 'rat look' or something? I had Vespers when I was a mod… you know? We used to ride down to Brighton on weekends for a rumble with Rockers… motorbike boys, you know? Ever hear of them?" Danny adds nonchalantly. His blasé attitude disturbs Tomic and Pitbull. They're disconcerted at how he's not scared of them. Perplexed, Tomic and Pitbull remove their helmets so they can better assert themselves. This gives Danny a good look at their faces. Tomic realises he's made a mistake, as not only does this person know what he looks like, his boyish features wouldn't frighten anyone.

"Listen, you old fucker, if you don't delete that pic I'll fuck you up! I will fuck you up good, bro. I'll fuck you up right here and now!" screams Tomic, his voice crackling and breaking. Everyone in the pub thinks he sounds more pathetic than frightening.

"Look lads, there's no need for that," says Danny coolly. "If it means that much to you, I'll delete the photo." Danny deletes a random pic from his phone. "There? Okay?"

"I wanna see, bruv," demands Tomic.

"Don't push your luck, sonny," Danny says coldly and stares at Tomic face to face. Sensing something's about to happen, the pub falls silent. Feeling as if they've been exposed, Tomic and Pitbull turn and make a big show of stomping out of the pub trying to appear tough. Several locals jeer at them but the pub manager tells them to shut up, fearful that they'll take their revenge on him.

"See, Alby, they're just kids. Just stupid bloody kids!" says Danny, picking up his pint of beer and emptying it in one. "Your round I think," he says waving his empty glass.

"Look, Danny, I know these kids. They won't take what you did well. The best thing you can do is leave right now and never come back!"

"No chance!" says Danny, snorting disdainfully and laughing.

"It's no laughing matter. They'll come back with reinforcements to put everyone in their place!"

"You're serious?"

"I am. I've seen it before. They never forget. Go back to Camden and stay there. If I'm over that way I'll call and we can meet up… now go!"

The drinkers in the bar back up what Alby said and urge Danny to leave as quickly as he can and not come back. Just as Danny's leaving, Alby spies a couple of Tomic's spotters and tells him to use the emergency exit at the rear of the pub. It suddenly starts to feel real to Danny and he puts himself on high alert; *just like the old days*, he thinks as he realises he likes danger, *I've missed this!*

Leaving the pub via the emergency exit, Danny finds himself in an alley full of bins and mountains of rubbish swarming with flies. The situation reminds him of ops in Vietnam when he'd had to extricate himself from a village after assassinating a warlord. *Look like you fit in. Do what a normal person would do!* Taking the advice of his inner voice, Danny throws his jacket over his shoulder, saunters across the road to the bus stop and checks the electronic arrivals matrix. According to the display, there's a bus for Camden due in ten minutes. It still amazes him that this type of information is at every bus stop. Just then, Danny notices a spotter pointing him out to a kid on a bike who then cycles away along the pavement.

To be cautious, he catches the next bus that comes along and goes to the upper deck where he takes the back seat to see if anybody is following him. The coast is clear, nobody seems to be following him. When Danny goes to get off at the next stop, so he can catch the bus to Camden, he spots seven scooters, all of them two up, speeding towards his bus. He waits to see if they pass by. They don't. Instead, they pull up twenty feet behind the bus and the riders exchange words with one another. One of the scooters races past the bus, heading its next stop, while the other scooters only move off when the bus does so. The scooter at the head of the pursuing pack is being ridden by Tomic and another by Pitbull. Danny's palms begin to sweat, not out of fear but in anticipation. He rubs them together like a mystic performing an incantation; he feels excited, alive, just like when he was on ops in Vietnam. With adrenaline coursing through his veins, electrifying his brain, Danny pumps his muscles up ready for action. He feels good; better than good, he feels invincible! The words, *you're going to get the fright and the fight of your life Tomic me old mate!* Percolate in Danny's head. He goes to stand on the lower deck of the bus and stares out of the rear window at Tomic who gestures that he's spotted Danny by pointing two fingers back and forth between himself and Danny. Danny does the same to Tomic and takes pics of him and the other scooter riders to annoy them.

Weighing the possibility that two gang members are waiting for him at the next bus stop, Danny stands by the middle doors as though he's preparing to get off the bus. At the next bus stop are five people, two wearing crash helmets. One of them signals for the bus to stop. The driver pulls in and, just as the bus comes to a halt, Danny steps out of the middle doors onto the pavement. Both crash helmet wearers come towards him. Danny walks towards them, which surprises them, they'd expected him to run. Once within reach of the scooter riders, Danny knee stamps the closest of them and throat chops the other just below the chinstrap of his helmet, which acted as a guide for Danny for where to hit him. It's over in the blink of an eye. Danny's "moves" prove to be devastatingly effective. The one who got knee stamped is left rolling around the floor in agony while the other is holding his throat and croaking like a demented frog that he can't breathe and begging passers-by to help him. Fight over, if it could be called that, Danny calmly steps back onto the bus and signals for the driver to move off. As the bus pulls away, Danny looks back at his handiwork with great satisfaction. None of the pursuing pack of scooters stop to check if their mates are okay, they follow the bus instead.

As the bus comes to a halt at a set of traffic lights, Tomic is in two minds whether he should leap from his scooter, enter the bus and stab Danny but in his moment of hesitation the lights turn green, the bus moves off and his chance has gone. The scooter riders are continuing their pursuit of the bus when they come to the attention of a special police unit set up to tackle scooter crime. The scooters and riders don't look right to the cops so they give them a flash of the blues. The scooters immediately "starburst", racing off in all directions like scalded cats. The cops give chase but quickly lose the scooters in heavy city traffic. The officers put out a police alert on the scooters and their riders. The majority of officers listening know precisely who the riders are but they also know the scooters will be ditched by now and the riders gone to ground. It being a complete waste of their time, in their opinion, to go chasing shadows when they have criminals of their own to deal with, they all ignore the call. Besides, none of them go onto Tomic's patch if they don't have to and often choose not to.

*

Half an hour later, Tomic and a posse of wannabees turn up at The Oak pub. Tomic orders the bar manager to turn off the CCTV. Everyone knows why they are there and turn away, hoping not to catch Tomic's eye. Alby, on the other hand, is playing pool and pays them no mind whatsoever. Sauntering over to the pool table, Tomic picks up a cue; *if you look like you're gonna use that on me I'm gonna break your head!* Thinks Alby, staring fixedly at Tomic and the pool cue he's holding.

"Your mate," says Tomic through gritted teeth, trying to sound tough. "The one who took the pic of me and Pitbull. Who is he? What's his name?"

"No idea. He just came in and we got talkin', that's all," says Alby nonchalantly and lines up his next shot.

"Fuck off Alby, you don't talk to no one, everyone knows that, bro!" snaps Tomic when out of the corner of his eye he spots several of Alby's crew shaping up by cracking their necks from side to side like weightlifters do before they're about to lift a really big weight. Tomic's bros notice this too and get nervous, these guys are big and not to be messed with.

"You know, Antoine, you shouldn't come in here bein' rude and pushin' people around, it's not polite. I told you I don't know who this guy is and that's that. Now, if you don't mind, I've got to practise my game, we've got a big match comin' up against The Northern Star and there's a lot of money ridin' on it so..." says Alby while indicating to Tomic to move away from the pool table with a wave of his cue.

Tomic hates it when people call him Antoine and wants to make a big show about it but looking around at the faces of the drinkers, he sees they're not as scared of him as he would like them to be. Alby's a big guy and well liked on the estate, so Tomic doesn't want to push things with him and so leaves The Oak with his bros at his back while all issuing random threats over their shoulders. Once Tomic is out of the pub, Alby's crew come over and ask if he wants something about Tomic. Alby says to leave off for the time being and to watch their backs as he's got a feeling the shit's about to hit the fan in a big way; not before time, in DS Dean's opinion.

CHAPTER FOUR

Four hours after his skirmish with the scooter riders, Danny is on his way back to Camden. He could've gone there earlier but has been playing soldiers. He could've simply changed buses after the police gave chase to Tomic and his gang and he'd've been home in twenty minutes but pumped up full of adrenaline and with a head full of memories of things he'd done in Vietnam he wanted to practise surveillance evasion. After he disembarked in Whitechapel, Danny mingled with the crowd, ensuring he moved at the same speed as those around him; this is known as "moving with the herd" so as to blend in and not stick out. He'd walked for miles along busy streets, glancing sideways, at various angles, at reflections in shop windows, checking to make sure he wasn't being "followed". He crossed and re-crossed roads several times and reversed direction after stopping to pretend "window shop". While doing this, he checked out pedestrians on his side and the other side of the road as well as passing traffic. *Not bad... not bad! Still got it! You're kidding yourself!* After so many years as a civilian, Danny needs all the practice he can get. Then, dodging into Liverpool Street station, Danny takes the Metropolitan line to King's Cross and, after switching lines no fewer than six times, catches the Northern line to Camden Town; his home ground, the best ground for him and the worst for any enemy. *Game over.*

While Danny practised "evasion tactics", he did some scheming in his head and needed to return to his flat to execute the first phase of his plan. However, right slap bang in between Camden Town tube station and Danny's flat is The Manor pub, so he stops in for a pint. *Shame not to go in for a beer.* On entering the pub, Danny spots Gaz and Jacko; it's not difficult, they're sat in their usual places. They spot him and nod a greeting. In response, Danny jiggles his hand, asking if they'd like a pint. They think he must be grief-stricken at what's happened to his daughter to offer them a beer without any arm-twisting. Nevertheless, they both nod "yes".

"We heard about Lucy," says Gaz sympathetically.

"Yeah... saw it on the telly news," adds Jacko equally sympathetically.

"Suppose you've been up at the hospital then?" says Gaz.

"Yeah... Kel and Joebyjoe are there and so's the ex and her husband. I was the first one there, though, after I got the call."

"How is she?" asks Jacko.

"They've put her in what they call 'a medically induced coma'. They had to do it because she was..." Danny falls silent. Talking about Lucy takes the wind out of him.

"Bet you'd like to get hold of the bastards that did it, eh?" says Gaz. His words bring Danny back on track.

"Yeah... yeah. In fact, I went to the spot where it happened to see if I could see anyone."

"What d'ye mean like?" asks Gaz.

"The detective in charge of the investigation told me where she got attacked and I went there... you know, to see if I could bait them into trying to rob me."

"What!" gasps Jacko in disbelief.

"Why?" Gaz asks.

"Why'd you think?"

"How'd you get on?" asks Jacko.

"No good, I saw a spotter for the gang that did it though; Scooter Muggers they call them. Nothing came of it so I ended up going for a pint in a pub called The Oak. Met a bloke there called Alby. Good lad he is!"

"I know The Oak, good pub," says Gaz who believes all pubs are good.

"Wasn't that a bit dangerous, you know, baiting these Scooter Muggers, like? I've seen things about them on the telly. Nasty bastards they are! You want to be careful Danny Boy. Just leave it to the police."

"Leave it to the police? Don't make me laugh! They're hopeless. The detective told me he knows who it was that attacked Luce, they all do, but they can't charge them with anything! There's no evidence and no one will make a statement against them!"

"Danny, mate, I'm telling you, leave it to the police. If these Scooter Muggers get hold of you they'll kick the shit out of you or stab you or something!"

"Yeah, Gaz's right. There's so many of them. You'll have no chance against them!"

"Yeah, maybe you're right," says Danny, pretending to take their advice. "Maybe you're right."

"Look Danny, at our ages we've gotta be careful. A kick or punch in the wrong place and it's all over for the likes of us! Remember old what's-his-name? The one who ran after a couple of lads down by the tube station? They put him in hospital… never came out! Left behind a missus and a couple of handfuls of grandkids. Poor bugger!"

"Yeah, you're right, I'll leave it to the police. Before I forget, that bloke I mentioned, Alby. I told him that if he's ever around this way he's to drop in for a pint, so if he shows up treat him like family."

"What, borrow money off him and don't pay it back?" jokes Gaz, taking a swipe at Danny for not paying his beer debts.

"Or do you mean after borrowing his car return it back to him with no petrol in the tank," jokes Jacko, taking a swipe at Danny for not filling his car up the last time he borrowed it.

"Yeah, that's right," laughs Danny. "Very funny. But seriously though, he's a big lad and could be handy to know if you know what I mean?"

Neither Gaz nor Jacko felt Danny hadn't meant what he'd said about not getting involved and leaving things to the police. Though he'd never told them much about his time in the army, they had the feeling he wasn't just a run-of-the-mill grunt like they were. There was something about him that Gaz and Jacko have always been uncomfortable with which made them wary of him. They tell people he's not the sort of person you want to cross or mess with. When asked what they mean, they say it's not something they can put a finger on, it's just a feeling they have about him.

*

After wolfing down a cheese sandwich to soak up the beer, Danny changes his clothes, puts on a disguise, grabs a pile of cash from his emergency fund and makes for the tube station. He's going to a shop he knows south of the river in Southwark. Sitting on the other side of the carriage to Danny are two men in their early twenties. They're chatting on their phones and have their feet on the seats opposite. Danny gives them a look as if to say, "Get your feet off the seats, you wouldn't do it at home!" One of them stares at Danny who stares back. The other man looks to see who his friend is staring at. "You got a problem, pal?" he asks. Danny politely tells them to take their feet off the seats as people shouldn't have to sit where someone has put their feet. He says someone could get something nasty on their clothes. The men ignore Danny and continue mindless phone-chatting with mindless mates. Danny says he hopes that when they grow up they'll be rich and successful and one day sit down where someone has had their feet on a seat and get their trousers covered in dog shit. The men laugh and call Danny a sad old wanker. He's just in the mood to launch his "moves" on them when they look up from their phones, realise they're at their stop and get off, hurling obscene abuse at Danny as they do so. He has an excellent memory for faces and puts theirs in the bank in the hope he'll come across one or both of them one day somewhere nice and quiet with no CCTV around.

He'll sneak up on them, nice and quiet like, and chop-kick them in the backs of their knees, wrecking their ACLs and sending them sprawling and screaming to the ground. The idea makes Danny so happy he muses about what he'll do to them once they're on the floor rolling around in agony. *Knee stamps and throat chops are favourite... not done an eye poke in a while... bowling ball... yeah, bowling ball... or nose slam? Nah, too dangerous... bowling ball it is!*

When Danny arrives at Southwark tube station, he heads west along The Cut towards Waterloo. The area's changed so much since he was a lad he hardly recognises it anymore. It used to be famous for boxing clubs, there's even a pub called The Ring, *but now*, he thinks, *it's lost all its character. It's just full of pubs selling overpriced beer to City types and theatres with plays I can't afford to go and see. I used to love going to the theatre when the kids were small... Pantos, they loved pantos. We must go again before I die!*

After a ten-minute walk, Danny stops outside a shop that looks like it's been closed for years. The windows are filthy inside and out, and windblown rubbish is piled up against the door. Squinting through the reinforced window in the shop's front door, Danny spies movement inside, so he knocks. A voice shouts, "Who's there?" Danny shouts back, "It's me, Danny Deacon." The voice shouts, telling him he'll have to wait as she's dealing with a customer. Understanding the need for privacy, Danny moves to a doorway two along from the shop. This one's been closed for years but Danny peers through the window for something to do. As the customer leaves the shop, Danny returns and knocks on the door again. A voice shouts, "Who is it?" Danny answers, "It's me again." After the click of a lock, the slide of a bolt and the turn of a key, the door opens ajar. Half of a woman's face fills the gap. After eyeing Danny up and down, she says, "Come in," and opens the door just wide enough for him to enter the shop and then shuts and bolts and locks it as soon as he's inside. The room is dark and musty. Danny sniffs the air and thinks the place smells only slightly better than his flat.

"Can't be too careful these days," says the woman as she waddles behind the counter. "If it's not thieves trying to rob you it's the police... can't tell them apart at times!"

"Too true," says Danny.

"Now then, what can I do for you my love?" she asks, reaching under the counter for a can of cactus spray but stops when she recalls Danny to memory, a customer she's not seen for a while.

"I'm after a mobile phone. It's got to be a good one that can get the internet and stuff."

"How much do you want to pay?"

"I'm a pensioner, so not much money rolling in. I'm looking for a good deal. Can you help me out?"

"You and my Wilf used to be pals didn't you?"

"Yeah, sorry to hear about him by the way."

"I've got this one," the woman says, placing an almost new Samsung on the counter. "Got all the bells and whistles... loads of memory and stuff." Danny picks up the phone and examines it, though what he's looking for he has no idea.

"Nice. How much?"

"Well, I had to pay to get it unlocked and it cost me quite a bit but, seeing how's you were a mate of my Wilf, I can let you have it for what I paid for it, plus a twenty for my trouble... eighty quid all in!"

"Deal," says Danny, not sure whether the phone's cheap or not but that's not the point, it must be untraceable. The woman asks if there's anything else she can help with. "Not right now but... never mind. Another time. I'll see you again."

After leaving the shop, Danny makes his way to the nearest phone shop and purchases, with cash, a pay-as-you-go SIM with ten-pounds' credit on it. Now he's ready to execute his plan of delivering righteous justice on Tomic and his gang.

Danny makes his way to London Bridge station, somewhere he knows he can make free, untraceable WhatsApp calls from. It occurs to him the phone he's in possession of could've stolen by the very Scooter Muggers who attacked his daughter. He even considers it could be Lucy's phone, *but hers was an iPhone*, he thinks; *what the hell does that matter!* Scolds his internal voice. Deep down, Danny knows by having a hooky phone he's complicit in the crime itself and that such crimes beget crimes like burglary and drug dealing. "I don't have a choice," he mutters to himself. His internal voice disagrees with him.

Once inside London Bridge station, Danny makes for a quiet spot, logs into the free Wi-Fi and downloads WhatsApp onto his phone. He next logs on to a website for army veterans and heads to the noticeboard used for keeping in touch with buddies. Little does Danny, or any veteran, know, the website is funded by the US Secret Service to keep tabs on who is in contact with who, what they're doing and what they're saying. Danny's an infrequent user and on this occasion wants to know who's dead and who's alive from his old IPEF unit. He sees many more have died since he last logged on; *I suppose that's to be expected.* Some, however, have gone "off-grid"; and who can blame them, considering the suspicious circumstances in which many of his comrades have met their ends since returning from Vietnam. After making a note of which of his old oppos is still around, it's a short list of half a dozen "possibles" for what he has in mind, Danny enters their numbers into his phone and from there into WhatsApp. The first name on the list is his former Sergeant, Charles "Chuck" Henderson. Chuck's surprised to hear from Danny as they haven't spoken in over two decades and, according to the vets' website, Danny hasn't logged on for almost two years.

"I thought you were dead and nobody posted it," says Chuck dryly. Danny notes a certain "suspicion" in his tone.

"Nope, still alive. Are you still living in Virginia?"

"I sure am... how about you? You still in London?"

"I sure am," Danny replies, mimicking a dreadful American accent. "What about your boys?"

"San Francisco. Yours?"

"Two of my lads are in Bristol and the other one's in Leeds. One of my daughters lives in a place called Solihull, just outside Birmingham in the Midlands, and the other's in Edinburgh in Scotland."

"I know which country Edinburgh is in for Christ's sake," jokes Chuck.

"How's the wife?"

"Left me."

"Oh… sorry."

"Don't be, I was always a P in the A to live with… especially after 'Nam. What about you, did you ever remarry?"

"Yeah, but it didn't last. Then I was busy looking after kids and trying to make ends meet. By the way, are you in touch with any of the guys from 'B' Company?"

"To be honest I try not to be and, again to be honest, I'm kinda spooked you've called. So, why'd you call Danny?" asks Chuck on full alert.

"I… I… my daughter got attacked and now she's lying in a coma in hospital. The police know who attacked her but they can't do anything because there's no evidence and everyone's too afraid to speak. Even if the police get something on them all they'll get is a slap on the wrist or could even get away with it thanks to some smart-ass lawyer!"

"Tell me about it! The same shit happens here all the time. At least we have guns in the good old US of A and we know how to settle things! Hey, you're not going to ask me to send you some guns are you?" Chuck asks hoping the answer is "no" for a million reasons.

"No!" Danny cries emphatically. "But I do want something. In fact, I've already done something. I tried to bait the scumbags that attacked my daughter. Got nowhere but I pissed a couple of them off when I took a photograph of them."

"That'll work," Chuck laughs. "So, Danny, why are you calling?" he repeats coldly. Danny takes a deep breath.

"I want you to help me get justice for my daughter... for old times' sake."

"Hey man, you're not interested in justice, you're after revenge. I get it and I'd do the same in your position. What sort of help are you looking for?"

"I've got a plan. Remember Phnen Bin? Well, my idea is to get a few of the IPEF guys together and..."

"Whoa, whoa, whoa! Let me stop you right there man. Guys began holding reunions and get-togethers and the like and ended up dead in all sorts of weird ways... and so have some of their friends!" Danny guessed this from the veterans' website. "Nowadays, I stay away from "old IPEF buddies" and I keep my trap shut about what went on in Vietnam and I hope you do too!"

"I've never breathed a word of it to anyone... not even my kids. Surely, though, after all this time... I mean, who'd be interested?"

"Listen, man, the military never forgets... never! And the government want to keep what happened in Cambodia from ever getting out! Now, please don't ever call me again for both our sakes!"

"Chuck... please man... I'm begging!"

"Sorry, man, all that shit's behind me... behind all of us. Even if I was interested I'm way too old... we're all too old!"

"I thought so too but the thrill I got when I was out hunting them down and them chasing me on scooters... I tell you, I felt electric, I felt alive! What are you're doing that makes you feel alive, Chuck?" asks Danny accusingly. Chuck pauses before answering.

"Okay, let me think about it."

"What's there to think about? C'mon, Chuck, help me out for old times' sake."

"Who else you got?"

"You were the first person I thought of," Danny answers evasively.

"So, just me then? Let's keep it that way!" insists Chuck to dissuade Danny from contacting anyone else and thereby alerting those monitoring IPEF veterans.

"Yes, but…"

"Tell you what. You stand down and let me contact a few guys I occasionally chat with on the dark web. We use aliases and so far it's all good. They could be interested but if they're not then they're not and that's that. Okay?"

"Okay. Thanks Chuck, I'll never forget this."

"No, please, forget it! I mean it, man, forget it. The least said the better."

"Just to let you know, I'm using an untraceable phone and calling on free Wi-Fi from a railway station so no one can trace me. Don't call me, leave a message on the vet-site noticeboard saying: 'Hey D, see you soon,' if you're coming, or, 'Sorry D, no can make it,' if you're not."

"What'll you do if the answer's no?"

"I'll get them one way or another but I'm staying positive and as soon as I hear that you're coming over I'll send you details of the plan."

"Oh, you actually have a plan," says Chuck sarcastically, "well, that's good to know. Don't call again," he adds, ending the call.

With all that's happened to his IPEF comrades since Vietnam, Chuck's understandably nervous about Danny contacting him out of the blue and before he contacts anyone else, he'll check Danny's story out to make sure it's legit. *Should be straightforward enough. If it stinks, I'll have to do something about Danny. Can't have him putting anyone at risk!*

Feeling pumped after his call, Danny's certain Chuck will fly in to help him. Before leaving the railway station, Danny WhatsApps the photo he took of Tomic and Pitbull outside The Oak, along with those he took of the scooters chasing the bus, to Chuck. He captions the pics: "This is what we're up against. They don't stand a chance. Tomic is their leader. He's the one riding the scooter by the traffic lights. The pillion is called Pitbull. Pitbull, what an idiot!"

*

With a thirst on him, Danny dives into the nearest pub to London Bridge station for a beer. *You're an alcoholic!* Sneers his internal voice. *I'm not an alcy! I am not an alcy!* Argues Danny unconvincingly. The pub is full of City types having a couple of drinks before going home to suburbia. They're talking so loud, Danny can't help earwigging on conversations. The things they're talking about are: money, how much they earn, how much they spend on this and that, what car they drive, what car they're buying next, where they're going/have been for their holidays, how much their houses are worth and who they're shagging. Danny's shocked that women are fully engaged with the men talking about shagging and wishes they'd've been like that when he was young. Some drinkers turn to stare at Danny as he's clearly out of place but they soon return to their conversations, unconcerned about him, who he is or what he thinks, they just think he's out of place. *Maybe it's the disguise that's making them stare?*

One pint is all Danny can afford at the overpriced pub; *they're even robbing you south of the river now! Where can a man go for a cheap pint?* He thinks, downing the dregs. After depositing his glass on the bar, Danny makes his disgruntled way to the nearest tube station. The station's so packed, staff are regulating the number of people allowed in to keep platforms from becoming overcrowded. Going by the number of people and the time of day, it seems to Danny that the "rush hour" is getting longer and longer. By the time he gets on the tube, Danny's mood has turned sour and angry. When he changes to the Northern line it's comparatively empty. He knows why, it isn't headed to the leafy suburbs, but it's packed enough that Danny has to stand. To his right is a teenager taking up two seats with bags and he has his feet on the seat opposite. This sort of behaviour has always pissed Danny off and whenever he's said anything, with his ex or his kids with him, they'd tell him not to worry about it but this is one of Danny's pet hates over the years. He tells the teenager to move his bags because he needs to sit down. The teenager's on his phone and looks up just long enough to sneer at Danny and tell him to piss off. Danny, again, tells the teenager to move his bags so he can sit down, "and take your feet off the seat, it's not nice!" he adds with a smile. Again, the teenager looks up from his phone just long enough to sneer at Danny and tell him to piss off. Passengers who travel the tube regularly develop a sixth sense for trouble and know when to look away and that is exactly what they all did at exactly the same time. No one wants to get involved. *Who knows what he's carrying or what he's capable of,* they're all thinking, when they'd've been better thinking about Danny and what he's capable of!

There're no threats of violence, nor any noticeable change in his breathing; Danny brings his right foot down hard on the teenager's knees while simultaneously throat chopping him; two of his go-to classic "moves". From experience, Danny knows the teenager's knees are shattered, having been reverse bent, meaning he'll never walk properly again, while the throat chop has permanently damaged his voice box; *something to remind him, for the rest of his poxy life every time he speaks, to be polite and careful of what he says. Especially to OAPs!* Muses Danny wistfully.

Being as how he's in disguise, Danny doubts anyone would be able to pick him out in a line-up but he's in a carriage full of people, all of whom are potential witnesses; some might even try to carry out a citizen's arrest. Needing to extricate himself ASAP, Danny's military training kicks in. He knows he has to do two things: first, and most important, he must distance himself from the scene and, second, not to look anyone in the eye as they're more likely to be able to identify him if he does. The tube slows as it approaches the next station. Danny feels a hand on his shoulder. Without looking at whoever put it there, he brushes it firmly away and as soon as the carriage doors open, his head bent to the floor, Danny barges his way through the scrum of people waiting to get off and continues in a direct line towards the exit. Everywhere, people are yelling at him but he neither stops nor turns around, he just continues on his way. Approaching the ticket barriers, Danny taps his travel pass on the reader. He's had trouble with it recently and hopes it works first time instead of the barrier beeping and attracting the attention of tube staff. The barriers fly open and he's through them in a flash. Moving at the speed of the herd, Danny exits the tube station. Once on the street, he takes the first road on his left; it's always left, that's what his training says he must do. Turning the corner, Danny finds a place from where he can launch an ambush on anyone following him. In war zones, oppos know this and will signal their presence. Anyone not signalling is an enemy and is taken out. Danny loves playing soldiers in his mind.

Standing stock-still for a whole minute isn't easy when you're being pursued but it's necessary when trying to ascertain if you're being followed. Danny's heart and mind are both racing, his breathing is loud, despite him trying to quiet it. His blood, being saturated with adrenaline, makes Danny's muscles twitch but this keeps them warm and ready for action. Voices are approaching Danny's location. He considers which of his "moves" he'll carry out on anyone following him. *If there's two of them that's okay but…* he doesn't want to think there might be more than two of them. After another thirty seconds, Danny's breathing and heart rate slow. He believes he's in the clear but, to be certain, he remains in the shadows for two more minutes to pass. With no sight, sound or sign of a pursuit, Danny crosses the road, using parked cars for cover, in the direction of a pub he'd spotted while lying in ambush. *I need a drink to calm my nerves! Nah! No I don't… I don't need excuses, I just fancy a beer, that's all, and that's okay because I'm not an alcy! It's a celebration!* "Yeah, a celebration," Danny mutters to justify him needing a beer. *A celebration of what?* Asks his inner voice acerbically. *A celebration of me, because everyone'll thank me for doing the things they're too scared to do! What a load of rubbish you talk in your head! Good job you don't say it out loud otherwise the men in white coats'll cart you off to the loony bin!*

Approaching the pub, Danny catches sight of himself in its windows. After his exertions, his disguise is dishevelled, *Christ! I can't go wandering around looking like this!* Urgently needing to change out of his disguise, Danny dashes into the pub toilet. Checking himself in the mirrors above the sinks, he sees his wig is lopsided, he's lost one of his sideburns and his "makeup" has rivulet lines through it due to him sweating. *Bloody hell! I look like an old drag queen! And not a good one!* As Danny is washing off his makeup, a man enters the toilet, gives him a look and smiles. Danny ignores him and disappears into a cubicle to change his clothes, which the man takes as an invitation for some freestyle cottaging and, pressing his foot hard against the cubicle door, tries to force it open. The door holds firm. He tries again. "Go away," Danny hisses beneath the cubicle door, "it's not what you think!" The man returns, disappointed, to the bar after taking a three-pints-of-beer piss. After changing out of his disguise, Danny goes to leave the pub but, believing it sacrilege to do so without having at least a pint of beer, checks out the pumps to see what's on offer.

"A pint of Pride please," says Danny to the barman/maid.

"Anything else I can get for you?" [s]he asks salaciously. *Still got it!* Muses Danny.

"Do you have free Wi-Fi I?"

"We do love. The PW is sixtynine, no spaces, all lower case."

Logging on to the pub's Wi-Fi, Danny sends Chuck a message saying he's got some ideas about the ideal location to carry out obs on Tomic and his gang. His intention is to prompt Chuck into action and hopes it doesn't piss him off. As Danny turns around, his pint is on the bar. It's more expensive than he's used to paying. *I'll either have to rob a bank or give up the beer!* He thinks half seriously. *Am I an alcoholic? I hope not, you can't afford to be one*, answers his inner voice. *I hope not too, I don't want to be scrounging off me mates or beg for beer money outside pubs*, he thinks gloomily. With that disconsolate thought, Danny sips his beer slowly to make it last and once it's gone he places his glass on the bar and leaves the pub despite that he fancies another pint. *I love beer.*

Standing outside the pub, Danny decides to visit Lucy before going home. Arriving at the ICU, he spies his favourite nurse and asks if it's okay for him to visit Lucy. She gives Danny a contemptuous look and tells him his sons are with "the patient" at the moment and as only two visitors are allowed at a time, he'll have to wait. Danny asks if she'll tell his sons he's waiting. She says she will when she has time and carries on with her duties. Danny's puzzled by the nurse's attitude and is standing outside the ICU when his ex shows up with husband number four.

"Where the hell have you been?" Joyce screech-hisses at Danny as quietly as she can.

"What d'ye mean, 'where the hell have you been'. I was here yesterday!"

"You haven't visited for three days! Three days!"

"Rubbish! I was here yesterday!"

"No you weren't, it was Sunday! I'm worried about you, Danny; do you think you might've had one of your blackouts?"

"No, no I haven't!" Danny hisses defensively. "Anyway, I just had the cold shoulder from the nurse and she won't tell Kel and Joebyjoe that I'm here so I can visit Luce."

"Serves you right."

"Thanks very much."

"You stink of beer!"

"That's because I've been drinking beer."

"Where have you been? What have you been up to?"

"Look, I'm a pensioner who lives all alone in a crappy little flat at the arse end of Camden and don't have anybody to help me do stuff so I have to do all the stuff that needs doing myself," Danny says indignantly. "Anyway, stop your moaning!"

"Hey! That's my wife!" protests Jeff with indignation.

"Serves you right!" Danny replies with a smirk. "Now, John, if you don't mind, we've got things to talk about that don't concern you so off you popski!" says Danny, giving Jeff a cold dead-eye stare. Despite him being quite a bit bigger than Danny, Jeff doesn't fancy his chances against him, mainly because of the things Joyce has told him about when Danny was in the army, so he walks away in a huff.

"That was rude!" Joyce hisses.

"I know, but what can you expect, he's from Essex?" replies Danny with a grin Joyce recognises from old and still loves. "Anyway, where were we? Oh yes, visiting our daughter, which I'd like very much to do if you wouldn't mind getting Kel and Joey to make room!"

"How much are you drinking these days, Danny? The boys said you stunk of beer the other night too!"

"For Christ's sake I only had a pint. One pint! That's all, one pint."

"Truthfully, how much are you drinking? I worry about you. I know you don't like to believe it but it was the drink that was the final straw. I hated it when you got drunk."

"When did I ever get drunk? I like a beer but I never got drunk... usually."

"I'm not going to argue with you. I'll ask the nurse to have a word with Kel and Joey. Jeff and I will head off home, we've already seen Luce today so we'll leave her to you."

As Kelvin and Joey exit the ICU, they spot Danny. Kelvin walks right past him without saying a word but Joey stops and asks how he is. He says he's fine. Joey smells beer on his breath and shakes his head, "Cut down on the drinking Dad, you'll die if you don't. Everyone's worried about you, even Kel, though he won't admit it," Joey whispers concernedly. "I'll try son. I'll try," says Danny in a non-committal way.

Slipping through the curtain around Lucy's bed, Danny, for some reason, is expecting to see his daughter sitting up reading. But she's not, she's lying there, her arms at her sides connected up to an array of machines and wires and her eyes are taped shut. The sight of his daughter looking like this causes Danny to break down and cry. A minute later, his favourite nurse appears and hands him a cup of tea, "I've put two sugars in... you need to cut down!" she jokes and gently pats and then rubs Danny on his back the way people do to the elderly to comfort them. When the nurse removes her hand, Danny realises how much he misses the warming touch of a female. It's been so long since anyone has shown him the slightest affection. "Aye, it's not only sugar I need to cut down on," says Danny. The nurse just smiles and pats him on the back again.

Following the nurse's departure, Danny notices, apart from the hissing of ventilators and beeping of machines, the ICU is silent. Intrigued, he peers through the slit in the curtain surrounding Lucy's bed. No one's around, everyone's gone; he's literally the only one there. Returning to his chair, Danny pulls close to Lucy to talk quietly into her ear to give her the latest news.

"Hello Luce love. Sorry, haven't been in for a while, been busy... you understand. Anyway. Where did we get to last time? I was telling you about me going to where you was mugged and trying to bait the so-and-sos that attacked you but they didn't show up so I went for a pint and met a geezer called Alby. That's right isn't it? Anyway, I went back to see Alby because I reckoned he grassed me up to Detective Sergeant Dean, the copper in charge of the case, about me going to see where you was mugged after he'd told me I should stay away. I think you know what I mean? So, Alby and me, we had a bit of an argument. Anyway, I think he probably did grass me up so I've got my eye on him. We got talking about the ones who attacked you and I asked him what they looked like and he says to me to look out the pub window because they were outside on a scooter, like the one used to rob you, by the traffic lights. I took a photo of them but they clocked me doing it and came into the pub. All the locals at the bar looked away. They were scared, terrified of these kids they were. So, one of them, Tomic they call him, comes up to me and asks me what I thought I was doing taking his photo and I told him I was taking one of his scooter because I like scooters. He tells me to delete it so I deleted a different photo and he wants to see my phone to make sure I deleted the photo and I tell him to get lost, sort of thing, and he and his mate, Pitbull they call him, idiots, they leave the pub in a right huff. Anyway, Alby tells me I'd better leave sharpish before this Tomic comes back with more of his gang. So I get on a bus and when I look out the back window I see about seven scooters following it and one of them is being ridden by this Tomic. I probably shouldn't tell you this but… at the next stop two of them were waiting for me so I got off the bus and faced them down. I probably shouldn't tell you this either but when they came at me I… I got in first and put them both out of the game. I won't go into detail but they won't forget me in a hurry.

"Y'know, Luce, everyone, including that detective, says that even if they catch the ones that attacked you, and even if they go to court, and even if they get found guilty, they'll probably just get a slap on the wrist because they don't have criminal records because no one will be a witness and testify against them because they're too frightened to. I couldn't stand it if that happened; sitting there in the court and watching those… bleeps… get away with it. They'd be all smiling and high-fiving one another and cheering and sneering at you and me. I can't let that happen, Luce, I couldn't live with myself if that happened. Remember what I used to say when you were kids about if anyone ever hurt you I'd… I'd make them pay? Because, one way or another, Luce love, I promise you, they're going to pay!

"And on that subject, I got in touch with one of my old Vietnam oppos and asked him, as a favour for old times' sake, to help me get justice for you… revenge he said it was. He said he'll get in touch with a couple of guys and get back to me. "Get back to me" sounds like the job interviews I used to go to when they said that and never did. Anyway… anyway. I never told you about Vietnam, did I Luce? Though, to be totally accurate, I never told anyone, y'know, about what happened there. I wanted to tell someone but… but I didn't because it would be dangerous for them to know so that's that. I think keeping it to myself was what really broke your mum and me up. She said it was the drinking but I only drank because… anyway.

"Listen, Luce love, as it's just you and me here, and you're in a coma, I'll tell you about what happened in Vietnam. Ready? After I left Germany, I got volunteered to join a special military unit. It had a weird name, one I'd never heard before: "International Pathfinder Expeditionary Force", it was called, IPEF for short. We weren't under the control of battlefield commanders. I'm not even sure where our orders came from. We even had our own base near a place called Phnen Bin. I interrogated prisoners there. It turns out we were expendable. All of us. Imagine, a hundred and fifty highly trained soldiers, mostly special forces, being "expendable"? I'm getting ahead of myself. Anyway, one day we get orders to rescue a couple of American officers that had been captured by the NVA, that's the North Vietnamese Army. Intelligence said they were being held in a village in Cambodia. No one was supposed to operate in Cambodia but that didn't stop us or the NVA. What we didn't know was it was all a set-up! The NVA knew we were coming and were waiting to ambush us and ambush us they did. About half of us fought our way out and carried on with the mission while the other half were either killed or taken prisoner. From what we knew of the NVA you'd be better off dead than be captured by them.

"After slogging through the jungle, we got to the village at about three in the morning. Looking through our night scopes we could see the place was well guarded. We snuck around and came at the village from the north. It went well except the people guarding the American officers weren't NVA, they were villagers. We slaughtered them. They didn't stand a chance. With all the gunfire, the whole village woke up; there were kids and women crying everywhere. They told us they'd been forced to guard the American officers. We'd found them tied to metal frames next to banks of car batteries. They'd been tortured... electrocuted. Somehow, they were still alive. The lieutenant ordered us to look for an attaché case. He said it contained secret plans for an offensive against the NVA. Some of the guys reckoned this was bullshit, they didn't believe it. They said we'd been set up. We were going to take the officers with us but they were in bad shape… too far gone… and we were a long, long way from home. The lieutenant ordered us to leave the hut and, when we got outside, he shot them.

"We were in the middle of the jungle, over a hundred klicks from the border, and we didn't know what to do or which way to go for the best. A few of us wanted to retrace our steps to rescue our buddies. Fat chance, there were hundreds of NVA there so we headed east. It was the shortest route back to base but we could've ended up north of the border and that would've made things a whole lot worse. Anyway, we made it back, and over the following few days some stragglers turned up. You'd think we'd've been treated like heroes, but we weren't. We were taken away and interrogated. We were warned never to speak of the operation in Cambodia to anyone… ever… but we talked about it among ourselves. Some of the guys reckoned the officers had been sacrificed to make the north believe an offensive was going to be mounted and we were sent to rescue them to make sure they swallowed the story. In actual fact, there was no offensive, it was all a cover for the Americans to evacuate Saigon… the war was over. I couldn't wait to get home. When I got back I called one of my oppos. His wife answered the phone. She said he was dead, killed along with fifty of his buddies in a plane crash leaving 'Nam. A couple of days later I got a call from my old sergeant warning me, whatever I do, not to speak to anyone about what happened in Cambodia. He said about half the people who got back from the operation were dead and so were some of their friends and family. He told me never to call him and hung up.

"Sorry to put that on you Luce, but it feels so good to finally get it off my chest! I've kept it bottled up for years. I didn't think it mattered, I thought I was okay, but I wasn't. All this time I've been totally screwed up inside." Danny lifts his head and listens for signs of people or movement. There is none but, nevertheless, he gets up, opens the slit in the curtain and calls out, "Hello, anyone there?" No answer. "Good. Good. Well, Luce, now you know why your dad is so mad," Danny says with a childish grin. "That was more than I wanted to tell you, wanted to say, but once I got started I couldn't stop. Sorry. Boring."

A minute later, a nurse appears and tells Danny that his sons are asking if he's finished his visit as they want to sit at their sister's bedside. Danny kisses Lucy on both cheeks, gives her hands a squeeze to check for signs that she's regaining consciousness. There are none; she remains sleeping, princess-like, motionless and catatonically unconscious. On his way to the lift concourse, Danny passes Kelvin who tells him he's a disgrace and should be ashamed of himself for not visiting Lucy and doesn't he realise that his daughter is lying in a coma and might not come out of it! Danny yells at Kelvin not to even think that. "Listen, brainiac, Luce is going to pull through! You mark my words, boy, Luce is going to pull through!" Joey moves between his brother and his father to stop them coming to blows. "Okay, that's enough you two! Go home Dad, we'll see you later," he says, putting his arm around his father's shoulders and walking him to the lift. "Never mind Kel, Dad, he seems like he's handling things but he isn't. He doesn't know what to do… none of us does. We all feel helpless. Now go home and get some sleep," pleads Joey. "You look shagged out!" Danny agrees to go home and tells Joey he'll see him and Kelvin later if they decide to visit him. Reaching the ground floor, Danny logs on to the veterans' website for messages. There are none.

CHAPTER FIVE

Over the next two days, Danny is on tenterhooks waiting for Chuck's message to be posted on the veteran website, but there is none. In his distraction, Danny doesn't visit Lucy, something his ex-wife, Kelvin, Joey, and now Brad, get onto him about. He's so happy that Brad has arrived in London and arranges to meet him in a pub by King's Cross station.

*

Danny and Brad are cut from the same cloth, which is an everlasting joy to both of them. Even when Brad was a small child, he always took Danny's side in things but, remarkably, remained on good terms with his mother and siblings. He seems to be blessed with an indefinable quality that people find alluring, captivating and reassuring. When he was a teenager, Brad's friends got up to all manner of mischief, including theft, but he'd tell them straight that he wasn't interested in whatever it was they were doing, and leave on good terms to catch up with them another time, with no hard feelings. The same applied after he left school and began work. When it came to not "doing the job" he'd call people out, telling them if they were lazy but no one ever took offence, and usually worked harder as a result. This quality was recognised by Brad's bosses and wherever he worked he was given promotions. Even when he was at school, Brad worked from nine to midnight stocking racks, rails and shelves in department stores and, despite him being only fifteen, he'd be picked out as the most reliable worker and promoted to manage workers who happily fell in behind him. With his natural leadership abilities, Danny had wanted Brad to join the army, like he himself had done, but his mother put paid to that idea as she wanted him to go to university but Brad, being a realist, knew he wasn't the academic type and went travelling instead. "Everybody loves Brad!" is what the family and everyone said, and they were right.

*

As Brad came through the pub doors, Danny threw his arms around him; "Great to see you son," he says, almost weeping. "You too, Dad," says Brad, bear-hugging his dad. Danny had set up a couple of pints on a table in the corner and the pair take their seats. As Brad is as straight and direct as they come, he tells Danny what he thinks about him not visiting Lucy. Danny tells he's been waiting on some news and it's occupying his mind.

"So, then, what have you been up to?" Brad asks accusingly.

"What d'ye mean?" Danny answers guiltily.

"I know you, Dad, you're up to something! Joebyjoe thinks so too. He told me the copper investigating the case told you where Luce was mugged and he reckons you'll try and sort things out yourself. Well, are you?"

"I wouldn't tell any of the others this, and I don't want you telling them either, but I went to the spot where Luce was attacked."

"You did what? Why? What did you do that for? Are you stupid? I hope you didn't do anything stupid!"

"Like what?"

"I don't know, you tell me!"

"I expected more from you Brady boy!"

"Don't give me that old pony! So, Daddio, what did you do then?" asks Brad as if speaking to a naughty child.

"I… erm… when I got to the place where Luce was attacked I got my mobile out and waited to see if the Scooter Muggers turned up to nick it but they didn't! There! Happy?!"

"You were trying to bait them weren't you? Dad, I love you to pieces but you're an idiot. You do realise you're getting on a bit, you're old, and if they get hold of you you'll get badly hurt? You know what they're like, especially in London!"

"No need for you worry about me, son, I can still look after myself y'know! I know I'm getting on a bit but I can still look after myself!"

"Sure you can, Dad, sure you can. I reckon you're still good to take on one at a time, maybe even two, but these pricks will be armed. They'll cut you to pieces and leave you bleeding in the middle of the road or down some alley! You're not in the army anymore, Dad, and all that stuff you used to do was a long time ago. Please, promise me you won't go looking for the ones who mugged Luce."

"Too late son… I've got have a plan. Now don't ask me what it is but I've got a plan… a good one it is too!"

"I hope your plan includes hiring the A-Team because if it doesn't then you'll probably end up next to Luce in intensive care!" *I used to love watching the A-Team!*

"Cheers, son, that's a nice thought," says Danny, clinking his glass against Brad's. "I remember you used to be more supportive of your old dad. You used to back me up!"

"I'll always back you up, Dad, but you going looking for the people who mugged Luce is dangerous and I can't be here all the time!"

"So, does that mean you want in?" asks Danny, sensing he's guessed right.

"Drink your beer!" says Brad, ignoring his dad.

After an hour reminiscing about the old days, Brad returns to St Thomas' Hospital and Danny goes back to his flat.

That evening, Danny's stood outside a pub leeching off their Wi-Fi. Logging on to the veterans' website, he checks out the noticeboard. There's a message for him. He clicks it open. It says, "Hi D, we'll see you soon." *We'll see you soon… we'll… he's got some help! Bingo! Time to roll!* Immediately after reading the message, Danny sends Chuck a WhatsApp with instructions of where he and the others will stay along with the address of the hooky shop in Southwark from where they'll buy their mobile phones. Danny knows Chuck and the others won't need telling but reminds him to tell the others to wear disguises whenever they're out and about, only use cash and ensure to only use free Wi-Fi in public places and never from their hotels.

Feeling confident Tomic and his buddies will soon be toast, Danny goes for a celebratory pint of beer on his way to St Thomas' Hospital to tell Lucy the good news about his Vietnam oppos coming over to London to help get justice for her.

Exiting the lift outside the ICU, Danny comes face to face with his ex-wife, Kelvin and Joey. They're standing in a huddle talking. Their body language gives Danny a bad feeling. He asks if everything is okay. "You'd know if everything was okay if you visited more often," Kelvin snaps. Joey tells his brother and his mum to go away and he'll talk with his dad. Joey tells Danny that Lucy's vital signs took a dip and are fluctuating. He says the doctors told them that if things continue this way, then Lucy's internal organs could be permanently damaged or could even stop working altogether. Danny emphasises the word "could", and says to Joey that doctors have been known to be wrong in the past and asks if Brad is with Lucy. Joey nods and says he'll keep his mum and Kelvin out of the way for a couple of hours because they're angry with him. "Truth be told, Dad, I'm angry with you too," admits Joey. Danny says he can't do anything about how other people feel about him. Joey disagrees, "You can, Dad, you can, all you've got to do is be a dad…

a dad that comes and sits at his daughter's bedside while she's lying in hospital in a coma she might never wake up from!" Joey's words sting Danny. He feels ashamed and wants to tell him what he's been doing, what's he's up to, what's going on, but suspects that if he does his son will shop him to his ex and the police.

The nurse on duty tells Danny he can go straight in to see his daughter. As Danny enters behind the curtain around Lucy's bed, Brad is about to leave and asks his dad if he'd like him to stay but Danny shakes his head no. Brad kisses Lucy on both cheeks, squeezes her hands, tells her he loves her, says goodbye, tells her he'll see her again soon and leaves, blanking Danny as he does so.

"I thought he'd never go!" Danny jokes as soon as Brad's out of earshot. "Anyway Luce, it's on! I just got a message from my old Vietnam sergeant, Chuck Henderson. He and some others are coming over. Hopefully, they'll get here in a couple of days and then we'll see some action! The police are useless. They can't do anything but I can... we can. You wait and see!

"Brad was just here. We met earlier for a pint in a pub by King's Cross. He told me off for going to see where you was mugged but I reckon he'd want in if I asked him but I don't want him getting involved. Anything could happen if I told him what's going on; he might bubble me to that detective or he might get hurt and I couldn't live with myself if that happened. Anyway, this is a job for professionals and with what I've got planned they won't know what's hit them; they'll be bagged up and carted away before they know what's happening. We've done it before, in Vietnam. There was this so-called "warlord", vicious he was... even to his own family! Orders came down to take him so we did. When we got him back to Phnen Bin you should've heard him... sang like a canary! Said there was no need for torture or violence, he'd tell us everything. Said he'd even work for us... be our boy, like, and spy for us. We didn't believe a word of it! Some of the lads sliced and diced him just like his lot had done to scores of ours. It was horrible it was, they were just left in the jungle, tortured and left hanging from trees where we'd find them. Sadistic animals.

"Well… last time I was here, I didn't exactly tell you the truth. The bit about us heading to the border after finding the American officers? It wasn't like I said. Only the ones who'd been wounded or were in a bad way headed for the border. There's an army saying that goes, 'no one gets left behind,' so we headed south to rescue our oppos or die trying. Sounds corny when I say it aloud but knowing that is what gives captive soldiers hope. Anyway, after about twenty klicks we came across six of our lads. They'd all been skinned alive. Imagine what they went through? Some of us wanted to bury them but the lieutenant said no because if we did the NVA would know we were around and come after us. We had to leave them there for all sorts of things to feed on them. I still see them, Luce, I still see them. It can happen anywhere… anytime… but mostly at night. I drank to try and block it out but alcohol doesn't work, nothing works!

"Anyway… after about another ten klicks we heard screaming in the distance so we split up into four squads and made our way towards the screaming. I was in the most westerly group so when we came across the NVA camp we had the sun at our backs. They were looking right at us but couldn't see us because the sun was in their eyes. When the east group got in place, the lieutenant gave the order to start shooting. The NVA hid behind everything they could but they were being fired on from all directions so there was nowhere for them to hide. It was like shooting fish in a barrel, they had nowhere to go. After they stopped returning fire, we went into the camp. To make sure they were dead we shot them all in the head one after another. You should've seen what they'd done to our lads, Luce. It was terrible! They'd crammed them into little bamboo cages, like ones used to take pigs to market. Tiny they were. I don't know how they got full-grown men inside them. They were all twisted and cramped… and naked. Every one of them was naked! Some of the cages were stacked on top of others so those above pissed and shat on those below. Some of the lads had been positioned for the NVA to… they'd raped them. Men raping men! After we released the lads they took whatever they could find and battered and smashed the dead NVA soldiers to pieces. No one tried to stop them but what did it matter? They were dead anyway.

"Two days later we were back at Phnen Bin. The rest of what I told you is true… you know, being interrogated and ordered never to mention anything about the mission to anyone ever. It's a good thing you're out of it, Luce, because if you ever blabbed to anyone about what I told you you'd be in danger. I know that sounds dramatic but it's true nonetheless. All of C Company are dead because when the survivors got back to America some of them went to the press with the story but it got shut down. Not one of them died from natural causes or an illness, they all died in accidents like plane crashes, hit and runs and falling out of tenth-storey windows! There aren't many of us left now so I hope it all comes out before we die," laments Danny.

"Mr Deacon?" a nurse says, poking her head through the curtain, "Sorry to disturb you but we need to bathe and turn your daughter and check everything is as it should be. Would you mind stepping outside please?" she asks. Danny is terrified that the nurse might've overheard what he'd said to Lucy.

"No… certainly… I hope you weren't upset by what I was talking to my daughter about? It was all a very long time ago when I was in the army… you know?"

"It's okay, Mr Deacon, I didn't hear a word of anything you said. It's hard to hear over the noise of ventilators and the beeping of machines," the nurse adds reassuringly.

"Anyway, I've been here long enough… let someone else have a go. I'm off home if anybody wants to know."

*

Enroute back to his flat, Danny receives a call from DS Dean. He says he's calling to bring Danny up to date with what's happening with the investigation. "Don't suppose you've arrested any of them have you?" Danny asks bitterly. DS Dean says not but the scooter used in Lucy's mugging has been found and forensic tests are being carried out on it. Danny asks what the likelihood is of getting something to tie the muggers to the scooter. The detective says he's not hopeful for a multitude of reasons but wanted to tell Danny before he reads about it in the newspapers. This winds Danny up. Dean says he hopes Danny's behaving himself and staying away from where Lucy was mugged and then ends the call abruptly. *That Dean's getting on the last of my nerves, he says one thing but his voice tells me to do another!* thinks Danny. Returning to his desk at New Scotland Yard, DS Dean congratulates himself on winding Danny up. He's absolutely positive he'll do something about those who attacked his daughter and then, hopefully, he'll get to arrest Tomic, *and his gang too but it's Tomic I want!* DS Dean's so desperate to arrest Tomic before he retires that he's prepared to do anything, including sacrificing a pawn like Danny Deacon, to achieve this ambition.

*

Danny and Chuck are in constant contact refining the operational plan. Danny's been using the free Wi-Fi at London Bridge station but he's started to attract the attention of station staff and British Transport Police and so moves to King's Cross station; *handier for home and not too bad for St Thomas'*; another plus for Danny is there's a good selection of pubs nearby.

The operational plan calls for Chuck and the others, Glenn Biedermeier and Tony McCann, both of whom are known to Danny, to travel to London, bringing plenty of cash with them, and go to their hotels; each chosen by Danny because a) they accept cash and b) proximity to multiple free Wi-Fi locations. The morning following their arrival, Chuck, Glenn and Tony travel separately to the shop in Southwark where they purchase a smart phone each, buy PAYG SIMs, head to London Bridge station to WhatsApp

Danny so he has their mobile numbers and then wait for his call. Despite them crossing paths several times during the morning and now being at London Bridge station together, the most observant surveillance expert, let alone a casual observer, would never connect them. After he arrives at King's Cross, Danny creates a WhatsApp group using Chuck's, Glenn's and Tony's phone numbers; he names "Vigilantes". When the WhatsApp call connects, the group name brings smiles to Chuck's, Glenn's and Tony's faces.

"Hi guys, thanks for coming over, it's appreciated," says Danny. "First off, some house-keeping. We'll hold daily update calls at fifteen hundred hours on WhatsApp. Calls must only be made from free Wi-Fi zones making them virtually untraceable. In emergencies, it's okay to use SMS. Disguises must be worn when you're doing obs on the streets. Never drive wearing a disguise or even when you're in a vehicle."

"Is there an obs plan?" asks Glenn, the inveterate worryguts of the group.

"There is. I'll send it right after this call."

"Just so we're clear," says Chuck, "the aim is to do this inside one hundred and twenty hours... in and out? Yes?"

"That's the plan," says Danny confidently.

"What about equipment... fake IDs and so forth?"

"I'll send a location pin of where the snatch van's parked. There's no CCTV in the street, or even close by, so you're okay to approach anytime; just keep a watch out for nosey locals. The keys are in the exhaust pipe... about ten inches in so you'll need a wire or something. Fake driving licences et cetera are in the glovebox. The van's insured for any of you to drive so you shouldn't have any problems with the police or ANPR."

"ANPR?"

"Automatic Number Plate Recognition. It's how the police here keep track of vehicles."

"We have the same thing in America!"

"Oz too!"

"Any intelligence update on T1… his movements?"

"No, I've been staying away since they chased me on scooters. You'll never guess! The detective investigating the case called me to let me know they've found the scooter they used in the attack on Lucy. He told me they're doing forensic tests on it but he's not hopeful. Wound me right up he did. It's like he's doing it on purpose! Like he's getting a kick out of it! Anyway, even if they find DNA, they can just say the scooter's been used by everyone!"

"Same shit in Oz, man!" says Tony.

"Okay, guys, if there's nothing else let's bug out and get on with the job!" says Chuck, taking charge as he'd been their sergeant in Vietnam. "Glenn, Tony… I'll see you on the ground at zero eleven hundred hours tomorrow."

"Don't worry Danny, they're toast!" says Tony confidently.

"To be on the safe side, I reckon we should do an obs run-through tonight … say, twenty-two hundred hours?" suggests good old, careful old Glenn.

"Okay, twenty-two hundred it is. Bug out in five-minute intervals; first me, then Glenn, then Tony."

None of those milling around London Bridge or King's Cross stations during the WhatsApp call could've possibly guessed at what had passed through the ether of the virtual world surrounding them, penetrating every fabric of their beings, concerning commissioning a criminal act. In fact, the very phones the criminal act was being planned on were themselves proceeds of criminal acts, they having been stolen in the very same way Lucy's phone had been stolen; one of them on the very same night. If the passers-by could somehow visualise, make solid, the virtual world surrounding them, they'd be horrified by the messages of infidelity, lies, deceit, duplicity, coercive control, fraud, sexting, phishing, smishing and pharming, and all interspersed with the banality of posts by "Internet Sensations" and "Social Media Celebrities" alerting the real world to every little thing in their dull, pathetic, shallow, finger-sitting, meaningless existences.

During the obs run-through that night, Glenn told the others he'd found a route to and from the RVP avoiding CCTV. Typical of Glenn, he reminded Chuck and Tony to top up their travel cards to avoid problems at ticket barriers which could attract the attention of tube officials, ticket inspectors or the Transport Police. He reminded them, too, that taxis are to be avoided except in an emergency. He'd even prepared a story for them to use should they come into contact with the police while wearing a disguise.

*

At eleven hundred hours, the three former soldiers converged on the RVP and signalled to one another that they were "clean and clear", in other words they'd arrived without being tailed.

To commence obs of the area, Chuck and Glenn took up positions north and south of the intersection where Lucy was mugged while Tony acted as their spotter. Each is wearing earpieces and thread mics with voice recorders, connected walkie-talkies. In the event they're eavesdropped, they communicate using the IPEF obs jargon each of them is versed in. Thirty minutes later, Glenn checks the photos Danny had sent them as he thinks he's spotted T1, target one, Tomic. "Possible eyeball T1, tracking S to E," speaks Chuck into his mic. "Confirm T1 S to E, show-time," speaks Tony into his mic. Chuck taps his shoulder, signalling to Glenn and Tony that he's going to follow Tomic and for them to fall in behind him to keep their profile thin. The three old soldiers constantly switch positions with one another to avoid being noticed by the target. Tomic has no idea he's being followed, he's far too busy bigging himself up to everyone he passes and hassling shopkeepers to give him free stuff, which they reluctantly do. All the shopkeepers hate Tomic and his gang and yearn for the day when he's either dead or in prison but none of them has the guts to do anything about their situation for fear of reprisals; each knows that if they stand up to the gang, or make statements to the police, or testify against them, they or their loved ones could pay with their lives. What's worse is, if they get up the guts to make statements to the police, or testify against Tomic or his gang, they'd be labelled as grasses and have to leave the estate or suffer the consequences; a catch-22 situation that mystifies all police officers, including DS Dean. They can't comprehend how supposedly rational human beings would rather keep schtum than talk to the police about criminals and this is why he, and the police in general, often delay emergency responses and let victims of crime suffer in the hope they'll turn on the criminals. DS Dean has a dream that one day people will get so sick and tired of being robbed and beaten and sexually assaulted they'll form neighbourhood groups against the scumbags who make their lives such a misery.

All the while they're following Tomic, Chuck and the others record where he goes, who he sees, what he does and so forth. What they are looking to identify is routine in Tomic's everyday actions because in routine lies danger for the target and opportunity for the snatchers. After they identify a routine, the former soldiers can plan when and where is best to snatch Tomic. When Tomic meets gang members, Glenn and Tony surreptitiously take their photographs, using body-worn cameras, to identify future targets. It's Chuck's job to watch his comrades' backs in case they're made. Everything is carried out exactly as in a military operation and all three old soldiers are absolutely loving it. They haven't done anything like this for years and realise what they've been missing.

As fifteen hundred hours approaches, Chuck and the others discontinue obs and locate to a free Wi-Fi zone for the daily check-in call. There's little to report, so it lasts barely two minutes. The main item of interest is Danny has obtained half a litre of surgical grade anaesthetic and a box of hypodermic syringes: essential kit when it comes to snatching people off the streets. "Let me know when you're ready and I'll deliver it to the van," says Danny. *Just like in 'Nam; drop off, pick up, do the job*, think Chuck, Glenn and Tony.

*

At eighteen hundred hours, Tomic and several of his cronies enter a local chicken takeaway and demand food and cans of Coke for free. The young man serving behind the counter protests. This earns him a beating and customers are chased off the premises. Not wanting any trouble, the owner gives Tomic and his cohort a tub of chicken wings, another of chips, and eight cans of Coke. The gang lounge around inside the takeaway eating, drinking, throwing food around and generally making a nuisance of themselves. After finishing their food and drinks, Tomic and his cronies kick the empty tubs and cans around the shop in a game of football which ends with them kicking in the bottom pane of glass of the shop door. Tomic says to the owner, "You don't give us no grief, you just give us what we want. Understand?" The owner says he does and the gang leave after kicking in the Formica panels at the front of the serving counter. The damage the gang caused will cost the shop owner over two grand; which is two grand a business like his simply cannot afford. "I'm feeling hungry," Chuck speaks into his mic. "Glenn, you follow T1 and Tony and I will go get some food." Glenn says to get him some fried chicken, salad, if they have it, and a sparkling mineral water. Chuck and Tony enter the chicken takeaway and stand at the counter eyeing up the menu and the damage.

"Looks like you've had some trouble?" Chuck says to the owner, nudging the remains of the Formica panels with his knee.

"Not really. What can I get you?" the owner asks.

"This sort of thing happen often?" asks Tony, pointing at the smashed glass in the shop door and the empty food tubs and cans scattered around the floor.

"Soony, clear up this mess!" shouts the owner into the back room. Soony appears, dabbing his bruised and bleeding face with a damp cloth. "It was just some stupid boys, that's all. They get carried away. Now, what can I get you?"

"Do you have CCTV?"

"Are you CCTV salesmen?" the owner asks, sounding peeved.

"No, we're not," Chuck answers in such a cold way the shop owner realises he'd better watch his mouth.

"Do you have CCTV?" repeats Tony.

"Yes… but it's not working," the owner lies.

"Okey dokey," says Chuck in an overly-friendly way as he peruses the menu. "I'll take three servings of fried chicken, two of French fries, one green salad, one portion of salad dressing, two cans of Coke and a sparkling water… and a copy of your CCTV for the last thirty minutes!" he adds, handing the shop owner a USB stick. The owner knows better than to argue with this man and tells Soony to download the last thirty minutes of CCTV onto the stick.

On leaving the chicken takeaway, Chuck calls Glenn to ask his location. He's barely a hundred yards along the road. When they meet up, Glenn tells Chuck and Tony about Tomic and his buddies going from shop to shop taking pretty much what they liked, except one, a hairdressers run by a formidable black woman who shooed them out of her shop on the end of a broom. This brings a smile to Chuck's face. "They took money from most of them," says Glenn, "like it's a protection racket they've got running!" Chuck passes Glenn the USB stick from the chicken takeaway and the trio resume their surveillance of Tomic. They fit right in, as many locals are eating and drinking while walking along the streets. Tony notices there's a large number of CCTV cameras around the place. "They're on shops, houses, pubs… everywhere," he says, pointing a couple out. This is bad news for plan "A"; throw Tomic into the van, drug him and then drive away with him. Continuing with their surveillance, Glenn spies a CCTV camera atop a high pole, protected by a ring of spikes, and is scanning back and forth, "It must be remotely operated," says Glenn. "We'll need to be especially careful about where we carry out the snatch," says Chuck. "I'll bring it up with Danny at the next check-in call."

When the gang reach the end of the street, Tomic turns and says something to them and they disappear into the estate. Tony wants to follow them but Chuck says it'll blow their cover, "We'll stick out like sore thumbs in there! We'll just have to sit it out and wait until they resurface," he adds and sends Glenn and Tony to cover the outer perimeter of the estate in case they exit there. Not long after taking up their positions, six scooters, each two up, come roaring out of the estate heading towards Central London. With nothing to do but wait, Chuck, Glenn and Tony rendezvous at a Wi-Fi zone on the off-chance Danny's online. He is. They tell him about the huge number of CCTV cameras in the area where they intend snatching Tomic, "There's some on top of poles with a ring of spikes around them, they look like they're remote-controlled?" says Glenn. Danny says they're probably the council's CCTV cameras and are monitored twenty-four seven. "That's bad news for the snatch," comments Tony.

Two hours later, when Tomic and his gang return to the estate, Chuck and the others assume they'll ditch the scooters and surveillance can resume. They're mistaken, instead the trio witness three "scooter muggings", one immediately after the other, in which mobile phones are stolen and one victim gets knocked to the ground, just like Lucy had been. They'd not seen anything like it before. It was all over in a matter of seconds with none of the victims seeing it coming. After choosing their targets, people lost in their own little worlds ogling mobile phone screens, the Scooter Muggers coast silently along the pavement, getting right up to their victim before the pillion reaches out and snatches the phone. The driver then hits the throttle and they're both out of reach before the victim can react. Chuck calls it a night and they return to their hotels after agreeing to have a debrief later that night. On his way back to his hotel, Chuck messages Danny about the debrief and invites him to attend.

Danny's on his way to St Thomas' Hospital with Brad when Chuck's message comes through. He's unsure what to do as his ex, Joyce, has drawn up a "Rota" and it's Danny and Brad's turn to visit Lucy. Joyce claims she drew it up due to the number of people wanting to visit Lucy but Danny suspects she's done it to guilt him into visiting more regularly; he hopes he can visit Lucy and make the debrief too. *I'll come back and visit Luce after the call too. Hopefully, that should keep everyone happy!* Sitting at Lucy's bedside, Danny appears agitated. Brad asks his dad what's up. He says he has something on his mind but refuses to elaborate. Brad thinks it's probably to do with money, *it usually is with him!*

At ten thirty, Danny says he has a bit of business to take care of and will see Brad back at the flat later. Brad asks Danny what he's doing that's so secret. He denies being secretive and says it's something he's had arranged for a while. Brad says he wants to tag along and after the bit of business is finished, they can go for a beer and a takeaway. Danny says it's better if he goes alone and leaves the ICU. After making sure Brad isn't following him, Danny heads to Waterloo Station and logs onto the free Wi-Fi. At twenty-three hundred hours, the "Vigilante" group call comes through.

"What's up Chuck?" Danny asks. "Any problems?"

"I just wanted a debrief of the first day's obs, that's all," says Chuck casually. *Here we go, you were just the same in 'Nam!* "Things went pretty well. We got eyes on T1, no problem, and followed him and his gang around; you know, checking out what they do, where they go, what they get up to, how they operate, how they interact and so on. At eighteen hundred hours, they entered a chicken takeaway. We observed them wrecking the place and they terrorised the owner into giving them free food."

"You should've seen them, Danny, they acted like they owned the place!" says Tony angrily.

"I can't believe an entire neighbourhood is afraid of a handful of dweeby punks!" adds Glenn.

"That's the thing, see," says Danny, "I thought that too but then I spoke with a geezer, a really big geezer," Danny adds with emphasis, "called Alby and he told me there are literally dozens of wannabes who'll do anything… robbery, beatings, stabbing, drugs, anything to get into the gang!"

"How many of them are there do you think?" asks Chuck.

"I don't know but this Alby got stabbed by a group of them a while back and, understandably I suppose, even he won't go up against them. I don't think he's scared of them… more wary of what they're capable of and if someone like him can get stabbed then who's going to stand up to them?"

"There's something else," says Chuck.

"Sounds ominous. What is it?" Danny asks.

"After they terrorised shop owners all along the road, the gang disappeared into the estate. We couldn't follow for obvious reasons, so we took up positions around the perimeter and waited. They came out after about ten minutes riding scooters and headed for the city centre. Obviously we couldn't follow them. When they returned we expected them to ditch the scooters and split up but they didn't. Instead, they snuck up on people and robbed them of their phones…"

"Just like they did with Luce," interrupts Danny as if talking to himself.

"Yeah, just like they did with Lucy. They coasted up, real quiet like, and after they snatched the phones they hit the gas and were gone before the victims knew what was happening."

"Did any of them get knocked to the ground?" Danny asks.

"One did."

"Yeah, luck of the draw I suppose," Danny says again as if talking to himself.

"There's a couple of things we need to discuss… decide on," says Chuck. "First, we need a plan for disabling CCTV cameras, and second, we need to decide if, in future, we're going to pursue the gang into the housing estate or on the road and, if so, how? Do we get scooters and tail them? Do we get a car? We can't use the van for obvious reasons."

"First things first; disabling CCTV cameras. That's easy. We're going to paintball the lenses. I've seen it done before. A while back, I was walking through Camden Town in the early hours when this car drives up the road like a bat out of hell, window winds down and next thing there's a sound like a weapon fitted with a silencer. Turns out it was a paintball gun! The buggers paintballed every CCTV camera in the road and sped away. Next day, in the pub, I heard that a load of shops got burgled where the CCTV cameras got paintballed. We'll do the same. I'll get us some paintball guns from the shop where we got the phones. Okay, that's the CCTV sorted. Now, about following the gang into the estate or on the road. Bad move. Strangers are easily spotted on housing estates. And, what's more, this lot are switched on. I told you, T1 and his mate confronted me in The Oak after I took a photo of them. I reckon they're always on the lookout for things that don't fit. Same story with scooters… do any of you even know how to ride a scooter? Anyway, it's a no to both, you'll be spotted and that'll be that, the op'll be burned!"

"Okay, Danny, but the clock's ticking. We're only here until the beginning of next week and then we're out of here."

"Don't worry, there's plenty of time, all you've got to do is spot a routine and snatch him like we done dozens of times in 'Nam. Simple. I'll get the paintball guns sorted and you just stick close to T1. He'll mess up, he's bound to, he's an arrogant little prick who thinks he's invincible. We'll see how invincible he is when I've got hold of him."

"Speaking of which, where are we delivering him to?"

"My place," Danny replies casually.

"Are you trying to get us busted?" chorus Chuck, Glenn and Tony in unison.

"Calm yourselves down. He'll be stashed in the basement. No one uses it and I've got the keys. It's perfect for what I've got in mind. Don't worry about it. No one will be able to connect you guys to it."

"What about CCTV around where you live and this ANPR?"

"Leave it to me, I'll sort the cameras out. While I think on, I'll get you a set of false number plates for the van so you don't get tracked coming to my place. Don't worry, the plates'll match an identical van so it won't get picked up. Everything'll be fine!" Danny says confidently. "In any case, the roads are so full of white vans, yours'll get lost in the crowd!"

None of them is entirely convinced that Danny's "false plates" plan will get them to Camden undetected, or go as smoothly as he says it will, but they've done far more dangerous things in the past with far ropier plans than this one so they're not put off.

*

After the debrief call, Danny returns to the ICU to sit with Lucy. No one's around, it's just him, Lucy and two lines of beds occupied by patients having their breathing done for them. They're hooked up to machines so nurses know they're still alive. Pulling the curtain around Lucy's bed, Danny draws close and holds her hand.

"Hello Luce love… it's me again… Dad. I just had a call with my old Vietnam oppos; they're here at last! They're a bit more jittery than I remember but maybe it's just their age. You know Luce, love, I hate getting old. When you're old it's like you're invisible… like you don't exist or you don't matter. Kids give me all sorts of verbals and cheek. They wouldn't've done it when I was in the army, no way, they'd've got smacked! Sometimes, I fantasise about what I'd like to do to them. I even find myself on the brink of actually doing it, especially to them who put their feet on seats on the tube. I can't stand people putting their feet up on seats. It does something to my innards. I always politely ask them to take their feet off the seats.

Most do but some don't and I find that the older I get the more don't do it. I'd like to smash their knees so they won't walk properly again or throat chop them so they'll never speak properly again. I'd love to do it but I know what would happen if I did, I'd end up in the nick so I don't... like to though... like to.

"Anyway, where was I? Oh yeah. Oppos. Things are going well. They're doing what's called "obs", observations, not sure that needed an explanation, on the leader of the gang, you know, Tomic, he's been designated as T1 for target one. They're watching him to find out what his routines are. Everyone has routines and there's danger in them because if he does something consistently we can lie in wait for him and snatch him. Once we get hold of him he'll be dropped off at my place so I can have a word with him to find out who it was did this to you and then we'll take them too... and the rest of them if we have time. We can't go on indefinitely though because sooner or later the police will get suspicious that something is going on and come looking for us. I'll be happy with eight or ten of them but I'm not going to put a number on it. How does that sound?

"Well, that's about all for now. Oh yeah, did you know your mum's done a rota? She reckons she did it because so many people want to visit you. Rubbish! She's done it to guilt me into coming in regular, but you understand I can't always get in because... you know. Anyway, see you next time my darling girl. Night night."

*

When Danny arrives back at his flat, he finds Brad's watching TV, who tells his dad that a Detective Sergeant Dean was there earlier looking for him. Danny asks what he wanted. Brad says he didn't say but he'll be in touch soon. Danny doesn't like it. He doesn't believe in coincidences and wonders whether Dean somehow knows about the obs on Tomic and his gang. *Maybe the cops are keeping surveillance too and have spotted Chuck and the others... nah... no chance, not that useless lot!* But then he thinks police snitches might've spotted them but decides to keep his suspicions to himself, for the time being at least. *Anyway, if they do get picked up, they won't've actually done anything wrong so they can't be arrested. If the police interrogate them they'll get the shock of their lives! They won't've questioned anyone like them before! It'll be the cops who get interrogated!* Danny's confident of this because all IPEF personnel received "Resistance to Interrogation" training. Equally, he's confident his oppos would spot any third-party surveillance being carried out on Tomic and this, he believes, is another reason for keeping his suspicions to himself.

"There's a takeaway in the fridge for you," says Brad. "And I got you some cans of beer. Where have you been, by the way, I've been waiting for you for hours?"

"After I finished my little bit of business I needed some time alone to clear my head so I walked home from Waterloo."

"What were you doing by Waterloo? There's nothing there!"

"I told you, it was a little bit of business, that's all, nothing for you to go poking your nosey little nose into!" Danny jokes, ruffling Brad's hair like he did when Brad was a child.

"I can tell when you're lying Dad, your lips move! You'd better not be doing anything about the gang who mugged Luce!"

"Listen, son, there's no need to worry on that score. I promised you and the police that I won't go anywhere near where your sister was mugged. Okay?"

"I know you, Dad, you're up to something and if it's anything to do with what happened to Luce then you need to tell me." Danny considers his reply for a moment.

"Okay. I've told you, or if I haven't then I should've, but I've definitely told your brothers, the police know exactly who attacked your sister but they can't do anything about them because no one will come forward to identify them or make a statement or go to court as a witness. Why? Because everyone's terrified of them, that's why!"

"And with good reason. These sorts of people are on the telly all the time! They're criminals and psychopaths!"

"No son, they're not psychopaths, they're just a bunch of jumped-up little punks who need to be taught a lesson, that's all."

"And who's going to teach them this lesson, Dad? You? Look, Dad, I know what you're like, and, I hate to say it, but you're old… you're getting on a bit and these kids could kill you if you get involved! They're armed with all sorts of things and aren't scared of using them. I don't want you to die, Dad, I don't want you to die!"

"I'm not the one who's going to die, son, so don't go worrying yourself on that score!"

"What do you mean, Dad, 'I'm not the one who's going to die'?"

"Okay, Mr Nosey. I'm going to tell you something and I swear that if you breathe a word of it to anyone then you and me are done! I won't want to know you! So, boy, do you want to hear it or not?" Brad nods. "Well, I'm not going anywhere near where Luce was mugged because I don't have to. I got in touch with some old oppos of mine from Vietnam and they're carrying out obs on the gang's leader."

"That's a job for the police!"

"Wrong son, because even if they get caught and get charged and get found guilty, some do-gooder social worker or smart-mouth lawyer will give the judge some sob story about how they didn't have this or that chances in life and how they were treated bad as kids and how they grew up in poverty and shouldn't be sent to jail. You see it all the time on the telly! Some little scumbag does an old lady's house over, frightens her to death, robs her of everything she holds precious, usually sentimental stuff, and gets a slap on the wrist. I couldn't stand it if that happened to the scumbags that put Luce in a coma! Do you remember me saying when you were a kid that if anything ever happened to any of you I'd sort it out myself because the police are a joke?"

"I do, Dad, I do!" answers Brad, getting irritated.

"Well then, it's getting sorted out."

"So, what are these old 'oppos' of yours going to do?"

"They're going to watch the target and plan how they're going to snatch him."

"Target? Target! You're not in the army anymore, Dad, but you're talking like you still are! And what do you mean by 'snatch him'?"

"I never told you about what we did in Vietnam, for your own safety, and I'm not going to tell you now, but we've done this sort of thing before... many times."

"Now you're really starting to worry me, Dad. Please, please, please stop whatever it is you're doing and leave it to the police."

"Sorry, son, this is 'a done deal', as they say. We're going to take these scumbags off the streets."

"Scumbags... plural?"

"First, we're going to take the main target and then the others."

"You're out of your mind!"

"We'll see who's out of his mind, son, we'll see!"

"So then Kojak, what's this plan of yours?"

"Simple. We're going to watch what his routines are and when we find one we like we're going to snatch him off the street. As I said, simple!"

"You've been watching too many films you have. That sort of thing doesn't happen!"

"Oh yes it does, son, it happened all the time in Vietnam, all the time."

"Well, Dad, this isn't Vietnam and there are millions of CCTV cameras all around the place watching what people do. You should know that from the telly!"

"Oh, I know alright, son, I know. But what you don't know is what we're going to do to the CCTV cameras!"

"Okay, tell me then, what are you going to do to them?"

"Simple. We're going to paintball every last bloody one of them! Let's see how well they work then!"

Brad is both dumbfounded and impressed and even tells his dad he thinks it could work. Danny says he knows it'll work and reminds Brad to keep his mouth shut.

CHAPTER SIX

It's coming on midday and, so far, there's no sign of Tomic or his cronies. Chuck uses his walkie-talkie to tell the others he's going on a scouting mission. They ask him what he means but he doesn't answer.

The very second he enters the housing estate, Chuck's presence is clocked by several spotters on BMXs. They call around the "youngers", as they're known, using mobile phones stolen the previous night, to alert them that an "undercover" is on the prowl. Within two minutes twenty pairs of eyes are on Chuck. Realising he's under obs, Chuck darts into the nearest shop, hoping it has a back door. The shop owner asks if he needs any help. He asks if there's a back door. She asks why he wants to know. He tells the shop owner he's a tourist and believes he's about to be mugged. Chuck points to several spotters riding up and down the street on bikes and says he needs to get away. She says he should call the police. He says he'd rather not. She tells Chuck that as soon as the police show up the bike riders will disappear. Chuck says he doesn't want to attract attention. Lalonde's lived on the estate long enough to know it's better not to ask why he doesn't want to attract attention and points Chuck to the back door. Opening the door a sliver, Chuck peers through the gap. It's no use, spotters are already in the alley. Chuck asks the shop owner to go into the alley and... before he can finish his sentence, the bell on the shop door rings and in walk Tomic and

Pitbull. The shop owner knows who they are and asks them what they want. Tomic asks who was the man that came into her shop a few minutes ago and where is he now? She acts embarrassed and says, "He's a friend of mine... from America and he just... you know... dropped by to... you know... give me a surprise, like," she adds, flashing Tomic a knowing look. He says, from what he's heard, her "American friend" is old enough to be her father. Lalonde just smiles. Tomic and Pitbull, as they have people to see and places to go, leave Lalonde's shop after helping themselves to forty pounds from the till. As soon as the coast is clear, the shop owner puts the closed sign and locks and bolts the door.

"Who are you and none of this bullshit about you being a tourist?" exclaims Lalonde angrily. "You just cost me forty quid and you're not leaving until I get my money back or I'll..."

"I'm sorry. I shouldn't've come in here. Of course I'll give you your money back," Chuck says, handing Lalonde five twenties and telling her to keep the difference. She hands him three twenties back.

"I don't want your money! I want to know what's going on!"

"It's no big deal. I'm a private detective working a divorce case, that's all. When I saw the hyenas moving in on me I had to get off the street. People in my business can't afford to attract attention... if you know what I mean?"

"So, you're a private detective? Who are you spying on then? Is it a him or a her?"

"I shouldn't say but it's a him."

"Who's he cheating with?" Lalonde asks, intrigued.

"It's kind of messed up. He's found himself a... a man."

"That's not messed up! That's okay. Love is love! Live and let live, that's what I say!"

"Maybe I'm just a bit old-fashioned."

"Are you married?"

"Used to be. Tell me though, that guy, the one who took your money, does he do that very often?"

"No, not really."

"What do you mean by 'no not really', because in my experience that usually means the opposite."

"You don't want to know."

"Tell you what I do want to know is your name. We haven't been introduced... I'm Harry, Harry Henderson, pleased to meet you," says Chuck, using his middle name and holding out his right hand. *Harry and the Hendersons?* thinks Lalonde, smiling to herself.

"Harry Henderson? Really?" says Lalonde sceptically. Chuck nods. "Well, Harry Henderson, I'm Lalonde Willian, pleased to meet you," she says, taking Chuck's hand. "And the guy that took my money is called Antoine Blake though he goes by Tomic. He's just a lowlife but he's got a gang behind him, a big gang! He's bad news. Stay away from him... I'm telling you, stay away from him or you'll wind up getting hurt, badly hurt! I mean it!"

"Thanks for the advice and thanks for protecting me."

"You should be okay to leave in about a quarter of an hour."

"Why a quarter of an hour?"

"Because the coast will be clear then because he'll be sneaking over to his best friend's place to fuck his woman! If that ever gets out, by the way, every kind of shit will hit the fan!"

"Don't worry, Lalonde, no one will hear it from me," says Chuck, smiling. "Does he usually go for his booty call around this time?" he asks, believing he could've identified a potential routine for Tomic.

"No, he's running kind of late today. He usually goes around eleven."

"Regular?"

"Yeah, I see him passing along the street most days around that time... weekdays at least."

After waiting fifteen minutes, Chuck sets off in the direction Tomic took. But he's not on a booty call, he's in a cuckooed house barely a hundred feet from Lalonde's shop. Spotting Chuck through a window, Tomic points, saying to everyone that he's the old man

93

he was telling them about that's banging Lalonde. They all fall about laughing and mimic fucking one another like they imagine a pensioner would fuck someone. Pitbull asks if they should sort him out. "Nah, bruv, he ain't worth it and anyway he probably hasn't got many years left in him so let him have his fun with Lalonde... I did!" Tomic says with a dirty grin which launches a round of jeering and yahooing from his sycophant cronies. But Tomic's not there to grin. He's there to extract, one way or another, drugs debts from the two badly beaten and tortured men lying tied up and gagged in the corner. In an attempt to keep their fingers from being cut off with a rusty old pair of secateurs, the men tell Tomic about a drugs grow house he can tax that's not far away. When Tomic gets the address, he's well satisfied as he knows the grow house must belong to the rival postcode gang he hates most.

*

After searching for Tomic all around the estate for over two hours, Chuck realises it's almost time for the check-in call, so he races to a free Wi-Fi zone, reaching it just in time. Glenn and Tony are already there. Neither says a word to Danny about Chuck going AWOL, they're just glad to see nothing bad has happened to him. After the check-in call ends, Glenn and Tony quiz Chuck about where he'd been, what he's been doing and why his walkie-talkie was off. Omitting no detail, Chuck runs them through the events of the past several hours. Glenn and Tony can't believe what they're hearing and are both convinced their cover is blown. Chuck says it's exactly the opposite. "In fact," he reckons, "I can wander freely around the estate without rousing suspicion. I'll go and see Lalonde later and afterwards do a bit of scouting on the estate." What Glenn and Tony are mostly intrigued about, however, is what Chuck told them about Tomic fucking his best mate's girlfriend. "I think you may've found our routine!" says Glenn. "You gotta promise me, though, you won't tell Danny about... you know... going into the estate, I don't want to have that conversation with him, okay?" Tony assures Chuck he'll keep schtum but good old, careful old Glenn says, "You do realise, don't you, this has got fuckup written all over it… you do realise that don't you?" he repeats but then says that he too will keep schtum about Chuck disobeying orders.

*

The reason Glenn and Tony agreed not to say anything about Chuck disobeying orders is because they want the job done and dusted so they can go home. Despite them having the best time they've had in years… decades probably, more than anything, they want nothing more than to go home and, as far as they're concerned, the sooner the better.

*

Many people believe routine is a good thing as it grounds, calms and centres us, while just as many believe it's a bad thing, despite them inevitably having routine somewhere in their lives. Routine is said to have many psychological as well as health-giving benefits, one of which is that it relieves stress, something which can adversely affect our health and can even lead to a heart attack; and no one wants one of those. Is brushing teeth a routine or is it something we do to maintain our health? It is, of course, both. Some people can't go to sleep without brushing their teeth, no matter how drunk they get or how tired they are. A good many people have nightly routines to help them fall to sleep; reading, for example, or having sex. Can there be too much routine in our lives? There can, especially when it's at the exclusion of spontaneity. There is, of course, depending on what's going on around us, danger in routine because if someone who means to do us harm locks onto one of our routines, then they are in control and we are in peril. Chuck, Glenn and Tony have been looking for one of Tomic's routines to aid them in snatching him off the streets without getting caught and they believe they've found just the one they've been looking for. The only thing that could put a spanner in the works is Tomic's best friend finding out he's shagging his girlfriend. Chuck, Glenn and Tony consider disappearing the friend but as that could attract unwanted attention they agree to leave well alone in the hope that, before they snatch Tomic, his best friend doesn't find out about his unfaithful girlfriend and his treacherous best friend banging each other's brains out, and if he does, then they'll have to look for another of Tomic's routines, assuming, that is, his best friend doesn't kill him.

*

That evening, Chuck, Glenn and Tony are on obs on the fringes of the housing estate. All is eerily quiet. Glenn suggests, as Chuck can now enter the estate, that he has a mosey round to find out what's going on. Keen to test he's as safe as he thinks he is to enter the estate and to see what Lalonde gets up to of an evening, Chuck disappears into the labyrinth of streets and winding high-rise walkways that connect tower blocks together. It's an extremely dangerous place, especially at night, but Chuck's confident he can avoid becoming an easy target if he adopts a purposeful stride. Reaching Lalonde's shop, he presses the buzzer to the flat above. Lalonde's voice comes over the intercom, "Who is it?" she asks abruptly. "It's me Harry, Harry Henderson… from earlier today," speaks Chuck into the intercom. Lalonde asks what he wants, though she thinks she already knows exactly what he wants. He says his "case" has gone to bed for the night and he'd like to repay Lalonde for her kindness. She asks what he has in mind. "A drink? A walk?" he suggests, more in hope than expectation. She says she'll be down five minutes.

As Lalonde exits the door to her flat, she asks Chuck if it isn't too early for his "case" to be in bed. He reminds her that his case is one of sexual infidelity and smiles; "Early night," he says. Chuck asks Lalonde if she'd prefer to go for a walk or a drink, "or perhaps something else," he adds suggestively. She smiles and says there's a park close by which they can walk around. "Around?" asks Chuck quizzically. Lalonde tells him it's not the sort of park you want to go into at night, "or even in the daytime for that matter," and tells him that during the day the park's used by gang members to gather and talk without being overheard as one of them found a "bug" in his flat a couple of months ago, "or so he said but I think he was just bigging himself up to look like a bad-ass gangster." Chuck asks what else happens in the park at night. "Drugs, prostitution? How the hell would I know? I've never been in there at night!" snaps Lalonde. Chuck laughs. He likes her feistiness and says, as they're supposed to be an item, they should hold hands otherwise it'll attract suspicion. Without glancing Chuck's way, Lalonde puts her hand in his and gives it a squeeze. *You could be alright here... yeah, you done good!*

*

Glenn and Tony are on the outskirts of the estate waiting for their walkie-talkies to come to life to let them know Chuck is okay. After receiving two transmission clicks two seconds apart, they're relieved that he is. They know not to confirm the clicks and, with nothing better to do, they retreat to a café on the main road to await further communications.

On entering the café, Glenn and Tony spot a group of young males wearing clothes they recognise from photographs Danny sent had them. While Glenn is ordering coffees and sandwiches, Tony takes a table in the corner. He enters the café's Wi-Fi password into his phone; he'll delete it from the phone's memory as soon as he logs off. Tony notices several of the young males eyeing up his phone. Glenn notices this too and slides a leather cosh down his sleeve into his hand, *just in case.* As the pair sit and drink their coffees and eat their sandwiches, two of the males go outside and make phone calls, glancing edgily at Glenn and Tony as they do so. The former soldiers know exactly what's going on, they've been identified as targets for Scooter Muggers to steal their phones. Tony sends Chuck an SMS to let him know they're being lined up for a hit by Scooter Muggers. He replies, ordering them to sit tight and tells Lalonde a colleague messaged him that his "case" is back on the streets and he has to make a phone call.

While out walking with Lalonde, Chuck had noticed a payphone in a pub they'd passed and goes there where he makes a 999 call to the police, informing them that a big drug deal is going down at the café. Turning around, Chuck finds Lalonde standing next to him.

"Who are you really and what's going on? And no lies this time mister!" says Lalonde loud enough to alarm drinkers at the bar.

"It's best you don't know," Chuck replies quietly but firmly.

"Who are you?" she hisses, further alarming the locals, many of whom are ex-cons. They believe Chuck could be undercover police by the look of him and start moving towards him.

"I'll tell you, but not here," Chuck whispers; he smiles at the locals to assure them all is okay.

"Where then?" asks Lalonde.

"Your place?" suggests Chuck with a broad grin.

As Chuck and Lalonde make their way to her flat, they spot four police cars racing down the main road in the direction of the café. As soon as the young males see the flashing blue lights, they're off like scalded cats on their scooters. Seeing known gang members making off from the scene of a reported drugs deal, the police go in pursuit of the scooters. A high-speed chase ensues but is soon over when one of the scooter riders loses control and ends up under an oncoming bus. Another skids and slams full force into a wall. A crowd quickly gathers and fire and ambulance services are called to the scene. The scooter rider that ended up under the bus is dead and the one that slammed into the wall is taken away unconscious in an ambulance.

"Okay, so, here we are, in my flat. Now, tell me you're not the police!" Lalonde says accusingly.

"I'm not the police," Chuck replies, giving nothing away.

"So… who are you then because you aren't no private detective?"

"I'm with the military."

"What's the military doing around here?"

"You asked me who I am and I've told you but I can't tell you any more than that."

"Why not?"

"It's… secret."

"Are you spying on people?"

"Sort of. We call it obs… observations."

"Who or what are you observating?"

"As you most probably know, the police are unable to get convictions against gang members for fear of reprisals against those making statements or giving evidence in court. The government wants to appear to be tough on crimes like scooter muggings, and, as the police have been ineffective, I and my team have been sent in to work undercover so arrests can be made."

"So, you are a spy then!" snaps Lalonde. Chuck laughs.

"No, I'm far too thick to be a spy. I'm just a soldier."

"I see, but you've done this sort of thing before?" Lalonde asks.

"Yes."

"But not in England with that accent," she says, mimicking Chuck's accent.

"No ma'am," Chuck replies in a southern states drawl for a joke.

"Where then?"

"If I told you you'd be in genuine danger. I'm not kidding!" The way Chuck says this leaves Lalonde in no doubt he's telling the truth.

"Is Harry Henderson your real name?"

"No… and please don't ask me what my real name is because I can't tell you for security reasons."

"Is there something I can do to help?" Lalonde asks, believing Chuck will twist her words into an opportunity to have sex with her. She's surprised by his answer.

"Yes there is. You can tell me everything you know about Tomic and the name and address of his best mate's girlfriend."

*

As the former soldiers make their ways back to their hotels, they ponder on what a complete and utter shambles the night has been, but it so easily could've been a lot worse and they know it. What was meant to be a straightforward piece of observing and reccying had turned into a disaster. Everything should've been low-profile, under the radar, but now, thanks to them breaking cover, at least one of Tomic's gang is dead, meaning the police will be crawling over the whole area for days to come and time is fast running out. Not only that, Tomic will now be on high alert wondering who called the cops. *What a shit show! What a complete and utter shit show!* During the small hours, Chuck messages to say they should not tell Danny what happened. Glenn and Tony agree with him.

*

When DS Dean hears one of Tomic's gang is dead and another is lying in a critical condition in the ICU at St Thomas' Hospital, he sets off to investigate how this came to be. He learns that a 999 call was made from a pub reporting a major drug deal going down at a local café so several cars full of Drugs Squad officers get dispatched to raid the premises. Business as usual. Spotting blue lights approaching at speed, Tomic's cronies depart the scene on stolen scooters. Business as usual. However, what was unusual is that the 999 call was made from a public payphone some distance from the café. *Who uses payphones these days?* Dean asks himself and goes to where the 999 call was made from. As DS Dean enters the

100

pub, the whole place falls silent as the locals know him very well. The landlady asks what she can do for him. He demands to see the CCTV from the previous night. She tells him the CCTV isn't working. He doesn't believe her and asks to see for himself. She tells him to come back with a warrant. He says he won't bother getting a warrant because by the time he returns, the DVR will have disappeared. DS Dean shouts around the bar, asking if any of them were in the pub the previous evening. They all shake their heads. He announces that he'll check the council CCTV and if any of them are lying, he'll arrest them for "Obstructing a police officer in the execution of his duty! Now, I'm going to give you lot thirty seconds to reconsider!" The landlady asks DS Dean what it is he's looking for. He says, loud enough so everyone can hear, "A 999 call was made from the public payphone next to the toilets at around ten last night and I want to know who made the call." Dean knows if anybody talks to him publicly they'll be branded a grass and so shouts again saying to call by two that afternoon with the information he's looking for or he'll come back with arrest warrants and start pulling people in, "and nobody wants that, do they?" he adds threateningly and leaves.

The landlady tells one of the pub's regulars to look after the bar and she goes off to speak with Lalonde about the man she was with the previous night who, she assumes, made the 999 call. DS Dean sees her leave the pub. He doesn't follow her as he's on the phone to the council's CCTV team. He tells them to pull the video from the previous evening, "Between nine and eleven o'clock and send it to me at New Scotland Yard." Next, Dean goes to the café to question its owner who tells him it was just the usual crowd that was in, "plus a couple of strangers," he adds. Dean asks about them. The café owner says one of them was American, "He looked like he was wearing false sideburns," and the other sounded Australian or Canadian or something, but he wasn't sure, though he thought it was put on. A name comes to DS Dean's mind; *I wonder if the man with the dodgy accent was*

Danny Deacon? Dean would be delighted to find he's involved as it would mean he hasn't been frightened off.

The DS calls Danny, who, going by the noise in the background, is in a pub. He asks Danny where he is. He says he's in The Manor. Dean tells him to stay put and he'll be there in ten minutes. Danny says not to bother as he's just about to go and visit his daughter. "Great, I'll give you a lift, save you the tube fare," Dean says and hangs up. When the detective arrives at The Manor there's no sign of Danny so he races to Camden Town tube where he spots him outside the station. Dean stops the car and tells Danny to get in. He refuses.

"Look, Danny, you can play silly buggers if you like but I need to speak with you and we can either do it here or I can take you into New Scotland Yard if you like! I'm doing you a favour!" shouts the DS. Danny looks around, anxious that nobody he knows spots him getting into a policeman's car.

"You'll get me fingered for a grass you pillock!" hisses Danny, pulling his baseball cap low over his eyes.

"Leave it out, Danny, everyone knows about your daughter and won't be surprised or suspicious or whatever if you and me speak to one another!"

"What do you want?"

"Have you heard what happened to a couple of Tomic's gang last night?"

"No."

"Really? I'll tell you all about it then. Last night, we got an anonymous tip-off that a drugs deal was going down at a café just around the corner from where Lucy was mugged. This caf is a well-known hangout for Tomic and his gang. The Drugs Squad went to raid the place but spooked the gang and they jumped on their scooters and…anyway one of them ended up under a bus, he's dead, hurrah, and another one crashed into a wall or something and guess where he is… go on guess?" Danny refuses to play. "He's in the ICU at St Thomas'. Probably lying next to Lucy."

"So, Sherlock, why are you telling me this? It's nothing to do with me, if that's what you're implying? There's nothing for you to worry about on that score! I promised I'd stay away and stay away I have!"

"I'm sure you have, Danny, I'm sure you have but I reckon you're involved in this somehow."

"Involved in what?"

"I went and spoke with the café owner where the deceased and his mates were hanging around just before he ended up under a bus. He told me there were two strangers there last night: an American and someone with a dodgy accent. I reckon that someone was you!" the detective says accusingly. Danny's furious at what his oppos must've done but disguises his anger well.

"Have you been smoking your socks or something Dean?" says Danny, mocking him.

"Come off it Danny, when you and me spoke that time, I could tell you're a man of action. You're the type of person who's not going to listen to what the police say or sit back while the scumbags that attacked your daughter are out walking the streets enjoying themselves. That's not the type of man you are!"

"You sound like you want me to do something about it because you can't."

"I'm just saying, right, that you don't strike me as the sort of person who'll sit by and watch the scumbags who attacked your daughter get away with it… because that's exactly what they ARE doing!"

"Anyway, I wasn't in any caf last night. I went to see Luce and after that I went to the pub to have a few with my mates. You can check if you like."

"No need to, Danny, no need to," Dean says reassuringly. "If, as you say, you were in the hospital and then the pub you'll have been seen by staff and you wouldn't be so stupid as to give an alibi that wasn't true now would you?"

"I don't know what your game is, Dean, but if you think I'm going to…"

"I don't think anything, Danny. I just want justice for poor Lucy, that's all."

"Were they the ones who attacked Lucy? Y'know, the dead one and the other one?" Danny asks.

"No, but that doesn't really matter, does it? About a dozen phones were nicked that night and if they'd've been cruising near the bus stop Lucy was mugged then it would've them that done it. See? They're as bad as one another! They're as guilty as one another!"

DS Dean and Danny don't talk for the rest of the journey to St Thomas'. Peering out of the car window, Danny's lost in thought about what Chuck and the others were doing going in a café. *They've lost it! They've bloody well lost it! They wouldn't've done that in 'Nam! No way!* When he arrives at Lucy's bedside, Danny's so visibly agitated that Brad tells him to take a walk. He asks Brad to go with him. As they leave the unit, Danny stares at the curtains surrounding patients' beds, wishing he had X-ray vision so he could see which of them the Scooter Mugger is lying behind.

*

After walking aimlessly for fifteen minutes, Danny and Brad find themselves outside a pub at the back of Waterloo Station. They go in, order beers and sit at a table in a quiet corner so they can talk and not be overheard. Danny tells Brad about his conversation with DS Dean. Brad tells him to be careful as he doesn't trust the police in general and, "This DS Dean in particular"; he reckons cops are only out for themselves and his dad should have nothing to do with any of them. Brad wants to know whether his oppos had anything to do with the scooter riders crashing. Danny's evasive at first but eventually says they could've been involved. Brad can tell by the way his dad's speaking and the words he's using he's unhappy about the turn of events.

Danny looks at his watch and sees it's almost time for the daily check-in call with his oppos. Knowing he won't make it to the free

Wi-Fi zone in Waterloo Station in time, he logs on to the pub's free Wi-Fi after first explaining to Brad what he's about to do.

"No matter what, you have to keep quiet, okay… don't say a word, okay… but if anyone comes close," says Danny scanning the bar, "let me know, okay?" Brad gives his dad the thumbs-up sign.

"I see we're all here," says Danny, checking his phone screen. "I just had a very interesting talk with Detective Sergeant Dean," he says cryptically. "He told me that some of Tomic's gang were in a caf last night that the Drugs Squad was going to raid and the whole lot of them took off on scooters. Long story short, one of them ends up dead under a bus and another ends up getting so badly hurt he's lying in the ICU in St Thomas' Hospital just a few yards from my daughter! Did you hear anything about that?" Glenn goes to interrupt. "Wait, there's more. Apparently, there were a couple of strangers in this caf last night… an American geezer and someone with a dodgy accent who Detective Sergeant Dean thinks is me. Well, it weren't me, were it? I don't suppose you lot know who it was in the caf, do you?"

"Look Danny, there was nothing happening so we went for a coffee and something to eat and…"

"So… let me get this straight… you decided to go to a caf for a coffee and something to eat… just around the corner from where Luce was attacked? What sort of idiot amateurs are you? Dean said there was two people. One was obviously Chuck or Glenn, so I assume the other was you, was it, Tony?" hisses Danny, apoplectic with rage.

"Yeah," replies Tony, not bothering trying to defend himself or his actions.

"So… who was the other one?"

"Me," Glenn admits.

"So… Chuck… where were you?"

"I was keeping obs in case any of the… look, I know we fucked up, but…"

"I thought I was working with professionals. I thought I could trust you to be professional but I was wrong!"

"It's…"

"I remember what you… what we… were like in Vietnam. How we moved in and out without being seen, without leaving a trace but it seems the years haven't been kind to us. We've lost it. I think it best if you guys go home and pray the police never find out what you were doing here."

"What do you mean?" asks Chuck nervously.

"You do realise, don't you, that we're involved in a joint enterprise, a conspiracy to kidnap and murder someone?" says Danny, delivering his words staccato fashion. "I hope you at least covered your tracks because I don't want to spend the rest of my life in jail and I don't think any of you do either!"

"It won't come to that," says Tony.

"Okay, Danny, I agree, but last night wasn't a complete bust," interjects Chuck, "we've identified a routine for Tomic and we'll snatch him in the next couple of days!"

"Oh really? So what's this routine of Tomic's then?" Danny asks, suspicious that Chuck has suddenly identified a routine for Tomic.

"You're going to love this… word on the street is Tomic is screwing his best friend's girlfriend. He sneaks around there most every day. He can't afford to be seen which means he takes backstreets and the like. We just have to follow him, pick our spot, make sure it's clean and clear and do the snatch. He won't see it coming!"

"Fine… but no more screw-ups! Okay?" hisses Danny. "Send me the plan before the snatch," he adds and ends the call abruptly so there is no argument.

Having heard his dad's end of the call, Brad tells him to stop whatever it is he's doing or he'll end up in jail or dead. "These oppos of yours don't sound like they know what they're doing, Dad! I'm telling you, leave it to the police. Please, just leave it to the police," pleads Brad. Danny says he'll think about it but Brad knows he won't. "Look, Dad, I have to go back to Leeds for a few days, maybe a week. My job's not like Kel's or Joebyjoe's, I actually have to turn up to work if I want to get paid!" Danny asks how he's getting back to Leeds. "Driving… got a call from the garage a couple of hours ago that my van's all sorted and good to go. Hopefully it'll get me up and down the motorway, for the next few months anyway," he adds, not sounding too hopeful. Danny tells Brad he'll do his best to save a few quid and help him buy a newer van. "Thanks Dad but I think you need the money more than I do," says Brad, "anyway, I should get off before the traffic builds," he says, looking at his watch. Danny says he's going to stay for another beer and will visit Lucy later so won't be going back to his flat. "See you soon. Love you Dad," says Brad. "Love you boy," says Danny, giving his son a big hug. After ordering another beer, Danny returns to the table and remains there until he's sure all visitors have left the ICU.

*

"Hello Luce love… it's me… Dad," whispers Danny brushing Lucy's hair off her face with his hand. "Well, what a day it's been! I was in the pub having a quiet pint with Gaz and Jacko when I get a call from that copper, Dean; the one investigating your case. He says he wants a word with me and tells me to sit tight as he's coming round, so, naturally, I leave sharpish. I'm outside Camden Town tube when he pulls up next to me and tells me to get in his car. There was all sorts of people I know looking at me, embarrassing it was, but I had no choice so I got in. He tells me one of the scumbags from the gang who mugged you ended up under a bus, he's dead apparently, and another one's hurt so bad he's in here somewhere… in the ICU. They were in a caf just beforehand and in that same caf was a couple of strangers; one with an American accent and the other one, so Dean said, had a dodgy accent who he thought was me but I told him I was here last night… sorry for lying… and then I was in the pub… which isn't a lie. I know what you're thinking, I go to the pub far too much. Maybe you're right. Anyways, I reckoned the two strangers in the caf were probably a couple of my Vietnam oppos. According to obs protocols, they shouldn't've been anywhere near a place like that!

"But anyway, when we had the check-in call, I tell the others the story Dean told me and ask if they know what the hell's going on. Surprise, surprise, turns out the two 'strangers' in the caf were Glenn and Tony. They'd gone there for a coffee. Idiots! This caf is just around the corner from where you was mugged! They know to go out of the obs zone to get something to eat or drink or answer a call of nature or whatever, but they got lazy… or maybe stupid. After they admitted it I said we should call the whole thing off and hoped they haven't left any evidence because we could all get done for conspiracy to kidnap and murder. That shut them up! Put the wind right up them I did.

"But it wasn't all bad news because they reckon they've identified a routine for the gang leader, Tomic. Remember I mentioned him before? I think I did anyway. This getting old malarkey and forgetting things drives me crazy! Anyway, this Tomic is having a bit of how's your father with his best mate's girlfriend and… well, the details have got to be worked out but I reckon they'll snatch him in the next day or so, so I'll have to get things ready for when they do. Sorry, Luce, this is going to have to be a short visit because… best you don't know."

As he exits through the curtain surrounding Lucy's bed, Danny looks up and down the ICU; *I wonder which curtains he's hiding behind?* One by one, he pokes his head through each set of curtains in turn. The first few beds are occupied by older people but then; *that's him, it has to be him!* Slipping through the slit in the curtains around the bed, Danny picks up and reads the name on the clipboard hooked over the end of the bed: *Gary Wilson.* The name seems so ordinary, so innocuous. *Gary Wilson.* Danny pulls a chair close to the head of the bed and sits down. Looking at the machines Gary the Scooter Mugger is hooked up to, Danny notices they're exactly the same as those Lucy's hooked up to. *But there's a difference isn't there, eh Gary? She's here because she was attacked, if not you then by one of your mates! Another difference is she's a good, kind person who's never done anyone any harm to anyone in her entire life and you're a scumbag!* An urge comes over Danny to put a pillow over Gary Wilson's face and suffocate him. *Some bloody alarm'll probably go off I bet!* He then wonders what would happen if he injected air into the line going into Gary Wilson's neck and looks round for a syringe but doesn't find one. *There's loads of them at home,* he recalls. *But they're spoken for,* he adds, knowing their intended purpose. But Danny doesn't give up, he opens the drawers, and then the cupboard, of the bedside cabinet; still no syringe! *I wonder where the bloody hell they keep all the bloody syringes?* Noticing how flimsy the breathing tube is, Danny has a thought, *if I kink the tube and hold his nose at the same time, that should do it!* But this still leaves the problem of an alarm going off. *Sod it, I'll kink the tube anyway and take the chance the alarm doesn't go off and if it does, I'll leg it.*

Just then the curtain around Gary Wilson's bed is pulled open and in walk two people. One male, one female. "Hello," says the man, "are you Gary's doctor? I'm Bob, Bob Wilson, Gary's dad and this is my wife Mary. Is our son going to live, doctor?" Danny tells them he's not a doctor but a hospital visitor. "My name's Danny, Danny Deacon," he says calmly. Bob says he's been told it's a rule that only two visitors at a time are allowed and asks Danny to leave but, instead of leaving, Danny tells Mr Wilson he knows the rule because his daughter is lying in a bed in a coma just a few feet away. Mr Wilson wonders why Danny is sitting with his son instead of his own child and says as much. Danny tells him there's a connection between Gary and his daughter and asks Mr Wilson if he can guess what it is. He can't. "Yeah, well, you see, Bob, my daughter's in here because she was mugged for her phone by the same street gang your son's in. She got knocked to the ground and hit her head on the kerb so they brought her here. They put her in what they call a 'medically induced coma' to stop her fitting and control her breathing so she doesn't die. She's not expected to come out of the coma," says Danny, speaking in a matter-of-fact monotone. Hearing Danny's story, the colour drains from Mr Wilson's face. "We're so sorry, Mr Deacon," says Mary, "we tried our best with Gary and his brothers but if they don't join a gang they end up getting hurt, or worse. We tried to move away but we can't afford the rents so we had to stay where we are. There's no jobs, especially for youngsters and everyone's broke. We're living in poverty!"

Mary's words strike a chord with Danny, but not in a sympathetic way. They remind him of his own upbringing. "Don't you dare talk to me about poverty! I was born and raised in poverty; real poverty, not the toy stuff they have today! When I was a kid all I had was one pair of shoes, one jumper, one shirt, one overcoat, one pair of socks, one of everything except undies. There were no fat kids when I grew up because no one had anything to eat. In fact no one had anything full stop. Not like today. If people haven't got money for ciggies, drink, drugs, Sky telly, mobile phones, holidays, cars, two hundred quid trainers and stupid hats to wear backwards they think they're poor, they think they're in poverty! Don't you dare talk to me about poverty! People these days don't want to work for a living, they think they should just get stuff for free or go out and steal from hard-working people like my Luce! And it's no good you saying it's the environment they grow up in is the cause of them going off the rails! Me and my relatives didn't go off the rails and we had nothing... nothing! My youngest lad was brought up in a rough area but he never got into trouble. All his mates were involved in illegal stuff but he wasn't. He'd take on any work that came his way; stacking supermarket shelves... anything! One lot of cousins grew up without a dad, he died of cancer when the oldest was only eleven. The council moved them to the worst housing estate but not one of them, not one of them, ever got into trouble... ever! The eldest lad joined the Royal Navy and became an engineer and the daughter joined the NHS and worked her way up to be a matron! They're a lovely family. Now compare them to you and your scumbag son! My daughter's in here because of people like him, so as far as I'm concerned he deserves everything that's happened to him, everything bad that's coming his way! If he wakes up, and my daughter doesn't, there's no justice in the world!" A nurse comes to see what all the commotion is. As soon as she appears, Danny leaves the ICU.

Walking to the tube station, Danny's fuming thinking about what Gary Wilson's parents said and has it in mind that if anybody should cross him or annoy him he'll destroy them. But then he thinks what a stupid thing for him to do when there are CCTV cameras everywhere. He'd end up getting arrested and probably sent to jail. No, he had something important to do and this was not the time for him to get arrested.

*

Opening the door to his flat, Danny he calls out for Brad but gets no reply. *He must've gone back to Leeds already.* It's at times like this, especially after Brad has left, that Danny is at his lowest and loneliest. But he's got things to do and first on the list is break into the basement, clear space in the rooms, change the locks and prepare everything to receive Tomic. He starts, though, by sharpening his knives and cleaning his tools. He's on familiar ground and his head is in the zone.

CHAPTER SEVEN

As Danny, Chuck and the others had expected, the entire area is swarming with police investigating the events of the previous evening. Chuck makes his way to Lalonde's shop while Glenn and Tony stake out opposite ends of the housing estate. Lalonde tells Chuck that the "notorious" Detective Sergeant Dean has been snooping round, asking questions about the 999 call he'd made from the pub. Chuck asks her what's been said about it. She says no one's said anything so far but Dean's threatened the regulars at the pub that he'll arrest them for obstruction if they don't come up with the information he's looking for. Chuck says he can't do that. Lalonde says she knows that and so do the regulars but that won't stop them worrying or thinking that Dean will find something to arrest them for. Just then, Tomic appears from around the corner. He pays no attention to Chuck or Lalonde. Chuck says Tomic looks pretty pleased with himself. Lalonde smiles and says, "He's on his way to have sex with his best friend's girlfriend. This is his usual time!" she adds, tapping her watch. Chuck hails Glenn and Tony on the walkie-talkie to tell them that T1 is on the move and he's going to follow him, "I'll check in every couple of minutes. If I get made I'll double click the transmit button for you come to my last location." Lalonde asks Chuck who he's talking to and why he's so interested in following Tomic. He explains he's speaking to colleagues who are working undercover investigating street gangs and Tomic is a key PoI, "Person of Interest and we're gonna bring him down!" Lalonde still doesn't entirely believe Chuck but nevertheless wishes him good luck as she hates Tomic for the way he and his gang treat people on the estate; the way they steal from them, the way they intimidate them, the way they use them, the way they assault them, the way they treat females, the way they rape them and get away with it.

Tomic's usually hyper-vigilant but, with sex on his mind, he fails to spot Chuck shadowing him, which isn't so surprising as Chuck's a professional and Tomic isn't. It's a mere six minutes' walk from Lalonde's shop to the girl's flat. Tomic stops to send an SMS. Chuck guesses, correctly, he's checking to make sure she's alone. After receiving a reply, Tomic sets off with a spring in his step. He doesn't care that he's betraying his best friend because he thinks he's a chump for working and she doesn't think she's being unfaithful because everyone on the estate is fucking everyone else, including her boyfriend. Chuck updates Glenn and Tony on what's happening and then goes into a local caf where he orders a truly atrocious cup of coffee. He then takes a seat in the window to watch and wait for Tomic to emerge from the flat.

It's three hours before Tomic reappears. Chuck's impressed that the skinny little rat was on the nest for that amount of time. But then he notices that Tomic looks wasted and thinks probably more dope smoking than shagging went on. Being full of coffee, Chuck visits the toilet before resuming surveillance. Just as he's squeezing the last drops of urine from his penis, the toilet door opens and in walks Tomic. Quick as a flash, Chuck dashes into one of the cubicles and hopes Tomic didn't recognise him. Believing he's disturbed a cottager, Tomic kicks the door of the cubicle hard, almost taking it off its hinges. "It's okay, bruv," he hiss-whispers against the cubicle door. "I'm not the police or nothing. If you're looking to score I've got some really good gear bro. Real good price too bro!" he adds reassuringly. Tomic has no intention of supplying the cottager with anything and plans to rob him at knifepoint. Chuck hiss-whispers saying he's good for now but will catch him next time. Tomic's about to boot the cubicle door in when he receives a phone call. Whatever is said makes him leave the toilet in a hurry. On his way to meet his gang, Tomic thinks it odd that an American was in his local greasy spoon caf but gives it no further thought.

Hearing Tomic exit the toilet, Chuck is quick to follow him. Keeping his prey in sight, he hails Glenn and Tony on the walkie-talkie, updating them on what's happening. They ask Chuck if he wants them to join him. "Affirmative, intercept T1 NW of B street." Neither Chuck nor Glenn nor Tony has had the opportunity of saying "affirmative" in this context for so long it invigorates and excites them. Making their way into the estate for the first time, Glenn and Tony are concerned not to bump into anyone from the fiasco of the previous night. They'd been careful not to make eye contact, meaning there'd be doubt if anybody thought they recognised them.

When Glenn and Tony locate Tomic, they fall in behind Chuck and formed an ant-line, as it's called, changing positions every twenty yards to keep their target from making them. Tomic leads the trio to a row of lockup garages at the back of several blocks of high-rise flats where a dozen members of the gang are waiting for him; Chuck, Glenn and Tony recognise many of them from the photographs Danny supplied. To assert his dominance, Tomic kicks and punches several low-ranking gang members before they all high-five one another and ride away on stolen scooters. Unable to follow, Chuck and the others retrace Tomic's steps to check out potential locations for the snatch. Despite there being three directions Tomic can take when leaving the girl's flat, the most likely is the way he'd used that day and just along the pavement from the greasy-spoon caf, where Chuck had waited for Tomic to leave the flat; there's an inlet in the pavement, behind which is a blind alley. A bench is situated within the inlet, making it the perfect location to snatch Tomic. Not wanting to hang around too long in case they arouse suspicion, they return to the van; which they now refer to as the "base of operations", with the intention of returning to the proposed snatch zone to reccy the area.

*

While Chuck and the others are busy with their plans to snatch Tomic, Danny's preparing the basement beneath his flat to receive Tomic. Having cleared space in each of the rooms, he's now screwing industrial metal hooks into the joists from which he'll hang ropes and leather straps; *just like we used in Vietnam, they did the job there and they'll do the business here!* Concerned the hammering might attract the attention of the other residents, Danny's prepared a story. He's going to tell them the landlord asked him clear out the basement. *They'll ask why and I'll say I've no idea. No, I don't know what he's planning to do with the place. No, I don't know if anyone's moving in but if you're interested I'll let him know.* All that's left for Danny to do is drag in a pile of futons from his van in readiness for Tomic's arrival. He's changed the locks on the basement doors, front and back, just in case the landlord turns up unannounced. He thinks the delay in gaining access should give him time to remove incriminating evidence. *If the worst comes to the worst, I'll come clean and hope old Henry understands. Fingers crossed it doesn't come to that!* In truth, Danny's unsure what he'll do if the landlord finds out what's going on in the basement. *I suppose it depends on what he sees.*

Returning upstairs to his flat, Danny pours himself a glass of cheap, burn your throat, whiskey which he downs in four gulps while recalling to mind interrogations he'd carried out in Vietnam. He'd always used a script and repeated the same questions over and over again and then asked other prisoners the same questions to ensure all answers were consistent. Discrepancies were always delved deeply into, sometimes for days on end; the reason for this is there's truth in every lie, a lie that's been concocted in the heat of interrogation to hide the biggest secrets and it was Danny's job to cut through the lies and discover the truth. It's been several decades since Danny has interrogated anyone and he wonders whether he's got what it takes to get to the truth without reverting to torture. The real question for him, though, is whether he's willing to do whatever it takes to get Tomic to talk as time is running out for his oppos to leave the country.

"*They're not going to hang around you know, they'll be gone in a few days. You'll have to torture the truth out of him before they go home or some of them will get away!*" crows Danny's inner voice.

"*If there's going to be any torture, it'll be psychological torture,*" *returns* Danny.

"*You'll need to make it look like you know what you're doing or it'll all fall apart... it's been a while,*" whispers his inner voice. "*Time's short and you don't want them getting away with what they did to Luce do you?*"

"*Time is short. And yes, I need to get results before the others go otherwise some of them might get away.*"

"*Everything's all set up in the basement, so you have to do is do it!*"

"*That stuff's for scaring them, that's all!*"

"*But what if he doesn't talk, what then?*"

"*I'll show him the tools! He'll talk then!*"

"*And if that doesn't work?*"

"*I'll tell him about what happened in Vietnam. He'll definitely talk after that!*"

"*Now you're talking! But what if he's never heard of Vietnam?*"

"*In that case we'll educate him, tell him what it was like, what happened there, everything! I'll tell him about tying prisoner's ankles to helicopter skids, but not all of them, and taking them up to a thousand feet and chucking out the ones who weren't tied to the skids to make the others talk. I'll tell him it takes ten seconds for a person to hit the ground from a thousand feet and I'll count down from ten to one. That'll make him talk.*"

"*You'll need to be convincing, make it sound like it was you chucking prisoners out of helicopters!*"

"*But it wasn't.*"

"We know that but he doesn't! Anyway, it'll all be okay once he sees the tools. He'll talk then for sure!"

"D'ye reckon?"

"Yeah, it'll be fine!" Danny's inner voice mumbles unconvincingly.

Holding the knives he'd edged earlier up to the light, Danny checks them for how shiny and sharp looking they are. He knows from previous experience that the shinier and sharper they look, the more likely the prisoner will be to talk. As the time of Tomic's arrival draws near, the question weighing most heavily on Danny's mind is, if it comes to it, would he use torture to get Tomic to talk? He believes he must otherwise all this will have been for naught. *After you do it to him then the others will be easy… you know that, you've seen it before!*

*

Being an Aussie, and therefore more used to driving on the left-hand side of the road, Tony gets nominated to drive the van to minimise the possibility of attracting the attention of the police. He doesn't mention, to either Chuck or Glenn, however, he's on a driving ban in Australia, which could prove problematic if they get pulled over. Tony's not what people call a "good driver" and not telling the others he's on a ban makes him drive nervously. *Shit! Tony's driving has gotten worse over the years!* think Chuck and Glenn, recalling how terrified his driving had made prisoners, which was no bad thing in their experience. The van, a classic Ford Transit in white, has a sliding side door. It was specially chosen for the purposes of kidnapping Tomic and his buddies; a sliding side door making it easy to bundle people inside. It's all over so quickly that witnesses doubt what they've seen and only come to believe their eyes hours after they've had time to process the information or see something about the abduction on the news, and by then it's far, far, far too late as the kidnap victim has, by that time, been spirited far away or could even be dead.

They need to dry-run the plan to snatch Tomic. The start point is opposite Lalonde's shop just before the time Chuck had seen him on his way to the girl's flat. They know rats are creatures of habit and, sure enough, Tomic shows up bang on time. Chuck gets out of the van and follows on foot. He needs to make sure Tomic's going where he thinks he's going and six minutes later they're at exactly the same place Tomic had stopped at the day previous and, like the previous day, he sends an SMS to make sure the coast is clear. When Chuck returns to the van, Tony circles the area around the flat, primarily to check out the CCTV situation; with Chuck and Glenn filming and writing down observations as they go. After finishing reccying, Tony parks the van back at their base of operations and they congregate in the cargo bay to finalise how the kidnap plan works.

"What do you think of the bench? Good spot for the snatch?" asks Chuck expectantly.

"I've marked it down on the map," Tony replies noncommittally. "While we were driving round, though, I spotted a potential snatch site at the intersection thirty yards along the road from the bench. If I park the van right on the corner you two can dump T1 into the cargo bay no problem. Plus, if we carry out the snatch there, instead of the bench, we can drive straight out of the estate double quick whereas, at the bench, we could get boxed in by delivery vans or cars; they drive up and down the road all the time," says Tony. Chuck doesn't like it when anybody comes up with ideas which challenge his.

"That's my concern too," Glenn adds.

"The problem with the intersection is… it's too open… lots of windows looking down onto it," Chuck remarks disparagingly. "Look guys, let's not worry about which snatch site we use for now, what we need to concentrate on is the CCTV situation!" says Chuck to divert the conversation.

"Yeah, it's bad. Worse than I'd imagined," admits Glenn.

"There's a couple of cameras on top of poles that Danny said are owned by the council?" says Tony like he's asking a question. "And they're remote-controlled too!"

"Yeah, that could be a problem," says Chuck, still irritated by the suggestion of an alternate snatch site, "but let's not fixate on them, Danny'll come through with the paintball guns so we can take them out!"

"I noticed the ones on top of poles have wipers so they can be cleared after they've been paintballed!" says Tony to Chuck's great annoyance. Chuck's always thought of Tony as a "glass half-empty" type of guy but begrudgingly admits Tony's natural pessimism saved him, and a number of their IPEF Comrades, several times in Vietnam, including the disastrous raid to rescue the American officers.

"Okay, so there are wipers on the cameras! So what? We can't do anything about that. Did you count how many CCTV cameras there are on shops and houses? I got thirty. How about you guys?"

"Twenty-eight."

"Thirty-one. There could be cameras inside shops too covering the road through the windows."

"Okay, council CCTV cameras apart, I don't see anything that presents a problem. Do you?"

"Not really."

"We'll need to paintball the cameras just before we carry out the snatch so we'll have to be certain on the timing. Do it too early, or T1 doesn't show or takes a different route, or whatever, the shop owners'll clean the lenses."

"Don't worry about the shop owners. Even if they do check their cameras, and they're blacked out, who's to say they'll do anything about them?"

"Yeah, the main concern is the council CCTV cameras. One of them's right on top of the snatch site!"

"Look, if the lens gets wiped clean who's to say it'll be pointing in our direction when we do the snatch. I think it's an acceptable risk. You guys?"

"Agreed."

"Agreed."

"So, let's go and park up outside the caf and wait for T1 to finish his afternoon delight. We need to follow him to confirm timing."

"What about getting him over to Danny's place?"

"Well, according to Danny, he reckons because we're driving a white Ford van it'll blend in so we'll drive over to Camden once it gets dark."

"Whoa, whoa, whoa," cries Tony. "You're saying we'll be travelling with a comatose bloke in the back of a van hours after the snatch? Risky. He might be reported missing or someone sees us snatch him. What'll we do if we get pulled by the police?"

"The van's legal so there's no reason for the police to stop us!"

"Yeah, so long as Tony drives properly," jokes Glenn.

"Piss off!"

"Look, the police won't know T1's been snatched for at least twenty-four hours so they won't be looking for him. In any case, it's not like people like him keep regular hours!"

"Agreed. So, after the snatch, we park up in the usual spot and as soon as it gets dark we'll drive over to Danny's place and drop him off! Simple."

"Yeah, by the time anyone misses him he'll be in Danny's basement!"

"I hope you two are right!" whines Tony.

At the daily check-in call, Chuck informs Danny they're ready to snatch T1 so long as he's ready to receive him. Danny says he is and he'll drop off the paintball guns at the van that night. "I'll bring the false number plates too. They're registered to an identical van in South London so ANPR won't pick it up." Glenn asks about ANPR and CCTV cameras on the route to Camden. "There's no need to worry on that score because if the police figure out what's happened you'll be long gone. But to set your minds at ease, I'll do random paintballing to set them on the wrong path." Chuck asks what Danny means. "If I do the ANPR and CCTV cameras leading straight to my place then the police might work out I'm involved but if do random paintballing they'll get confused! Get it?" Glenn and Tony say Danny's is a good idea, something else for Chuck to get hissy about.

*

"Hello Luce love… it's me… Dad. Well, everything's in place. The lads are ready, I'm ready and, hopefully, by this time tomorrow or the day after, the leader of the gang that did this to you will be a guest in my basement. To be honest, I'm a bit nervous about it but I know I'll be okay when the time comes. I'm always like this before an op. I remember once, I was going out on really dangerous patrol and as I was getting kitted up I had to run to the bog and puke. I wasn't the only one. Some of the lads got nervous diarrhoea. Their guts were in so much turmoil they could hardly leave the toilet but when the time came we all… you don't need to know the rest. The point is, I'm feeling nervous! It's good to be nervous, it's stops you being complacent. All sorts of things can go wrong in ops like this and you never know where they'll come from neither! Again, to be honest, I'm a bit worried about the lads. Do you remember before when I said they sounded jittery? Well, you should've heard them on the catch-up call today! Right mess it was. They don't seem to remember what we decided! I'm not that sure myself! I'm putting it down to old age! Gotta laugh haven't you!

"I know what you'd say if you were awake. You'd tell me to stop what I'm doing and leave it to the police, but like I've told you before… I think I've told you before… the police can't do anything about these Scooter Muggers. Even if they get them to court all they'll get is a slap on the wrist and I couldn't live with myself if they got away with doing this to you Luce because of some senile old judge or a smart-arse lawyer gets them off with it! Sorry about the language Luce. Remember when you were little and I used to say that if anybody did anything bad to you I'd sort them out because, even back then, you'd see how criminals got off for doing all sorts of things?

"Anyway, anyway... last time we spoke, I told you how one of the Scooter Muggers is in the ICU? Well I found him. Gary Wilson's his name. I went and sat by him. I was all alone right next to him and I got to thinking about offing him... killing him like. I was going to smother him with a pillow but that would've set some alarm off; I've seen it on the telly when a patient stops breathing, all hell breaks loose. Then I thought about injecting air into the tube in his neck but I couldn't find a syringe. Can you imagine not being able to find a syringe in a hospital? Crazy! Then I came up with the idea of putting a kink in his breathing tube. I don't even know if that would've worked but thought I'd give it a go anyway.

"I was just about to do it when two people walked in and one of them asks if I'm a doctor. Me! They're only the Scooter Mugger's mum and dad! We got talking and they gave me some sob story about how tough things are for kids like their son. I saw red. I really gave it to them. I told them their son's in the same gang that put you in a coma. I told them what a decent, hard-working person you are and scumbags like their son deserve everything they get. Anyway, a nurse came in to see what all the kerfuffle was about so I left sharpish. I was in such a temper, if anybody had've crossed me I'd've killed them. To set your mind at rest, nothing happened because I had to get things ready in the basement for this Tomic geezer so I went straight home. Okay, love, that's all for now. I'll let you know how we get on. Nighty night my darling daughter. I know you'll wake up, I know it, and when you do we'll have the biggest party this family's ever seen. See you soon my angel."

As Danny leans forward to kiss Lucy goodnight, his emotions get the better of him. He wells up and, for the first time, tears flow down his cheeks which he wipes away with his coat sleeve. "No!" he barks, shaking his head. "No tears, no tears Luce! If I cry, then I'll... no, no tears for you my darling girl. Nothing but love, love in my heart for you my baby daughter," he whispers and kisses her cheeks. He tastes salt and wonders whether it's from him or Lucy. He touches the tape on her eyes to check but his rough fingers can't tell if it is or not. Holding his breath, Danny concentrates on Lucy's taped eyes to see if there's any sign of movement but there's not. He leaves her bedside convinced the salt he tasted was his own.

On his way out, Danny discusses Lucy's condition and treatment with one of the nurses. Receiving no good news, he trudges, head bowed, to the lift concourse and presses the down buttons for the lifts. When a lift arrives, the doors open and there are Kelvin, Joey and Detective Sergeant Dean, who walks right past Danny, but his sons stop next to him. "According to your mother's rota, you two aren't due to visit for an hour yet," Danny jokes. Kelvin replies dryly that nobody's adhering to the rota any longer and if he visited Lucy more often, he'd know that. Joey intervenes to stop the pair coming to blows and tells Kelvin to go on ahead. Joey asks his dad how he's been. Danny replies, somewhat sarcastically, that if he visited him more often, he'd know how he's been. Realising his dad is taking a pop at Kelvin's starchiness, Joey laughs and gives Danny a loving hug. "He's always been like that Kel has," says Danny. Joey says he knows what he means and asks how he's been. Danny says he's been keeping busy. Joey says he hopes he's not keeping busy by snooping around where Lucy got mugged. Danny says not and asks Joey when he and Kelvin and their families are coming to visit him. He knows Joey and his wife, Frances, and Kelvin and his wife, Gillian, hate visiting his flat and, rather than go there, arrange to meet him at some pretentious, posh, expensive place he feels uncomfortable in; *probably as uncomfortable as they feel in my flat*, he's thought more than once. Danny, however, is mostly upset about not seeing his grandchildren and hopes that if and when Brad has children, they'll all stay with him.

It's obvious to Danny that Joey is eager to visit Lucy, so he looks at his watch and says he must be on his way but then asks, "Has yours or Kel's missus been to see Lucy?" Joey says they've both visited several times but returned to Bristol the same day, "Because the kids need looking after and there's school and homework and stuff and with Kel and me being here all the time there's lots of extra things for them to do; you know, home-life-type stuff… socialising and stuff. Fortunately, me and Kel can work from anywhere so long as we can get online, but it's not the same as being in the office so Frances and Gillian have to go into the office occasionally to do work-type stuff for us," explains Joey. Danny says it'd be lovely to see Gillian and Frances next time they're in London and Joey should let him know so they can get together. Joey promises he'll do just that, though Danny knows the wives will make up some excuse not to visit him. "Bye son, take care and give my love to Gillian," says Danny. "Frances, Dad, I'm married to Frances!" returns Joey before realising his dad is having a joke with him.

After watching Joey disappear into the ICU, Danny presses the lift buttons again. *Blimey, these hospital lifts are soooooo slow! I should've used the stairs! You think I'd've learned by now!* On the way to the tube station, Danny concludes the last thing he needs at the moment are visitors so he won't mention anyone visiting his flat again until Tomic and his cronies have been dealt with.

*

Once back at his flat, Danny races downstairs to the basement to check nobody's tried to get in while he's been out. Everything looks okay. For security, he'd placed a wet hair across the opening side of the door and left a matchstick leaning up against it so if the door had been opened the hair would be detached and the match would've fallen over; both are still in place. Danny double-checks everything is ready for Tomic. He tightens the hooks one more turn into the joists and then loops a rope over them to make sure they'll take the strain that'll be put on them. *Perfect, they'll do!* He recalls seeing this setup in Vietnam. It's worked well. The only thing missing are electrodes and a bank of batteries to hook prisoners up to.

Checking his watch, it's time for Danny to deliver the supplies to the van; three paintball rifles, three 5-25x56 telescopic sights, two hundred paintballs, one hundred rubber-coated ball bearings, three boxes of syringes, six vials of surgical grade anaesthetic (labelled as distilled water), a pack of cable ties, six futons for when Tomic is flung inside the cargo bay and a set of cloned licence plates for an identical white Ford Transit from South London. The anaesthetic being labelled as distilled water will help if they get stopped by the police, even the paintball rifles shouldn't be a problem. However, should the police come across the syringes they might look more closely at the liquid in the vials. The mislabelling is so Chuck has plausible deniability for carrying anaesthetic but Danny knows it'll get confiscated, which will put a serious dent in his plans.

*

The morning of the snatch, Chuck, Glenn and Tony rendezvous at the van. The police presence on the estate has already reduced, making the kidnap phase of the op far easier to execute. Chuck opens the side door. In the middle of the cargo bay is a grey blanket covering a mound. After pulling away the blanket Chuck calls out, "We must've been good little boys because Santa's paid us a visit and left us everything we asked for." Glenn and Tony climb into the cargo bay alongside Chuck and slide the door shut behind them.

"Nice scopes," says Tony, shouldering one of the rifles. "Good balance and light as a feather! Wonder what they cost?"

"Jesus, you could kill someone with one of these!" says Glenn, holding up a box containing rubber-coated ball bearings.

"I reckon we should stash them, British cops are touchy about ammo like that."

"Yeah, but we'll keep them as an option if necessary," says Chuck without elaborating on what he means by "if necessary".

"So, today's the day?" Glenn says nervously. He's eager to get the job done and return to the US as soon as possible.

"Depends," says Chuck. "We have to take care of the CCTV cameras, tonight maybe? And make sure T1 does what's expected."

"I gotta be honest guys, I want to be heading home so I say we get on with things."

"Okay, so let's follow T1 and if he goes to the flat as usual, and leaves by his usual route, and we can be pretty certain he does that the majority of the time so if he does the same tomorrow morning we'll snatch him straight after he leaves the flat. Agreed?"

"Agreed!" says Glenn reluctantly.

"Agreed!" says Tony just as reluctantly.

Tony parks the van opposite Lalonde's shop. Five minutes later, right on cue, Tomic comes round the corner. He crosses the road and heads in the direction of the girl's flat. Chuck spots Lalonde peering at Tomic through the shop window. He leaps into the cargo bay so she doesn't spot him and tells Tony to follow Tomic. Lalonde gives the van a long hard look and makes a note of the licence plate.

Tony's careful not to get too close to Tomic. He drives for ten yards, parks up and repeats the process until they're outside the greasy-spoon caf from where they can keep surveillance on the girl's flat. As on previous occasions, Tomic sends an SMS to make sure the coast is clear. It is. He appears to be particularly happy this morning, and clicks his heels in the air as he makes his way to the girl's flat where he opens the front door with his own key. "That's new," remarks Chuck almost as an aside. "I don't like new things. Something must've happened. Something must've changed. I don't like it when things change. Tony, use a scope to look into the flat. See what's going on." Tony grabs a telescopic sight and focuses it on the front room. "Okay... T1 looks like he's rolling a joint. He is. He's lit it. He's passed it to... F1. She's blowing smoke into T1's mouth. He's now smoking it. Now he's blowing smoke into F1's mouth." This commentary continues until the joint is finished. "T1 and F1 have left the front room. I think they're in the bedroom," says Tony, putting the telescopic sight back. "The key thing?" says Chuck. "Maybe the boyfriend's off the scene? Maybe they've split up and she's given T1 a key?" he adds with a sigh for his failed relationships. "Whatever has or hasn't happened," Chuck says, "we need to be extra vigilant. If the boyfriend's off the scene maybe T1's routine will change."

Two hours later, rather quicker than usual, Tomic exits the flat and makes his way to where the van is parked. Chuck and Glenn slide over the front seats into the cargo bay to avoid being seen by him. Tony stays put and pretends he's with his mobile phone. As Tomic passes the van, he notices Tony's phone and thinks he can get a hundred quid for it from the hooky shop in Southwark. He considers grabbing it and running but, being worn out from his exertions, he goes to the lockup garages to meet up with his cronies. They've got a smash and grab on a nearby jewellers planned as a practice run for an exclusive jewellery shop in Bond Street in the heart of Mayfair.

*

At the check-in call that afternoon, Chuck doesn't mention to Danny about Tomic having his own front door key to the girl's flat but does tell him they plan to snatch T1 the following afternoon and intend paintballing all the CCTV and ANPR cameras that night. "And you need to do the paintballing you said you'd do," says Glenn to Danny, who says he'll take care of it. "Just so you know, we're going to snatch T1 on his way to the girl's flat, not after. He'll have sex on his mind and won't be on his guard," says Chuck. Danny says he wants time to think about this but that doesn't go down well with the others. "Look," begins Danny, "the later you take him the heavier the traffic will be and the better you'll blend in," he says convincingly. Chuck's not happy with Danny's interfering and says so. "At least tell me you're going to use the false number plates!" Danny says insistently. "Hey man, if we're paintballing CCTV and ANPR cameras, and you're doing the same around Camden, then what's the need? Also, with the increased police presence it makes more sense not using false plates. Who knows, the guy that owns the genuine set might be wanted or something and at least with ours we know they're clean and clear!" answers Chuck equally insistently. To add fuel to the fire, Tony sides with Danny as they'll be parking the van back up at the base of operations after snatching and dropping off T1. *Way too many fucking cooks!* thinks Chuck. *This has got fuckup written all over it!* thinks Glenn while, at the same time, Danny wonders if his oppos are past it.

After a heated argument, Danny agrees to snatching Tomic on his way to the girl's flat, though stating he's none too happy about it, "But," he adds, "at least use the false number plates like I said because there'll be lots of white Transits on the road during the evening rush hour so you'll blend in. Trust me, there's no chance of you getting pulled by the police if you use them... believe me, I know what I'm talking about!" says Danny, driving his point home. Though Tony agrees with Danny, Chuck and Glenn remain unconvinced that it's such a smart idea.

After the check-in call is over, Glenn and Tony ask Chuck why he hadn't told Danny that Tomic has a front door key to the girl's flat or that he'd left early that day. "We shouldn't be keeping stuff like that from Danny," say Glenn and Tony. "You do want to go home don't you?" Chuck asks. Glenn and Tony both nod. "Well, if we go telling Danny every little thing that happens this will never get done and we won't be going home anytime soon!"

*

That night, instead of visiting Lucy, Danny phones the ICU to ask whether there's any change in her condition. A nurse tells Danny to hold while she fetches the ward sister to speak to him. This alarms Danny; fearing the worst, his pulse races, his brain pounds inside his skull and his blood runs cold in his veins with thoughts that Lucy might have died or deteriorated badly.

"Mr Deacon?" asks a stern female voice.

"Yes," Danny whimpers in reply.

"Mr Deacon, I'm Senior Ward Sister Williams and I've received a complaint about your conduct from the parents of one of the patients under my care in the ICU. Do you know to whom and to what I am referring?"

"I'm not sure I do," replies Danny disingenuously, "but I spoke to a man and a woman while I was there recently. They said they were the parents of Gary Wilson in bed six. He's one of the gang that mugged my daughter and put her in your ICU, but I think I was very well behaved and very calm under the circumstances!"

"Mr Deacon, St Thomas' cannot tolerate such behaviour, particularly around such seriously ill patients."

"I understand. I promise it won't happen again," says Danny, contrition dripping from every syllable.

"I'm sorry, Mr Deacon, but I'm going to have to ban you from the hospital and its grounds for at least a week. By that time, Mr Wilson should've moved to another ward but if not then the ban will be extended."

"You can't do that! My daughter's lying in a coma in your ICU thanks to Gary Wilson and his mates! The reason he's in St Thomas' is he was legging it from police on a stolen scooter and came off second best!"

"Believe me, Mr Deacon, I do sympathise with you and the sense of injustice you must be feeling, but if I don't ban you, and things did get out of hand, and it might not necessarily even be your fault that things got out of hand, and someone gets injured or worse, then can you imagine the consequences? For starters, the press would have a field day! I can see the headlines now! I'm sorry, Mr Deacon, but if you turn up at the hospital, security will be called to remove you and you might even get arrested."

"Tell me, Senior Ward Sister Williams, what happens if Gary Wilson doesn't come out of his coma and has to stay there for years?"

"I probably shouldn't tell you this Mr Deacon, but I will so that you can see light at the end of the tunnel and some hope for your daughter, but Mr Wilson has already come out of his coma and if he continues to recover the way he has, and there are no complications, he'll be moved to general ward in the next four or five days to continue his recovery."

"You know, Sister Williams, I read in the London Metro that Wilson's parents are suing the police. They're blaming them for what happened to their turd of a son and a bunch of bloody do-gooders, pardon my French, are helping them to do it! Where are the do-gooders for my Luce, Sister Williams? Who's on her side? She's a good girl, never done no one no harm, worked hard all her life, and ends up like this thanks to bastards, pardon my French again, like your precious Gary Wilson!"

"As I said, Mr Deacon, I do sympathise with you, believe me I genuinely do, but I am charged with the responsibility for safeguarding the welfare of all patients under my care without fear or favour, including the Gary Wilsons of this world, and can't take the risk of someone like you taking the law into your own hands and attacking him! Now, if you'll excuse me, I have a great deal of work to do and it won't do itself. If you feel you're being treated harshly you can write to the Board of Trustees, though, to be honest, they only meet monthly, and not for another two weeks at least, by which time your ban should be over. Please do feel free to ask to speak with me next time you visit the hospital and I'll be glad to see you. Goodbye Mr Deacon."

Danny is so angry at the injustice of it all, in desperation, he calls DS Dean to see if he can help get his ban lifted. Dean says to meet him at The Rose & Crown south of the river in an hour to see what he can do for him. When Danny arrives at the pub, DS Dean's already there. He's talking to a couple of dodgy-looking characters who disappear as Danny approaches the table.

Eager to get down to business, Danny comes clean about his confrontation with Gary Wilson's parents. Dean, of course, knows exactly who they are as they're taking legal action against the Met for its police officers having the temerity to do their jobs by chasing after criminals. Danny, burning with indignation, explains to Dean why he can't visit Lucy, "And guess what?" he adds, "the bugger's had the nerve to come out of his coma!" hisses Danny, absolutely seething. DS Dean tells him to calm down and not to attract attention. Danny asks if the police are any closer to charging those responsible for attacking his daughter. Dean says regrettably not, and that's not likely to change unless something drastic happens like one of them confesses or witnesses come forward. Danny asks Dean if he's joking. He says he wouldn't put it that way but, in all honesty, he sees little chance charges will ever be laid. Dean then remarks he's surprised that Danny listened to him and stayed away from where his daughter was mugged. Danny asks how he knows this. "I've got eyes everywhere," Dean whispers in confidence. "In that case, why haven't any of these eyes come forward about the attack on my Luce?" asks Danny with unnerving calm. DS Dean says Danny knows why, "It's the same old story, no one's prepared to be a witness or give a statement. I know you don't want to hear this but you can't blame them. They all live on the same housing estate together... victims of crime, Scooter Muggers, burglars, fraudsters, benefits cheats, prostitutes, drug dealers... they're often one and the same thing! How are you ever going to separate them? They can't afford to move out and can't live where they are and be a grass!" says the detective, his voice barely audible over the hubbub of the pub. Danny asks what's so great about living where they are that they wouldn't want to leave! "And where would they go?" asks Dean matter-of-factly. "You've changed your tune you have!" says Danny accusingly. DS Dean says he hasn't changed his tune at all, he's just being realistic. "These people have no choice. They're all on benefits living in crappy council flats on a council estate. They can't afford private rents, so which borough would take them? Even if they found one that would, they probably couldn't afford to move! And you've got to remember, everything and everyone they know, for better or worse, lives on the estate. Their only hope for the future is to band together against criminals... but that's not going to happen anytime soon."

Changing the subject to what he'd come to speak to DS Dean about, Danny says he'd appreciate it if he would speak to the ICU ward sister about removing his ban on visiting the hospital; "I can't stand the thought of not being able to visit Luce," Danny whispers to prevent others hearing his plea. Dean says he'll give it try but Danny thinks, going by his tone, he won't. "I must say, Danny Boy, I'm surprised at you. I mean, there's Gary Wilson lying in a coma in the ICU and there's you sitting all alone with him and you don't do anything," says DS Dean casually. Danny asks him what his game is. "There's no game, I just think I misjudged you, that's all. I had you down for a man of action… someone who'd… never mind. Anyway, I'm glad I'm not having to arrest you for doing something stupid. Look, Danny, I'll do what I can to get your ban lifted. Okay?" says the detective and indicates, with a flick of his head, that it's time for Danny to leave. As he stands, Danny remarks that he might yet surprise Dean, who asks him what he means, but Danny just walks away. On reaching the door, Danny turns to see the two men he'd seen talking with DS Dean when he'd first entered the pub go over and sit with him whereupon they lean in close as though they're plotting something and don't want to be overheard.

*

Standing on the pavement outside the pub, Danny considers he's best calling Brad to explain to him, before everybody finds out, that he's been banned from St Thomas' Hospital for at least a week. *He'll understand. I'll just tell him it's a week though.*

"Hello son… got home to Leeds okay then did you?" Danny begins nervously.

"What? Of course I did you mad old man," laughs Brad.

"Good… good. Listen, I've got something to tell you."

"Go on," replies Brad, assuming the worst.

"Now don't get angry, son, but… I've been banned from St Thomas' Hospital for a week," says Danny sheepishly.

"What! Jesus wept Dad, what did you do to get banned from a hospital?"

"Oh, nothing really, I just... did I tell you that one of the scumbags that's in the gang that attacked Luce ended up in the ICU just a few beds down from her?"

"No, but what did you do Dad?"

"Well... I went and sat with him and..."

"You did what? Are you crazy? Are you?" yells Brad into the phone.

"I didn't do anything, I just... I was going to smother him with a pillow but I knew that if I did he'd stop breathing and the alarm would go off so I didn't do it. Okay?"

"No, not okay. Not killing someone just because you thought you might set off an alarm isn't okay! Did anyone see you? Is that why you got banned?"

"No, no one saw me."

"Then why'd you get banned?"

"His mum and dad came to visit and found me sitting there next to him; Gary Wilson's his name by the way, what a stupid poxy name, Gary bloody Wilson! Anyway, I told them who I was and that their son's one of the gang that attacked Luce and put her in the ICU and they had the cheek to try and tell me how hard things had been for him and this and that about what it's like for kids round their way so I lost it and gave the dad a right talking to. Anyway, they complained to the hospital and when I phoned to check on Luce I got told I'm banned for a week. But here's the kick on the bollocks, that little scumbag is out of his coma! Can you believe it?"

"Dad, I know this isn't easy for you... or for any of us... but you can't go round doing things like this. It's not the olden days like when you were in the army. These days things are different. Everybody's got rights. Everybody's got mobile phones with cameras and social media and there's CCTV everywhere so it's easy to make things look like how they want them to look and things won't look good for you if it gets out that you were sitting by this Gary Wilson's bed in the ICU while he's in a coma. Do you get it?"

"Yeah, yeah, yeah, everybody's got rights alright… everybody's got rights… by the way, Luce has got rights! Who's sticking up for her rights? The police? The public? The newspapers? Lawyers? No! No one's sticking up for Luce's rights except me!"

"What do you mean Dad, except you? You're not going to do anything stupid are you?"

"What son? Me son? No son!" says Danny disdainfully.

"You said that like you're hiding something. Tell me straight, Dad, are you up to something?"

"You'll just have to wait and find out like the rest of them!"

"Whatever it is Dad, stop! Stop whatever it is you're up to. I mean it! I'll drop you in it if I have to!"

"No you won't. Besides, I'm not involved in anything yet, so there's nothing you can tell anyone!"

"I'll call that copper, the one that's on Luce's case, and tell him that you're up to something and he needs to have a word with you."

"Go ahead, be my guest! To be honest, he's been goading me to do something right from the start. He warns me not to get involved but then acts surprised when I don't. I reckon he's fed up with people like these getting away with things and wouldn't mind if someone like me did something about them because the police sure as hell can't do anything to them."

"Dad, leave it to the police. Please leave it to the police. These people are dangerous and if you are up to something and it backfires you could end up dead. Please, Dad, leave it to the police, I'm begging you."

"They've had their chance son, so now we're doing things my way."

"Has this got anything to do with these old oppos you told me about?"

"Might have," Danny replies cryptically.

"Right, that's it. Sorry, Dad, but I'm calling the police on you! You'll thank me for it later!"

Brad ends the call and phones Scotland Yard and asks to be put through to whoever is in charge of the investigation into the attack on his sister. He's put through to Detective Inspector Christine Haynes. Brad tells her he thinks his dad might be planning to do something to the gang that attacked his sister Lucy. DI Haynes interrupts Brad, telling him that she's aware, via the staff at St Thomas' Hospital, of his father's confrontation with the parents of a supposed member of a street gang which resulted in him being banned from the hospital grounds and she advises Brad to talk some sense into his father to not do anything like it again, adding that she'll pass his concerns about his father onto Detective Sergeant Dean, the officer responsible for the day-to-day running of the investigation into the case. DI Haynes then asks Brad if there's anything else he'd like to speak with her about. He considers telling her that his father thinks DS Dean is goading him into taking matters into his own hands but doesn't like her demeanour and so says there's nothing else he wants to discuss and ends the call. Brad is so furious with the DI he throws his mobile phone across the room. "I can see why Dad wants to do things his own way with idiots like her around!" he screams, wishing he'd said the same to Detective Inspector Haynes.

CHAPTER EIGHT

That night, the three old soldiers get little sleep as they go over, in their heads, again and again, the plan to snatch Tomic. When they rise out of bed at zero three thirty, they're in a complete mental fug of tiredness as they make their way to their base of operations.

Wearing nondescript hoodies, they disguise themselves with spectacles and facial hair for the journey, and once at the van, they alter their appearance through taking on a different disguise. They're all aware that a van cruising around a dodgy housing estate at four in the morning would attract attention from the police, so they wait for traffic to build and, while waiting, they practise taking one another to the floor of the Transit and simulate injecting anaesthetic into thighs, backsides, necks and abdomens so they're ready for however T1 ends up in the back of the van.

By five, traffic has built up sufficiently to drive Tomic's route to paintball CCTV cameras. They'd decided the previous evening not to paintball them at night but wait until morning and risk being spotted. They believed this was an acceptable risk. Before they set off, Glenn swaps the licence plates with fakes belonging to an identical van. They'd argued over when was best to use the plates, before or after the snatch. Tony and Glenn won out. Chuck is not happy. Tensions are at max. Their starting point is Lalonde's shop. Chuck asks, "We ready?" Getting no response, he puts it down to pre-op jitters. Chuck peers up at Lalonde's bedroom window and wonders if she's alone. In the cargo bay Glenn preps the paintball rifles, sets the range on the scopes, loads each magazine with twenty paintballs and connects the CO2 canisters; each being good for fifty shots, they don't intend changing them unless something unforeseen occurs. Tony parks up ten yards from the council CCTV camera overlooking the snatch point. Glenn takes it out while Chuck takes out six shop cameras and four covering houses. They're such expert shots, it's the work of seconds to blot out the lenses of all eleven CCTV cameras. After Chuck and Glenn take a final reccy to make sure they got all the cameras, Tony drives to the next spot and so on until every CCTV camera along T1's route has been paintballed.

After blotting out twenty-four CCTV cameras, Tony drives to the snatch point where he parks up with the sliding door adjacent to the bench. Further along the street, he notices three additional CCTV cameras outside the house. Despite the cameras not being on their route, Chuck says they can't take a chance they might capture something and orders Glenn to pop them, which he does just as a resident is leaving home for work. The noise, slight though it is, attracts his attention. Looking around, he notices the rear door of a white Transit van closing. Thinking it's probably kids up to no good, the man just shrugs his shoulders and carries on walking to the bus stop. *Shit, that was close*, they think, hoping there'll be no more screw-ups.

Taking a moment to admire his work, Chuck spots the wiper on the council CCTV camera clearing the lens and calls out to the others. Peering through a telescopic sight, Tony reports that the lens isn't clear, it's smudged. Check takes a look and instead of re-paintballing the lens he reckons it's smudged enough to blur any images, "If we paintball it again it might make them suspicious and send someone out to clean the lens and we don't want that!" says Chuck. They all agree to leave well alone. "Besides, there's nothing to say it'll be pointing our way when we do the snatch!" says Tony optimistically, an unusual type of sentiment for him. *Must be his age*, Chuck thinks with a smile. "Well, guys, this is it. It's on!" Chuck says excitedly. "Man, I feel alive! Alive!" Glenn adds, high-fiving the others. "I've missed this!" he admits, as if talking to himself. "Yeah, me too. I'm so pumped!" says Tony, keen not to be left out.

*

At a quarter to eleven, Chuck takes a walk to Lalonde's shop from where he'll follow Tomic to the snatch point. Glenn will be sitting on the bench reading a newspaper. The plan is simple. As Tomic reaches the bench, Chuck will close in on him and he and Glenn will grab Tomic and throw him inside the van where Tony will dose him with anaesthetic. Tony has three additional syringes ready in case things don't go according to plan. There are three futons spread on the floor of the van to minimise noise and the blanket that covered the paintball rifles is to be used to cover Tomic. Nothing fancy, just the essentials, enough to do the job; less to go wrong!

At ten past eleven, Chuck hails Glenn and Tony on his walkie-talkie. Tomic is a no-show. Chuck says he'll stay on station for another thirty minutes. Thirty-five minutes later, Chuck arrives at the van.

"Where the hell is he?" asks Chuck.

"How the hell should I know?" Tony replies, irritated at Chuck's accusatory tone.

"The Q was rhetorical, it needs no A!" Chuck snaps.

"Cool it guys! We've seen it all before in 'Nam. Shit happens. We just need to come up with a plan," says Glenn to keep the peace. Just then, right in front of them, they spot Tomic coming out of the flat.

"Shit! He must've spent the night there! Quick, Glenn, you and me on the bench, now! Tony, get ready with the syringe!"

"Are you sure? This has got fuckup written all over it!" says Glenn.

"Look, there's hardly anyone around and we might not get a better chance. He'll be relaxed and off guard! C'mon, it's now or never!"

Chuck and Glenn exit the van, leaving the side door wide open, and go to the bench while Tony positions himself in the cargo bay, ready to inject Tomic. Before reaching the bench, Tomic goes into the greasy-spoon caf. Glenn looks at Chuck as if to say, "Told you, this has got fuckup written all over it." Chuck whispers, "Don't worry, he's done that before. He'll probably head into the toilet looking for someone to rob or sell drugs to, who knows, but he'll come out soon." A minute later, Tomic leaves the greasy-spoon caf heading towards the bench. Chuck and Glenn's bodies are like coiled springs ready to grab him and throw him into the van. Chuck nods at Tony to let him know the snatch is about to go down. Tony shows him the syringe. Ten feet from the bench, Tomic's mobile phone rings. He stops to answer it. Glenn goes to move on him but Chuck holds him back by his wrist. "He's right there. He must only weigh one sixty, we can easily pick him up and throw him in the van!" hisses Glenn. Chuck just shakes his head and whispers back, "No, wait for him to come to us!"

A minute passes and Tomic is still on his mobile phone. He's all smiles. Chuck and Glenn think, going by his face, he must be talking to a female, maybe the same one he'd left five minutes earlier. Still on his phone, Tomic ambles towards the bench, sliding the soles of his shoes on the pavement as he goes. Finishing his call just as he reaches the bench, the next thing Tomic knows is he's being picked up and thrown into the back of a van. He lands with a thump and screams out, "You don't know who the fuck you're messing with!" It's then he realises that one of the men who threw him into the van is the same man he'd seen with Lalonde. "What? You havin' a laugh, bruv?" he yells and goes to stand up but he falls back instead. He hadn't felt a thing when Tony injected anaesthetic into his thigh. Tomic's last waking words are, "You're dead… you're fucking dead!" and then everything went black.

When Tony returns to the driver's seat, he calmly adjusts his mirrors and sets off back to the base of operations, confident that no CCTV camera will record the journey. Bad driver though he is,

Tony knows to drive normally; not too fast, not too slow, as to drive otherwise could attract attention. As soon as they park up, Glenn swaps the fake licence plates for the genuine ones and returns to his seat. "I'll go and do the post," says Chuck. He walks to the nearest Wi-Fi zone and logs on to the veteran website where he places an anonymous message on the noticeboard: *Bird in hand.* Danny's been logged in to the site all morning. As Chuck's message arrived quite a bit later than he expected, it leaves him concerned that things had not gone according to plan, but, no matter, the message was clear; they had Tomic and would deliver him to Camden that night. *Sure you're up to it? I am. Sure? Certain!*

"Okay guys, I sent Danny the message. Man, I feel great!" cries Chuck, punching the air. They gather in the cargo bay to check Tomic to make sure they hadn't OD'd him, and go over, time and again, what they'd just done. "It's just like the old days man!" says Glenn, though they all knew it wasn't really like the old days. This was grabbing a punk off the streets of North London, not spiriting away NVA informers, traitors, criminals or warlords, never to be seen again, but it made them feel like it was.

Immediately after they'd snatched Tomic, a change came over Chuck and Glenn and Tony. Gone were the doubts, fears, anxieties and uncertainties they'd harboured over whether they could actually pull off the snatch at their ages, replaced by a calmness and a self-assuredness that they'll take the rest of the gang members, one after another, off the streets and then head off back home after a successful mission. The thrill of it all electrified them. They were invincible, just like in the old days.

*

Danny waits on tenterhooks, pacing the basement, for Tomic to be delivered. He wonders what he'll feel like coming face to face with him again, this time under markedly different circumstances. Deep down, he's still unsure whether he can go through with it, knowing that once Tomic sees his face there'll be no going back, he'll have to die; the irony being that if he doesn't go through with it, and releases Tomic, the thought of him going to the police and making a statement against him and testifying in court, something people are too scared to do against him, angers Danny.

"*You're an idiot!*" yells Danny's inner voice, "*Just wear a mask! Then he won't be able to see your face, if that's what you're worried about. And if he doesn't see your face then he can't…*"

"Shut up, shut up, shut up!" cries Danny aloud. "*I can't go through with it! I can't go through with it! I'll get them to give him a quick jab and dump him in a park or something. He won't know what's happened… or anything about me.*"

"*No! No! No! You're not just doing this for Lucy, you're doing this for all the poor sods whose lives have been made miserable by scumbags like Tomic and his gang! You've got to go through with it! You can't chicken out now!*"

"*You're right. I've got to go through with it… all of it… all of them!*"

"*Yeah, but put on a mask to keep the old options open, eh? Yeah, keep the old options open, that's best,*" says Danny's inner voice to calm him.

"I will, I will!"

At that time of day, traffic in North London being what it is, Danny estimates it'll take between twenty and forty minutes for them to drive to Camden. To kill time, he re-checks everything to make sure he's ready to receive Tomic: hoods, bar-gags (that's all the hooky shop in Southwark could get at short notice), cable ties, cord, noose rope, leather straps, syringes, metal bars, anaesthetic, interrogation kit (knives and tools), questionnaire script. Danny reads the script again to make sure he's got everything covered. Once again, doubt rises inside him; *am I doing the right thing?* he asks himself. *Of course you are! If not you, then who else will get justice for Luce?* snaps his inner voice. "I know, I know, but once it starts I have to go through with it because if I don't I could end up going to jail for kidnap and false imprisonment and stuff and at my age that means I'll never get out! I'll die in prison!" Danny mumbles to himself. *Then you have to go through with it!* argues his inner voice logically. *I couldn't do it in Vietnam so I doubt I can do it now,* returns Danny. *But this is different, this is Luce we're talking about. You're her only hope. You know that!* "No, I'm calling Chuck and telling him to dump Tomic somewhere." *He's probably seen their faces!* "Even if he has, they'll be okay, they'll be out of the country inside forty-eight hours. The police'll never find them!" *They're going to be very pissed off that you've wasted their time!* crows Danny's inner voice. *Shut up! Shut up! Shut up! Let me think!* he cries inside his head. *Don't take too long, the clock's ticking. They'll be here in less than five minutes if the traffic's light.* "That's it, I'm calling Chuck. I'll tell him it's a bust... I'll say the landlord's shown up or something!" Taking his mobile out of his pocket, Danny's thumb is hovering over the call button when a heavy knock comes on the back door to the basement. *Christ! Frightened the life out of me! I hope it's them and not the police!* As soon as Danny releases the catch on the back door, Chuck and Glenn burst in carrying Tomic; he's out cold. They're immediately followed by Tony, who slams the door shut and locks it behind him.

"Where do you want him?" asks Chuck matter-of-factly.

"On the futon," says Danny, pointing.

"On the what?" Tony asks, taking the piss. He doesn't usually behave like this but, like the others, he feels so elated by what they've done he's drunk with success.

"The futon... the mattress thing on the floor!" Danny replies irately. "How'd everything go? Any problems?"

"Nope, all sweet, man, all sweet," answers Chuck, feeling as elated as Tony and Glenn.

"It was just like the old days in 'Nam. I gotta tell you, it felt great! I feel great! We all feel great!" cries Glenn, feeling like he's twenty again.

"Great," says Danny, "great. Nice to hear. I told you snatching Tomic before he got to the girl's flat would work best!" he adds, attempting to take some of the credit for the smoothness of the op.

"Actually," begins Glenn hesitatingly, "he was in the flat before we got to the snatch point. Something must've happened with the boyfriend. We think he's moved out and he's moved in," says Glenn, nodding towards Tomic.

"Anything else?" asks Danny.

"Like what?" Chuck asks casually.

"I don't know, Chuck, you tell me!" snaps Danny.

"Look, man, it's all good, it's all good," interjects Glenn on Chuck's behalf.

"We kept to the plan as much as we could but, as we all know, things change because not everything is in our control," says Chuck. Danny gives a snort of derision. "Look man, we handled it, okay? We handled it and it's done!"

"How much jungle juice did you give him?" asks Danny, nodding at Tomic.

"Not much. He should've come round by now," says Tony.

"He might be playing possum. Kick him," says Chuck. Tony kicks Tomic who moans like someone who's not quite awake.

"Sounds like he'll come round soon. Okay, we'll be heading back to our hotels now and resume obs tomorrow. As soon as you find out who the others are let us know so we can finish up here and head home."

"Yeah, we need to bug out ASAP! Don't want to be hanging around if you know what I mean?"

"Good luck Danny, hope it all goes well," says Tony, shaking Danny's hand.

"Good luck to you too," says Danny. "Hey Chuck, you have to admit, this got the old heart pumping didn't it?"

"It sure did, man, it sure did but my old bones ain't what they used to be and they're longing to sleep in their own bed again, know what I mean?"

"Amen to that brother, Amen!"

*

After blind-folding and gagging Tomic, Danny also puts a hood over Tomic's head and cable-ties his wrists behind his back before rolling him onto his front and cable-tying his ankles. Next, he connects the cable ties with a length of cord, hogtying Tomic. Finally, Danny slips a noose around Tomic's neck and pulls it tight, causing him to gurgle and choke. When Tomic comes round a few minutes later, he finds that he's blindfolded, gagged, hooded and trussed up like a turkey and struggles to free himself but can't. Angry and agitated, Tomic mumbles in such a way he makes Danny think he's eager to be heard.

Moving an ear close to Tomic, it seems to Danny he's making death threats on whoever the fuckers are that snatched him. To discipline his prisoner for using bad language, Danny, without warning, slaps Tomic hard across his face. The shock of it silences him, but only momentarily. He goes to roll away in an escape attempt but this only tightens the noose around his neck. Desperate to relieve the pressure on his throat, Tomic attempts to stand up but Danny knocks him down, giving him rope burns around his neck. Getting the message, Tomic lies still. His mumblings turn into what sounds to Danny like he's pleading with whoever it is that has him not to hurt him anymore. Danny whispers in Tomic's ear asking him if he'd like his blindfold and hood removed. Tomic nods feebly in response. Before removing Tomic's blindfold and hood, Danny places a hood over his own head to keep his identity a secret for now. *It'll be a nice surprise for you later on when you see my face.*

When Tomic's eyes adjust to his twilit surroundings, he sees there's only one person there in the room with him and, going by his physique, Tomic can tell he's old. He takes encouragement from this in the mistaken belief that he'll easily be able to overpower his captor. Seeing a glint in Tomic's eyes, Danny waggles his forefinger from side to side as a warning to him not to try anything. The warning has little effect, so Danny takes a cut-throat razor from his toolbox, opens it, and waves it at Tomic. The sight of the razor makes Tomic's eyes almost stick out on stalks like in a cartoon. He's terrified, and sensibly so; here he is gagged and bound in a basement with a hooded nutcase waving a cut-throat razor at him. To drive home just how sharp the razor is, Danny slices a sheet of paper in half in one slow, smooth motion. In response, Tomic makes noises that sound like sobbing, and he is. Danny lifts Tomic's head and whispers, "Not so tough now are you?" Tomic looks puzzled. To further terrorise his prisoner, Danny gently rests the blade of the razor against his cheek, so gently he hardly feels it but there's no mistaking the warm wetness of the blood gathering, and then dripping from his chin. Looking down, Tomic sees blood droplets landing on the futon, where they're quickly absorbed, leaving a dark stain on the material. His sobs turn to full-blown crying and wailing and begging for mercy. "Mercy? What mercy do you show to the people you steal from? Where's the mercy for the people you attack? Where's the mercy for the people you threaten and beat? Don't speak to me of mercy, Mr Antoine Blake, because you'll find none here!" Hearing his name emanating from his captor's mouth causes Tomic to have a full-on panic attack. As he can hardly breathe, Danny removes the noose from around his neck and cuts both cable ties. "If you try and make a break for it I'll cut your Jacobs off," he hisses holding the cut-throat razor inches from Tomic's testicles, "do you understand?" Despite him having no idea what his "Jacobs" are, Tomic nods despairingly, curls up in the foetal position, hugs his knees and sobs like a child.

Danny knows to go no further at present. He can't go too far too soon, otherwise Tomic might become obstinate and clam up; he's seen it before in Vietnam and Tomic clamming up would necessitate him having to resort to torture which, in turn, could make him even more obstinate and he'd get nothing out of him. Danny will use all his experience and training to get the most out of Tomic in the shortest possible time, because time is not on his side. Leaning close to Tomic's ear, Danny whispers that he's going to let him rest for a while but warns him not to make any noise or call out, "Do you understand?" he hisses; Tomic nods in return. Danny bets that, if he could, Tomic would be sucking his thumb right now just like he'd sucked on his mother's teats. *I bet you were a biter weren't you!* Before departing the basement, Danny doses Tomic with a small amount of anaesthetic, which instantly sends him to sleep.

*

After returning the Transit van to its usual spot, the former soldiers split up and go their separate ways: Glenn to a tube station and Tony to a nearby bus stop, while Chuck sneaks to Lalonde's shop. He's surprised to see it's still open. As she's talking to a couple of women, he waits across the road for them to go but when Lalonde disappears into the back room and then reappears carrying three cups of coffee Chuck goes to the greasy-spoon caf as he hasn't eaten for hours.

As he passes the bench where they'd made the snatch, Chuck recalls the thrill of grabbing Tomic, hoisting him up and throwing him through the air into the back of the van just like he'd done dozens of times before in Vietnam. *I've really missed days like this!* Moving on towards the caf, Chuck glances up at the council CCTV camera. The lens has had the paint cleaned off it. *Shit! I looked right at it! They'll have my face! Fuck! Fuck! Fuck!* Turning his face away, Chuck makes for the sanctuary of the caf from where he checks out the council CCTV camera through the window. He's unsure which way it was pointing when he'd looked at it. *It might not have captured my face after all but I won't make the same mistake when I leave!*

Following an epically bitter, thin-tasting coffee and a bun that'd seen better days, Chuck returns to Lalonde's shop. There's no one in the shop so he ventures inside. Lalonde asks him what he wants. He says he was just passing and thought he'd drop in and say hello and ask if she'd like to go to dinner with him. Suddenly, a huge commotion erupts in the street. Lalonde says something must be going on because gangs have been fighting one another all evening. She notices Tomic is absent. "Maybe he's fucking his best friend's girlfriend," suggests Chuck with a grin. "I hope you haven't told anyone about that? I told you in confidence!" says Lalonde, giving Chuck the stink-eye. He assures her that he hasn't told a living soul about Tomic's tomcatting and asks about their dinner date. She tells him to pick her up tomorrow at eight and take her "somewhere nice and expensive". Before leaving the shop, Chuck leans in for a goodnight kiss but Lalonde gives him her cheek to kiss which makes him smile. "I'll take what I can get," he says, smooches Lalonde on both her cheeks and bids her goodnight.

*

Due to the disturbances, the next day there's a large police presence across the entire housing estate so Chuck, Glenn and Tony keep well apart from one another so as not to attract attention. The PoIs, Persons of Interest, are not around as, unbeknown to Chuck and the others, the police swept up a large number of gang members the previous evening and most have not yet been released. The estate is so quiet but there's nothing they can do but wait. Bored minds wander and Chuck's mind wandered to thinking about his date with Lalonde that evening and how he hopes it'll end. Looking at his watch, it says 14:55. Chuck has barely five minutes to get to a Wi-Fi zone before the daily check-in call begins so he races to the pub from where he'd made the 999 call. The landlady recognises him immediately and flicks her head in the direction of a man standing at the bar. She mouths "police"; it's DS Dean come, just as he'd promised to do, to harass the locals. Chuck mouths back, "thanks" and steps outside. Fortunately, the pub's Wi-Fi signal is still strong. At three, the "Vigilantes" group call comes through from Danny. Chuck asks if he could make it a quick one because he's standing in the street.

Danny asks which street he's in. Chuck says he doesn't know but he's on free Wi-Fi, so it's all good. Danny's suspicious but says nothing. They want to know about Tomic. Danny says he's sleeping but his interrogation will commence when the call ends and, because they're in such a hurry to return home, they're to snatch T2 ASAP, reminding them that he's the pillion passenger in the photograph with T1.

Immediately following the check-in call, Danny goes down to the basement. Switching on the light, a single bulb hanging in the middle of the ceiling, he finds Tomic's nowhere to be seen and sings out, "Antoine, Antoine, come out come out wherever you are! If I have to come looking for you I won't be very happy and if I'm not happy it'll be bad for you!" Hearing a muffled mumble emanating from behind an old sofa, he pulls it away from the wall to reveal Tomic lying in a crumpled heap. How he'd gotten there Danny can't imagine but warns him not to do anything like it in future. Tomic nods curtly. Danny asks if he'd like his gag removed. Tomic nods again, more enthusiastically this time.

"Now, Antoine, I tell you right now, if you call out or scream, or whatever, I'll take Mr Cut-throat Razor here," says Danny waving it in front of Tomic's face, "and I'll cut your tongue out of your mouth. Do you understand?" Eyeing the razor, Tomic nods vigorously, so Danny removes his gag.

"Hey, c'mon bro, what's going on? Why am I here, bruv? I ain't done nothin' to you, fam!" Tomic whines the moment his gag is removed.

"You're here, Antoine, because you've been a naughty boy… or would you prefer me to call you Tomic?"

"I don't know what this is about, bruv! Is Billy behind this?"

"Billy?"

"You know, Sandy's man. I know I shouldn't've, bruv, but, you know, it's not like he's keeping his cock in his pants! Is this to do with Billy? Does he know?"

"Oh, I see. You think you're here because you've been shagging your best mate's girlfriend. Some mate you are. If only it were that simple, Antoine, if only it were that simple. No, Antoine, you're here because your gang mugged my daughter for her mobile phone!"

"What! Is that it? Are you a fucking nutter? All this for a fucking phone! Let me go right now or I will fuck you up. I swear to God I'll fuck you up!"

"Antoine, I don't like bad language. I occasionally swear myself, but only very rarely, and if you swear again I'll slice your nose open and cut off your ears. Do you understand?" Tomic nods but doubts the old fool in front of him would do it. Merely having such a thought in the situation he's in is an indication of how utterly dense Tomic is. He's completely failed to comprehend, recognise, or understand the effort, organisation and planning that's brought him to where he is.

"Look granddad, if it's a mobile phone you is after for the one your daughter lost, let me know which one and I'll get it for you, bro and if you let me go right now it won't go no further, innit. Okay?"

"No, not okay. In fact, if you speak again I'll cut your tongue out. You see, when your scumbag cronies robbed my daughter's phone they knocked her over and she hit her head on the kerb and was taken to hospital and she had to be put into a coma to save her life. She's still in a coma and might not ever come out of it. Do you think this is about a phone you dumb fuck? Now see what you made me do? You made me swear! Make me swear again and I'll cut you to pieces! Lots of little pieces!"

From the training he's received, Danny understands perfectly the "Psychology of Interrogation" and knows that threats without action will embolden a prisoner, so he takes the cut-throat razor and nicks Tomic's cheek with it. Feeling blood running down his face onto his chest, Tomic cries out in shock and fear but, recalling Danny's warning, remains silent. *See, Antoine, you can be trained!*

"Now, Antoine, you may speak to answer questions or if you have something to tell me," says Danny, displaying unnerving calm.

"Please, please, please fam, don't hurt me," bleats Tomic, rubbing the blood from his cheek with his shoulder. "I'll do anything, just don't hurt me... please!"

"Well, Antoine, that's up to you isn't it? Give me what I want and I might let you go," says Danny with sincerity, knowing that prisoners must have hope of a future no matter what their situation. "The first question I have, Antoine, is, if maybe I do let you go, will you and your mates come after me when you're free?" asks Danny, cunningly leading Tomic from "might" to "maybe" to "when" he's free.

"How can I come after you, bro? I don't even know who you are, bruv, or what you look like and the other guy, the one I saw with Lalonde, tell him I won't come after him either."

"Who are you talking about?"

"American guy. Big guy! You know? Come to think of it..." Tomic stops speaking and quietly swallows his words as the realisation dawns on him that the man in the toilet cubicle in the greasy-spoon caf must've been the same man he'd seen with Lalonde, the same man who picked him up and threw him into the back of the van. Things are now starting to sink in for Tomic.

"What big American?" asks Danny, seething inside that either Chuck or Glenn hasn't been following protocol.

"Yeah. Big guy. Blond hair. Looks like he dyes it. Nice Rolex." With the mention of a big, blond-haired American wearing a Rolex, Danny knows it was Chuck that Tomic had seen with this "Lalonde".

"Rolex? Funny you clocked that, no pun intended." The pun didn't register with Tomic. "Thinking of mugging him were you?"

"No... yes... look I won't lie, I wanted the watch, innit?"

Now the ice is broken, it's time for the interrogation to begin proper. Danny will start by asking simple, easy to answer questions that appear to give little or nothing away; essential to building rapport with the prisoner, or interrogatee, as Danny prefers to call them. He begins by asking about "Lalonde".

"Lalonde? That's an unusual name. Where's it from?"

"You should see her, bro. She's in her late thirties but tidy… know what I mean? Great body. Been there, bruv," adds Tomic to let Danny know he's fucked her.

"And what was she doing with this American?"

"Dunno. We went into her shop and he was there. She said she knew him. We let him wander around the estate so we could keep an eye on him. Know what I mean, bruv? He might've had something interesting."

"Like a Rolex watch for example?"

"Yeah, it's a nice one innit? But with him throwing me in the back of a van, wish I'd sussed him and had him took care of… know what I mean, bro?" says Tomic, completely failing to appreciate the crass stupidity of his remark.

"You know, Antoine, I'd like to know more about you; what makes you tick sort of thing. Know what I mean?" says Danny, employing a moronic phrase to gain Tomic's confidence. "Tell me, bro, what it was like for you growing up. Where were you born? Where did you go to school? That sort of thing. I'll make notes if you don't mind."

With very little prompting, Tomic tells Danny his life story, embellishing the parts he thinks will win him favour with the man in the hood. After finishing his sorry tale, Danny tells Tomic he's earned himself a drink and something to eat. Tomic asks for a can of Coke and chicken nuggets. "You're in luck, I think I've got both," says Danny. "I don't drink anything but Coke, bro," Tomic says thoughtfully. "Okay… I'll go and heat the nuggets up for you," says Danny. "Do you have tomato sauce and mayo to dip them in?" Tomic asks. Danny says he thinks he's got some sachets somewhere. "Now listen Antoine, while I'm gone, if you make any noise or shout out or try to hide or escape, I'll cut your Jacobs off. Do you understand?" says Danny with a snipping motion of his fingers. "Listen, bro, what's my Jacobs?" Tomic asks. Danny points at his testicles. The mere thought of having his testicles cut off makes

Tomic swallow hard and go light-headed. "Now Antoine, sit still, I'm going to gag you and cable-tie your wrists and ankles. Understand?" Tomic nods. Danny knows this type of treatment makes prisoners more accepting of their situation and can even make them docile and compliant.

Following protocol, before leaving to fetch the chicken nuggets and can of Coke for his prisoner, Danny slips the noose around his neck, telling him he'll pull it tight if he tries anything and ties the rope off around the doorknob. Whenever interrogation prisoners were fed in Vietnam, they were made to stand on tiptoe before the noose was tied off but Danny felt this was unnecessary with Tomic as he believed this might disincline him to answer questions. When Danny returns to the basement, he removes Tomic's gag and cuts the cable ties securing his wrists so he can feed himself, but not before reminding him that should he try anything, he'll pull on the noose and break his neck. To demonstrate, he tugs lightly on the rope, "One good pull on this and it's all over for you Antoine!" he says handing Tomic the chicken nuggets, can of Coke and the tomato sauce and mayo sachets he'd taken from the stockpile of condiments he'd built up from local takeaways.

Immediately after Tomic's been fed and watered, Danny commences the interrogation. All he wants to achieve at this stage is to build trust, so only asks questions that are easy for Tomic to answer because they're so innocuous; Danny doesn't even bother writing down his responses. At half past seven, Danny preps a syringe, flicks out the air bubbles and ejects the excess to ensure the correct dosage will be administered. "What's that for bro?" Tomic asks nervously. "Don't worry, Antoine, you won't feel a thing. You'll just fall asleep and when you wake you'll feel right as rain. I'll even let you have a can of Coke for your breakfast. Goodnight." With that, Danny jabs Tomic and ten seconds later he's out cold making it simple for Danny to gag him, cable-tie his wrists and hogtie them to his ankles, and loop the noose around one of the metal bars he'd fitted between the joists. Believing it unnecessary, Danny doesn't hood his prisoner.

*

As soon as Danny returns back upstairs to his flat, he sends Chuck an SMS saying they need to talk. It's almost midnight before Chuck replies.

<Hi. Everything okay? How's things going with T1?>

<Whewre are you? What took you som long to rply>

<Only just checked my messages. What's up?>

<Who's Lalond>

<Someone I met>

<Whered you mee4t her?>

<I went into her shop when I was surveilling around the estate and got to know her.

<T1 recognided you>

<Thought he would.>

<What a=else are tyou keepwnhg form mje?>

<Nothing! I didn't tell you about Lalonde because I knew you'd be like this but there's nothing else. ok?>

<I suppose it'll have to Be. what's doenm ids done. No more surpoises. okay?>

<You're shit at typing>

<Do G and T know about Lalod? just relaiesed G&T>

<Yeah but don't blame them I didn't give them a chance to speak.>

<I'm not blamignnthem, I blameg you ypou";re their boss>

<Received. We'll get back out tomorrow and get T2 for you<D'Onlt dleciver him until I say So. okay?>

<How fat are your fingers?>

<No more surprise4s. are yloi gojng to tell G&T abo9t this?>

<Yeah, they deserve to know.>

<agree>

Danny believes he'd been right all along to be suspicious of Chuck, and resolves to be more watchful of him in future, but so long as he delivers the goods he won't take things further at present.

*

After a remarkably restful night's sleep, Danny wakes to chiming and buzzing from his phone; he'd forgotten to mute it the previous night just like he'd forgotten the night he got the call from St Thomas' Hospital. *Shit, St Thomas', I'll give that Sister Williams a call later and ask her if it's okay for me to come and see Luce if I promise to behave myself.* It's Brad calling. "Brad? Brad?" says Danny, acting the fool. "Do I know anyone called Brad? Oh yeah, I've got a son called Brad. You wouldn't happen to be him by any chance would you?" Danny asks light-heartedly. Brad laughs and says, equally light-heartedly, "It's not always up to me to call, you know, you can call me anytime you like! Anyhow, what have you been up to you mad old fart? I hope you've been behaving yourself and not getting involved in things you shouldn't!" Danny assures Brad he's keeping his nose clean but says it's not easy because the police aren't doing anything about the gang that mugged Lucy and they're still at it. Brad asks how he knows this. "It's in all the local papers," Danny replies plausibly. Brad says he doesn't believe him. "Well, it's a fine thing when your own son calls you a liar," responds Danny, feigning indignity. Brad says he'll be back down to London soon but in the meantime Danny's to behave himself and not get into any more trouble with the hospital. Danny asks when, precisely, he'll be coming to visit him. This question raises Brad's suspicions. "Maybe tomorrow, maybe next week or maybe this weekend, it all depends on when I can get away," Brad answers noncommittally to keep his dad on his toes. *I'll have to move things along before "Brad the Bubbler" pays a visit!* thinks Danny in a panic.

Following a meagre breakfast of a mug of tea and a round of toast, Danny goes down to the basement to check on Tomic. He's confident he'll find him exactly where he'd left him the previous evening; he is, Tomic hasn't moved so much as a toe off the futon. "Are you hungry?" Tomic nods eagerly. "And thirsty?" he nods even more eagerly. "I haven't got much in so it'll have to be tea and toast. Okay?"

says Danny, removing Tomic's gag. He says he hates tea and reminds Danny that the previous evening he'd said he could have a can of Coke. "I think I might have one in the fridge but if not then tough luck!" Danny checks Tomic's bindings before leaving the basement; they're all secure. Returning to the basement with Tomic's breakfast, Danny goes through the procedure for feeding prisoners, which ends with him cutting the cable tie securing Tomic's wrists. "Here's your breakfast," says Danny, handing it to him with one hand while holding onto the noose with the other. While interrogating prisoners in Vietnam, it was common practice to slip sedatives, hallucinogens and other medications into their food to achieve quicker results, especially in time-critical situations, and as Brad could show up at any minute, Danny had put a little something on Tomic's toast.

With considerable experience interrogating prisoners, Danny knows Tomic's bodily functions will be in a state of dormancy due to stress; this is similar to when people go on holiday or move house or change job, they get "bunged up". When Danny first arrived at Phnen Bin, he didn't take a dump for a week and is hoping Tomic is going to be the same. Pissing, however, is an entirely different matter and Danny knows Tomic will need to piss out the Coke he's drunk, and has a plastic bowl ready for the purpose.

"Now, Antoine, before we begin, do you need to piss or take a shit?" Danny asks. "Because if you say you don't and you want one after we begin I won't be happy!"

"I could do with a piss," answers Tomic, hoping there could be a chance for him to get the jump on Danny, who, of course realises this and removes a paintball gun from his toolbox.

"This, Antoine, is a gas-powered paintball gun loaded with ball bearings," says Danny, pointing the weapon at Tomic's testicles. "If you get hit in the bollocks with one of these you'll know about it. Do you understand?" Tomic answers with a curt nod. "You can take a piss in that plastic bowl over there," says Danny, pointing the muzzle at the bowl, "and I warn you, if you try anything you'll wish you'd never been born."

"Look, bro, I'm sorry for what happened to your daughter, okay!" says Tomic, relieving himself into the bowl, "but it weren't me, I had nothing to do with it, bruv, honest. If you let me go I'll find out who done it and tell you. I promise, I've learned my lesson, bro, and, if you let me go I won't do anything again," he says, giving his penis a shake and a squeeze before putting it back in his tracky bottoms.

"It was interesting hearing you telling me about what things were like for you growing up but you left out the most important parts."

"Like what, bro?"

"Like the crimes you committed. Like all the misery you spread. Have you ever raped anyone?"

"No! No bro, honest. I think rapists are the lowest of the low. I would never do anything like that, fam, believe me, I'm not even lying innit!"

"Before we begin the interrogation, I've got a surprise for you," says Danny. "But first I need to retie your wrists. Turn around. Make one wrong move and I'll shoot you in the bollocks," says Danny, removing a cable tie from a pack on the floor.

"Don't worry, bro, you don't have to worry about me, I'm cooperating all the way, bruv, know what I mean? I've got nothing to hide, bro, honest. Question me all you like and you'll find out I'm not a bad person. I'll tell you anything you want then you can let me go innit. Okay?" Once Tomic's wrists and ankles are securely hogtied together, Danny removes his hood and throws it to the floor.

"Here's the surprise I mentioned," says Danny icily. Tomic recognises his captor immediately. "Ah, I see you remember me then!"

"What the f… what's going on, bro?" cries Tomic, stopping himself just in time from swearing. "You… you was in the pub with Alby that time!" Despite Tomic being monumentally thick, he immediately understands that, with the man having removed his hood, things cannot be good for him.

"Are the pieces falling into place Antoine?" Danny asks matter-of-factly.

"Look… bro… sorry if… you know…" mumbles Tomic as he starts blubbing.

"Sorry? Sorry for what, Antoine? Sorry you threatened me, a poor, feeble pensioner? Sorry you and your mates followed the bus I was on? What were you going to do to me if you caught up with the bus?"

"C'mon, bro, don't be like that. You know how it is round where I live. Everyone's at it. If you don't get on it then you go under innit."

"Don't try and kid me! You love being you. You love playing the big gangster with everyone being scared of you!"

"I'm not a gangster, bro, honest! I'm just a foot soldier, that's all. You want the ones at the top, the olders. I'm just a younger. They tell me what to do and I do it because if I don't do what they say then I'm gone!"

"Nice try, Antoine, nice try. You see, boy, I've done my homework and you are definitely running things. I got given a few names, like Pitbull, but I need the rest. I want the top dogs, understand? And if you lie to me I'll cut things off and if you carry on lying then I'll cut some more things off and some more until you've no fingers, no toes, no ears, no nose, no cock or bollocks!"

"You… you… you've got it wrong, bro, I'm just a foot soldier, honest! I'm not even lying innit!"

"You know, Antoine, I was a soldier once. A real soldier not a make-believe one like you. One of the places I served in is a country called Vietnam. Ever heard of it? As a matter of fact, the men who snatched you are old oppos of mine from my Vietnam days. We've been through a lot together and they were more than happy to help me to get justice for what happened to my daughter. You see, Antoine, you're up against professionals not a bunch of civilians who don't know how to do things. Professional what, I hear you ask? Professional everything! We've interrogated, tortured and killed hundreds of people," Danny exaggerates for effect, and the effect it has on Tomic makes him blub like a baby.

"Please bro, please, please bro," cries Tomic howling, "I'm not even lying, I'm just… I'm just… I'm just nothing… just one of the gang innit!"

"Can you imagine what's going through my mind, Antoine? Can you? Imagine what I'm thinking about doing to the scumbags who attacked my daughter, putting her in a coma. The doctors say there's hope but they've got to say that because if they say there's no hope and she wakes up they look like right idiots. Get it?"

"It weren't me, bro, I had nothing to do with it, honest, I'm not even lying!"

"Now, Antoine, I'm going to ask you some questions and write down your answers and then I'll ask you the same questions again and if your answers don't match I'll cut your lying tongue out of your lying mouth. Do you understand? Good. Here we go!"

Danny drones out question after question in perfect monotone, just as he'd been trained to do when interrogating prisoners, concerning the members of Tomic's gang. He tells Tomic he wants their real names, their street names, aliases, address, family members, friends, relatives, associates, appearance, crimes and more. Tomic starts by giving up everything on Hakeem, street name Pitbull, before going on to Luke, street name Lukey; Jamal, street name JJ; Kevin, street name Muff; Omari, street name Chip; Sammy, street name Smirfy; Treyvon, street name Tee Ess; Gary, street name Ga; Simon, street name Syko.

While comparing Tomic's answers, Danny muses how the police should use the same questioning methods as him; *they should ask questions using the exact same words exactly the same way. If they're telling the truth, they'll get the same answers… but only if they're telling the truth. I'll suggest it to Deany next time we meet. Nah, screw him!* Despite time is of the essence, as Brad could show up at any minute, Danny doesn't hurry his questions, he keeps the same rhythm, uses the same tone of voice, the same everything, all to prevent Tomic from forming answers to meet Danny's expectations.

It's extremely difficult and tiring speaking in constant monotone but it's essential as it makes it all but impossible for the prisoner to "read" what the interrogator is looking for. It's even more vital when repeating the questions as it keeps variables down to one, the answers, thereby making lies easy to spot. After completing three gang members' profiles, Danny says it's time for a break. This is more for Tomic than for himself as the time-out gives the prisoner time to consider their answers. This is an uncomfortable time for a liar and, often, if they have lied, they ask to change their answers and tell the truth. After a coffee, which Tomic was not happy with drinking, a slice of buttered toast and a piss break, involving the cutting and redoing of cable ties et cetera, Danny asks Tomic if he'd like to change any of his answers. He asks Danny to read them back to him. He refuses and begins questions for T4, Jamal; street name JJ.

*

All the time Danny is interrogating Tomic, Chuck, Glenn and Tony are sat in the cargo bay of the van at their base of operations planning where to carry out snatch on T2. They know they shouldn't be using Google, as it leaves a tech footprint, but as Danny hadn't said not to, they'd agreed between them they would and not tell Danny about it. To speed things up, the former soldiers are building files on gang members based on the photographs Danny had sent.

With Chuck seemingly able to come and go as he pleases inside the housing estate, and with Glenn and Tony patrolling its borders, they soon ID everyone in the photographs and put names to them just by listening to shouts between gang members and conversations with locals, shop owners and people angry at the goings-on.

"They wouldn't've gotten away with doing things like that when we were young!" says Glenn, referring to a street robbery occurring over the road from where Lucy had been mugged.

"I know, but what can you do? The police don't do nothing!

They just let them do what they like! Crazy!" replies the old woman he'd struck up a conversation with.

"I know. I saw that one over there in the red hoodie acting suspicious the other day like he was dealing drugs or something."

"I know, they do it all the time right out in the open. Why don't the police do nothing to stop them?"

"I know, they should do something! Right?"

"That's a nice accent. Where's it from? America?"

"Sure is, ma'am, Kentucky," the Californian replies, flicking the peak of his baseball cap in a salute.

"Do you live over here now?"

"No, ma'am, visiting relatives. See! There's that one in the red hoodie again. He's running away from something!"

"It won't be the police," the old woman laughs.

"Look, a young woman's running after him. She's shouting that he's stolen her phone."

"They do that all the time. A young girl was attacked right here last week or something. I heard she's in a coma. Poor thing."

"That one in the red top, I heard someone shout his name. It was something like…"

"He's called Sy or Syko or something. Simon McVey's his name. He used to be such a nice little boy," the old woman says sorrowfully.

And so Glenn opens a file on Simon "Sy/Syko" McVey. Now he had a name, it was a simple task to add to it by talking with shop owners, people in the street and pub-goers. Glenn likes carrying out investigative work in pubs. Not just because he loves beer, but because alcohol loosens people's tongues and lowers their inhibitions. He has to be careful, however, because ask too many questions in a neighbourhood like this one and it could be interpreted that you're an undercover cop, and he and the others know being labelled as one means everyone would clam up. Word would soon get round and you'd be in danger of being attacked or even killed.

CHAPTER NINE

"Want something to eat?" Danny asks Tomic after double-checking the answers he'd given second-time round matched the first. "I've got sausages, beans, egg, bacon, fish fingers and a few frozen chips."

"No chicken nuggets, bruv?"

"No."

"Fish fingers are a bit like chicken nuggets… I'll have them."

"Please!"

"Please. Coke?"

"I think there's a can in the fridge but if not it'll have to be water as you had a right moan about tea."

"I hate water."

"It's not a hotel you know! But, tell you what I'll do because I like you, if I've run out of Coke, I'll run round to the Co-op and get some for you," says Danny to keep Tomic sweet.

"If you go, bro, can you buy some chicken nuggets too innit?"

"Is that all you eat, chicken nuggets?"

"They're tasty bro!" returns Tomic sounding aghast that Danny shouldn't know that.

"Okay, if I go the Co-op I'll get you some chicken nuggets. By the way, Antoine, does your mate Pitbull like chicken nuggets?"

"Yeah, why?" Tomic asks nervously.

"No reason, just curious to know if that's all you lot eat, that's all."

There's no Coke in the fridge so Danny goes to the Co-op and buys a dozen cans of classic red Coke; a dozen in anticipation of other gang members arriving shortly, and a monster bag of frozen chicken nuggets. Leaving the shop, Danny runs into Gaz and Jacko. They're on their way to The Manor for an afternoon session. Jokingly, they ask Danny if he's given up beer as they haven't seen him around as much as they used to. He tells them he's a little bit broke at the minute but says, after his pension comes through, he'll see them in the pub. "No wonder you're skint if you're shelling out for cans of Coke and chicken nuggets," says Gaz. "I just fancy them occasionally, that's all. It's important to have a varied diet and... anyway, it's no big deal, I just fancied them, that's all," Danny replies defensively. Gaz and Jacko think he sounds nervous but leave him to enjoy his Coke and chicken nuggets as they're keen to get to The Manor. Back in his flat, Danny sees he's got eleven missed calls; most of which are from Brad. Thinking Lucy could be dead, he calls Brad who tells him that Kelvin and the others are furious that he hasn't been to visit Lucy. "Thank goodness, I thought something had happened to her. I've been meaning to tell the others about me being banned from the hospital but didn't because I thought I could butter the ward sister up to let me visit but I forgot to call her. Don't ask why I forgot to call because I don't want to talk about it!" says Danny defensively. Brad tells him that because Lucy's stable, they're thinking of moving her off the ICU into a side room. Danny says he thinks that's a bad sign. Brad agrees with him and both struggle to hold back their tears. When Danny regains his composure, he tells Brad he'll definitely call the ward sister to see if he can get his ban lifted. True to his word, Danny calls Ward Sister Williams immediately after his call with Brad but she tells him that as Mr Wilson is still on the ICU, she can't risk lifting Danny's ban. Before ending the call, she tells Danny that as Mr Wilson is breathing unaided, she'll see about moving him onto a general ward in a day or two. Danny thanks her and repeats his promise not to do anything like he'd done ever again; *well, not in your ICU anyway.*

Returning to the basement, Danny goes through the noose, cable-tie cutting and feeding process, after which he re-cable-ties and nooses Tomic and resumes the interrogation. Having readily given everything up on Pitbull, Lukey, JJ, Muff and Chip, Tomic just as readily gives up everything on Smirfy, Tee Ess, Ga and Sy/Syko. "That's enough for now, well done," says Danny encouragingly. Tomic asks when he's going to release him. "First, I need to reunite you with your friends and see what they have to say. If any of them contradict what you've told me then that's going to be a problem for you and them." Tomic asks Danny what he means by "reuniting him with his friends" and whether it involves setting him free? Instead of answering, Danny decides to tell Tomic about his time in Vietnam as he'd found it cathartic telling his comatose daughter about it and wants to feel more of the same.

"I told you I was in Vietnam but what I didn't tell you is what went on there. I got volunteered, as an Interrogation Specialist, to a unit known as IPEF. We got up to all sorts of things; mostly bad things. A couple of journalists even wrote an article about us. It never got published but in it they called us a bunch of lawless, mercenary cut-throats and murderers. The plane they were travelling back to America on crashed in the middle of the ocean. No one ever found out why.

"Anyway, the war was coming to an end. It was vital that the evacuation went smoothly, and, by smoothly, I mean minimal casualties. To achieve this, the Americans needed an 'evacuation window' to get all their personnel out of Saigon without them having to fight their way out. They tried to strike a deal with the North but they refused, so the Pentagon, I guess, came up with a plan to convince the North that the evacuation was a ruse and America was going to mount a major offensive against them.

"Two American officers were carrying out the battle plans when they got captured by the NVA, the North Vietnamese Army. Let me tell you, you didn't want to get caught by them; they did all sorts of things to prisoners, horrible things. Everyone reckoned you were better off dead than being taken by the NVA. If you've seen the film *The Deer Hunter* you'll know what I'm talking about. Anyway, US Military Intelligence found out that the officers were being held in a village in Cambodia so the Pentagon, the CIA or whoever, lined us up to carry out a rescue mission. No one was supposed to operate in Cambodia but everyone did. The place was used as a corridor between the North and the South. What we didn't know at the time was the US government didn't want anyone finding out about what IPEF had done in Vietnam so sent us on a suicide mission, killing two birds with one stone; one, the North would think the plans were genuine and, two, IPEF would be wiped out trying to rescue the American officers. You look puzzled, I'll explain shortly.

"All five IPEF Companies, over a hundred and fifty highly trained soldiers, slipped across the border into Cambodia and headed north. Here's where it gets nasty. The NVA knew we were coming. They'd been tipped off and were waiting to ambush us. It was only by a stroke of luck we weren't all massacred. Lots got killed or taken prisoner but A Company and B Company, my Company, and a couple of guys from other Companies carried on with the mission and made it to the village where the American officers were being held. It was dark when we arrived. Everyone was asleep. It was obvious which hut the American officers were in because it was the only one being guarded. We circled around and killed the guards. The Lieutenant and a couple of guys went inside the hut.

"Next thing all hell broke loose. The villagers had woken up and wanted to fight us! We slaughtered almost all of them. They didn't stand a chance. There was a young woman who kept on yelling that we'd killed her grandfather. She kept on and on screaming and wouldn't shut up. One of the guys shot her... killed her right in front of her kids. I went in the hut where the American officers were being held to make sure the lieutenant and the others were okay. I'll never forget what I saw. The American officers were in bad shape, bad, bad shape. Looking at them, it was obvious they'd been tortured. The lieutenant ordered us to leave the hut and next thing there's two shots and he comes walking out. 'We couldn't've taken them with us the condition they were in,' he said. Then he said we were bugging out straightaway.

"We couldn't leave our Comrades behind so, those of us that could, headed south to look for them. The rest, the injured, the wounded, headed east to the Vietnam border. A few hours later we came across an abandoned NVA camp and found six of our guys hanging from trees by their wrists. They'd been skinned alive. One of them was… wasn't dead. We couldn't tell who he was and he couldn't speak. The lieutenant wadded up a shirt and choked him with it to put him out of his misery. He had to, you see, because we couldn't make any noise. The sound of gunfire would bring the NVA down on us. Some of the guys wanted to bury them but the lieutenant said no. He said if we did that the NVA would know we were around and hunt us down. With our numbers, we'd've had no chance against the NVA so we said a silent prayer and left the poor sods hanging there for the birds and animals to feed on.

"We came across an NVA camp. They'd crammed our guys into bamboo cages. They were naked. They were all naked. The cages were piled on top of one another so the lower down you were the more covered in piss and shit you're… just like life really. Some NVA picked up one of the cages and put it on top of an empty cage away from the others. They poked the guy inside with bamboo sticks to force him against the back of the cage and took turns raping him. They'd probably done this to all of them.

"The lieutenant ordered us to skirt the camp. Once we were in position we opened fire. The NVA tried to hide behind things to protect themselves but were caught in a crossfire. Sitting ducks they were, sitting ducks. Once the shooting was over, we walked among the NVA and shot them all in the head to make sure they were dead. We killed every last one of them. When we released our guys from the cages you should've seen them. They smashed the NVA bodies to pieces for what they'd done to them. We all swore never to speak of it and here am I telling you. We knew with the noise from the shooting the NVA would soon come down on us so we cut east. We reached the border by nightfall and a day later we were back at camp. The first thing we noticed was the place was full of strangers. Most of them weren't in uniform. That should've been our first clue.

"After we were debriefed we got packed into trucks and driven to an abandoned training camp and interrogated. Night and day they interrogated us but how stupid was that? We'd been trained in Resistance to Interrogation, Conduct After Capture and S.E.R… Survive, Escape, Resist. Before we were released they ordered us to keep our mouths shut about what happened in Cambodia. When we got back to camp we found out IPEF had been disbanded and we were all being flown out. We could understand them disbanding IPEF but not flying us out! Most of us requested transfers to active units but they turned down.

"Anyway, long story short, the NVA didn't fall for the bogus plans and when the Americans evacuated Saigon it was a complete shambles; they barely got out in time. I heard through the grapevine that some of the guys wanted to tell the story of how two American officers were sacrificed by the US government to sell a lie to the North. Soon after that a plane carrying former IPEF soldiers crashed. There were no survivors. Guys just kept on dying and disappearing. Everyone left in A Company banded together to tell their story, they even got the backing of a Congressman, but they got posted and every last one of them was dead within six months. It seemed that those who wanted to blab died so the rest of us went dark.

"Everyone in B Company agreed we'd never to talk about what happened in Cambodia and, by and large, we've been left alone. I reckon, in all, there's only about twenty of us still alive out of over a hundred and fifty men. So, Antoine, now you know a little about me I hope it's given you a flavour of what'll happen to you if you lie to me or mess me about!"

After telling his tale, Danny felt a warm glow surge throughout his entire body, purifying it, and his soul too, and thinks, *I must do this more often!* His tale turns Tomic's innards to jelly with fear. He has no doubt that the story is true given the way he'd been snatched off the streets in broad daylight. A sudden realisation of his true situation comes over Tomic and terrifies him. "Please, bruv, don't kill me, bro. I'm cooperating with everything, innit, so there's no need to hurt me or nothing, innit?" he says imploringly. Danny makes no reply, he just stares at him. "I'm telling you everything, bruv, and I ain't even lying so please don't kill me!" pleads Tomic. Again, Danny offers no response. Thinking about the sharp things in Danny's toolbox, Tomic whines that there's no need to torture him either, "I'm not good with pain, bro… don't like blood, innit?" Tomic's constant use of the non-word "innit" irritates the hell out of Danny but he continues with the silent treatment which has a toxic effect on his prisoner.

*

Generally speaking, Danny has refrained from using torture, but he's never been in a situation like this, as Brad could show up at any minute, so he's keeping his options open. It must be recognised, however, that killing is an entirely different matter to Danny. During his military career he'd killed when it was necessary or when he'd been ordered to but this is different; he's dealing with those who attacked and injured his daughter, and this is different for many reasons, not least that he'd made a pledge to her, and his other children, that if anything ever happened to them, if they ever got injured or killed by criminals, he'd get back at whoever did it as, even back then, he had little confidence in the police to deliver justice. Why should he, a soldier who's been trained to deal with any situation he finds himself in, stand by and watch those that attacked and robbed and injured his daughter for a lousy mobile phone, get away with it when he has the wherewithal to do something about it?

He'd made that pledge to his children and is determined to deliver on it, every last syllable of it! *Luce is lying in a hospital in a coma because of the likes of you and you're going to pay for it! You're all going to pay for it!*

*

At the check-in call, Danny tells Chuck to deliver Pitbull and, as he has the rest of the names from Tomic, will send over details of those that need snatching. "I'll link the names to the photographs I took from the bus so you'll recognise them by sight," he says. "Did you torture T1 to get the names?" asks Glenn, knowing, of old, Danny's reluctance to use torture. "No need to. He was happy to answer all my questions," replies Danny, as if making a point. "Would you have tortured him if he hadn't blabbed?" Tony asks. "You know I don't use torture but, to be honest, I'm keeping my options open on this one. Anything's possible!" replies Danny; his answer surprises and pleases Chuck and the others. "Okay then, message me when you've bagged T2 and I'll jab T1 so he's out of it when you arrive."

They'd never understood Danny's reluctance to torture prisoners and, to their knowledge, he hadn't used torture while they'd been stationed at Phnen Bin. They're keen to get the job done as quickly as possible, so if torturing a few punks achieves quick results, they're all for it. Chuck has always maintained that Danny was responsible for several ambushes carried out by the NVA on American units when, had he tortured prisoners, hundreds of American soldiers' lives might've been saved.

*

With little more to be gained from continuing to interrogate Tomic, Danny calls it a day and asks him what he'd like to eat. "Chicken nuggets and chips," mumbles Tomic, his voice barely audible as he's still very shaken after hearing Danny's tale. "Chicken nuggets and chips what?" snaps Danny. "Chicken nuggets and chips please," answers Tomic still mumbling. *See, they can be trained.* After arriving with yet another meal of chicken nuggets, accompanied by chips and the obligatory can of Coke, Danny goes through the noosing, cable-tie cutting, feeding, drinking, pissing, re-cable-tying and de-noosing ritual, and, loading a syringe with a large amount of anaesthetic, he jabs Tomic with it, sending him off into a deep, coma-like sleep.

*

It's late. Danny's tired. He's about to go to bed when a message comes through from Chuck: *T2 in the bag. With you in thirty minutes.* Danny returns to the basement to ensure everything is ready to receive Pitbull; Tomic is out cold. Half an hour later, a knock comes on the outer door of the basement. Danny peers through the spyhole and, seeing Chuck and the others, unlocks and unbolts the door. They rush inside carrying a bundle wrapped in a sack. Glenn throws it on the floor next to Tomic but Danny tells him to take it into the next room. Shouldering the sack, Glenn takes it into an adjoining room and throws it onto one of several futons lying about the floor where it lands with a thud followed by a groan.

"Where the hell you getting all these futons from man?" Glenn shouts.

"Fire sale," returns Danny sarcastically.

"How's things going?" asks Chuck.

"Great," answers Danny.

"Got everything you need?"

"For now," Danny replies coldly.

"Look, man, if you're pissed about Lalonde then say so!"

"Okay, I'm pissed about Lalonde. You know you shouldn't be chasing women while you're on a job like this and you guys should've told him that! Christ on a bike!" yells Danny. Regaining his composure, he asks, "What about the others? Have you ID'd any of them yet?"

"Yeah, it was easy, they're always hanging together. I reckon we should be able to take two or three at a time, get this thing over with and get out of here... go home."

"I told Tomic about Cambodia," Danny says out of the blue.

"What? Are you fucking crazy? You'll get us all killed!" screams Tony in Australian rage.

"Relax. Who's he going to tell, he's not going anywhere," replies Danny, drawing a finger across his throat.

"Why'd you do it?" Glenn asks quietly. Danny knows this is a bad sign, as Glenn's dangerous when he speaks quietly.

"To be honest, I find it cathartic, you should try it, though the story comes out different every time I tell it."

"Christ! Who else've you told!" yells Chuck.

"Don't worry, it was only Lucy. I talk to her whenever I visit the ICU. The medics said talking to her might bring her round," says Danny, not sure they had.

"What if someone heard you?" Glenn asks quietly.

"I checked, no one was around. I've got to tell you, it felt great telling someone after all these years and telling it twice was even better! You should try it!"

"No thanks. Anyone else?"

"I thought I might tell Pitbull and the others."

"What if they escape and..."

"Trust me, they're not going to escape."

"I'll stay here and make sure that..."

"No, you do your job and let me do mine. Want a coffee before you go?" says Danny as a way of letting them know it's time for them to leave.

There being no takers for Danny's atrocious coffee, Chuck and the others leave and he locks the door behind them. Back in the van, Chuck says Danny's lost his mind. Glenn says they should quit while they're ahead and go home. Tony says they should finish what they started. Chuck ends the discussion saying they'll sleep on it and decide in the morning.

Before going to bed, Danny binds Pitbull securely. As with Tomic, Pitbull's wrists and ankles are cable-tied and then hogtied together, a noose is around his neck and looped over a joist and with the end wrapped around and around his legs he looks like a Sunday joint of beef. A quick pull on the noose tells Danny that Pitbull's going nowhere. *A little jab and it's sweet dreams for you Pitbull my son. We'll get acquainted tomorrow!*

*

Next day, Danny's up with the lark. Having, once again, unburdened himself about what happened in Vietnam, he feels like a new man, refreshed, as if some great weight has been lifted from his shoulders. After breakfast, Danny makes buttered toast for his prisoners and grabs two cans of Coke from the fridge before making his way down to the basement. Now there are two prisoners he knows he needs to be extra cautious. Placing the toast and cans of Coke on the floor, Danny unlocks the cellar door and shoves it open with considerable force in case someone is standing behind it. After first checking that Tomic is exactly where he'd left him, Danny collects the toast and Coke and enters the basement. Tomic's frantically mumbling something so Danny removes his gag. "Thank f… thank God you're here, bro, I need a shit… real bad, innit!" he groans as he writhes in agony. Danny thinks Tomic might be trying to distract him; *maybe Pitbull's gotten free and they're going to jump me*, so, whipping the cut-throat razor from his toolbox, Danny races into the room where Pitbull is being held and finds he's still lying on the floor, bound, gagged, hooded and noosed. Having heard Danny enter the room, Pitbull snarls threats through his gag. In response, Danny kicks him hard in the guts and tells him to shut up. "Who you talking to, Fam?" yells Tomic from the other room, "Who you got in there, bro?" he shouts. Danny ignores him.

Believing Tomic probably does need to shit, Danny cuts the cable ties on his ankles and points to a plastic bucket, "Take a dump

171

in there," he says. "I need paper, bruv," says Tomic after squeezing out four plasticine-like turds. Danny throws him some old newspaper from off the floor to wipe his arse with, giving him a look that says not to complain. Tomic asks again, "Who was that you were talking to next door, bruv?" Danny says he'll find out soon enough and re-cable-ties his ankles. After covering the plastic bowl with sheets of old newspaper, Danny hands Tomic a slice of toast and a can of Coke, placing the rest out of reach. "Who's that for, bro?" Tomic asks, "You?" he asks. Danny says nothing. While Tomic eats his toast and drinks his Coke, Danny doesn't take his eyes off him for a second and, as soon as he's finished, pulls on the noose, re-cable-ties his ankles and hogties him. With Tomic secured, Danny goes into the other room and removes Pitbull's hood. On recognising Danny, Pitbull screams through his gag. Tomic shouts, "Who you got in there, bro?" Not answering, Danny hoods and gags Tomic and returns to Pitbull's room, shutting the door behind him.

"Hello Hakeem. I see you remember me, just like Tomic did. He's in the next room but you know that already because you heard him shouting. 'What's he doing here?' I hear you ask. Well, he's here for the same reason you are. You see, over a week ago now, my daughter was mugged for her mobile phone by some of your mates. During the attack she was knocked to the ground and hit her head on the kerb and now she's lying in a coma in St Thomas' Hospital. I know which of your gang did it but I want to hear it from you!

"In case you're thinking about escaping or getting revenge or whatever, you need to know a little bit about me. I was in the army for over twenty years. We used to get up to all sorts of things… killing people and stuff. In fact, the people who snatched you are buddies of mine from my time in Vietnam.

"So, Hakeem, why are you here? What do I want from you? I'm glad you asked. I'm going to ask you some questions and write down your answers. Now, if you lie to me I'll cut your tongue out," says Danny waving the cut-throat razor in Pitbull's face which sends his terrified eyes out on stalks. "Nod if you understand. Good. I've already asked your mate Antoine these questions and if you give different answers I'll find out which of you is lying and cut their tongue out. If I can't decide who's lying I'll cut both your tongues out. Nod if you understand. Good.

"I bet you're hungry? And thirsty too? I did you some buttered toast for breakfast and there's a can of Coke to drink. For dinner it's chicken nuggets and chips and a can of Coke… assuming you make it that far. Okay? Good.

"Now, Hakeem, I'm going to cut the cable tie on your wrists so you can feed yourself and take a piss if you want. I'll be holding onto the noose so if you try anything I'll pull it tight and break your neck. Okay? Good. You'll soon get used to how we do things around here."

After explaining the de-noosing, cable-tie cutting and redoing processes with Pitbull, Danny cuts his wrists free and removes his gag so he can eat and drink. Before asking his questions, Danny cable-ties Pitbull's wrists behind his back and warns him of the consequences of using bad language. The smell from the contents of the plastic bowl in the other room is overpowering, which is something, given the background stench which pervades throughout the entire building; *at least any smells coming from the basement should go unnoticed!* thinks Danny.

*

Questioning Hakeem takes barely two hours as Danny's not interested in his background or what makes him tick, he just wants to know about the other gang members and the crimes they've committed. Just like Tomic, Hakeem makes no mention of his crimes or the attack on Lucy. At the end of the questioning, Danny compares Pitbull's and Tomic's answers and they're close enough to give him confidence they're not lying. The next phase of Danny's plan depends on the rest of the gang being brought in. At the daily check-in call Danny is pleasantly surprised by what he hears.

"We grabbed Luke, Jamal and Kevin and half an hour ago we grabbed Omari. The word on the streets is Sammy, aka Smirfy, is dead. Seems a rival gang murdered him in a revenge attack over some postcode vendetta. Fucking idiots!"

"According to DS Dean, Luke and Jamal were the ones that attacked Lucy," says Danny, "so I look forward to meeting them. Are you sure this Smirfy is dead?"

"If he isn't we'll snatch him. You know Danny? I really do miss doing this sort of thing," says Chuck. Glenn and Tony say they do too.

"Makes you feel alive doesn't it? Do you know what we should do?" says Danny mischievously.

"What?" asks Glenn.

"Remember The A-Team? We should join forces and fight crime on the streets of London."

"Very funny," says Chuck dryly.

"You were just like this in 'Nam. You weren't funny then and you're not funny now!" says Tony.

"C'mon guys, just kidding… where's your sense of humour!"

"Sense of humour my arse!" yells Tony which makes everyone laugh.

"I used to love The A-Team," Glenn says nostalgically. "Wouldn't work in England though."

"Why not?" Tony asks.

"First, no guns allowed!" says Glenn, holding up a finger. "Second, there are no bad-ass vans over here," he adds, holding up a second finger, "and third, no hillbillies that need rescuing."

"Are you jokers fucking serious?" roars Tony, making everyone laugh. "Get fucking real will you!"

"We used to have fun though didn't we? Even when things were bad, we always had fun, we always found ways to have fun." Everyone's thoughts turn to past times.

"Okay you guys, let's get back to business," says Chuck, bringing everyone down to earth with a bang. "Thanks to Tomic's disappearance, folks on the estate are getting jittery. And with this Sammy guy being killed everyone's on their guard."

"You'll need to move quickly and snatch the others in case they decide to bolt," says Danny.

"Agree. We'll drop-off what we have tonight. Make sure you're ready," says Chuck.

"Don't you worry, I'll be ready!" replies Danny, relishing the thought of coming face to face with Luke and Jamal. *We'll see how tough you are then you little shits*, speaks Danny's inner voice.

*

At nine that night, a white Ford Transit van with a side sliding door arrives outside Danny's flat and, one by one, Luke, Jamal, Omari and Kevin are carried, unconscious, into the basement, laid on futons in the third and fourth rooms and secured with cable ties. Chuck and the others see Danny has been busy. Nooses are looped over pipes and there are leather straps hanging from joists; cable ties litter the floor. "Useful things cable ties," Tony remarks absentmindedly. "Danny, as soon as we bag the rest we're out of here," says Glenn, meaning he, at least, is going home after they've snatched the remaining names on Danny's list. Danny asks if they'll stay a few extra days depending on what he gets out of the prisoners. Chuck weighs in first, saying he'll stay as long as Danny needs him, leaving the others little option but to say they'll stay also. Danny suspects Chuck's motives for agreeing to remain are probably due to Lalonde but doesn't say anything as he doesn't care anymore as he's got what he wants.

As soon as Chuck and the others depart, Danny goes into the room where Luke and Jamal are stashed. They're still out cold and for what Danny has in mind for them they need to be fully awake, meaning it'll be morning before they're conscious enough to appreciate what's happening. Before leaving the basement, Danny inspects the leather straps hanging from joists. He swings on them to ensure they can support his weight. This arrangement is designed so Danny can string up Luke and Jamal with their arms behind their backs. He'd seen this done in Vietnam and later discovered it was an interrogation method used in mediaeval Italy, known as the strappado. For maximum effect, Luke and Jamal would be dropped from ten or twelve feet but Danny is restricted to the height of the basement ceiling. He'd never used the strappado on prisoners but thought it looked like agony personified when he witnessed it in Vietnam. Essentially, what happens is the prisoner has their hands tied behind their back while the other end of the rope is fixed to a high beam. They are then made to drop and are stopped from hitting the ground when the rope reaches its full extension. The sudden jerk almost pulls arms out of sockets. This process is repeated until the mere thought of the drop is sufficient to loosen any tongue. But Danny isn't concerned with loosening tongues, he wants Luke and Jamal to pay for what they did to his daughter; *it's not torture, no, and it's not revenge either, it's justice for what they did to Luce. This way won't leave it to chance that the police and the courts get their act together or some smart-arse lawyer gets them off. This way Luce will get justice and they will receive punishment for what they've done, and that's fair!*

Before returning upstairs to his flat, Danny checks to make sure his latest prisoners are all properly cable-tied, noosed, gagged and hooded. Satisfied, he ensures that Antoine and Hakeem are also secure, and that they're still breathing as he'd dosed them fairly heavily with anaesthetic. Tomic's eyes momentarily flicker open. Danny strokes his forehead, whispering, "Sleep, Antoine, sleep deep, for tomorrow the fun begins," and turns out the lights.

*

When Danny opens the door to his flat he gets the shock of his life! There, inside, are all three of his sons waiting for him. Kelvin asks why he hasn't been to visit Lucy for almost a week. Danny yells at him not to exaggerate. Joey intervenes before an argument ensues and asks Danny to explain why he hasn't been to see Lucy. Before Danny can say anything, Brad jumps in and tells his brothers about him being banned from the hospital and the circumstances that brought it about.

"You're lucky they didn't arrest you!" yells Kelvin angrily, outraged that his father could do something so stupid and selfish.

"Who'll arrest me, Kel? The nurses? I don't think you're as smart as you think you are!" Danny says with a grin.

"What's that on your hands, Dad?" asks Joey. "It looks like dried blood." Danny looks down at his hands. They're both stained with blood!

"Oh, it's nothing. I was just doing a bit of DIY for a mate and must've got cut. See, it's only a little nick, that's all," says Danny, showing his sons a neat slice below the thumb.

"That's a neat cut," says Brad. "It looks like it was done by… a razor?"

"That'd make sense. I was trimming a thin bit of MDF that was just a bit too big so I used an old cut-throat razor to trim it down so it'd fit better…" Danny stops speaking because he sees his sons aren't buying it.

"So, Dad, what's this ban of yours? When's it up?"

"The ward sister said a week or after they move this 'Gary Wilson' to another ward. You'll never guess? He was only in a coma for a day before he came out of it! Where's the justice, eh lads, where's the justice in that?"

"Justice doesn't work that way, Dad, I don't think you're as smart as you think you are," replies Kelvin with a smug, self-satisfied grin. Danny feels he'd like to punch Kelvin in his smug face at times.

To avert an argument erupting, Joey grabs Kelvin and says they're leaving, but Brad says he's staying. Danny tells him he doesn't have to stay but Brad insists. As soon as Kelvin and Joey depart, Brad asks, "How did you really get that cut and don't give me any old malarkey about trimming MDF!" Danny says he's surprised he cut himself, "It must be my age, son," he adds, laughing. "Anyway, I'm going to wash up and then it's time for something to eat... fancy a takeaway?" asks Danny. Brad simply says okay. "Chinese or Indian?" Danny asks, "or we can have finch and chimps if you like." Whenever Danny substitutes silly words for proper words it reminds them both of what a great time they had whenever Brad came to London to stay after Danny's divorce. "Tell you what, let's grab a takeaway by Camden Town tube and then go and visit Luce," says Danny. "What about your ban?" asks Brad. "If they say anything I'll just say Sister Williams said it was okay," replies Danny. "What if she's there?" asks Brad. "Ah yes, but what if she's not?" replies Danny impishly, which makes them both laugh.

*

"Mr Deacon, what are you doing here?" asks Senior Ward Sister Williams sternly.

"Oh hello Sister Williams, I got a call from somebody saying that Gary Wilson's condition's improved and he's been moved to another ward so it's okay for me to visit my daughter... you know, the one that's lying in a coma."

"Mr Wilson has indeed... never mind. I think you're lying about the call but as the rest of your family are here I'll admit you but you must not ever do anything to cause me to regret my placing my trust in you. Do you understand me Mr Deacon?"

"Loud and clear, ma'am," Danny replies, saluting the ward sister to Brad's amusement.

"As it's late, and visiting time is almost over for the day, I'll allow you to join the other visitors around your daughter's bed but... NO NOISE OR DISTURBANCE OF ANY KIND!" Sister Williams says, wagging a finger in Danny's face.

"Oh, so you've finally decided to put in an appearance have you?" Joyce asks, vitriol dripping from each and every staccato syllable. "You haven't changed one little bit Danny Deacon, but why should I expect you to?"

"Hello Joyce, I…"

"Don't bother, Kel told me all about it. What were you thinking? Oh, that's the problem, you don't think, do you?"

"Do you mind, Sister Williams told us to keep the noise down," Danny replies playfully, making Brad and Joey choke back a laugh and Kelvin to snort derisively.

"Very funny, Danny, very funny. Everything's a joke with you isn't it? Our daughter is lying in a coma and you can't be bothered visiting her in her sick bed and even when you do you make jokes. Well, they're not funny and you're not funny!"

"To be accurate, I couldn't visit her because I was banned…"

"Like that's an excuse! You getting banned from the hospital shouldn't've stopped you. You seem to be able to do just about everything else except visit your daughter!"

"You're not making any sense, you…"

"Will you two stop it please?" urge Joey and Brad in unison.

"At least you don't stink of beer!" says Joyce mockingly. "I… I've been reminded by the nurses of the importance of speaking to Lucy as a possible way to help bring her out of her coma. She was always a Daddy's girl so… over to you to do your bit!"

"I'll do better in future."

"You'll do better in future or you'll try to do better in future?"

"I'll do better in future. Promise. Now, if you don't mind, I want to hold my daughter's hand," says Danny apologetically.

"I've been here long enough today anyway so I'm off back to our hotel," says Joyce to nobody in particular. "By the by, I've noticed no one's sticking to the rota but as your father and his little shadow are now visiting we should reinstate it to avoid overcrowding at the bedside. Goodnight."

Danny and his sons remain at Lucy's bedside until one of the night nurses asks them to leave so she and the ICU team can attend to the patients. Taking turns kissing Lucy on her cheeks, each says goodnight. While on the concourse waiting for a lift to arrive, Danny says he knows a place where they can get a beer if any of them are interested. Kelvin says he isn't very keen but Joey says he is and Brad always fancies a beer, so off they go together. Danny takes them to the drinking club DS Dean took him to after that first time he went to visit Lucy in the ICU. All the same crowd is in, including DS Dean. He's engrossed in conversation with several dodgy-looking characters and ignores Danny. The underworld regulars check out the newcomers but recognising Danny they return to the drinks and conversations.

"Nice place, Dad, nice place," remarks Joey, nudging Kelvin in the ribs while laughing.

"I love it," says Brad, taking in the atmosphere.

"How did you find this place?" Kelvin asks. "It's a bit off your patch," he adds, looking around disdainfully at the regulars.

"The copper investigating Luce's case brought me here. That's him sitting over there actually," says Danny, pointing at DS Dean who notices him but continues to ignore him.

"What! You're joking!"

"No, that's definitely him, I'd recognise him anywhere," jokes Danny.

"I don't mean that. I mean what the hell is a copper doing in a place like this!"

"Well, you know what they say? Police and criminals are different sides of the same coin."

"C'mon Dad, we're leaving and, in future, stay away from that copper. I've got a bad feeling about him!" warns Brad and, taking Danny by the arm, escorts him from the drinking club, followed closely by Joey and Kelvin, who's especially glad to be out of the place.

CHAPTER TEN

After leaving the drinking club, Joey and Kelvin take a taxi to the friend's house they're staying with and Danny and Brad catch the last tube to Camden.

Entering the flat, Danny asks Brad if he'd like a nightcap. "Yeah but just the one!" he replies in a way as to make it clear he really means "just the one!" Danny fetches a bottle of whiskey from beneath the kitchen sink. Brad doesn't recognise the label. "I think it's the store's own brand," says Danny dubiously. After taking a sip, Brad coughs and chokes and compares it to drinking paint stripper. "That's the worst whiskey I've ever had," he complains, sputtering. "Let me see the label. There's no country of origin on it. I think it's the law that it has to have the country of origin on it!" cries Brad, inspecting the bottle from top to bottom. "What do you expect for a tenner a bottle?" Danny asks. "You were robbed," jokes Brad. The pair fall about laughing and Danny fetches a bottle of good stuff from his wardrobe. "I was saving this for Christmas," he says, pouring out two large measures. "Jesus, Dad, that's better!" says Brad, swilling the malty goodness around and around his mouth before swallowing.

"Do you remember when you was a lad and you'd come and visit me after your mum and me split up?"

"Of course I do."

"Every weekend you'd come... rain or shine... winter and summer. I used to say to you, 'You don't have to come every weekend you know son, you should be spending time with your mates,' but you'd say you could see your mates anytime and preferred coming to visit me."

"Yeah, but I was young and stupid then," jokes Brad. They both laugh. "We used to have a great time together though didn't we Dad? Remember when…"

As always happens when Brad is with his dad, especially after a few drinks, they reminisce about how Danny would drive down to Kent to pick him up on a Friday night and drop him off on a Sunday afternoon and how they did everything together.

"Remember when we put that electric shower over your bath that time?"

"Yeah. That was funny that was!"

"You thought you'd soldered all the joints but you'd missed one and when I turned the mains on, the joint burst open and water sprayed everywhere! You kept on shouting, 'Turn it off, turn it off!' and I kept shouting back, 'What?' because I couldn't hear you properly. The loft was in a right mess by the time I switched the water off. What a laugh!"

"Yeah, brought half the ceiling down that did," says Danny, laughing in fond remembrance of the fun times they'd had when Brad came to stay. "And what about the time we went on that skiing holiday?"

"That was brilliant… and the activity holiday you took me on! Remember when the boat sank and I had to be rescued?"

"Yeah. That was funny that was! That was so funny!"

Danny and Brad reminisced about everything from football to the first time he beat his dad at table tennis, thereafter never losing to him again, and disastrous, and sometimes successful, DIY projects. Brad recalled how, every weekend for a year and a half, he and his dad travelled to Danny's parents' place up north as his father, Brad's grandfather, was dying from mesothelioma from when he'd worked in the shipyards. After each visit, Danny and Brad left to drive home at two forty-five in the afternoon so they could listen to football commentary on the radio during the journey back to London.

"You're a good lad Brad," Danny says weepily.

"You're not going to go crying on me are you Dad?" Brad replies joking, but not really.

"No son, I'm not going to start crying, not yet at least."

"Not yet? You mean Luce, don't you Dad?"

"Yeah, son, I mean Luce. I'm scared she might not make it. Do you remember when you were all little? Remember what I used to say to you about if ever any of you got hurt by anyone? Remember what I said I'd do to them?"

"I do," Brad replies coldly.

"You know, son, I'd love to get my hands on the bastards that hurt Luce. Know what I'd do to them if I got hold of them?" Brad doesn't answer, he just shakes his head. "I'd kill them. I'd kill each and every last one of them."

"You're starting to worry me now, Dad. I hope this is just the booze talking and you're not planning on doing something stupid."

"Can I trust you son? I mean can I really trust you?"

"What the hell, Dad! What's going on? Have you and your idiot army mates done something?"

"You know as well as me that even if they catch the ones who attacked Luce they'll probably just get a slap on the wrist or, if they get a smart-arse lawyer, they might even get off altogether!"

"Yeah, you've mentioned that a few times before," says Brad sarcastically. "What do you mean by asking me if you can really trust me? What's going on? Tell me what's going on Dad! What have you done?"

"Okay, I'll tell you, if that's what you want. Better still, I'll show you. You'll have to wear one of these," says Danny, throwing Brad a hood with eyeholes cut into it.

"I'm not putting that on until you tell me what's going on and even then I might not put it on!"

"Okay… but don't react straightaway… okay? I've got the

scumbags that attacked Luce tied up in the basement," Danny says calmly and hoping Brad will keep calm.

"What! You're kidding!"

"No, I'm not kidding. In all there's… there's six of them down there with more to come. One of the ones we're after is supposed to be dead and, obviously, one's in St Thomas' Hospital."

"Dad… if what you're telling me is true you could end up going to jail for the rest of your life. It's kidnapping and false imprisonment! Or maybe worse? Anyway, I thought there was only two of them?"

"That's right, but to find out who they were I had to… never mind… details. Now, if you want to see them you have to put the hood on! And don't say a word when we're down there, I don't want them being able to identify you if things go tits up or they get rescued or get away or something!"

When Danny and Brad reach the basement door, Brad grabs his dad by the shoulder and spins him around. "If they're in there, I can't guarantee I won't set them free," Brad says in a low voice. "You won't do that son, you'll think of Luce and you won't be able to set them free." Danny opens the door and switches on the light. Lying in the middle of the floor, Brad sees a crumpled figure of a young male; he's gagged, bound with cable ties and has a noose around his neck. "His name's Antoine but he goes by Tomic… it's a street name… they all have them, apparently," Danny informs Brad matter-of-factly.

Brad checks to see if Tomic is breathing. He is. Brad is very, very relieved. "When he didn't move when you put the light on, I thought he was dead. Why isn't he awake?" asks Brad. In answer, Danny holds up a hypodermic syringe and a vial of anaesthetic. "The ones that attacked Luce, Luke and Jamal they're called, are in that room," says Danny, heading for the far door to his right. Inside the room, Luke and Jamal are laid out comatose on futons. Brad spots that they're trussed up identically to Tomic. After checking the prisoners' pulses, Brad says, "They're not in good shape, Dad, their pulses are very weak. You should let them go. You should let them all go before something happens to them," he adds, genuinely concerned for the prisoners and his dad. "Don't try and kid a kidder, son, you're wasting your time. There's nothing wrong with their pulses. What is it you kids say? 'This is not my first rodeo?' Is that right? I used to do this sort of stuff all the time in 'Nam so save your breath!" says Danny. Brad begs his dad to let the gang go, saying the last thing they'll do is go to the police so he should be safe. Danny asks, "But what if they come looking for me? No, for the time being, at least, they're going nowhere!" Brad wants to ask his dad what he plans to do with them but he's afraid of the answer he might get and warns him, "You've gone too far this time Dad, way too far!"

After showing Brad the rest of the haul, they return upstairs to the flat. Neither says much, except goodnight, as Brad beds down on the lounge floor on yet another futon and Danny slides into his lumpy old divan. Despite their long day, neither Danny nor Brad fall asleep. Danny lies thinking whether he's done the right thing by involving Brad, while Brad lies staring at the ceiling thinking how he can get his dad to see sense and let the gang go. Just before the dawn, both drift off into sleep, with each dreaming very different dreams.

*

Danny wakes at eleven. There's no sign of Brad anywhere in the flat. Fearing the worst, he checks his trouser pockets for the keys to the basement. They're not there. Racing downstairs to the basement, he finds the door is locked. Knowing he can't hammer on the basement door or shout, as he doesn't want to attract attention, Danny phones Brad who answers immediately. "Where are you?" he hisses. "Where are you?" hisses Brad back. "Don't be funny. I'm standing outside the basement door! Where are you?" Seconds later the basement door opens and Danny rushes inside. Tomic is exactly where he'd left him. He's fully conscious and there's a look of fear in his eyes. Danny wants to know what's going on. Brad leads him to the room occupied by Jamal and Luke. Each is hanging from the joists, strappado fashion, with their arms wrenched out of their sockets. They're in bad shape, both having been severely beaten. Danny knows, despite Brad's slender build, he has a terrible, freakish strength in him and had single-handedly lifted Jamal and Luke onto the strappado, no mean feat. It's obvious to him, looking at Brad's knuckles, he's used them as punchbags.

"I came down to let them go while you were asleep. I was sorting things out but they laughed and joked about what they did to Luce. It made me realise it's a mistake letting scumbags like these back out on the streets so I... I want in, Dad. I want to be involved in whatever it is you're going to do to them!"

"Son... you should've covered your face with the hood. They've seen you now!"

"It doesn't matter. Their DNA is all over me and my DNA's all over them; both our DNA is all over the basement! It'll be everywhere! There's no getting away from it so I'm in whether you like it or not!"

"I hoped you'd come round but not like this. We're two peas in a pod you and me, we always were. You can't be around for the last part though," Danny whispers in confidence. Brad immediately understands his dad's meaning.

"We'll see," says Brad.

"No, we won't see, and that's all there is to it!"

*

Meanwhile, on the housing estate, local grasses have alerted the police that Tomic and several of his gang have gone missing. News of this gets back to DS Dean's boss, DI Haynes. She's of the opinion that they haven't gone missing at all but have gone into hiding following the murder of Sammy "Smirfy" Bluskin. DS Dean says that's very unlikely. "More likely," he adds, "they'd've hit back following Smirfy's death and there'd be a war going on." DI Haynes ignores DS Dean's opinion and orders him to investigate matters and report his findings back to her. *Yeah, right, I do all the fucking donkey work and you claim all the fucking glory. Well, Missy, fuck you! I know you fucking fast-track lot! Cunts! Every last one of you are cunts!*

DS Dean phones around his snitches and gets told about an "incident" involving Tomic and Pitbull that took place in The Oak a little while ago. *Alby's local. I bet he's involved!* The snitch tells Dean that a stranger took a photo of Tomic and Pitbull which they took exception to and told him to delete it. "Tomic wanted to check he'd done it but the bloke refused to show him and they lost their bottle and went away with their tails between their legs. Fucking funny it was!" DS Dean asks what the stranger looked like. The description he gets sounds exactly like Danny Deacon and, what's more, he was drinking with local villain and hard man, Albert "Alby" Gray. DS Dean's impressed if Danny was with Alby as he's not known for befriending strangers in case they're undercover police. Immediately following his call with the snitch, DS Dean visits The Oak and sits down at the same table as Alby who, after his "friends" leave, asks what he can do for him. At that moment, all eyes look away from them. DS Dean asks Alby about his new mate, "Danny Deacon". Alby says he doesn't know anyone called Danny Deacon. DS Dean says he has witnesses putting them together during an incident involving Tomic and Pitbull, "Something to do with a photo that was taken of them that they took exception to?" says the detective, carefully watching Alby for a reaction. "Oh yeah. I remember now. They got in a shot this guy was takin' of the buildin' over the road and axed him to delete it and he did. No drama," says Alby, cool as you like. The detective says he'd heard Tomic and Pitbull weren't very happy. Alby says they seldom are and gets up and leaves. Dean's about to follow him when he gets a call from DI Haynes ordering him to return to New Scotland Yard immediately and hangs up abruptly. "Yeah, that's right, Missy," Dean hisses to himself, "I've fuck all better to do than fanny around after you!" he snarls and orders the pub manager to send him the CCTV of the incident involving Tomic, Pitbull, Danny Deacon and Alby. "And if you don't send it P D fucking Q, I will fuck you up. Believe me, arsehole, I will fuck you up good and proper if you mess me around. Got it!"

*

In the area where Tomic, Pitbull and the others were snatched from, shop owners, over several days, report to local PCSO's, Police Community Support Officers, that their CCTV cameras have been vandalised by having their lenses spray-painted. Statements are taken and collated and an investigation into what happened begun. After CCTV footage was analysed, it didn't take long to establish that the cameras were all vandalised on the same day but revealed no clue as to who spray-painted the lenses. One minute all was okay, the next everything went black. However, when the footage from the council's CCTV from outside the greasy-spoon caf is analysed, PCSOs are astonished to see what they believe is a kidnap taking place. The image is blurry due to the wiper blade smudging the paint on the camera lens. "That looks like Tomic, that does," says a constable pointing at the screen with her police baton. Her colleagues agree with her. Senior Officers gather around the screen and run the footage over and over again in an attempt to make out the identities of the men picking Tomic up and throwing him into a van, but all they can tell is that the men are bigger built than Tomic and have either blond or grey hair. The duty officer calls the council's CCTV supervisor to discuss the footage.

"Didn't anyone notice someone being kidnapped?" asks the DO.

"I'll ask. Hey!" yells the CCTV supervisor to her colleagues in CCTV Central. "Did any of you lot notice someone being kidnapped on camera 114b? It was just after the lens wipe the other day, apparently. Is anyone awake?"

"Nobody saw nothing. What probably happened is because there's a whole bank of screens it's easy to miss stuff."

"Yeah, and around that time, we'd be organising the sandwich run so would've been even more shorthanded. It's the cutbacks is what it is, the cutbacks. Means we're understaffed." The DO hears the goings-on over the phone.

"Detective Sergeant Dean is heading the investigation. Send him what you sent us…"

"To be honest, chief, it'd be easier and quicker if you sent it… know what I mean?" the CCTV supervisor says resignedly.

The DO calls DS Dean and briefs him on the council CCTV footage of Tomic being kidnapped before sending him a copy. On viewing the footage, DS Dean is enraged. His outburst attracts the attention of DI Haynes. She asks him what's up. He says nothing's up. She notices CCTV footage is running on his laptop and orders him to play it for her. She's astonished by what she sees.

"That's a kidnapping," says DI Haynes, her mouth open wide in shock. *I can see why you're on the fast-track to the top, love,* thinks DS Dean.

"I believe it is ma'am. I just received it and…"

"What is it about the footage that enraged you, Detective Sergeant Dean?"

"The sheer bloody audacity of it, ma'am. It was broad bloody daylight for goodness' sake!" he yells. DI Haynes doesn't believe him. She thinks something else has angered him.

"Has either the victim or the perpetrators been ID'd?" *I just told you, didn't I, I only just got the fucking thing!*

"The victim is possibly one Antoine Blake, aka Tomic. He's been missing for a few days I believe. He's the leader of a postcode street gang."

"I know who he is!" snaps DI Haynes. "Has CCTV in the area been checked for better footage of the kidnapping?"

"According to the DO at Holloway Road, they'd all been vandalised; had their lenses spray-painted or something he said.

From the footage, you can see Tomic getting chucked into a white Ford Transit van and driven away." To put DI Haynes on the wrong track, Dean tells her it was probably the same people that killed "Smirfy" Buskin.

"Really? Those men look… going by their gait… to be quite old! According to intelligence, Buskin was killed by a rival postcode gang, not a pair of old codgers!"

"I'll send the footage to the lab to see if it can be enhanced, ma'am."

"There's something going on, Sergeant. There's definitely something going on!"

"What d'ye mean ma'am?"

"Well, Antoine Blake gets kidnapped in broad daylight, Smirfy Buskin gets murdered and several gang members go missing. They could've been kidnapped! Really, Detective Sergeant, I'd've thought you'd've been aware that…"

"Missing ma'am? Kidnapped? I doubt it, ma'am. They're probably lying low planning a revenge attack. I'll have a word with my narks to see if they know anything."

"No, Sergeant, there's something going on. This kidnapping was far too well organised for a rabble like the local gangs… far too well organised. I mean, why kidnap anyone? They usually just gun them down in the street. No, kidnap is too risky and it's not their style. Run the CCTV again, Sergeant," the DI orders; her very voice and words are like poison dripping into DS Dean's ears.

After viewing the CCTV footage more than a dozen times, DI Haynes declares the kidnap was carried out with military precision and says she wouldn't be surprised if the kidnappers are, or have been, soldiers. "They looked like they might've done this sort of thing before… so precise!" *Really? You're a fucking genius at stating the fucking obvious you vacuous cunt!* thinks DS Dean but says he's of the same opinion as her, that the kidnappers are probably soldiers. "Ex-soldiers, I'd say due to their obviously advanced years." *They've definitely got a few miles on the clock those two have.* DI Haynes orders DS Dean to concentrate on the van, "Run the registration through ANPR to see where it went and whether it returned to the area after the kidnapping." *What! You think the people who pulled off an operation like this didn't use false plates? Checking every white van caught on CCTV will tie the investigation up for months you fucking idiot!*

Ignoring DI Haynes' order, Dean considers his next move; *Danny Deacon's involved in this somehow and, if he is, he has to know the kidnappers. They were definitely ex-military! I wonder if Danny is too?* With that, DS Dean phones around his contacts in useful places to check whether Danny has a military record. The following morning, he checks his inbox to find an email from FreddyFox101. It contains a file titled *Military Record – Charles Daniel Deacon*. Opening the attachment, it's just Danny's name, his DoB and a notice of pending BAoR posting in Germany, but that's all. Everything else, every line, every entry, is totally redacted. Not a single word, letter or number can be made out. *Shit! He must've been some kind of spook or something! Who'd've thunk it?* Try as he might, DS Dean fails to find anything out about Danny's time in the military. Nevertheless, he prints out a copy of his record as it shows, at least, that Charles Daniel Deacon served in the British Military and must've been involved in some serious shit and that, in itself, could be powerful knowledge to have in your back pocket.

*

Waiting impatiently for the final delivery of gang members, Danny sedates Tomic and the other gang members so he can visit Lucy. The cheapest way to get from Camden to St Thomas' Hospital being by bus, Danny and Brad catch the 214 to King's Cross where they'll change to the number 1 to Waterloo Station and walk from there. The bus is jam-packed. "I hate buses," says Danny to Brad, "always have!" Brad jokes that he's never mentioned it before and laughs. At the next stop, a gang of teenagers get on the bus via its middle doors. Drivers don't like this, as that door is for people to alight from. The driver calls out, telling them to make sure they "tap in" to pay their fares. He receives a jeer in response for his trouble. This behaviour puts Danny's heckles up which puts Brad on high alert to stop his dad from doing something stupid.

"Excuse me," says Danny to the nearest teenager. "I think you forgot to tap in," he speaks loud enough for all the passengers to hear.

"Fuck off and mind your own business!" the teenager replies.

"Look at this," Danny announces to the passengers, "he hasn't paid his fare and now he's swearing and threatening a pensioner!" Some passengers are on Danny's side but others tell him to be quiet and leave the lad alone. The teenagers make their way towards Danny, puffing themselves up to make themselves look bigger than they are.

"Hey, granddad, how old are you?" one of them asks. Danny doesn't reply. "How did someone with such a big mouth get to live so long!" he yells. The teenagers all laugh as Brad closes in behind the one threatening his dad and stands sideways on to him.

"I'm warnin' you, bruv, you're going to get yourself seriously hurt!" another teenager says to Danny.

Without saying a word, Danny stands and throat chops the nearest teenager, takes another to the floor by pulling his floating rib, causing him to roar in agony, and stamps down hard on the inside of the knee of a third teenager, shattering his kneecap. It's all over in seconds. The remaining teenagers retreat and then race forward. They do this several times but remain at a distance. Some passengers implore Danny to stop what he's doing and get off the bus. Brad grabs his dad and drags him to the middle doors where he presses the bell to stop the bus. While they're waiting for the bus to come to a halt, neither Danny nor Brad make eye contact with anyone, making identifying them difficult. As Danny and Brad alight the bus, a couple of the teenagers spot their chance to take retribution on Danny but Brad leg-sweeps them and while they're on the floor, he bangs their heads together, rendering them unconscious. Some passengers applaud the vigilantes but others call them idiots. "Should know better at his age he should," says one old woman to another. "I taught you well, didn't I? You remembered not to look at anyone! Well done son!" says Danny, dragging Brad into a side street. "Yeah, Dad, you taught me well, but I'd rather not get involved in punch-ups on buses if it's all the same to you. I love you Dad but if you carry on like this some fucker's going to stab you or something! I don't want you getting hurt so please don't do anything like that ever again!" Brad pleads but looking at his dad's expression he knows he's wasting his time, his dad won't stop being who or what he is for anyone or anything.

*

When Danny and Brad arrive at the ICU, they find there's no change in Lucy's condition but she's still on the main ward, at least, which they take as a sign that the doctors haven't given up on her. Brad chats to her about some of the things they did together as kids which Danny doesn't know about; in fact, he does know about them but feigns surprise at each "revelation". The more childhood tales Brad recounts, the more his eyes well up and the more thoughts of seeking vengeance race around inside his head. At the end of their visit, Danny squeezes Lucy's hand. There's no response; he hadn't expected one but he hopes and prays and dreams that one day she'll squeeze his hand back. Exiting the ICU, Danny receives a call from DS Dean saying to meet him back at his flat, as he has something to discuss. Danny tells Dean he's with his son and he'll meet him at The Rose & Crown down by the river instead. Dean tells Danny to come alone and hangs up. "Sorry son, you'll have to make your way back to the flat without me, the copper in charge of Luce's case wants a word with me." This suits Brad as it'll give him some alone time with the prisoners.

Danny arrives at the pub ahead of DS Dean, so he buys two pints of beer and takes a table in the furthest dark corner of the bar. When Dean arrives, he joins Danny at his table.

"Good choice of table Danny. Nice and secluded and private. If I didn't know any better I'd say you're ashamed of being seen drinking with me!" Dean says, laughing.

"Cheers," says Danny, clinking glasses with the detective. "You wanted the meet so what can I do for you?" he asks.

"What would you say if I told you that I've just seen CCTV of Tomic, the mush I told you about on the night your daughter got mugged, getting kidnapped in broad daylight!"

"I'd say... great?" Danny answers quizzically.

"It was really slick the way it was done; with what you might call military precision."

"That's nice."

"Yeah, very! It got me thinking it did. I thought, I wonder if these geezers could be ex-soldiers. I thought ex-soldiers, not serving soldiers, because, going by their gait, they're a bit too old to be serving soldiers."

"Couldn't you tell from their faces how old they were?" Danny asks cunningly. His question makes DS Dean even more certain that Danny's involved.

"About that... it seems the lenses on all the CCTV cameras in the area had been spray-painted. We wouldn't have seen anything at all only the council CCTV camera has a lens wiper to wipe dirt and stuff off to keep it clean!"

"That's handy."

"Yeah, dead handy. But going back to the lenses of CCTV cameras being sprayed; it's like it was planned and coordinated to coincide with the kidnap, just like soldiers would do!"

"If you say so."

"I do. And you'll never guess what?" Dean asks, staring at Danny who doesn't flinch or flicker an eyelid. "I got one of my contacts to do a check on you to see if you've ever been in the military."

"Oh aye?"

"Guess what he found out?"

"No idea."

"I think you do. He found out you were in the army but you knew that already. Oh, you were in the army alright, Danny, but apart from a side note about a posting to Germany everything else is redacted… blacked out! Totally blacked out! Who are you Danny Deacon or should I say Charles Daniel Deacon? What are you hiding?"

"Hiding sir? Me sir? Nothing sir!" Danny replies in military fashion. "What's someone like me got to hide? Lots of stuff gets redacted on military records but it doesn't mean it's secret, it's just the way the MoD does things. I've got nothing to hide. Ask me anything. As for these 'experts' you say did it, they're probably not experts at all, everyone gets their ideas off the telly these days."

"Ask you anything? Okay, how about you come with me to New Scotland Yard and make a voluntary statement? That's what I'd like to ask."

"There's no need, I've told you everything."

"Not quite everything, Danny, not quite everything. How about you making a voluntary statement about a confrontation you had with Tomic and Pitbull in The Oak pub on Holloway Road just days before he was kidnapped."

Danny realises DS Dean must've been snooping round big time and, as he has no desire to be ambushed by sneaky questions, he tells the detective he wouldn't call it a confrontation, "It was more an exchange of views," he says and, downing the dregs of his pint, he makes to leave the pub. As Danny walks away, DS Dean calls to him to talk to the shop owners around where Tomic was snatched and they'll tell him he can be trusted, as he's always dishing out summary justice to gang members who hassle them. Danny promises he'll do so and carries on walking. "Don't you want to know where Tomic was snatched from or do you already know?" the detective shouts. Danny just keeps walking. *One nil to me*, thinks DS Dean.

*

Following his encounter with Dean, Danny resolves to remain totally schtum on anything concerning Tomic and his gang until after he's finished doing what he has to do, what he must do! At the check-in call that afternoon, Danny's disappointed to learn that the outstanding targets have gone into hiding. "What about Gary Wilson? He's tucked up in St Thomas' Hospital," says Danny. "No he's not, against medical advice he discharged himself," replies Chuck sounding really pissed off. "Shit!" hisses Danny. "Listen guys, the detective I told you about, Dean, reckons he's got CCTV of T1's kidnap. He said it looked to him like a military operation so he got hold of my army record." Danny's news is met with stunned silence. "It's a bust," murmurs Tony eventually. "That's it, I'm off back to Oz!" Glenn says he's off back to the US but Chuck makes no comment. "What about you, Chuck? What are you going to do?" they all ask. "I'll tell you what I'm going to do. We haven't finished what we set out to do and until it's done I'm staying here. You guys can go home if you want and I won't hold it against you." Chuck's words hit Glenn and Tony hard so they agree to stay to snatch Treyvon, Gary Wilson and Simon McVey, aka Syko. "Okay, but if things start going sideways then the op stops and you all go home. Okay?" says Danny, eager that the next phase of his plan is executed ASAP in case the police catch up with him. "Let's hold off these calls for a week," suggests Chuck. Everyone agrees.

*

Danny returns to his flat intending to let Brad know that DS Dean is onto him and things are likely to go tits up, so he needs to scarper back up north, but Brad's not there when he arrives. Danny calls him but his phone's off. A glance at the nail on the back of the bedroom door tells Danny that Brad has the keys to the basement. He races downstairs. The door's locked, so Danny presses his foot against the bottom panel to try and spring it but it's no good, it doesn't budge. Hearing a creaking noise at the basement door, Brad presses an ear up against it.

"Dad? Is that you Dad?" Brad hiss-whispers.

"It is, let me in!"

"No. I want to know what you and that copper talked about?"

"He reckons he's got CCTV of my oppos snatching Tomic and to him it looked like a military operation… and he knows I was in the army and that my record is heavily redacted. He's telling the truth, he's not bluffing. He's onto us, so you need to scarper up north as quick as. I don't want you involved in any of this!" says Danny. Brad opens the basement door.

"But I am involved, Dad, very much so," says Brad, offering his dad his battered and bruised knuckles.

"What have you done son? You haven't killed them I hope!" cries Danny in despair.

"No but I banged them up pretty good!"

"If Dean puts two and two together the cops'll turn up with a search warrant and…" Brad stops Danny from talking by nodding towards Tomic who he suspects is pretending to be out cold to keep from being used as a punchbag.

"What are we going to do with them Dad? We can't let the cops find them here!" Brad hiss-whispers as quietly as he can.

"I think we both know the answer to that, son!" replies Danny, drawing a finger across his throat. Out of the corner of his eye, Danny sees Tomic squirm. *He's awake the sneaky little bugger!*

"I thought you'd say something like that, I'll go and get some…"

"You'll do nothing and there's no 'we' in this, Brad, there's only me. Now pack your bags and go back to Leeds… now!"

Brad protests but he knows deep down he's a liability now that things are hotting up and so he hugs his dad, packs his bags and leaves for Leeds, telling Danny he'll come back in a week or so. "Don't come unless I call!" says Danny, giving his son a final hug. "Love you boy," he whispers. "Love you too Dad," Brad whispers back.

Having earwigged on Danny's and Brad's conversation, Tomic realises he's dead and mumbles through his gag, promising he won't go to the police or come looking for Danny if he lets him go. Danny asks, "What about your mates? Do I let them go too?" Tomic mumbles, "Fuck them, bruv, they're the reason I'm here innit? I told you, bruv, I never touched your daughter! Please… please let me go bro! I never done nothing, bruv, you know that fam!" pleads Tomic tearfully. Under the circumstances, Danny disregards Tomic's bad language, along with his pleas, and begins filling the line of syringes full to the brim with anaesthetic. Tomic knows about injecting, due to his knowledge of drugs abuse, and deduces there's enough liquid in the syringes to kill. Believing, quite correctly, that he's about to be OD'd, Tomic panics and frantically writhes about on the floor, trying to break free of the cable ties, but Danny and he both know it's futile. After dragging the prisoners, one by one, into Tomic's room and arranging them in a neat, orderly line like soldiers on a parade ground, Danny starts injecting them, beginning with Pitbull. As each life-light expires, Danny glances along the line towards a terrified Tomic who's now kneeling, rocking back and forth, seemingly in acceptance of his fate. *He's going last so he can fully appreciate the magnitude of our vengeance.*

After the deed is done, and Tomic and his oppos have breathed their last, not for the first time, Danny sits in silent meditation surrounded by death. It's something he's gotten used to over the years. After what he considers to be an appropriate amount of time, Danny sends his oppos a coded message telling them what he's done and orders them to snap their SIMs and mobile phones and head home; he doesn't even thank them but they never expected him to. After hitting the send button, Danny snapped his SIM and mobile too. *Let them sort that one out if they can!*

That night, Danny slips commando-fashion into the lockup garage where he keeps his van and locks the doors behind him. Out of sight of prying eyes, he swaps the van's number plates to those of an identical van he knows to be insured to avoid hassle from ANPR.

Arriving at his flat, Danny parks adjacent to the external door of the basement. He doesn't get out of the van immediately. Instead, he sits waiting for his eyes to adjust to the darkness so he can check if anyone's watching him. It's all clear, no one's around so he enters the basement carrying a pile of dust sheets covered in splats of paint from his DIY sideline and, after shutting the door behind him, switches on the light in the room housing the corpses. *How pathetic, how puny, how small you all look!* "Need to get you ready for your trip," says Danny, throwing dust sheets over the corpses and, one by one, he wraps each of them in its own shroud. He makes a good job of this because he's had experience of doing it before, a long, long time ago. "There, you'll do," says Danny, recalling saying those exact same words to his children after getting them ready for special outings like Christmas or birthday parties.

After loading the bodies into the back of his van, Danny returns upstairs to his flat and makes himself a cup of tea and a slice of hot buttered toast. *Thank goodness there's no need to make any more bloody chicken nuggets!* he says to himself. Re-entering the basement, Danny takes a last look round, for what, he doesn't know. Before setting off, Danny throws ladders, dust sheets, cans of paint, old newspapers, anything he can lay his hands on, over the corpses to cover them up. He's surprised at how little room the bodies of six twenty-somethings take up. Despite driving a van in the small hours is risky because you're more likely to get pulled by the police, Danny knows he has to act before DS Dean turns up with a search warrant. "If I get pulled, hopefully they won't look under that lot," says Danny, talking to himself and looking over his shoulder at the pile of gear covering the bodies. Having studied his route using an old AA Road Atlas, Danny sets off on his journey to an old oppo's place in Dorset. He hopes his van will make the journey, and not break down, and return him back to London before daylight.

*

Thankfully, the drive down to Dorset is uneventful, as Danny was mindful to keep to the laws of the road and do nothing to draw attention to himself or his van. Arriving at his destination, Danny phones his old oppo, who tells him where he can find the keys to the excavator. Having worked on building sites for many years, operating the massive machine is no problem for Danny, and he quickly digs a ten-feet-deep trench before dropping, one by one, the dust-sheet-covered bodies into it. After the last of them is cast into the pit, Danny backfills the trench with dug earth and disguises the burial site with brushwood before setting off, lickety-split, back to London. Halfway home, he stops to change the van's number plates to another false set. During the last leg of his journey, Danny ponders on what to do about the three that got away, *the three that have escaped his justice*: Treyvon, Gary Wilson and Simon "Syko" McVey. They too had to die, but for the present, uppermost in Danny's mind is getting away with the murders he'd already committed. Once inside his lockup garage, Danny fits the genuine registration plates to his van and destroys the fake sets. *Let's see them sort that lot out!*

Despite his extreme tiredness – after all, when all is said and done, he's a pensioner – Danny goes directly to St Thomas' Hospital to visit Lucy. Arriving at the nurses' station, he's shocked to learn that she's been moved to a private room. He's been told many times by many people that this is a bad sign. He demands to know what's going on and doctors tell him there's nothing more they can do for Lucy and that, in their experience, it's better for the patient to be in a private room so family can visit anytime. "They can even stay overnight if they wish," says Lucy's neurologist, stroking Danny's shoulder; this serves to remind him of how much he misses the soothing caress of a woman. The CN guides him to Lucy's room where he sits sobbing and holding Lucy's hand tight as memories of her childhood come flooding into his head. As they're alone, Danny takes the opportunity to tell Lucy of the fate of her attackers while simultaneously unburdening his conscience.

"Hello Luce… it's Dad here. You can't tell, but they've moved you into a private room. It sounds good but, from what I've been told, it's not. Anyway, before anyone arrives I've got some news for you. I can't remember where we're up to but I told you I got hold of the scumbags who put you in here? Yes? Well, there's nothing to worry about on that score anymore. They've… I've taken care of them. I won't go into detail but… they're dead… well, those I could get hold of are but the others won't be around for much longer either. Actually, I'm just back from… disposing of them… disposing? Yeah, disposing is the right word for rubbish like them! I had to get on with it because the detective I told you about, Detective Sergeant Dean's his name, is getting close and I didn't want him finding them and letting them go so after I offed them I took them to an old mate's place down by the coast so they can spend eternity together. I hope they get on," jokes Danny. "Just so you know, because I know it'd be important to you as a humane person, they didn't suffer. I just sent them all into a nice little sleep and they didn't wake up. Not like you Luce. Not like you. They got it better than you did my darling little girl."

Danny's words trail off into sobbing and he's still sobbing as his ex-wife, Joyce, enters the room. She joins in with him sobbing and they hold hands across the bed. Wiping his eyes, Danny tells Joyce he's said his goodbyes and will leave so she and her new husband can say theirs. "I'm not ready to say goodbye," says Joyce. "She's going to pull through and when she does she'll find me at her bedside. I've ordered a couple of mattresses so… you know… you can… if you like?" Danny thanks his ex and heads for home; he has things to do to ensure he gets away with his crimes. Joyce can't understand what's gotten into Danny, he was always the one who insisted Lucy would make it, she'll pull through, and wonders what could've happened to change that.

*

When Danny arrives back at his flat, it is his intention to destroy any evidence but he goes straight to bed instead; he's not as young as he used to be and his exertions have taken their toll on both his ageing frame and his mind. He wakes just after midday of the following day and, as usual, he switches on the TV. There's an outside broadcast being covered by a reporter who's ducking for cover. "All hell is breaking loose on the streets of North London as rival gangs fight to take over their rivals' postcodes," says the reporter before being moved back by police. Danny grabs the remote to see what else is on. The violence is on every news programme on every channel. *Hope they all kill one another.* Just as he's about to go downstairs to the basement to commence "Operation Cleanup", a knock comes on the door of his flat. "Who is it?" he shouts. "It's the police, open the door!" yells DI Haynes. "No one's in, this is a recording, leave a message after the tone. Beeeeeeep," replies Danny, rendering an immaculate imitation of a voice message. Outside the door of the flat, DS Dean is grinning at Danny's little joke but DI Haynes isn't amused and repeats her words more harshly. Opening the door with a wild flourish, Danny takes both detectives by surprise. "What can I do for you ladies?" he asks. DI Haynes says they are there to question him over the kidnapping of Antoine Blake as well as the disappearances of several members of his gang. Danny says they're wasting their time, "I've never heard of this Antoine Blake character and by extension can't know who is and isn't in this gang you say he's in." DI Haynes tells Danny he can either answer their questions at his flat or they'll take him to New Scotland Yard for questioning. Danny chooses option "A". DI Haynes informs Danny that, a single council CCTV apart, every CCTV camera in the area where Antoine Blake was kidnapped had been sabotaged, "Which shows a high degree of planning and the kidnap was executed with military precision," says the DI. Danny remains poker-faced.

"The council CCTV footage shows two men throwing Mr Blake into the back of a van which was then driven away from the scene by a third person."

"Well," says Danny, "you got CCTV, that's it, game set and match!"

"Not quite, the CCTV's… a bit blurry."

"Oh, that's a shame," says Danny, feigning concern and disappointment. "I bet that would've come in handy if it had been clear," he adds with a smirk.

"Quite. I mentioned the kidnap was carried out with military precision so imagine my surprise when I discovered that you were in the army for over twenty years!" says DI Haynes and glaring at DS Dean. He's shocked that she knows Danny was in the military and, given the dirty look she'd given him, suspects she must've found the redacted military record he'd hidden in his desk.

"I don't understand why you're surprised I served in the army, lots of people have served in the army."

"But that's not the most disturbing aspect of the discovery. Can you imagine what that is? No? Your entire military record is heavily redacted. In fact, it's more redacted than any other document I've ever seen!" This confirms DS Dean's suspicion that DI Haynes had found the printout he'd made of Danny's service record.

"I've no idea why that would be the case," Danny replies casually.

"Charles Daniel Deacon, I am arresting you on suspicion of conspiracy to kidnap Antoine Blake. You do not have to say anything but it may harm your defence if you do not mention when questioned something which you later rely on in court. Anything you do say may be given in evidence."

Having arrested Danny, DI Haynes orders DS Dean to handcuff him and take him away. As they depart, a team of detectives enter to search the flat. Danny shouts at them over his shoulder, "If any of you lot find any money down the back of the sofa it's mine so keep your thieving hands away from it!" DS Dean can't help but laugh at Danny's remark but DI Haynes isn't amused and shows it. *Miserable cow, that was funny that was. Moments like that make life worth living and I bet the lads loved it too. Quite impressed with the police caution she gave though; word perfect. Fucking bitch!*

On their drive to New Scotland Yard, DI Haynes attempts to engage Danny in conversation and mentions that the missing people are suspected members of the gang that attacked his daughter. Danny says nothing, he doesn't even look in the DI's direction, he simply sits and stares out of the car window for the whole trip. On arriving at New Scotland Yard, Danny is booked in and when the duty sergeant asks what the charge is, DI Haynes answers, "Kidnap and murder." Danny doesn't flinch at hearing the charge. Before placing Danny in the cells prior to questioning him, DI Haynes asks if he'd like a lawyer. "No thanks," he answers, "lawyers are for the guilty and as I haven't done anything why would I need one?" During questioning, Danny doesn't say a word; he doesn't even go "no comment", he just sits looking straight ahead. In fact, apart from him refusing a lawyer, asking for a cup of tea, milk and two sugars, giving his name and date of birth for the interview recording and taunting the detectives to keep their thieving hands to themselves, Danny hasn't said a word for over three hours. "Yours is not the behaviour of an innocent man!" yells DI Haynes, completely losing her self-control; much to DS Dean's satisfaction. *Brilliant job you're doing there Ms Fast Track!* At the end of the interrogation, Danny is returned to his cell where DS Dean asks for the code to his mobile phone which Danny gives him without hesitation. "What about laptops and tablets?" the detective asks. "Well, if you've got a headache, there's a pack of paracetamol in my bathroom cabinet, if you're going that way, but a police officer, especially one of your age, shouldn't be going to those sorts of clubs!" Danny jokes. "I like you Danny, I do, I really do. Now, I know that you, or those mates of yours, kidnapped Tomic and his mates but I hope that's all you've done. I've been after that little shite for years and I want to bang him up, just once, before I retire. That's all. It's not much to ask, is it? So, tell me, Danny, where is he? Where are Tomic and his mates?" Without acknowledging DS Dean, Danny lies down on the bed in his cell, pulls the thin sheet up over his shoulders, closes his eyes and lies smiling with his arms folded across his chest like a corpse in a shroud.

Next morning, mug of tea in hand, Danny is returned to interview room four. After he confirms his name and date of birth for the interview recording, DI Haynes asks if there's anything he'd like to say about what the detectives found while searching his flat. Danny knows she's bluffing and says, "Okay, Detective Inspector Haynes, I admit it, you got me bang to rights… the DVDs are mine but the bloke I got them off said they were legit, though I had my doubts going by the silhouettes bobbing up and down like they were in a cinema or something." Once again, DS Dean smiles at Danny's humour and, once again, DI Haynes isn't amused in the slightest by it and nor is she amused by DS Dean finding Deacon's behaviour funny. After thirty minutes of Danny giving the detectives the complete run-around, DI Haynes speaks the time into the microphone, followed by her saying that the interview is over and storms out of the interview room after ordering DS Dean to return Danny to his cell. Had Haynes or Dean known that Danny had been trained to resist, obfuscate and bamboozle interrogators, they wouldn't have expected him to say anything, lawyer or no, that he didn't want to say, want them to know or want to tell them. It was he that was in control, not them.

With the custody clock counting down to zero, DI Haynes applies for a twenty-four hour extension, which is refused. As a consequence, Danny is released, given back his possessions at the custody desk and bailed to reappear in four weeks' time but he's seen enough cop shows to know this is nonsense; he'll either be rearrested on new evidence or get a call telling him not to bother coming in and clogging the place up. Outside New Scotland Yard, DS Dean catches up with Danny and asks to meet him at The Rose & Crown. He agrees. *Keep your friends close and your enemies closer!* each thinks.

*

When Danny arrives at The Rose & Crown, he finds DS Dean's already there. He's sitting well away from everybody else and has a couple of pints lined up.

"Thanks for meeting me Danny," Dean says cordially. *That's polite for him, wonder what he wants?* "Just to let you know, we won't be talking about the case. Okay?"

"Good, but we both know you can't talk to me about the case anyway. So, what do you want?"

"I just wanted to talk to you about what's been happening in N7 since Tomic and his mates went missing."

"Why would I want to know about what's going on in Tottenham? I live in Camden."

"Because I think you'd be interested, that's why!" snaps the DS. "To be frank, whoever disappeared Tomic and his gang did everyone a favour, a big favour! On the one hand, gangs are at war with one another over Tomic's postcode but on the other hand we're arresting dozens of gang members for all sorts of crimes; it's like shooting fish in a barrel. The local community are happy Tomic has gone and equally happy we're taking so many criminals off the streets; win-win! It's only a week but crime and burglary rates have fallen through the floor! There's a feeling of optimism on the estate I've never seen before! There's even talk of setting up Neighbourhood Watches and opening a Crime-Stoppers hub. Incredible. Unbelievable. Who'd have thunk it? As I said, whoever disappeared Tomic and his gang did everyone a big favour and whoever it was, everyone, including me, owes them a big debt of gratitude!"

"Well, that's nice. Are we finished? Is that all you wanted to talk to me about? I could've got that off the telly!"

"Hey, did you ever contact the shopkeepers around where Tomic was snatched to see what they say about me? You know, whether I can be trusted or not?"

"Not yet but if you're in so thick with them why aren't they telling you about what happened to Tomic? Surely they must know."

"Who says I'm not talking to them? You know, Danny, I'm not your enemy. You can trust me. That's all I'm saying, you can trust me. I've got your back in ways you can't imagine."

"That's good to know," Danny says sarcastically, "but now, I'm off."

"Don't worry about answering your bail. It won't come to that."

"I know."

"What about Lucy? How's she doing?" asks DS Dean, attempting sympathy.

Danny tells DS Dean that Lucy's been moved to a private room, "So relatives can visit her whenever they like," he adds. Dean knows what that means and places a consoling hand on Danny's shoulder. "I'll pray for her," he says. "I wouldn't've thought someone like you believed in God," says Danny acidly. "I don't but I can't see how it can hurt," replies the detective, ignoring Danny's obvious contempt for him. Danny says he'll pray too, though doesn't say for who.

CHAPTER ELEVEN

The following morning, Danny wakes up cold and alone in his flat and with an empty feeling deep inside of him. *What the hell have I been doing?* he asks himself. *You should've been concentrating on Luce instead of... but I've been... I don't even know what I've been. I could've got them anytime, anytime! I just hope Luce never finds out!* Danny is so consumed by self-loathing and shame at prioritising revenge over his daughter and wonders if he'd done what he'd done for her or for himself. As Tomic and the others are no more, Danny resolves, in future, to visit Lucy as much as he can; *I'll visit at least twice a day! I'll put a mattress on the floor next to her bed... they said that was okay! Who are you kidding, you'll never keep it up?* his inner voice mocks. Danny knows it's right, he'll never keep it up.

After forcing down a slice of hot buttered toast with a mug of black tea – he's run out of milk again – Danny shuffles off, tramp-like, to visit Lucy. Arriving at her room, he hesitates, scared of what he might find. Opening the door, Danny sees his ex-wife sitting holding Lucy's hand with Jeff, her latest husband, standing behind her; his hands are on her shoulders comforting her. Joyce looks tired. She smiles at Danny and asks where he's been. As there's no smell of stale beer, she knows he hasn't been to the pub at least. Danny takes a moment and decides to tell her the truth.

"I got arrested."

"What for this time?"

"The police think I kidnapped the scumbags that mugged Luce."

"Did you?"

"No! It's a load of rubbish! The police haven't got a clue so they're clutching at straws." *No point telling her about that!*

"I hope you're telling me the truth, Danny. You'd better not've done anything stupid because the kids'll need you more than ever once Luce goes."

"Don't say that! She's not going anywhere! She's going to pull through! Don't ever say anything like that ever again!"

"Danny, be realistic," says Joyce compassionately, "they've put her in here to..."

"Don't! Just don't!"

Danny exits the room and the hospital in a rage. He's angrier with himself, for having sought revenge instead of spending time with his daughter, than with his ex. He's also regretting not having been more kind to Joyce after their divorce, but that's the way of things with families in crisis, as there were many good reasons for things being the way they were or are. Rather than calming down, Danny's fury rises to the point where he's in the perfect mood to dish out righteous justice.

As he nears the tube station, Danny comes across a young couple having a heated argument. The man is much larger than the woman and is shoving her backwards towards the road. Danny steps in on the side of the female but she tells him to piss off and mind his own business. The couple quickly make up and leave the scene arm in arm with the male glaring menacingly over his shoulder at Danny. *Yeah, mate, give me a dirty look but that's all you'll give me!* Danny stares back at the male to goad him into a fight. He turns in Danny's direction but the female calls out, "Don't Gary, don't! Don't 'it 'im, love, he ain't werf i', he ain't werf i'. Let's go 'ome and leave the sad bastard to 'isself!" *Another Gary, another gobshite! Christ, the world's full of them!*

After the incident with the couple, Danny's mood darkens considerably. *What's wrong with people! All I wanted to do was to make sure that she was...* Danny's reverie is abruptly cut short when he spies a man in his mid-twenties staggering towards him, concentrating on the screen on his mobile phone instead of looking where he's going. Danny hates this because they think it's okay to delegate their safety to those around them who are paying attention to where they're going. As Danny and the male pass on the pavement, he shoulder barges the man. The collision is so violent, the man's phone flies from his hands and lands several yards away on the ground, smashing the screen.

"What the fuck!" the man cries. "Watch where you're going you old twat! My phone's fucked thanks to you! I'm going to fuck you up! I'm going to fuck you up good and proper!" says the man, slurring his words.

"I'm so sorry," replies Danny meekly. "I wasn't watching where I was going," he adds humbly.

"What! You weren't watching where you were going! You actually admit you weren't watching where you were going!" the man slurs.

"No. Sorry. Were you watching where you were going?" Danny asks innocently.

"Of course I was fucking watching where I was going you stupid old twat! What do you think I was doing?"

"I see. So, you were watching where you were going?" Danny says as if making sure of the facts.

"I just told you I was, didn't I? Are you fucking deaf as well as old and thick?"

"In that case, you bumped into me on purpose," Danny says menacingly.

"What?"

"I said, 'in that case, you bumped into me on purpose'. What's wrong with you? Why would you bump into me on purpose? Do you normally go round bumping into people on purpose?"

"I don't, I... what?" stutters the man, thinking he could be in a bit of trouble despite Danny's advanced years.

"You heard me. I asked is there something wrong with you?"

"No," says the man, backing away.

"Would you like something wrong with you because if you do I can make something very wrong with you!" Danny says with icy calm.

Before the man can utter another word, Danny stamps down hard on the inside of his knee. *That'll teach you to look where you're going!* As the man rolls around in agony, Danny retrieves his phone from the ground and uses it to call for an ambulance. After making the call he posts the phone down a nearby drain. It suddenly dawns on Danny that there could be CCTV in the area. He's relieved to find there isn't any and makes his way to the tube station to watch the ambulance arrive. He's glad he hung around, as the man, being drunk, lashes out at the ambulance crew and gets arrested. *Perfect!* says Danny's inner voice as he enters London's labyrinthine tube network.

Feeling in the mood for a celebratory beer, Danny stops at The Manor on his way back to his flat for a swift pint which turns into several. He sits and drinks all alone because neither Gaz nor Jacko are there to keep him company.

*

When Danny returns to his flat, he finds all the lights are on. "Who's there?" he calls out and is answered by Brad saying that he'd heard from his mother he'd been arrested and he wants to know all about it. "You could've just phoned," says Danny, though he's glad Brad's there. Danny recounts the story of his arrest to Brad and about the cops searching his flat. "Did they find anything?" asks Brad. Danny says no but if they search the basement, then he's done for. "We're done for, you mean," says Brad. Danny tells Brad he needn't worry because he'll tell the police his DNA is in the basement because they use it to do DIY down there. "If they ask what it was we did, just tell them all sorts of things like building shelves and stuff."

Brad says Danny's story is feeble and unconvincing but he's not to worry because he's come prepared. "We need to destroy the DNA evidence!" says Brad. Danny says he doesn't think that's possible but Brad tells him it is, "There are things called Oxy-Active agents as well as bleaches that degrade and destroy DNA on contact. I looked them up on the internet and brought a load down with me. Also, I 'borrowed' a couple of spray guns from work so it shouldn't take us long to douse the whole basement," says Brad, pleased with himself; in response, Danny gives his son a "playful" punch in the guts.

"It's lucky I didn't cut them up before putting them in the van," says Danny, making a bad joke, "so there shouldn't be too much mess down there!" he adds, grinning grimly.

"What? You carted the bodies away in your van? Are you mad, Dad? They'll have you on ANPR. Where'd you take them?"

"Don't worry, I covered my tracks. I paintballed CCTV cameras all over Camden and used false number plates on the van… two sets! They really shouldn't tell people on the telly how the police work, it makes it ten times easier to fool them!"

"They can still track your van on ANPR no matter what number plates you used! All they have to do is watch out for your van type and track it! Where did you take them?"

"To an old oppos place down in Dorset."

"Dorset! At least that's miles away!"

"I know."

"What time did you…"

"I started around midnight."

"What! There won't be many vans like yours on the road at that time of night and once they spot the same van with different number plates it won't take them long to work out what was going on!"

"Don't worry son, they can't link the number plates back to me and I destroyed them. Cut them up into little pieces and burned them. There's nothing left of them; not a shred of evidence, as they say!

"Dad, please, tell me where you buried the bodies. By the way, how did you do it? You know, kill them?"

"Like I already told you, I buried the bodies at a mate's place in Dorset and I killed them nice and humane, the way Luce would've liked, by putting them to sleep with anaesthetic… lots and lots of anaesthetic; they didn't feel a thing."

"Okay, you don't have to tell me exactly where you buried them, just say whereabouts so I can check online for ANPR and CCTV cameras in the area."

"Already done, son. Did it before I set off. There's no ANPR within fifteen or twenty miles of the burial site. See, I'm not so useless after all," Danny jokes, giving Brad a friendly dead-arm punch. "Anyway, if the cops work it out I'll worry about it when the time comes. Now, let's go to the basement and start spraying the place!"

*

After a night removing DNA evidence from the basement and generally making the place look less dungeon-like, the following morning Danny gets a call from Alby saying to meet him in The Manor at twelve. Danny tells him his son Brad is staying with him. "Bring him along, the more the merrier," says Alby and hangs up. Brad asks who was on the phone. "A geezer called Alby. I think I told you about him. I met him in a pub called The Oak near where Luce was… you know… attacked." Brad asks what this Alby wants. "He wants a meet in The Manor at twelve. You're invited!" says Danny. Brad says he'd rather not go but Danny insists, "Don't get me wrong, I like Alby and all that, but there's something about him. I think he's one of Deans' narks." Brad asks why he thinks that. "A couple of times after meeting with Alby, Dean found out I'd been up to no good and right after he tries to get all matey with me but got nowhere, and hey presto, now I get a call from Alby to meet up for a pint. Coincidence? I don't think so!" Brad warns Danny not to meet Alby if he thinks he's a snitch. "As I've always told you, son, keep your friends close and your enemies closer!" says Danny, slapping Brad on his back. "Yeah, so you keep saying, but here's another one for you: 'if you swim with sharks you're gonna get bit' and at your age that might prove fatal," returns Brad. Danny just laughs. "Don't worry about me, son, you just keep your eyes open for anything that doesn't look right!"

When Danny and Brad arrive at The Manor, Alby's already there waiting for them and greets Danny like a long-lost friend, which he finds suspicious. Looking over Alby's shoulder, Danny spies Gaz and Jacko who come over to join them. "Long time no see," says Gaz. "I was in here last night but you two lightweights were nowhere to be seen," bants Danny. Alby shows them to a table in the corner of the bar being guarded by two massive black guys. "I reserved us a table," he says, dismissing the table-minders so not even they can hear them.

"How's your daughter?" Alby enquires politely. Danny suspects he already knows from DS Dean that Lucy has been moved out of the ICU.

"They've put her in a room of her own. She still has a machine to breathe for her and a heart monitor and all that but she's in her own room. Her mother reckons they've put her there to die," says Danny. Brad's shocked to hear his dad say this out loud to strangers but doesn't react.

"Sorry to hear that, Danny," says Alby sincerely. "Let's hope she's wrong and your daughter pulls through and comes home soon."

"Yeah, let's hope so."

"Danny... I want to talk to you about what's goin' on since Tomic and his gang disappeared. Do you know anything about that?"

"About what?"

"Don't act stupid, Danny, I mean about Tomic and some of his gang disappearin'!"

"No," Danny says bluntly. Alby, of course, doesn't believe him.

"Since they went missin' it's total mayhem. There's open warfare on the streets! Police are everywhere… makin' life difficult for everyone." *For people like you, you mean,* thinks Danny.

"Sorry to hear that, Alby. I heard from that copper, what's-his-name, Detective Sergeant Dean? Yeah, Detective Sergeant Dean, he reckons that crime's down and the locals are forming Neighbourhood Watches and things are better."

"Depends on what you mean by 'better' but I suppose you're right, crime is down. The police are lockin' up gang members like there's no tomorrow… it's like shootin' fish in a barrel."

"Like shooting fish in a barrel?"

"Yeah."

"Funny, those are the exact same words DS Dean said to me just a few hours ago!" Infuriated by the obvious insinuation, Alby reaches across the table and grabs Danny by his collar. Brad goes to help his dad but Danny tells him to stay in his seat.

"You better not be accusin' me of bein' a grass!" snaps Alby, releasing his grip on Danny.

"No need for violence, Alby, no need for violence. Sorry if I offended you. We both know being a grass on an estate, especially one like yours, is dangerous so let's let things be and not do anything we might regret."

"That's twice you've accused me of bein' a nark, there'd better not be a third time or you and me are goin' to fall out big time!" snarls Alby. Danny doesn't react to Alby's threat because DS Dean has just entered the pub. He comes over and sits at Alby's table.

"Fuck off before I fuck you off!" growls DS Dean, pointing in turn at Alby, Brad, Gaz and Jacko.

"Cheers," Dean says, picking up a glass from the table and clinking it against Danny's.

"Yeah, cheers," Danny replies, taking a sip of beer. "What can I do you for Dean?"

"I believe you own a little white van," says the detective, his eyes boring into Danny's.

"I do. I'm thinking of selling it actually. Not looking to buy a cheap van are you?" Danny asks, smirking. "Good runner… six months MOT… never raced or rallied."

"I like you Danny, I really do. You make me laugh you do. Look, I want what you want: justice for your daughter. All too often scumbags go unpunished and, just like you, I want to see Tomic punished for the crimes he's committed but…"

"I've been thinking. How does that work?"

"How does what work?"

"You told me it wasn't Tomic that attacked Luce but instead of giving me the names of the ones that did, you gave me his name. Why did you give me his name?"

"He's their leader and…"

"You set me up. You goaded me into getting involved so you could get Tomic, didn't you? You used me as bait and I fell for it. You didn't care what happened to me! What were you going to get him on?"

"Don't you worry about that, I'd've found something."

"But what about me? What was going to happen to me? What if… I remember you telling me that you wanted to nail Tomic before you retire and I think that you were prepared to do anything and everything to get him!"

"I'll draw a scenario for you, shall I?" says DS Dean, directing the conversation onto the subject he really wants to talk to Danny about. "Being a military man, you'll know what a scenario is I suppose?" Danny just shrugs his shoulders. "Let's say a van… one just like yours for example… drives from London to Dorset and back again in the middle of the night. For what reason, I ask myself? To do what, I ask myself? Dispose of bodies?" hisses DS Dean quietly under his breath. Danny turns pale; he thinks he's done for. "No need to shit yourself, Danny, this is just a scenario I'm painting for you here. But it's good news for you because if you've been in the police as long as I have you've got friends everywhere… including ANPR HQ. Remember I asked you to speak with shop owners around where Tomic was snatched so you could ask them what I'm like? Did you go? Did you fuck. I need you to trust me Danny. I've done you a big favour and I want one back. But first, I'm going to do you another big favour, I'm going to tell you that Detective Inspector Haynes, remember her, is, at this very moment, getting a search warrant for SOCO to search your flat... and the basement below it." After dropping his bombshell, DS Dean leaves the pub.

"What the fuck did he want?" chorus Alby, Gaz and Jacko returning to Danny at the table.

"He wants me to turn grass," Danny replies unconvincingly. The others, rightly, don't believe him.

"So, what did you tell him?" asks Alby, playing along.

"What d'ye think I told him? I told him no way. Now, me and Brad need to get off, we've got some DIY stuff to do before he heads off back to Leeds. C'mon son," says Danny, draining his glass.

On the walk back to the flat, Danny tells Brad what went on with DS Dean. He so regrets ever getting Brad involved, but he wanted in, so he got in, and it's too late now. Brad tells his dad he reckons that the spraying they did will have destroyed all the DNA but suggests they do another spray. "Just to be on the safe side, son," says Danny, "I reckon we should set the place on fire!" Brad looks at his dad in horror before realising he's joking. Continuing their walk, they jostle one another along the pavement, cracking up with laughter. "You're a silly sod," says Brad, wrapping a loving arm around his father's shoulders. "Listen, son," says Danny seriously, "if it comes to it, don't hesitate to drop me in the shit to save yourself." Brad tells his dad he'll never do any such thing and he's not to suggest, or even think, anything like that ever again.

After thoroughly drenching every nook and cranny of the basement with the Oxy-Active agent, Danny and Brad clean themselves up to go and visit Lucy. Danny thinks this might be his last chance to see her if SOCO find anything or DS Dean stops playing games and arrests him. *That sneaky bugger's up to something!*

What's his game? Does he think if he gains my trust I'll tell him where the bodies are? No chance! answers Danny's inner voice.

*

Entering Lucy's room, Danny sees Joyce and Jeff sitting at her bedside holding hands. *He shouldn't be here at a time like this. He should just go, he's not real family!* "Hello Brad, thanks for bringing your dad with you," says Joyce sarcastically. Brad ignores her and, seeing the look on his dad's face, invites Jeff to go to the cafeteria with him to get everyone coffee. Jeff takes the hint and leaves. Danny sits down opposite Joyce and they reach out over Lucy, holding hands and talking to her like she's awake, like she's a part of the conversation. Just then, Danny spots Lucy's eyelids flicker. He asks Joyce if she saw it too. "I did but I didn't want to say anything in case it got everyone's hopes up or I imagined it." They both stare at Lucy, talking to her all the time, but her eyes remain un-flickering. When Brad and Jeff return, Danny and Joyce tell them they saw Lucy's eyes flicker. "I thought I saw her eyes flicker," says Brad. "Did you see them Jeff?" He says not.

After five minutes of watching without so much as one of Lucy's eyelashes flickering, Danny tells a nurse what they saw. She tells a doctor who tells Lucy's consultant. "Would you all please wait outside so we can carry out some tests on the... on Lucy," says the consultant. Danny, Brad, Joyce and Jeff pace nervously outside Lucy's room. After thirty minutes the consultant emerges and tells them she detected no change in Lucy's condition and her eyes flickering could be a sign that she's dreaming. "Is that good?" Danny asks. "It's neither good nor bad, it's just something that happens with some patients." Danny says he knows it's more than that and Lucy will wake up. "Mr Deacon, may I call you Danny?" he nods. "Even if your daughter does eventually come round you have to be aware that there's likely to be some brain damage from the bleeds we discovered when she was admitted." The consultant's words deflate everybody and they go for a walk together to clear their heads. During the walk, Brad says he has to head back to Leeds and wants some time alone with his sister before hitting the road. The others understand and Brad, alone, returns to Lucy's room and tells her about his role dealing with the scumbags who attacked her and about DS Dean being close to finding out about it all. "I'd do the same all over again, Luce. I'm just like Dad in that respect, I couldn't've lived with myself if… you know. Anyway, Dad's dumped the bodies at a mate's place in Dorset so good luck to the police finding them! Goodbye Luce… love you to the moon and back," says Brad tears streaming down his cheeks. He places a tear on each of Lucy's eyes, kisses her on her nose and whispers, "C'mon Luce, c'mon, wake up… you can do it… wake up."

*

At six the following morning, there's a loud banging on Danny's front door. It's DI Haynes. She shows Danny a search warrant and tells him that SOCO will be carrying out a forensic examination of his flat, "and the basement below," she adds, watching Danny's face for a reaction but there is none, he gives nothing away. Danny says, as far as he knows, nobody uses the basement and that the landlord keeps it locked. She tells him the landlord is there and he's letting SOCO into the basement just as Team 2 enter Danny's flat. Danny had fitted the original locks on the basement doors shortly after his return from Dorset so when the landlord tries his key it works perfectly. DI Haynes tells Danny he's not allowed to remain while SOCO carry out their work and takes him to one of the police vans parked on the road outside his flat. Danny asks where DS Dean is.

"He's… otherwise engaged."

"Really?" says Danny feigning surprise.

"Look, Mr Deacon, I know that you're involved in the kidnap, and the likely murder, of Antoine Blake and his cronies and SOCO will find the evidence to prove it and then I'll arrest you and you'll stand trial for your crimes. Every contact leaves a trace as they say!"

"Look, Detective Inspector Haynes, as they say," begins Danny mimicking the DI, "I know you're just doing your job but you're wasting your time; I haven't done anything and while you're fannying around here, playing politics, the real criminals are laughing at you." DI Haynes knows her colleagues think she's more politician than police officer so Danny's remark stings her. "I heard that you've got a degree in sociology, or something equally useless, and that you're on the fast track to the top while real coppers are doing all the real police work and covering your arse at the same time. It's just like when I was in the army; the grunts do all the fighting and the cunts get all the promotions, as they say. Sorry, I don't usually use bad language, but I'm quoting."

"Oh, you don't have to be concerned about me, Mr Deacon, I've heard every swear word and curse in the book. But as you mentioned the army, why don't we talk about your time in the military?" Danny realises it was a mistake to have mentioned the army as it's given the DI a way in to question him about it. "I showed your military record, such as it is, to some spook friends of mine I was at university with and they say you must've been involved in some pretty nasty operations for your record to be so heavily redacted. I asked them, as a special favour to me, you know, as an old university buddy and all that, whether they could possibly get their hands on the originals for me. They tried and tried but couldn't get hold of them." Despite this casting suspicion on Danny, he remains calm and impassive, just like he'd been trained to be. "Tell me Danny, what the fuck were you involved in? What did you do that was so hush-hush?" the DI hiss-whispers into Danny's ear so no one else could hear; her warm, moist breath sends a shiver down his spine.

"Sorry, ma'am, can't say, Official Secrets Act and all that," Danny replies military fashion and salutes her.

Word flies around Camden that the police are giving some "old geezer's" place a proper turning over and a large crowd quickly gathers outside Danny's flat. They're soon joined by hordes of TV news crews and newspaper reporters. Seeing a crowd gathering, DI Haynes considers arresting Danny but, in her moment of hesitation, he steps from the van and approaches the crowd. He tells the throng that he's a just poor old pensioner who lives all alone whose place is being busted up by the police for no good reason. A BBC TV news reporter asks Danny whether he's under arrest. He says not and says he'd been arrested earlier and then released as there were no charges to face, and what's happening now is nothing more than harassment of an old man who's given the best years of his life in the service of his country. Danny's little speech brings the crowd to the brink of rioting. DI Haynes is just about to arrest him when she receives a call from her boss who orders her to pull SOCO immediately, stop whatever it is she's doing and return to New Scotland Yard ASAP.

After ordering SOCO to stand down, DI Haynes glowers at Danny with pure hatred burning in her eyes. Before she returns to New Scotland Yard, Danny walks up to her and tells her that this "fiasco" she'd orchestrated won't look good on her record and, hopefully, it'll lead to her getting fired so proper coppers can get promoted. *That'll wind her up good and proper!* Several news reporters hear Danny's remarks and ask him what he means. He pulls no punches in telling them that DI Haynes is widely regarded as a politician by her colleagues and she takes credit for their arrests. "When I was at New Scotland Yard the other day, I heard her colleagues say that she's on something called a 'Fast Track', apparently, whatever one of those is," says Danny disingenuously, "and that she's bound to make Detective Chief Superintendent, or maybe even Deputy Commissioner, before she's thirty, when good, honest, hard-working coppers doing proper police work aren't getting promotions. No wonder the police is in the state it's in!" Danny sermonises. He's asked to elaborate and replies by saying it's no secret that the police aren't able to do their jobs properly and it's because those at the top are a bunch of ineffectual self-promoting, self-aggrandising windbag politicians, just like DI Haynes is, and don't care anything about anybody as all they care about is their careers! Danny's comments cause a storm in the newspapers and on prime-time TV news programmes. One red-top headline reads: *Fast Track Cop Skids Out Of Control.*

Watching TV news programmes and reading the newspapers, DS Dean congratulates himself on leaking the raid on Danny's flat to his mates at the BBC as well as arranging for the local rabble to turn up outside Danny's flat to protest about his treatment. *She's fucked!* is DS Dean's thought on DI Haynes' career prospects in the Met, *or anywhere else for that matter.* Thoughts such as these make DS Dean extremely happy.

*

With the police having withdrawn from his flat, Danny goes to The Manor for a celebratory drink. As he enters the pub, bar staff applaud and give him a pint on the house. Twenty minutes later Gaz and Jacko turn up and in celebration of Danny having defeated "the fuzz" buy him a pint. *Two free pints is a good day!* thinks Danny. *Yeah, an alcy would think that!* Ignoring his inner voice, Danny downs three more pints in quick succession. The impromptu party is going well when Alby enters The Manor accompanied by four of what Danny, Gaz, Jacko, the pub's bar staff and patrons think are the four toughest-looking geezers they've seen in a long time. Alby directs Danny to a quiet corner of the pub and demands to know what happened to Tomic and the others. "When I was a kid, my dad told me that if I don't want people to know things then don't tell them!" Danny replies smugly. Alby says he's not interested in homespun philosophy and wants to know what happened to Tomic and his cronies. Given his previous conversation with DS Dean, and suspecting that Alby's a nark, Danny wonders if he's wearing a wire and so pulls him close, hugs him tightly and whispers, "Ask no questions get told no lies." As near as Danny can tell, Alby's not wearing a wire. Realising Danny's patting him down, Alby returns the favour. Both men stare icily at one another before breaking off contact. Right then, their attention is directed to the TV by Alby's heavies; it's a BBC newsflash. Alby shouts to the bar manager to turn up the volume. On screen, a BBC reporter is pointing towards a row of lockup garages beyond yellow police tape. Reading from notes on her mobile phone, she says, into the camera, that this is the closest she can get to the scene where police were called to earlier in the day following a tip-off from a member of the public. "According to locals I've spoken with," says the reporter, "the victims, all males, looked like they'd been tortured. Another witness told me that the bodies looked like they were in the process of being cut up and put into sacks." A police spokeswoman then appears on screen and makes the following statement: "Earlier today, the Metropolitan Police received a call from a member of the public to attend the lockup garages you see behind me. Upon searching the garages, the bodies of four young males were discovered. At this present time, the identities of the deceased are unknown and the Metropolitan Police urge members of the public to come forward with any information they may have concerning this incident. Thank you." The spokeswoman refuses to answer questions put to her by reporters. Suspecting the men's deaths were somehow connected with what he's done, Danny feels it's all getting out of hand, but the moment soon passes.

"That's a turn-up," says Danny as though remarking on an unexpected football result.

"You don't suppose that had anythin' to do with whatever happened to Tomic and his mates do you?" Alby asks disingenuously.

"I doubt it. I mean, why would it, it doesn't make sense and if things don't make sense then they're not right!"

"This is all gettin' out of hand, Danny," says Alby, echoing Danny's thought. "C'mon man, just between you and me," Alby whispers in confidence, "did you have anythin' to do with what happened to Tomic and his gang?"

"I told you, ask no questions get told no lies," Danny repeats to Alby's rising anger and frustration. Alby snorts, as if to say he knows Danny was behind whatever happened to Tomic and his gang. Danny returns Alby's snort while thinking, *you're better off minding your own business!*

With nothing more to discuss, Alby calls his heavies to heel and they leave the pub together; *where are they off to?* Danny would love to know!

*

While Danny's celebrating with his mates in The Manor, DI Haynes is sat waiting outside the DCS' office. It's six thirty before she's called in and, before he can say a word, DI Haynes gets in first.

"Sir, can you please tell me why you pulled the operation? I'm absolutely certain that Danny Dean murdered Antoine Blake, and possibly other gang members too, and I'm just as certain that he carried out the murders in the basement beneath where his flat is and there's evidence to be found there!"

"Quite possibly, quite possibly. However, I received a request, a 'hands-off' request, from," the DCS points to the ceiling before continuing, "I am given to understand it originated from the Security Service at the American Embassy. Please, allow me to continue. The request made it quite clear that any and all investigations into Mr Deacon are to cease forthwith and there are to be no further requests to the MoD, or any other department or agency, concerning Mr Deacon's background, military or otherwise. Do I make myself clear?"

"Yes but…"

"There are no buts DI Haynes and now I have to inform you that you are being promoted to the position of Assistant to the Commissioner, effective immediately. Congratulations, don't let the door hit your arse on your way out. Dismissed."

As the former DI leaves New Scotland Yard to meet up with friends for a champagne and cocaine binge to celebrate her promotion, her phone rings. Not recognising the number, she lets the call go to voicemail. Her phone rings again. It's the same number.

"Hello?" answers the former DI, barely audible.

"It's me," says an old uni buddy.

"Oh it's you! Didn't recognise the number. Got a new phone? Guess what? I got promoted. Fancy meeting up at Gino's for celebratory champers and sniff?"

"That's nice, you get a promotion while I got my fucking arse kicked from one end of the fucking building to the fucking other!"

"What the hell are you on about?"

"Your mate Danny Deacon!"

"You're not making any sense."

"I got cluster-fucked for 'abusing my position' by looking into his military background for you. You owe me a shag!"

"Still not making any sense."

"Seems he's got an angel and some angels can be devils. I'm afraid I'm going to have to give your celebration bash a miss. We won't be seeing one another for a while... like forever."

"You don't mean..."

"What? No! Christ! I mean it's best we forget each other until after lots and lots of people who know what we've done have passed away. Ta ta!"

"Wait a minute Harry, I just..." It was no use, the caller killed the call, or at least the former DI hoped he'd killed it and nothing more serious had happened to him.

*

Before visiting Lucy that evening, Danny goes to the local supermarket to buy a bottle of mouthwash to take away the beer smell from his breath, which it does but leaves behind an odour that says to anyone, *he's been drinking!* When Danny enters Lucy's room, Joyce grabs him by the hand and leads him to the "quiet zone". She asks him if he had anything to do with what's going on. Danny says he doesn't know what she's talking about. "I understand from the police that the people who attacked Lucy have 'disappeared' and now four young men have been found murdered and the news are saying they're the latest victims in a turf war caused by the disappearance of the people suspected of attacking Lucy! Full circle, Danny, full circle that ends up with you!" Danny swears he had nothing to do with any of it. After they return to Lucy's room, they sit either side of her bed and glare at one another across it. Danny looks at Lucy, asks how she's been and squeezes her hand. Lucy squeezes it back. "Joyce... she squeezed my hand! Luce squeezed my hand! She definitely squeezed my hand!" Danny cries ecstatically, disbelievingly. Joyce squeezes Lucy's other hand. She squeezes it back. "She just squeezed my hand too! She's coming out of her coma... she's coming round!" Joyce cries tearfully. "Just let the doctors say this means nothing!" cries Danny manically. Joyce runs and tells a nurse what just happened. She puts out a call for Lucy's consultant, who appears in seconds and whisks Lucy away for tests and a brain scan.

Danny and Joyce wait nervously until the consultant reappears. "I don't want to get your hopes up but... good news, there are signs of increased brain activity as if Lucy is trying to... but, as I said, I don't get your hopes up, there's a long way to go yet!" says the consultant wrapping her arms around Danny's and Joyce's shoulders. "All we have is hope, doc, so if it's all the same to you, we'll get them up!" says Danny, choking back his tears. Joyce can't speak, she just nods in agreement with Danny and they hug one another, their tears mingling as they run down their faces. Danny's phone rings. He looks at the screen. It's DS Dean calling. He sends the call to voicemail. The detective calls again and, once again, Danny sends the call to voicemail. DS Dean sends him a SMS: *Meet me in The Rose & Crown in half an hour. Come alone!!!!!!!!!!*

CHAPTER TWELVE

DS Dean is already at The Rose & Crown when Danny arrives. He's sitting at a table with the same dodgy-looking characters Danny had seen him with previously. As Danny approaches, they pick up their pints and leave. Reaching the table, Danny asks Dean if he's wearing a wire. He says not and asks Danny if he's wearing one. Danny replies not. Being distrustful of one another, they hug as in a greeting to pat one another down. They're both clean.

"I reckon you've done this before," says DS Dean.

"Not really. Funny enough, though, I patted down a mate of yours earlier today." DS Dean not enquiring who Danny was referring to made him think he'd been right all along to suspect Alby of being his snitch.

"Why didn't you take my call?"

"I was visiting Lucy, so I couldn't. So, what do you want?" Danny asks coldly, determined not to sully the good news about Lucy by mentioning it to Dean.

"I was very impressed with the interview you gave to the BBC. Even though you pushed all the right buttons, things didn't work out as I'd planned."

"I didn't do it for you, I did it for myself... for Lucy!" says Danny angrily.

"Tell me, Danny Boy, did you think it was an accident all those journalists turning up at your place?" DS Dean pauses for

Danny to ask what he means but he remains silent. "I wanted to derail Haynes' career or, preferably, get her fired, or maybe even transferred, and now she's the Assistant to the Commissioner so, she gets a promotion instead. That's 'Fast Track' for you, those fuckers can do no wrong! Here," says DS Dean, handing Danny a bundle of documents, "take a gander at this."

"What's this?" asks Danny, suspicious that Dean is setting him up.

"Open it and find out! I'm doing you another favour, though I don't know why!" Danny opens an envelope on top of the pile. It's a forensics report. A quick scan reveals that Tomic's DNA was discovered on two knives found at the scene of the murders of the four young men at the lockup garages in North London. Danny can't understand how that can be. "You look puzzled as if you know that can't be because he's already dead or something! D'ye know Danny, if you're really careful, you can transfer DNA onto virtually anything these days," says the detective. "That's science for you!"

"Why are you showing me this?"

"You're in the clear, Danny. Whoever carried out the murders at the lockups obviously involved Tomic somehow. DNA doesn't lie! Case closed!"

"What do you want me to say?"

"What I really want to know is what you did in the army?" asks Dean.

"Shhhhhhh," says Danny, kissing a finger and then pressing it on Dean's lips. "That sort of information, Detective Sergeant Dean, is on a need-to-know basis and you don't need to know!"

"Well then, why don't you return the favour by telling me what really happened to Tomic and his mates? That I gotta know!"

"Well, what I can tell you is, DNA doesn't lie, so what did SOCO find at my flat or in the basement?"

"You'll never guess, someone destroyed all traces of DNA using something called an Oxy-Active reagent. Ever heard of one of those? Never mind. As for me? Well, it seems some of my 'contacts' aren't as solid as I thought they were and one of them grassed on me for setting DI Haynes up. Maybe that's what got her promoted? Who knows? Anyway, I've been 'advised' to accept early retirement so maybe we'll bump into one another in The Manor or maybe even The Oak… who knows?"

"It's a free country, Deany, you can drink where you like. One thing though, if you do drop by The Manor, do everyone a favour and ignore me and my mates." As Danny leaves The Rose & Crown, the two dodgy-looking characters re-join DS Dean at his table.

Feeling relieved he's out of the frame for anything to do with Tomic, Danny has an urge to tell Chuck, Glenn and Tony about what's gone on. He knows it's risky but he has to let them know that they're all in the clear. That night, Danny posts four coded messages on the veterans' website which, when read in the correct way and in the correct sequence, is a clear message for those who know, and have a need to know, how to read them.

*

It's been six weeks since Danny posted his coded message on the veterans' website. He hadn't received a response but hadn't expected one. Detective Sergeant Dean is retired; he's just plain Paul Dean now. He sent Danny a postcard from Jamaica informing him he's on a month-long cruise around the Caribbean. Unbeknown to Danny or anyone else, that morning, Lucy has woken up out of her coma. She's lying alone in her room because Joyce and Jeff are on their way to the airport for a "much needed" break in Edinburgh. They're staying with Stephanie, Joyce's other daughter, and had left to catch their flight less than an hour ago. Lucy's vision is blurry. She opens her mouth to shout for attention but nothing comes out. She thinks she's dead and has gone to heaven. A junior doctor doing the rounds enters Lucy's room and sees her eyes are open. Lucy turns her head to look at him. He calls for colleagues and they come quickly. A brain scan is carried out. As far as medics can tell, Lucy is fully conscious and in good physical condition, considering she's been in a coma for over two months. While tests are being carried out on her, Lucy tries to speak, but still nothing comes out. She looks around concernedly at the medical staff. "Don't worry," says a nurse, "your voice will return once we take your breathing tube out." Lucy looks at her as if to say, "Take it out then!" which the nurse does. Lucy's consultant asks, "Do you know where you are?" and "Do you remember what happened to you?" Lucy croaks her answers. Unsurprisingly, her voice is weak but the doctors tell her it will soon return to normal.

In Camden, Danny's phone rings. It's Lucy's consultant calling him from the ICU in St Thomas' Hospital. Danny's heart skips a beat and then pounds; he goes light-headed and dizzy and almost passes out. He's expecting the worst. *She's dead, I know she's dead.* "Mr Deacon," says the consultant, "I have some very good news for you, Lucy has come out of her coma..." was all Danny heard before collapsing on the floor in a flood of tears of joy. As soon as he arrives at St Thomas', Danny heads straight to Lucy's room where he's met by a nurse. She tells him that his daughter is being examined at the moment and invites Danny to wait in the family room. He asks about his ex-wife and her husband, "Where are they?" The nurse says she thinks they went away for the weekend and explains they've tried to call them but, so far, haven't been able to contact either of them. Danny's delighted, in a schadenfreude way, that they've been unable to contact his ex, *that'll put the guilts on her for a change*, he thinks and smiles. Wasting no time, Danny calls around the family to let them know about Lucy coming out of her coma. They all have questions but all Danny can tell them is she's undergoing tests, and he's at the hospital and they should come there too. Kelvin and Joey are at St Thomas' within an hour. Danny's phone rings. It's Joyce. She's crying. He can't make out many words but "miracle" and "our baby girl," come out loud and clear which makes him cry too. *It is a miracle and if I've ever taken my little girl for granted I swear I'll never take her for granted ever again!* Danny's aware that this is the type of thing people say at times like this, but he doesn't care, he just hopes he can live up to the vow he's made.

The following day, the entire family, including Stephanie, are gathered in Lucy's room. Having been told not to overwhelm her, they sit quietly around her bed, saying little, stroking her hair and smiling a lot. Despite having slept for over two months, Lucy is exhausted and constantly drifts off to sleep. As she sleeps, she mutters things from her childhood which everyone thinks must be a good sign but her lack of movement and poor speech is concerning to them all. They ask the doctors about it and are told, "It's early days yet but the signs are good from the tests we've carried out. We'll continue monitoring her progress but don't expect too much too soon."

Over the following three weeks, Lucy makes slow progress, but she's out of danger at least. Having done their brotherly duty, Kelvin and Joey return to Bristol, and Joyce and Jeff return home, though Stephanie returned to Edinburgh two weeks ago after receiving a call informing her that her BF is putting himself about.

*

While Lucy continues her recovery, Brad stays with his dad but knows he'll have to head back to Leeds shortly, otherwise he'll lose his job. He and Danny visit Lucy twice every day and, with Brad's help, Danny's virtually stopped drinking, much to everyone's relief, including his. One Thursday, Brad gets a call from his boss telling him he has to be back at work at eight o'clock on Monday or he's lost his job. Brad tells Danny he has to go back to Leeds as he can't afford to get fired. Danny, thinking he won't be seeing his son for a while, says they should have a few beers and a takeaway; Brad agrees so long as it's not a "Beano".

While chomping on their takeaways, Brad, out of the blue, asks, "Have you heard anything from that copper, Dean?" Danny says not and asks him why he'd asked. "I was just thinking; it seems strange to me that he did what he did and wanted nothing in return. He didn't strike me as that sort of bloke. Why d'ye think he done it?" Danny says he has no idea but then a thought occurs to him. "He'd been after Tomic for years. I think it got to him. He was obsessed and, even though he doesn't know for sure what happened, I think he's glad he got what was coming to him." Danny's answer satisfies them both, despite it being miles from the truth.

That Saturday morning, as Brad is due to depart shortly, Danny insists they go to The Manor for a few pints followed by an afternoon in front of the TV watching the footy scores roll in and place a few bets, "I'd like a day of doing the stuff we used to do," he says, reviving memories of good times in them both. As Danny and Brad enter The Manor, they receive an ironic cheer from the regulars followed by shouts of, "Get 'em in moneybags," from Gaz and Jacko. Danny says he's skint but they don't believe him. "You haven't been in for weeks, you must be rolling in it!" banters Jacko. Danny's missed his drinking buddies and gives them both a hug. "What, no hug for me?" says a voice behind him. He turns to find Alby standing there with a couple of guys he recognises from The Oak. "Yeah, we drink in here sometimes," says Alby. "Regulars, more like," says Jacko, handing Danny and Brad their pints. "Cheers!" says Gaz, "Good to see you," says Alby, raising his glass to Danny. "How's Lucy? Recoverin' well?" Danny tells him it's slow but there's progress. Just then, old Mrs Gray comes in the pub. She looks pale and worried. The barman asks what's up. "I got my cat'lic converter stolen from under my car last night," she says miserably. She knows full well it's a catalytic converter but calls it a cat'lic converter because she thinks it sounds funny. The barman hands her a whisky on the house.

"They took six last night, they did. Six! Just from my street. I heard they took about ten more from the flats! Something needs to be done about them!"

"There's a lot of catalytic converters being nicked all over the place," says Alby, sounding knowledgeable on the subject.

"Yeah, that Detective Sergeant Dean says it's the next big thing in thievery," says Gaz.

"How do you know what he says?" Danny asks.

"Yeah, he comes in here quite a lot… especially since he came back from that cruise he went on."

"What's he doing hanging around here?" asks Danny.

"No idea."

"He was asking after you, actually," says Alby, implying there's something going on between them.

"Well, I've got nothing to say to him. C'mon, son, let's go."

Once outside the pub, Danny speculates why the former Detective Sergeant has been asking after him. Brad says he's always had a bad feeling about Dean and advises his dad to have nothing more to do with him. "You've no need to worry on that score, son, I've got no intention of having anything to do with him ever!" As they wander off back to Danny's flat, Brad carries on talking about catalytic converter thefts. "Why do they steal them?" Danny asks. "Simple, they've got precious metals like platinum in them, especially older types like the Prius. It's big business and replacing one costs a fortune… like fifteen hundred quid or something!" replies Brad. Danny's appalled. It goes against his sense of justice that ordinary people are being robbed and having to fork out such large sums of money to get their cars fixed. "Hey Dad, I've seen that look in your eyes before. Keep your nose out! It's nothing to do with you!" says Brad. "Do you know son, when me and the lads sorted out Tomic and his cronies, we felt alive, like we were doing something useful, worthwhile. We felt like we used to when we were in the army," says Danny passionately. Brad tells him to find another way to get his kicks. Danny smiles and says he'll take up knitting.

Following his arrest, whenever Danny and Brad are in the flat, they're careful what they talk about in case the place is bugged. Despite them believing they're off the hook for murdering Tomic and his cronies, neither would put it past the police to plant a couple of bugs, as they're so small and easy to hide. Thinking about what Mrs Gray had said in the pub, Danny asks Brad if he knows anything else about catalytic converter thieves. Brad reluctantly tells him all he knows, which isn't much, and, once again, warns his dad not to get involved, "Don't do anything stupid. These people don't mess around. They even steal them in broad daylight and don't care who sees them. If anybody gets involved they use violence on them. They even stop traffic on main roads to steal them for Christ's sake so they won't think twice about doing you in if you get in their way!" Danny says he's just interested in the topic, that's all, and might call Dean to find out what the police are doing about it. Infuriated, Brad drags Danny out of the flat to speak openly with him and says, once again, that he's never trusted Dean and for Danny to keep well away from him, "Once a copper always a copper!" whispers Brad, careful not to speak too loud in case the whole place is bugged. "Do you think, for one minute, that if Dean finds out what really happened to... you know... he won't... you know?" mouths Brad. Danny tells him he worries too much. "Remember," he whispers back, "it's like I always say, keep your friends close and your enemies closer. I'll be alright son, don't worry. Besides, you never know, Deany might let something slip about... you know... things!" Realising his dad will do exactly as he chooses, Brad gives up, says goodnight, and goes to bed. Next morning he leaves for Leeds without saying goodbye to Danny which hurts him but it doesn't change his mind.

*

Four more weeks pass before Lucy has recovered sufficiently to be discharged from St Thomas'. To keep the promise he'd made to himself, Danny says he'll drive her home. Joyce asks if he's still driving his tatty old van. He says he is but will hire a car for the journey, "Can't have our Luce being thrown about in my old van, can we?" he adds chirpily. Joyce says she and Jeff should drive Lucy home in their BMW, "It'll be much safer and better for her, much more comfortable." Danny insists he'll drive Lucy home, "I really want to do it," he adds. Joyce relents but, knowing how broke Danny is, says if anything changes he's to let her know. Danny knows what she means and thanks her but says it'll be okay. They reach out and stroke one another's arms like they used to when they were married and, again, Danny realises how much he misses the warm touch of a woman.

The drive to Birmingham is free of traffic jams and uneventful. During the journey, Danny and Lucy talk about anything and everything under the sun. They haven't ever done such a long drive together, just the two of them, since Lucy was a child. "Is this what it's like when you and Brad are in the car together?" Lucy asks. Thinking of past road-trips with his son, Danny smiles and says, "Yeah… it was especially fun if we were driving on a Saturday afternoon. We'd tune into local radio stations along the way and listen to football matches. If we were on a long journey, we'd listen to footy commentary for hours and hours." Lucy feels a pang of jealousy having missed out on road-trips with her dad and says as much. "You were always busy with your mum or doing horsey stuff… but I'd pick you up from the stables sometimes… remember?" Lucy says she does and that she'd like to go back to that time and tell him to take the long way home so they could listen to the radio together. They laugh at this and Danny affectionately ruffles Lucy's hair like he did when she was a child. She hated it back then. "I remember you used to do that to me when I was a little girl," she says grimacing. "But I loved it when you ruffled my hair while I was lying in the hospital, it gave me hope," Lucy adds in a strange, distant, ethereal way. Danny's shocked by what Lucy said and asks her what she means. "It was weird. While I was in the ICU, I knew when people were there… you know, when they were speaking to me. I could sometimes hear them, not always clearly, and I wanted to speak back to them but I couldn't… sorry, Dad, can we stop chatting for a moment, I'm not feeling up to it." Danny wants Lucy to tell him whether she'd heard him speaking to her but she closes her eyes, leans her head back and pretends to be asleep, so he leaves her to rest.

Lucy wakes up just as they arrive at her home. Her children are stood by the front door waiting for her and they rush to greet their mother, wrapping their arms around her as soon as the car door opens. They're sobbing, which starts Lucy sobbing. Encircling her children with her arms, Lucy tells them how much she loves them and has missed them, and they tell her how much they love and have missed her too. Danny leaves them to their tearful reunion and goes inside the house to check on arrangements. Unbeknown to Lucy, he's organised for all the family to be there to welcome her home. They're all there; Joyce, Jeff, Kelvin, Joey, Stephanie and Brad, along with their partners and spouses.

Corks pop and champagne flows like water at the welcome home party and, just as it's winding down, Danny, his threshold for alcohol diminished due to his recent abstinence, pontificates about those who mugged Lucy going missing, saying that whatever happened to them they deserved and was made necessary by a system that is broken. Brad wants his dad to stop talking but he's pushed away by him. "The police can't do anything, the courts can't do anything and even if they get caught they get away with a slap on the wrist or some smart-mouth lawyer gets them off altogether! There's no such thing as justice anymore! Nobody tells the truth anymore! Nobody is guilty anymore! Lawyers tell their clients to say 'no comment' to everything in case it 'harms their defence'! How can telling the truth be harmful? They're a bloody disgrace! They're as bad as the criminals they defend. It's all just a bloody game to get away with whatever you can!" Danny's words anger Kelvin and Joey as each firmly believes that it must be left to the police to fight crime otherwise society will collapse and chaos would reign in its place, "And then where would we be? Hey? I'll tell you where we'd be, shall I, Dad?" spouts Kelvin with his trademark pompousness, "We'd all be held in the grip of whoever wields the biggest club, that's where we'd be!" Danny scoffs at Kelvin's assertion, saying that local people and their communities are in a better position than the police or the courts to deal with crime. "Don't be ridiculous,

Dad," cries Joey, "If that were the case then why don't communities rise up against the criminals and gangs who make their lives hell?" With his recent experiences of the estate where Lucy was attacked, Danny has no answer. Brad, of course, comes down on Danny's side, telling everyone he agrees with his dad because ordinary, everyday people are sick and tired of criminals getting away with their crimes and something has to be done about it, and if that something means people taking the law into their own hands then so be it! Brad's remarks enrage Kelvin. "Oh, you agree with Dad, do you? No surprise there!" sneers Kelvin, who then ridicules Danny by reminding everyone about how enraged he'd get with those who parked on yellow lines or in disabled spaces or used fake parking permits. "Remember when he had that dicky-fit in the Tesco car park?" he adds, fake-laughing his head off. Joey reminds everyone of the superhero costume Danny got Brad for his eighth birthday, "Tell you what, Dad, you should get one for yourself," he adds mocking his father, "you'd make a great 'Masked Avenger', you would; I can just see you sorting out crime in Camden! No, seriously, Dad, you'd be great at it!" he adds, laughing out loud. Danny takes exception to Joey's remarks but keeps his cool. Kelvin takes up where Joey left off. "Tell you what, Dad, as you're retired, and have so much time on your hands, I have to say I agree with Joey, you should give the old 'Masked Avenger' a go. I mean, other than drinking, what else do you do?" he adds snidely. Though Kelvin's remarks further infuriate Danny, he maintains his cool because, as far as he's concerned, Kelvin and Joey are behaving just as disparagingly and being judgemental of him as they've always been. Things are about to kick off with Brad grabbing Kelvin by the throat when Lucy steps in on Danny's side, telling her brothers they've gone too far and they should show their father some respect and apologise to him for their behaviour. "That bang on the head she got must've loosened something," Kelvin whispers to Joey. Lucy hears this and gives him a daggers look which elicits a rare apology from him.

With the welcome home party at an end, Lucy and her children stand at the front door waving off family, well-wishers and friends. Just as Danny is about to depart, Lucy whispers, telling him to remain.

"Are you sure?" asks Danny. "I'd love to stay but…"

"Is there anything you need to go off back to London for?" Lucy asks.

"To be honest, I haven't, to tell the truth," admits Danny.

"Then why don't you stay for a couple of days? I need looking after and who better to look after me than my daddy?"

"Wouldn't you rather your mum look after you?"

"Nope, I'd rather have you; besides, Jeff is a bit of a drip, he bores the arse off me and everyone else to be honest. C'mon, Dad, say you'll stay, it'd be great to spend some time with you," Lucy says, hugging her dad and nuzzling her head into his chest the way she did when she was a child.

"Okay I'll stay, but if you get fed up with me don't be afraid to…"

"Don't worry, I'll even pack your bags for you!"

*

With their mum home from hospital, Lucy's children are expecting to have a couple of days off school to spend time with her, but she won't hear of it and packs them all off before Danny is out of bed. After breakfast, she and Danny take the dogs for a walk in the fields down by the river. They chat all the way. Lucy's speech is improving but isn't one hundred percent, and she's still feeling weak, so, following Danny's advice, which is unusual for Lucy, they head home. When they arrive, Lucy's ex-husband, Simon, is waiting on the doorstep. She asks him why he's there and what he wants. He says he visited her while she was in the ICU and now that she's home, he wants to make sure she's okay. She asks why he went all the way to St Thomas' in London when he couldn't drive ten miles for their son's recital. He says he was scared she was going to die and wanted her to know about the arrangements he'd made for the children should the worst have happened. "I told you, so, somehow, you'd know the children would be looked after if… you know," says Simon, holding his arms open for Lucy to give him a hug. Instead, she asks about the arrangements. He tells her all about them and, to keep the children settled, he'd have moved back into the former family home. "And you told me all this while I was lying in a coma?" Simon says, "That's correct." "Was anyone else there with you?" Lucy asks. "No… just me," Simon replies stiffly. "When was this exactly? Was it in the morning or the afternoon or what?" Lucy asks. "It was in the early hours actually. I drove down after work and… Why are you acting this way?" Simon asks, acting hurt by Lucy questioning him. "Well, for starters, no visitors were allowed after eleven so how could you have…" Lucy lets Simon complete the question in his head. "The nurse said, as I'd come so far, she'd bend the rules just that once," Simon replies confidently. "Funny, other people came from much further afield but they weren't allowed to visit after curfew," Lucy answers coldly. "Look, Luce darling, I've not come for an argument, I was genuinely concerned about you, okay?" Simon says, trying to divert the conversation. "But you didn't visit me though, did you? You didn't sit at my bedside. You didn't say anything because if you had I'd've remembered," says Lucy. Simon asks her what she means. She tells him all the while she was lying in a coma she heard every word spoken to her and quotes things that Brad, Kelvin and Joey had said sitting at her bedside. As Lucy speaks, she looks towards her father, holding him in her gaze. He knows that her look means she'd heard every word he'd spoken to her while she was lying in a coma. "Look, Simon, I know what this is about. You want to know whether or not I'll be able to carry on with the business and run the house and look after the kids and the million other things I do, but not out of concern for me! No! You want to take everything; the house, the business, the kids… everything! You're probably pissed off I survived and not only survived I'm actually doing well and with my dad here everything's going to be… fine. Now, get in your car and get lost!" Realising the gig is up, Simon turns and leaves. He doesn't even say goodbye or ask about the children.

"Is he still with… you know… your friend… what's-her-name?" says Danny, trying to be delicate but making his usual mess of it.

"Don't know, don't care… but, yes he is. Just before I went to London, I heard from Steph that she's pregnant. Bastards. Bastards, both."

"You're better off without him, love. You've done so well on your own… c'mon, Luce, darling, don't cry."

"I can't help it, Dad. Sometimes I just wish things had worked out differently, that's all. We were happy. We were happy. What went wrong? Was it me? Did I… and now look at me! Bringing up four children alone and not even the least sign of a man on the horizon. As soon as they find out you've got a bunch of kids they can't get away fast enough!"

"I know, Luce, I know. When you were a little girl it was my job to protect you, but now? I feel so helpless. It kills me watching you going through… and when you got attacked, I felt like killing someone!"

"But, Dad, you did kill someone. You killed those bastards who attacked me! Don't look at me like that all innocent! I heard every word you said when you visited me and I've got a memory like an elephant so don't you try and fool me. We need to talk before the kids get home."

"So… how much do you remember of what I said?"

"Everything!"

"You not conning me are you?"

"Moi?" says Lucy, feigning indignation. "I could never con you Daddy," she adds with a coy smile. They both laugh in the knowledge of how she's always found it easy to manipulate her father. "I remember when you were in the army and we lived abroad. Everything was great… well, not great, but we were happy. We lived in nice houses and had lots of friends. But everything changed after you left the army and you had to make your own way in the world. You had terrible jobs, one after another! I actually felt ashamed of you. I used to think you were… a failure, but I didn't know about Vietnam."

"Luce, listen, you must never ever breathe a word about Vietnam to anyone ever. If… if… if it gets out that you know about what happened there it'll be over for everyone! Everyone! All of us. You, me, the boys, your mum… my oppos… everyone!"

"I know, you told me! Remember? Look, Dad, there's no point going over what you said, but I want to let you know that when you were telling me about Vietnam, and what you and your 'oppos' were up to, you sounded alive! Like you had a reason for living!"

"Yeah, it wasn't easy going from what I did to delivering letters!" jokes Danny. "The things we did in Vietnam were dangerous but they were exciting too! It was like a drug and after it was over I missed it. Look Luce, I don't want to sound mad or anything but if the government, theirs or ours, or the Secret Service or the CIA, or probably even MI6, ever get wind of what we did to Tomic and his mates it'll be all over for us so keep schtum about it."

"If what you told me is true it doesn't sound mad and, for what it's worth, I don't have a problem with what you did to the bastards that attacked me!" *That's my girl.*

"You know, Luce, it was great, really great, to be doing something exciting, something worthwhile, instead of putting up shelves for your mates or doing a bit of painting and decorating!"

"I understand," says Lucy, holding her dad's hand. "To be frank, when you told me about 'offing' Tomic and the others you sounded so matter-of-fact, deflated almost… probably because it was all over." Lucy notices a furtive look in her dad's eyes as she says this. "It is all over isn't it Dad?" she asks. "You're not going after the ones that got away, are you? Don't do it Dad. That'd be pushing your luck!"

"You should've seen us in Vietnam, Luce! We were unstoppable! We did all sorts of things, bonkers things!"

"I know, you told me! Remember? Are you feeling alright Dad?" Lucy asks, concerned by her father's change in demeanour. Danny waves her concern away. "I can't imagine being in situations like you were in and then having to lead an ordinary life. It must've been hard for you... drove you crazy!"

"To be honest, Luce, since we.... you know... did what we did, I've got a taste for it!"

"Now you're worrying me. What's going on, Dad? What're you up to?"

"I was drinking in The Manor with a couple of mates a few days before I came up here when old Mrs Gray comes in and tells everyone that her catalytic converter got nicked from under her car; she reckoned more than a dozen went that night apparently. I felt bad for her and all those that had to replace them... a grand and half each they cost! Anyway, the copper who investigated your case, Detective Sergeant Dean, he's retired now, he goes in The Manor occasionally and he left a message saying he wanted a word with me. Brad's always told me to stay away from him but we speak on the Q.T. He says he knows who's thieving the catalytic converters and, if I'm interested, we can stake out a few roads, do a bit of surveillance, and get them nicked by the local police. Went like a charm it did. Cops got them all, every last one of them, and they're off to court!"

"That's amazing, Dad, amazing! But you need to be careful, these people are dangerous!"

"Gave me a buzz it did. Anyway, Deany and I are thinking about doing more things together."

"That sounds a bit dodgy but if you got a buzz out of it then go for it. It needs to be something proper, though, maybe some kind of security consultant? I can hook you up with a couple of contacts if you're interested?!"

"That's not a bad idea Luce," says Danny not meaning it, "though I don't know about being 'proper' if it means starting a company and all that; don't fancy the paperwork! I'm not much at sitting behind a desk either, I need to be where the action is!"

"But no going after the ones that got away! Okay!"

"Okay Luce. Now, before the kids get back we have to speak, this is important, I want you to promise me you'll never ever mention anything that I said while you were in hospital to anyone. It's literally a death sentence if you do!" For the remainder of his stay, Danny and Lucy don't talk about what he'd said to her while she was in a coma.

As Danny's preparing to return to London, he hugs Lucy and says to her he's had the best time that he's had in years and promises to visit often. He meant it when he said it but they both know he probably won't make it up to Birmingham more than once or twice a year.

CHAPTER THIRTEEN

On his return to London, Danny arranges to meet with former Detective Sergeant Dean.

"How's your daughter doing?" Dean asks.

"Good. Really good, really good. By the time I left her you'd hardly have guessed she'd been in a coma. How'd it go with the catalytic converter gang?" asks Danny, desperate for news of their work.

"They all coughed for it so it'll just be a sentencing hearing. They'll get credit for pleading guilty."

"What do you reckon they'll get?" Danny asks eagerly, rubbing his hands together.

"Depends. They've got themselves a right smart-arse lawyer. Very expensive! He'll plead extenuating and mitigating circumstances, et cetera, and if the judge is lenient they could get off with a fine and maybe a bit of probation because none of them has a criminal record and haven't been in trouble with the police before. That doesn't mean they haven't been at it, it just means they've never been caught before."

"That's bloody ridiculous!" cries Danny, furious at the idea of violent offenders practically getting off scot-free.

"That's the way it goes, Danny, that's the way it goes. I've told you before, I'm actually all for criminals getting a discount off their sentences so long as they plead guilty in the first twenty-four hours. Saves the police loads of time investigating that can be used to convict more criminals! What winds me up, though, is these cunts who go 'no comment'. Yeah, sure, it's their right and all that but it wastes so much police time. It's their right to go 'no comment' but they should have to pay for the privilege… say fifty percent added to their sentences if they're found guilty. Same if they go not guilty. The amount of time police waste scurrying around trying to find bits of evidence while they just sit there with smug grins on their smug faces! But what really, really, really winds me up though are the ones that go 'no comment', plead not guilty, and then, when the case comes to trial, change their plea to guilty! They should get fifty percent added to their sentence for being cunts!"

"Yeah… I think you've mentioned something like that before," says Danny, knowing full well he's heard it all before. "The law's mad and the courts are too soft but none of this helps to put those scumbag catalytic converter gangsters behind bars!"

"You're right," agrees Dean. "Maybe we should do something about them ourselves? Y'know, dish them out some homespun justice maybe?" he suggests.

"Not sure about that," says Danny. "I promised my daughter I'd keep my nose clean."

"What do you mean, 'keep your nose clean'? Clean from what? You didn't tell her what you did to Tomic and his mates did you?" Dean asks concernedly. Danny realises he's said too much.

"Who said I'd done anything to them?" Danny asks innocently.

"Ever heard of a loan shark called Devo?" Dean asks out of the blue.

"Of course I've heard of him, everyone has, but that's as far as it goes. I've never had anything to do with him myself but I've heard he's a right nasty piece of work."

"He is… he is, but I mention him for a reason," says the former DS.

"Oh yeah, what reason's that?" Danny asks, playing along.

"He's a vicious thug who brings misery to thousands of people and uses violence if they don't keep up with payments. But no one's prepared to make a statement against him so the police are powerless to do anything. Sound familiar?"

"Just like when Luce was mugged!" says Danny pointedly.

"Right. I mentioned Devo because your mates, Jacko and Gaz, took out loans from him and from what I heard they can't keep up with the payments and are due a hiding."

"What! We should have a word with them, tell them to go to the police."

"I already tried having a word with them but they told me they're too scared to go to the police. Besides, if they do they'll get labelled as grasses and… well, you know what happens to grasses on estates!"

"Why are you telling me this?"

"We sorted out the catalytic converter toe-rags and we can do the same to Devo and his gang of wankers!" Danny's not sure about this as he doesn't have the same feeling he had with Tomic and his gang.

"It won't hurt to have a word with Jacko and Gaz, I suppose," says Danny.

*

When Danny and Dean enter The Manor, they go straight over to Gaz and Jacko and Danny tells them he knows they've taken out a loan from Devo and can't make the repayments. They ask how he knows and Danny tells them. They're furious with Dean, saying to him that they told him in confidence and expected him to keep it secret. Danny asks Jacko and Gaz how come they hadn't mentioned anything to him about taking out the loan but had told Dean. They tell him they were afraid to because they, and everyone, think he's behind the disappearances of Tomic and his gang and didn't want things to get out of hand. "Okay, just for the record, it was me that was behind Tomic and his cronies getting disappeared but that's a completely different thing, that was family!" Jacko and Gaz are shocked and horrified by Danny's confession but Dean's delighted by it. *I knew it, I knew you'd done them, I knew it!* Now, all Danny wants to do is help Jacko and Gaz out, "You know I haven't got much but I could lend you a bit of money to give you a bit of breathing space. How much do you owe?" Jacko and Gaz tell Danny it started off at six grand and now it's over double. Jacko says the debt collectors have visited and told him that if he doesn't start making payments, or if he goes to the police, they'll firebomb his house. Gaz says he's been told the same, "But I don't think they'd do it, I think they'll just give us a kicking," he adds, like it's to be expected. Danny tells them they have to go to the police and make a statement but they say that's out of the question. "Even if we made statements and they get arrested, so what? They'll get out on bail and even if they get jail-time they'll be back on the streets in a couple of months and then what? I'll tell you 'then what', we're dead, that's what!" Danny asks what they wanted the money for. They tell him it's too embarrassing to talk about. He jokes about doing a bank job to pay Devo off. They say they've already thought about it. After downing their drinks, Danny and Dean leave the pub.

Making their way to Dean's car, he says to Danny, "To all intents and purposes, Mr Deacon, you just confessed, in the presence of two witnesses and a former Detective Sergeant, that you murdered Tomic and his mates." Danny says he admitted no such thing. "C'mon, Danny, tell me where their bodies are. I know you buried them somewhere in Dorset, but where?" Dean presses. Danny asks why he wants to know. "Well, as I mentioned before, DNA can be transferred onto all sorts of things like we did on the knives in the murders at the lockup garages." Danny asks Dean who the "we" is. "Look, Danny, we're in this together, you and me, so tell me where the bodies are." Danny doesn't answer but he's beginning to comprehend how determined Dean is to get hold of Tomic's DNA. *What do you want it for? What are you going to do with it? I bet you'll* use it to fit me up! *Don't be stupid*, snaps his inner voice, *if he was going to fit you up he'd've already done it!* Danny agrees with the inner dialogue. The real reason the former DS wants Tomic's DNA is simple: he needs it to cover up past misdeeds, including a murder for which he remains the prime suspect.

Danny changes the subject from "where's Tomic buried" to Gaz and Jacko owing Devo a small fortune. "I couldn't stand it if anything happened to those two wallies!" he says. "There's no need for anything to happen to them if you tell me where the bodies are," says Dean, bringing the topic back round. "If you do, I'll use Tomic's DNA to fit Devo and his gang up!" Danny asks if there's another way to help Gaz and Jacko out of their predicament. "I'm already in as far as I can go," says the former DS. Danny doesn't really understand what he means but doesn't pursue it. "Tell you what, let's team up like we did for the catalytic converter gang. We'll carry out surveillance on Devo and call the cops in when he does something illegal!" suggests Danny. "Not a bad idea, not a bad idea at all. After he's arrested, the police'll turn his gaff over and if they find DNA evidence of something like, say, a murder, how much better would that be?" says Dean. Danny says he wants no part in planting evidence, to which Dean claims he was only kidding. "Tell you what, let's start with surveillance on Devo, for Gaz and Jacko's sakes, and see where it goes from there," says Dean. Danny reluctantly agrees.

*

The following day, Danny and Dean are sat in Dean's car waiting on one of Devo's money-collecting rounds, intending to gather video evidence against him. After four days of this they're nowhere, as only his heavies show up to collect payments. "I reckon Devo doesn't want to get his hands dirty," says Dean. "With you being in the Met for umpteen years, I'd've thought you'd've known that!" says Danny accusingly. Dean tells him that Devo always collected the money personally, which is a lie.

"Can I ask you something?" says Dean.

"Depends," says Danny, with Brad's words of warning ringing inside his head.

"C'mon, Danny, don't be like that! You need to remember what I've done for you! If I'd've wanted to I could've had you arrested but I didn't. Instead, I tampered with DNA and ANPR evidence so's you wouldn't get nicked! Now, tell me, do you trust me or not!"

"I don't not trust you," Danny answers cryptically.

"That'll have to do I suppose," Dean says acidly. "Look, to help Jacko and Gaz, we've got to flush Devo out into the open. Agreed?" Danny nods. "Okay… but if you don't like my idea say so because it'll be dangerous, especially for you!" says Dean.

"Dangerous in what way?" Danny asks.

"You need to get a loan from Devo."

"Why? What for?"

"Hear me out, just hear me out, okay?" pleads Dean. "I did something similar before and it worked out great. The details aren't important but, trust me, I know what I'm doing!"

"You wonder why people don't trust coppers!"

"Look, Danny, as a former military man, you know there are times when it's necessary to adopt 'creative' tactics and this is one of those times! Do you think Jacko and Gaz can pay off their debts? Of course they can't! How long do you think it'll be before they get a visit from Devo's boys and they get busted up?" Danny makes no reply. "Then just be quiet for a minute and listen to my plan!"

"Okay, but I make no promises!"

"You borrow five hundred from Devo. Then, when his heavies come to collect, you refuse to pay any of it back. Any of it! Devo has to put in an appearance, or he'll lose face, and we'll have the evidence we need to bust him. It's a simple plan so there's not much to go wrong! Okay?"

"If for some reason things don't go according to plan, what then?"

"If things don't work out for whatever reason, I'll pay the five hundred off for you. Fair enough?"

"Hang on though," interjects Danny, "as Devo doesn't get involved in collecting money, what makes you think he'll put in an appearance if I don't pay up?"

"As I said, he has to show up to save face. If someone doesn't pay on purpose, like you won't, he can't afford to have that sort of thing known around Camden or others might take it into their heads to refuse to pay up too. See?"

"Yeah, I'm not sure. If I was him, I'd just send my heavies to pay me a visit. Why would Devo show up for a poxy five hundred quid?"

"It's not the amount that matters, it's the principle of the thing that matters to people like him! Five hundred quid's fuck all but if lots of people stop paying then it's a problem, a big problem, for Devo because he's got debts too and they have to be paid!" says Dean lying through his teeth.

"I still don't see…"

"Look… when the heavies show up, you tell them to piss off and don't come back because you're not paying them a penny. That'll get Devo around to your place on the hurry up, you'll see. When he comes round, we'll have it on CCTV! Simple!"

"I'm not liking this, Deany, I'm not liking it one little bit. It sounds… sketchy."

"Look, Danny, just say if you don't want to do it but make your mind up quick because time's running out for Jacko and Gaz!"

Danny eventually agrees to go along with Dean's plan and calls Brad as soon as he gets home to tell him about it. Brad goes ballistic, telling him he's all kinds of a fool to trust Dean. Danny says he knows what he's doing. "In that case, Dad, why are you calling me?" Brad asks. "Insurance, son, insurance," Danny replies. The father and son discuss various scenarios and at the end of their discussion, the father tells the son that if things go bad then he's to go to The Oak pub, near where Lucy was mugged, and tell Alby what's going on.

The next day, Danny goes to The Manor to get the latest from Gaz and Jacko. They've both had a visit and been given until the end of the week to make a payment, otherwise arms will get broken. Danny asks if they're able to pay up. They say no. "Tell you what, I'll take out a loan, say a monkey, and you can use it to keep Devo off your backs," says Danny. Thinking only of themselves, they ask what'll happen after the money runs out as they won't be able to make further payments. "We'll worry about that when the time comes," says Danny. "Who are you getting the loan from?" asks Gaz. "Devo," replies Danny casually. They tell him he's crazy but Danny tells them not to worry, "It'll all get sorted," he says confidently. Given Danny's "admission" about Tomic, they're worried what he means by "sorted" but are relieved that their arms won't get broken, not for a while at least.

"Hi... a couple of mates gave me this number to call to get a loan," says Danny.

"How much you arter?" a male asks abruptly.

"A monkey... five hundred."

"I know what a fuckin' monkey is you muppet!" says the man. "Who put you onto us?"

"Jacko and Gaz."

"Never 'eard of them. Who else you know?"

"They said I could get the monkey with no questions asked and here's you asking questions!"

"Oaky, Mr Smartmout'," the man says, "listen up, a monkey's gonna cost you a couple of ponies a week. Do you want it?"

"Yes."

"Whereabouts are you?"

"Camden."

"What's your name?"

"Danny, Danny Deacon."

"Well Danny Deacon, go to the back of Camden Town tube at eight and no more fuckin' cheek! Bring something wid your name and address on it and you better not be connin'! Things happen to people who con! My man'll bring the money and tell you about payments!" The call abruptly ends. Danny's positive it was Devo he'd been speaking to.

*

Danny is behind Camden Town tube by eight. A heavy-set man approaches and asks his name. *I could take you easy*, thinks Danny optimistically. "Danny, Danny Deacon," he says. "Got some ID?" the man asks. Danny shows him his OAP bus pass and a council tax bill. "Good enough. I'm the tallyman, here's the money. Be home every Friday at eight and have my money ready, it's fifty a week! Okay! No messin' around, it's fifty! Not ten or twenty... fifty! An' no missin' payments! Got it?" Danny says he's got it, and after the tallyman leaves, goes to The Manor to meet Gaz and Jacko. As they see him enter the bar, they feel ashamed and yet relieved. Danny hands them half the money each and says, "That should keep Devo off your backs for a while." They pretend they're reluctant to take the money but when Danny forces it into their hands it quickly disappears into their pockets. "Thanks Danny," says Gaz quietly. "Yeah, thanks Danny, we won't forget this," says Jacko, his voice barely audible. "What about you?" asks Jacko. "Have you got enough coming in to make the payments?" asks Gaz. *It's a bit late to be thinking about that now*, thinks Danny. "Yeah, are you going to be alright?" asks Jacko. Danny tells them not to worry, it's all going to be okay.

It's eight o'clock on Friday and Danny's first payment is due. He's been in constant contact with Jacko and Gaz during the week to make sure everything's okay. His attention puzzles them and they asked him what's going on. Danny tells them not to worry about it and that their debts will soon be things of the past which, while deepening their suspicions about him, satisfies them so they ask nothing further. A knock comes on the door to Danny's flat.

Switching on his body-worn camera, which Dean supplied, Danny opens the door. He recognises the tallyman.

"What's that fucking smell man?" the tallyman asks, almost retching.

"Yeah, it's been like that since before I moved in. I think it's getting worse. You get used to it after a while. Anyway, what can I do you for sausage?" Danny asks, planting himself in the doorframe to keep the tallyman in shot of the CCTV camera pointing at them from the far end of the hall.

"What! You 'avin' a fuckin' larf you fuckin' Muppet?" yells the tallyman. "You are Danny Deacon an't you?" he asks to make certain.

"I am," replies Danny casually. "And what?"

"And what! And fuckin' what! It's fuckin' Friday, payday, granddad, and I'm here to collect a pair of fuckin' ponies on account of you borrowing a fuckin' monkey you old cunt!"

"Hey! Whoa there! Take it easy! Less of the old thank you!" Danny jokes.

"Funny guy!" snarls the tallyman. "Well, grandad, let's see how funny you think it is getting your fuckin' face smashed in!"

The tallyman darts towards Danny, who steps forward and stamps down hard on the inside of the tallyman's right leg, shattering his kneecap. With the tallyman rolling around on the floor in agony, Danny closes his front door and wipes the CCTV of the attack as it's evidence he doesn't want to keep. He then sits and waits to see what'll happen next. Twenty minutes later, Danny detects shuffling sounds in the hall outside his flat, followed by four heavy thumps hammering on his door. "Who is it?" Danny calls out. A voice answers, saying, "Never fucking mind who it is... we've come to collect fifty notes and give you a talking to about what you did to Simmo!" Danny knows what this type of talking to involves and tells the man it's late and he needs to call back tomorrow. The man says if Danny doesn't open the door, they'll smash it down. "Look, I'm a poor old pensioner," whines Danny pathetically, "so can you give me more time to pay, please?" The man says it's too late for that sort of thing and hammers on the door again. After checking to see that Dean's car is parked in the street outside his flat, Danny opens the door. "Are you the boss?" Danny asks. "No, I'm not the boss, I'm Stakis, you might've heard of me," the man replies. "Well, Stakis," says Danny, "if you don't mind, I'd like to talk with the boss so we can get all this straightened out." Stakis says that's good because the boss wants a little talk with him. Danny's escorted from the building by four of Devo's heaviest heavies. They drive to an abandoned warehouse in Southwark, just around the corner from the hooky shop where Danny and his oppos got their mobile phones from. As Stakis parks up, more heavies appear from the side door of the warehouse. They drag Danny out of the car and take him into the warehouse's basement. Going by the marks on the walls of the stairwell, many people have made this journey. Little does Danny realise, not many of them make it back out onto the streets again. In the basement is a man-monster known as "Big Rob" and in front of him is a metal-topped table with two "V" blocks sitting on it.

Anyone familiar with engineering will know what a vee block is. Even those unfamiliar with engineering can probably guess what one is but, for the sake of argument, a vee block is a precision jig made from steel that is used to support pipes while they're being machined. As pipes come in a variety of diameters, so vee blocks come in various sizes from those for supporting the smallest diameter pipe to those large enough to support pipes a foot or more across. Somewhere betwixt and between are vee blocks which are the right size to support something of, say, the diameter of a human arm. In fact, two vee blocks, properly spaced, are perfect to nestle an arm at wrist and elbow, when, for example, said arm is to be struck with a length of iron bar in order to break it. The pair of vee blocks sat on the metal-topped table in front of Danny aren't beautifully crafted precision jigs of the type used in precision engineering, these are rough offcuts, with crude vees cut into them, made from resin-rich Scots pine and have been stained dark over the years, not through the application of a mahogany wood stain or an all-weather preservative, but by the blood of debtors spilled over them. A rusty, three-feet-long iron bar sitting between the vee blocks completes the picture.

Two of Devo's heavies, Karl and Willie, grab Danny and tie him to a metal workshop stool. *This wasn't in the plan!* "Haven't got a cushion have you? My backside is freezing!" says Danny. Ali tells him not to worry about it because he won't be there long. As none of the heavies have, thus far, attempted to break his arms, Danny hopes things might work out okay, though the iron bar sitting crossways on the table in front of him makes him nervous.

"So, what are you waiting for?" Danny asks cockily.

"What? Shut up you old git!" yells Mehmet, spraying Danny's face with spittle.

"Waiting for Devo to show up are you? Can't do anything without Devo?" Danny mocks.

"I won't tell you again, now shut the fuck up!"

"Or what? You'll kidnap me, drag me to a basement in Southwark and tie me to a freezing cold stool?"

"Look, you old bastard, if you carry on I'll..."

Without notice, Big Rob punches Danny on the side of his head, knocking him and the stool to the floor. Mehmet is furious and warns Big Rob and the others not to touch Danny. "He's Devo's!" Mehmet says and moves everyone away from Danny. This is exactly what Danny needed to hear, Devo's on his way to sort him out personally. *I just hope Deany's done his bit.* As minutes tick by, Danny has time to think; *what if the cavalry don't arrive in time and I get busted up?* Another thought is, *what if it's all a wind-up and Deany leaves me here?* These thoughts make him regretful of ever having gotten involved. *Under the circumstances, what else could I do?*

The sound of a car skidding in the car park outside is followed by the slamming of the warehouse door and the stomping of a heavy-set man coming down the stairs to the basement. A shout from one of the heavies guarding the stairwell announces Devo's arrival. At this, the heavies turn and stare at Danny, their eyes moist and shiny in the gloom of the basement. The basement door bursts open and in walks Devo. The two heavies closest to Danny know the form; they grab his right arm and slam it, elbow and wrist, into the bloodstained vee blocks, holding it down by force. Danny turns and looks at the loan shark. His face is incandescent with rage while Danny's is the epitome of calm. He's been in situations like this before but that was all a very long time ago.

"This is him?" says Mehmet, pointing at Danny.

"Oh fucking really, is that why he's here?" snaps Devo sarcastically. "That old fart bust Simmo up?" he asks disbelievingly. "I'd never have guessed! Pass me the bar you fuckwit!" Mehmet passes Devo the length of iron bar that's been troubling Danny's thoughts since he'd been tied to the stool.

"Before you do anything," says Danny calmly, "you need to see what I've got taped to my chest."

"Didn't you search him?" snarls Devo accusingly.

"No! Why would we search him? We've never searched anyone before..." Mehmet tails his words off when he realises his boss isn't looking for an answer, just someone to blame.

"See what he's got taped to his chest!" orders Devo. Karl holds Danny by the shoulders while Mehmet rips open his coat and shirt.

"What's this?" Mehmet asks Danny.

"It's a police issue tracking device," answers Danny smugly, though doesn't mention he's wearing a covert police issue CCTV camera.

"Where'd you get it from?" Mehmet asks.

"Where d'you think I got it from? The Boy Scouts? Listen, the whole place is surrounded by Special Branch," Danny announces confidently. "Go outside and see for yourselves!"

"Willie... Karl... go and check!" orders Devo. The pair race up the stairs to the car park and return almost immediately.

"No one's there boss," chorus the heavies. Danny looks perplexed.

"You sure?" asks Devo.

"Positive," says Karl.

"Well, it looks like the cavalry aren't comin' to your rescue after all! Hold his arm down!" yells Devo to the heavies. Just then, the door to the basement opens and in walks former Detective Sergeant Paul Dean.

"Oh, you've decided to put in a fucking appearance have you?" yells Devo. "I wasn't sure you would!"

"I couldn't miss this now could I?" says Dean, glaring at Danny.

"What's going on Deany? Where are the…" Danny's words tail off to silence as he realises he's been set up.

"What's going on, Danny Boy, is because of you I was forced to retire early on half pension. And because of you I never got to arrest that little prick Tomic. All you had to do was wind him up, take a beating and I'd've had him! But no, you had to go all vigilante and… well, we know you killed him, you said so yourself, and now I want you to tell me where you buried the bodies."

"Why was it so important for you to arrest Tomic? You must've arrested hundreds like him!"

"True, but what you don't know is he burgled my lovely old Nana's house. The shock of it was too much for her and a week later she died. I swore he'd pay."

"I'm certain someone as bent as you could've…"

"Oh sure, I could've done this or done that but my name was in the frame, as they say, regarding Blake. If I'd've set him up it'd all come out in court and he'd've been untouchable after that. So, I bided my time. I've set up a dozen muppets like you over the years but unlike you they were all talk and no action so it was a waste of time! When he went missing I was the prime suspect! I've got form as they say. Thank fuck when that piece of CCTV came to light otherwise I'd've been well and truly fucked! Now, Danny Boy, I need you to tell me where Blake's body is so I can use his DNA to make it look like he's still alive so my reputation and my pension will get reinstated."

"So, what happens now?" asks Danny, hoping there's a way out of his predicament.

"Well… first of all… Devo's going to break both your arms, he has to for obvious reasons. Then, you're going to tell me where Blake's body is and, if you don't, I'm going to take this hot air paint stripper and start by burning your toes off, but let's hope it doesn't come to that!"

"I doubt you'll let me go whether I tell you where Tomic is or not," says Danny intuitively.

"But how much better a painless death than… tell you what, Danny, Devo won't break your arms if you tell me where Blake's body is," promises Dean. Devo looks pissed off, he enjoys breaking people's arms.

At that moment, the door to the basement whispers open and in walks Brad, followed by Alby and six of his heavies. Big Ron runs at the group and, with a single punch, Alby knocks him sprawling to the floor unconscious.

"I warning you Alby, you'd better leave now while you still can… don't get involved in things that don't concern you!" threatens Dean.

"Don't you go tretenen me, Mr Dean! You're not a cop anymore, you're nothin'!" replies Alby as his heavies face off against Devo's heavies who don't look like they're keen on fighting them. "An', Mr Devo, don't you go thinkin' that the ones upstairs are goin' to help, they're not in any fit state!"

"I told you not to trust him, Dad!" Brad says, pointing at Dean. "Didn't I tell you not to trust him?"

"How'd you know to come here?" Danny asks just as his old oppos, led by Chuck, enter the basement.

"You!" Dean cries, calling to mind the blurred CCTV images of Tomic's kidnap. "It's you! You're the ones who kidnapped Blake! Look, do the smart thing, don't get involved with these muppets or you'll end up going to jail for the rest of your lives. Call 999 and…"

"Save your breath, man, you're toast!" says Chuck, pressing a size twelve boot on Big Ron's back to prevent him from getting up off the floor.

"Look, bruv… it was all his idea," whines Devo, pointing at Dean, "it was him what came up with the plan. He said you couldn't resist helpin' your friends and I had to go along with him because if I didn't his mates in the Met would've sort me right out!" pleads the loan shark.

"Yeah sure," says Chuck, shoving the vee blocks off the table and replacing them with a brown leather Gladstone bag of the type used by doctors.

"So… what now?" Dean asks resignedly.

"You wanted to know about my military record," says Danny. Chuck shakes his head at this. "I won't go into detail," he adds to Chuck's relief, "but let's just say I've done some terrible, horrendous things I'm not proud of but they took the edge off me being squeamish… if you know what I mean?" Danny's words have the effect of draining the colour from Dean's and Devo's faces along with those of his heavies. "But all that was a very long time ago. I've mellowed. You offered me a painless death and now I'm offering you the same," says Danny.

"Don't be stupid, Danny. You'll get caught. You know you will. You watch cop shows all the time on the TV and people always make mistakes and, believe me, with these muppets involved," whispers the former detective nodding towards Alby and his heavies, "there'll be mistakes, loads of them, and there'll be evidence everywhere! And what about them?" says Dean, nodding at Devo and his heavies, "they're witnesses!" he hisses.

"Oh no we're not!" interjects Devo quickly, making certain everyone knows whose side they're on. "Look, bro, we ain't grasses. We won't grass to anyone! Never have, never will," Devo adds, getting nods of agreement from his heavies.

"Look, Devo, I don't like what you do and…"

"Don't worry! We'll get out of the loan shark business as of right now! You won't have to worry about us!"

"If it's not loans, it'll be something else," says Alby.

"No bruv, honest we won't…"

"C'mon, Alby, everyone deserves a second chance… except bent coppers that is! Why not give Devo and his gang a second chance and if they turn bandit we'll deal with them then," says Danny as Chuck fills the last of a line of hypodermic syringes with surgical grade anaesthetic.

"What're they for?" asks Devo, nervously pointing at the syringes.

"Don't worry," says Danny, "it's just insurance to make sure everything goes down quietly… no fuss. All's that'll happen is you'll have a nice little sleep and wake up after we've gone."

"But… but…" stammers Devo.

"If you prefer," says Chuck, "we can have Mr Browning here do the talking," he says, pulling a pistol from beneath his jacket. "Okay? Then lay on the floor… c'mon… bunch up nice and close and no funny stuff!" Danny and Chuck inject Dean and Devo and, one after the other, the heavies.

"Okey dokey," says Danny to Alby and the others. "Anyone that hasn't served in IPEF leave the basement now!"

EPILOGUE

The Scene: a soundproofed room beneath Washington DC's Capitol Building where a top-secret Federal Oversight Committee is in session discussing the budget for running America's Intelligence Services. The newly appointed SoS is present; it's her first meeting. She believes this appointment will greatly enhance her political career.

"Madame Secretary, the next item on the agenda is Operation Ophidian," says the chairman. "All those below level nine leave the room," he adds, not deigning to raise his eyes to them.

"Tell me, Mr Chairman," begins the SoS, "what's 'Operation Ophidian'; it eats up a lot of money! A lot of money!"

"Madame Secretary, Operation 'O', as we call it, has been running some fifty years now. It's entering sundown and hopefully will be mothballed soon," says the chairman quickly, keen to move on and avoid further questions.

"I can read and I can do the math," says the SoS coldly. "So... tell me, what's Operation Ophidian about?" she asks again.

"Madame Secretary," interjects one of the suits around the table. "Operation O is on a 'need to know' basis. It's classified seven levels above Top Secret," he adds to frighten the SoS off.

"And your point being?"

"Plausible deniability, Madame Secretary, plausible deniability," interjects another suit, smiling a snake-smile. "Just knowing the smallest amount of detail about this sort of operation can be career limiting… or even terminal."

"We're spending as much on Operation Ophidian as we do on fighting narcos!" the SoS says through gritted teeth. "What are the total numbers on it?" she asks.

"You don't want to know!"

"Oh yes I do. Get them up on the screen! Now!"

"They only go back five years," says the first suit.

"Madame Secretary, it might help you come to a decision as to whether or not you want to know about Operation O if I give if a short verbal report on it; then you can decide what you want to do," says the chairman greasily. Without the SoS agreeing to anything, the chairman continues, "We were planning to pull out of Vietnam, and couldn't afford any fuckups, so the Pentagon, or the Secret Service or whoever, planted phoney information on two army officers that made it look like we were going to mount a massive military campaign against the North and made sure that they fell into the hands of the NVA.

"Intelligence gathered indicated the North weren't buying the 'military campaign' story so IPEF was sent into Cambodia to 'rescue' them; to 'sell the lie', if you will. The NVA were alerted to the mission and intercepted them enroute. Many were killed, some were captured and the remnants, somehow, completed the mission and returned to Phnen Bin. They were taken to a special facility and interrogated. I understand, even then, some of them were suspicious that the whole thing was a setup and the officers and IPEF were sacrificed to sell a lie. We couldn't afford for something like that to get out, so actions were taken to plug any potential leaks."

"What actions?" the SoS asks coldly.

"Two aircraft full of IPEF soldiers didn't make it home. Word spread they'd been downed by the CIA because of what they knew. At the time, Phnen Bin was crawling with operatives reporting that some men were writing home telling their loved ones what was going on, what happened. The letters, of course, were destroyed, but we couldn't take any chances so the letter writers were 'sanctioned'. Operation Ophidian was born because one of those who died in the plane crash had written a dossier on the rescue mission and somehow managed to send it to his lawyer in Chicago. Fortunately, the lawyer was a patriot and handed it over to the Secret Service. He got sanctioned."

"How many people have been sanctioned?" the SoS asks even more coldly.

"There's no way of getting that number but it has to be… fifty… sixty maybe?"

"And how many are still alive?"

"Thirty… forty maybe?"

"You don't know the number?"

"Over time, some of them have 'dropped off the radar' so to speak. Sometimes they turn up; some dead, some alive."

"I'm confused. What's Operation Ophidian about?" the SoS asks quizzically.

"Because one of the soldiers wrote a dossier, we couldn't take the chance others hadn't done the same, so they had to be watched around the clock. We needed to know everything about them. Everything. We even have agents dress up as priests to make sure there are no deathbed confessions and the like!"

"No wonder this costs a fortune! It has to stop!"

"What do you mean, Madame Secretary, 'it has to stop'? What exactly are you saying?" asks a suit.

"I'm saying what I'm saying! It has to stop!"

"Madame Secretary, Mr Chairman, there's something you both need to know," another suit pipes up.

"Go on!"

"A situation concerning two IPEF PoIs has cropped up. They flew to the UK after Charles 'Chuck' Henderson was contacted and then messaged by a 'dropped' IPEF PoI, a Charles Daniel Deacon. During surveillance, a second 'dropped' nominal was identified: an Australian citizen named Anthony McCann. The second US PoI is Glenn Biedermeier; all four were stationed together in Phnen Bin.

"Here's why they were all in London. Mr Deacon's daughter was attacked by a street gang and ended up in a coma. Convinced the perpetrators would never be brought to justice, Mr Deacon sought the help of his old IPEF buddies to get revenge on them. They did a great job! A great job! Long story short, most of the gang are now dead but we've lost McCann, Henderson and Biedermeier. They might still be in London.

"Moving on. While Mr Deacon's daughter was lying in a coma, he sat by her bedside talking to her about all manner of things… as a kind of therapy to bring her round… including the IPEF mission in Cambodia. The operatives monitoring Deacon are convinced none of the hospital staff overheard him but, lo and behold, when his daughter comes out of her coma it turns out she'd heard it all… every bit of it and remembers it perfectly."

"How do you know this?" the SoS asks, knowing that people like the suit tell lies to cover their tracks as well as getting people sanctioned for no good reason.

"I have recordings from inside the hospital and others from the daughter's home after she returned there with Mr Deacon. So, Madame Secretary, what do you want to do?"

"What do you think?" she asks bluntly.

"Wait, hold on one minute! As Chairman of this committee, it's up to me to say what…"

"What we're going to do about it should've been done years ago, decades ago!" says the SoS, interrupting snippily. "It would've been far easier doing it then than now when everyone's online with social media that can reach millions in seconds! I take it we have files on each and every one of them?" asks the SoS.

"Most of them, Madame Secretary, most of them," answers yet another suit.

"Are they complete and comprehensive?" asks the SoS.

"It depends on what you mean by 'complete and comprehensive', Madame Secretary."

"Do their files say whether or not they've produced dossiers, whether they've talked to anyone, written a will... written a goddamn book about it maybe! We need to know everything, everything, everything about every one of them! Every last one of them!"

"And then?"

"And then we, and by 'we' I mean you, will take care of the survivors and anyone else who knows about what happened in Cambodia! And by 'taken care of' I mean sanctioned! This has to stop and it has to stop now in case these old farts get organised and the shit hits the fan!"

*

"Well, Mike, that's it, it's all over, Operation Ophidian is no longer in sundown mode, it's officially in sanction mode."

"No it's not."

"Sure it is. You heard what she said."

"Who cares what she said, she'll be gone inside a year... two at most."

"Yeah, but she'll want updates, progress reports, all that shit!"

"Yeah, so what? Investigations like these have to be thorough, very, very thorough. They take a long, long time and long before we're done, she'll be long gone."

"Why are you so interested in keeping them alive?"

"You saw what they did in London... and at their ages too!"

"What about it?"

"I'm going to put them to work. No one will ever see them coming!"